Hellfire Corner

Alaric Bond

for George and Amy

by the same author

Contents

Hellfire Corner

Prologue

The slender moon had risen now and was strong enough to divide sea from sky whilst also picking out a low mist that crept across their starboard bow. This was carried by the southerly breeze, unusually gentle for late September. And neither did it feel particularly cold, Harris decided from his position on the bridge; he had certainly known worse conditions. Off the port beam *MGB 97*, their sister Motor Gun Boat, was keeping pace in the low swell while, slightly closer to their port bow, a more modern craft carrying the flotilla's senior officer led the way. Harris briefly transferred his attention to the seas beyond, which still held nothing but gloom and haze, before returning to check his own command.

And there all was as it should be; Scott and Daly, the seamen gunners, were sweeping the horizon with binoculars as they sat huddled in their respective turrets. These were set to either side of the gunboat's aft superstructure and gave less protection than the metal outer plating suggested. But then fragility was not unusual aboard *MGB 95*; the entire vessel had been designed to deliver rather than receive, with many areas that would crumble at the impact of a heavy bullet, let alone an enemy shell. And even in the matter of delivery, the gunboat was lacking; both turrets were armed with single half-inch Vickers machine guns, worthy enough weapons in themselves although of doubtful value against the enemy they usually encountered. Further aft was something more solid; an Oerlikon manned by Ward and Lawlor – two experienced men who could be relied upon to get the best from their piece. But even a twenty-millimetre cannon was barely adequate and hardly justified the vessel's classification as a gunboat.

Of greater value were her engines; *MGB 95* was one of the last to be powered by a derivation of the Rolls-Royce Merlin, an inspired creation that currently graced many fighters. Combined, her two supercharged units could bring the boat close to forty knots – more if the conditions were right. But such raw energy did have its drawbacks; at anything over half that speed the noise was enough to warn even the dullest of their approach while the tiny engine room was cramped and, when at maximum throttle, the closest thing to hell Harris had ever known. The engines were growling more gently now, yet easily kept the forward section of the gunboat's sixty-three-foot hull free of the water as she tore across a placid English Channel.

But such progress could not last forever. Soon they would be drawing close to the enemy coast; Collins, the senior officer in their leading boat, would be signalling at any time. Then they would power down and lie cut allowing the enemy, in that night's case a slow-moving northbound convoy, to wander into the trap they had set. It was an exercise the three boats had performed before, and with moderate success. Even two years into the war, German coastal convoys remained small, usually consisting of no more than two or three merchants protected by a variety of escorts that ranged greatly in their capabilities. Armed trawlers were common and hardly the docile fishing craft the name suggested while minesweepers could be anything up to the size and power of a small destroyer. Either was capable of dealing with *MGB 95* without difficulty, providing they got a bead on the elusive little beast, for a well-handled gunboat could be as annoying as any fly. But there was yet another class of escort that could both trap and swat them with ease, and it was these that Harris hated, and feared, the most.

The British knew them as E-boats, and they were every bit as deadly as their larger cousins while being faster and much more manoeuvrable. Driven by three engines that comfortably outpaced those in the British craft, the E-boats were also larger and heavier, qualities that gave room for a truly substantial armament. The longer hull was also stronger, but the final difference was probably most significant; British gunboats relied on high octane petrol stored in poorly protected tanks for their propulsion, whereas the German craft could go faster, and a great deal further, on far less volatile diesel.

Faced with such an enemy, and without the torpedoes that could more easily sink a merchant, gunboat attacks appeared futile and were only made viable by one subtle advantage: the Germans had no wish to fight.

A northbound convoy was likely to be taking coal to Sweden whereas most southbound carried iron ore and either cargo was worth more to the German war effort than a chance of destroying an enemy launch. Consequently, it was usual for the enemy escorts to play a defensive role, protecting their charges with determination and vigour, though rarely continuing the fight when the British chose to retire. And even if the merchants could not be destroyed, the gunboats' intervention would surely slow them down while ensuring those that followed would be protected at least as well, if not better.

"No sign of a signal, sir," Sub-Lieutenant Simpson remarked, breaking a silence that had lasted for several minutes. The man was standing close by, but Harris did not need to turn as he could so easily imagine the cautious yet ingratiating smile. Simpson had been his second in command for nearly a month; throughout that time had barely changed and definitely not improved.

"It'll come, just keep your eyes peeled," Harris told him gruffly. The fact that the two did not get on was hardly surprising; he had nothing against the lad and was sure if their paths had crossed in other circumstances they might even have worked well together. But Harris was a professional seaman, Royal Navy trained from an early age and determined to make the Service his career. Conversely, until very recently Simpson had been a bank clerk whose only nautical experience was inland dinghy sailing or as a passenger aboard a steamer on a day trip to Ostend. With a little more effort on Harris' part the two might have managed better, but the older man really could not see the point. Even the strongest rapport would hardly improve Simpson's seamanship, nor the fact that the fellow simply lacked other basic qualities essential in a naval officer.

Almost as an antidote, Harris glanced across to Dave Chapman's boat as it gallantly rode the gentle waves two hundred yards off his beam. Harris first came across Chapman at Dartmouth and the pair had been through much together since. It was only luck that saw them posted to the same flotilla, but both were grateful for they had found themselves in the middle of what had quickly become a small ship war. And it was a private one, fought with tiny craft, reduced crews and limited communication. Rarely did their exploits reach the public's attention as damaging German small craft or delaying a consignment of coal seemed insignificant when compared to forcing a pocket battleship to scuttle. So those who were involved fought alone and in secret, yet all the while knowing survival depended on trusting the men they served alongside. And it was a trust that must extend to those in other boats as well as their own. Harris and Chapman had pulled each other out of several tight spots, something that probably accounted for neither having lost a man; a rare feat in Coastal Forces. So, if he had to serve with amateurs, Harris would prefer them to be his second in command rather than the captain of another gunboat, for at least when Simpson made one of his regular gaffs, he was usually around to see it put right.

"How far is the enemy coast?" Harris asked abruptly and, taken by surprise, Simpson took a moment to answer.

"I don't know exactly, sir," he admitted at last. "But I'd say a fair distance."

Harris made no reply. Navigation was one of Simpson's responsibilities; admittedly they were travelling in company and had only to follow the senior officer's boat but that would be of little use if action or an accident saw them suddenly on their own. Harris could set a course himself but for that he would need at least a dead reckoning position and Simpson had clearly not bothered, or been able, to keep the chart up to date. He supposed they might always turn to the east, which must bring them back to some part of England eventually, but it was typical of the sloppy seamanship Simpson practised, and at that moment Harris did not like it, or him, one bit.

* * *

4

On the other side of the bridge and trapped in the tiny copular that was one of many things he hated about the boat, Simpson was equally unhappy. He had been serving under Harris for long enough to know anything he did was likely to annoy and had now reached the stage when he ceased to care. With luck this would be his last patrol; his request for a transfer had been lodged some while ago and the base captain felt he could expect to be gone by the end of the week. That time could not come soon enough for Simpson.

When he volunteered for Coastal Forces it had been on the understanding he would be in actual contact with the enemy; to his mind the only honest way of fighting a war. Admittedly there was much he needed to learn, and the theory taught at Hove and *St Christopher*'s had been eagerly digested. But practice on active service was bound to be different and for this he had been relying on guidance from his commanding officer. From the outset, Harris proved a disappointment, and not the kind who provided encouragement. The two muddled along well enough he supposed, at least nothing too dreadful had happened, but Simpson was now thoroughly fed up with the arrangement.

"Reduce to twelve hundred," Harris ordered, and Simpson bit his lip. The two quick flashes from a blue-shaded Aldis aboard the senior officer's – or SO's – boat must have been sent and he had missed them. There was little consolation in both midships gunners, who doubled as lookouts, also failing to report; Harris was expecting Simpson to pick up the signal and, yet again, he had failed. It was another bad mark against him, another reproof to add to a list that felt endless, and the young man longed for his release all the more.

* * *

The three gunboats continued for a further mile under reduced power before their engines were cut completely. As they began to wallow in the gentle motion, no one appreciated the relative silence more than the two seamen gunners at *MGB 95*'s rear Oerlikon.

"That's a mercy," Sharkey Ward remarked as he stretched. "Think by now I'd be used to it, but that din gets to you after a while."

"Worse for them below," Lawlor remarked. "Deafening that engine room must be, and hot enough to cure tobacco."

"Well no one asked them to go down there," Sharkey

grunted.

"But they got no air, bach; it's not natural," the Welshman replied before considering further. "Do you think them on the bridge would notice if we had a quick burn?" he asked, waving a packet of Woodbines.

Ward snorted. "I wouldn't, not unless you want Jimmy the One to smack you with his feather duster."

Lawlor nodded and settled himself more comfortably on the gun platform. They had fired off several rounds on leaving harbour and a selection of brass cartridge cases now lay scattered about the bandstand mounting.

"It's TITS," the Welshman exclaimed cheerfully as he sorted through a handful.

"You think?" Sharkey enquired. "Well, if you know of a better hole..."

"No, T.I.T.S.," Lawlor insisted, holding up a cartridge case.

Sharkey glanced down at him. "What you on about, Taff?"

Lawlor sniffed at one of the cases luxuriantly. "Tracer, incendiary, tracer, semi-armoured piercing – TITS, see?" he declared. "It's how you remember the order for the magazine. They taught us that at *Excellent* and what the coding means but I never realised you could tell the difference by smell."

"Wonderful," Sharkey exclaimed without enthusiasm.

"Well, you can tell the tracers," Lawlor corrected as he continued to experiment. "Can't say I'm sure about the other two. And you can change the order, you know."

"Change it?"

"Yes, some teams do; add more tracer if they want a clearer sighting, though I'm told too much can dazzle, and we wouldn't want that now, would we?"

"I don't need to know the order and I certainly ain't going to change nothing," Sharkey stated firmly. "That's for other folk, my job is to point Betty here and it's what I do best."

"Oh, there's no doubt about that," Lawlor hastened to assure him. "No one finer in the flotilla so they say." The pair had been shipmates for a while and got along well enough, but Sharkey could be volatile at times and Lawlor liked to play it safe.

"Reckon we'll be due a spot of leave afore long," Sharkey mused. "Got any plans, have you?"

"I don't know, maybe get back to Pontypridd if we're given long enough."

"That's Wales, ain't it?" Sharkey asked. "Why should anyone want to go to Wales?"

"Ah, magical place," Lawlor declared as he gazed out at the mist-filled sea. "You should see it."

"Not me," his mate announced.

"Why not come along as well?" Lawlor suggested. "We'll have a high old time."

"Not on your life," Sharkey snorted. "I can have a high old time a darn sight nearer to home thank you very much."

"Fair enough," Lawlor agreed. He knew from experience the gunner spoke the truth and was secretly relieved.

"No, when our leave kicks in I'll finds me a decent pub and settle," Sharkey continued. "The only thing I know about Wales is I wouldn't want to be eaten by one."

* * *

Below and slightly further forward the two men who constantly maintained *MGB 95*'s engines were also supposedly at rest. But for the past three hours their charges had been running up to regulation speed; this was a mere eighteen hundred revolutions yet still the beasts needed attending to so Carter was rubbing down the starboard engine with a rag while Newman applied oil and love in equal measure to the port.

"Still reckon one of these head gaskets is on the way out," Newman claimed.

"But we ran a pressure test," Carter reminded him. As acting chief motor mechanic, he was in charge and Newman, a leading stoker, merely his assistant although the younger man's kindred spirit had long been recognised. He was gifted when it came to engines and Carter always listened to his comments.

"I know, but it still doesn't feel right," Newman insisted. "What say we whip the heads off next leave. Only take a day or two?"

Carter smiled. You couldn't fault the lad for enthusiasm, although he could think of better ways of spending his free time. "We'll run another test when we gets back," he said, compromising. "Just to be sure."

* * *

"Well there's nothing to be seen," Price, at the wheel, sighed. "Just a load of mist."

"Reckon the intel were off 'Swain?" Jelly called from the W/T office.

Price turned to look at the telegraphist; the man was squeezed into what was little more than a cupboard off the wheelhouse and his face glowed in the orange light from countless valves.

"Maybe, we'll find out soon enough."

"Don't bank on it," Jelly sighed. "Set's been buzzing all evening – reckon every boat available's at sea, both ours and Jerry's."

"It's the conditions," Price supposed. "Perfec' night it is. An' this time o' year – who'd 'ave thought?"

"Wait, there's something coming through now," Jelly snapped as he began to listen intently, his right hand occasionally tapping on a key in response. Then, after making a note on a pad and leafing through a small black book, he leaned towards the bridge voice pipe.

"Message from Dover Command, sir," he said after a pause. "Convoy's been tracked and should be in our area any moment."

He turned and gave the coxswain a grin. "Looks like things are starting to liven up," he said.

* * *

Harris snapped the brass cover shut on the speaking tube and considered the SO's boat again. Despite having been without power for a good half-hour they were keeping reasonable station; even Chapman, to his left, had hardly altered position. But it was time enough for the engines to have cooled slightly and, in Collins' position, Harris would have started them on getting the message from base. And it really wouldn't hurt to get underway again, then, at least when the enemy came into sight, they would be ready.

"Be good to get the engines going," Simpson suggested, and Harris looked to him in surprise.

"Just thinking the same myself," he admitted and was about to add more when a cry from Scott, in the port turret, cut into their thoughts.

"Signal from the SO!" he announced.

"One, two, three – three flashes!" Simpson reported. "That's the signal to be off."

Harris bent towards the engine room speaking tube. "Crash start both engines, Chief, and prepare to give me all you've got."

Looking up once more Harris noticed the phosphorescent glow behind Collins' boat as its screws began to bite.

"Half speed 'Swain," he ordered, this time to the wheelhouse. "Maintain station on leader."

A rumble aft was followed by a mild jolt as both engines engaged, then the gunboat was charging forward across the misty sea. In no time she had risen up on to the plane but already Collins' boat was drawing ahead.

"Open her up, 'Swain," Harris was having to bellow now but Price was an experienced hand and knew what they were about. As the engines' pitch increased the boat seemed on the very edge of taking fully to the air. Harris gripped the sides of the copular and looked across at Simpson again. He, too, seemed to have been caught up by their sudden call to action and for a moment their eyes met in something close to understanding.

"Vessels bearing green twenty!"

This was from Daly, in the starboard turret, and Harris strained forward into the mist. At first he could see nothing, then a slightly darker mass developed into the outlines of a large merchant ship and he knew they had found the convoy.

* * *

Ahead, the SO's boat had lengthened its lead and Harris glanced across to Chapman on the port beam. His boat was keeping pace well but slightly ahead, it made sense for him to take second place and Harris bellowed down to Price to hold back accordingly. Chapman took the hint and edged closer behind Collins' boat, keeping just to port of its wash. Without specific instruction, Price slotted *MGB 95* behind and to starboard until all three were powering forward at full speed in a ragged line ahead; the ideal formation for a gunboat attack.

To starboard, the leading merchant was now in clear sight and Harris knew that, despite their size, the British boats would be equally visible to the enemy; even if the Germans missed their glowing bow waves and similarly obvious wakes, they could not ignore the din of supercharged engines at maximum revs. There was still no sign of an escort, but that meant nothing; even the largest would be considerably smaller than any freighter and likely to be travelling wide of the main convoy. The trawlers would probably be sighted first, they being larger, slower and, although heavily armed, probably the easiest to avoid. It was the E-boats that caused him the most concern and, if he was to be facing any tonight, he would rather know about it as soon as possible. In the enemy escorts' position, Harris would have held back and kept his presence hidden until the British came close, although strangely the Germans were usually only too pleased to give the game away, and this time proved no exception.

They saw the low plume of wash from the first as it bolted out of the mist and fell upon the SO's starboard beam. It was well ahead and out of range, yet still Harris pressed the action gongs and a ringing of bells echoed about the boat. In both turrets the gunners shouldered their weapons and made ready while Ward and Lawlor, at the aft Oerlikon, closed up. A starshell burst overhead and hung fizzing in the air, but the added light would make little difference to the British plans and may even aid them. There was a brief exchange of tracer as the German boat closed with the SO's, then Collins veered sharply to port, sending up a positive tower of water to hide the rest of the action. Chapman's boat was next in line and could be expected to follow. As he did, Harris caught a glimpse of 97's midship turrets also opening up, presumably on the E-boat, before their wash also obscured his view.

"Hold your course, 'Swain," Harris bellowed down the speaking tube before turning to Simpson. "We'll carry on," he shouted. "Reckon that will be the main forward escort. If Collins and Chapman keep it occupied, we can have a crack at the freighter."

Simpson gave him a limp nod although Harris wondered if he had truly understood. But there was no time for further explanation, the merchant was growing ever closer; they would have to act.

"Depth charges!" he told Simpson, and for a moment the lad stared back at him in apparent confusion. "Depth charges," the captain repeated. "You take the starboard, Jelly can handle port – come on man, you know the drill!"

"But we can release them from the wheelhouse," the young man protested.

"And can we set the fuses?" Harris demanded. "And are we sure the mechanism will work? Damn it, you should understand my methods by now!"

Simpson's mouth opened and for a moment Harris thought he might start an argument. Then the boy saw sense and slipped down into the wheelhouse without a word.

"We're going to depth charge the merchant," Harris told Price through the speaking tube. "Are you happy to take her in?"

"Yes, sir." The coxswain's voice came back strong and positive. Bringing a speeding gunboat close enough to make the high explosives count was a job that required sensitivity and experience; attributes Price held in abundance and Harris was always happy to leave a job to an expert.

They were closing on the merchant now, their turret gunners spraying a line of tracer across her foredeck. There was still no sign of interference from starboard and Harris knew that, even if another escort was to appear from that quarter, the attack would continue: they were committed.

And then 95 was under the lee of the huge rusty bows; Price was doing well, holding them on a straight course that seemed destined to end in collision and only at the last moment swinging to port while almost cutting the engines. Then their klaxon sounded, and both depth charges were released.

The port charge would probably do little good other than aid the confusion but, if Simpson had done his job properly, two-and-a-half hundredweight of high explosive was currently sliding down the freighter's side. It was hardly a conventional use of the weapon but one that had become the norm through necessity. With no torpedoes and only limited firepower, gunboat commanders quickly adopted the practice on the understanding that anything that could open up a submarine's pressure hull would do serious damage to a surface vessel. And, though as dangerous as it was unorthodox, several German ships had already been sunk or seriously damaged by such a method.

Price hit the throttles as soon as the gunboat delivered her deadly load and they roared away with the guttural grunt of the Oerlikon joining the midships Vickers. Harris resumed control and glanced back. It would have been a simple operation to set the charges for almost immediate explosion; a quarter-turn of the key clockwise would do it, yet still he wondered if it had been right to trust such a task to his second in command. But his doubts were shamed as two columns of water rose up far above their own wake. The sight silenced 95's own guns, which had been robbed of a target, and was followed by the roar of an explosion louder even than the scream from their engines. The freighter would probably not sink; they could even have failed to inflict significant damage, yet chances remained strong that she would be unable to continue to Sweden so they had done all that was required of them.

"Good work," Harris told Simpson as he reappeared in the copular next to him. The lad looked shaken though apparently pleased with himself and Harris wondered if he had been hasty in judging the fellow. But before he could think further, Scott's Vickers, in the port turret, opened up once more and appeared to be aiming at something off their port bow. He looked across; light from the starshell was fading but enough remained to show an E-boat heading straight for them.

"Left standard rudder!"

Price, in the wheelhouse, may have missed the fresh danger but reacted promptly and soon *MGB 95* was heeling into a steep turn as both midships gunners sprayed the sea before them with red tracer. The manoeuvre had been Harris' only choice; turning to starboard, which had been his instinctive reaction, would have seen them trapped between convoy and the enemy coast. Further escorts must be coming up from astern, and they should certainly account for a single gunboat. As it was, he would still have to confront an E-boat at close quarters, which was not his ideal occupation, although one he had survived on several occasions. It was probably the same craft that had seen off Collins' and Chapman's boats, he decided. With luck, his comrades would not have gone far and could even be near enough to give assistance.

But first he had to make it past. Scott's Vickers was unable to reach the target now, but Daly's continued to send bolts of blinding tracer in the German's direction while Ward's Oerlikon also joined in. And the E-boat's forward gun was equally fast in responding; green tracer passed overhead: it could only be a question of time before the enemy found their mark.

And then it happened, while Ward and Daly peppered the oncoming boat's bridge and foredeck, a line of green played along the full length of Harris' own command. With the snapping of dry wood, a line of holes appeared as if by magic, sweeping the boat from stem to stern, ripping up deck, punching fist sized holes into the superstructure and missing their bridge by nothing less than a miracle. But the gunners continued to fire and Harris knew their concentrated efforts must be having an equally devastating effect on the oncoming craft.

Then it was oncoming no more. Either by accident or design, the E-boat suddenly veered to port. Seeing this, and dreading the attention of the aft mounting guns, Harris bellowed down to Price. "Port ten, 'Swain, and make sure Carter's giving her everything!"

The boat surged to the left, kicking up a fountain of water in her wake that in itself should grant a degree of shelter. But, once settled on the new course, it became clear the E-boat was no longer following. And neither was she continuing to fire. Harris gazed back as the enemy vessel disappeared into the night and knew they were finally free of danger.

"Vessel in sight off our starboard bow," Daly reported languidly adding, "looks to me to be the SO's, so it does," even more casually as Collins' craft emerged from the haze.

"That could have been a whole lot worse," Harris told Simpson, his gaze remaining aft. It seemed as if one of the Oerlikon's crew had been hit, and the other was attending to him. "Better have a nose around, check on casualties," he added before turning back to look directly at his second in command and noticing for the first time he was missing.

But that was not strictly true, as Harris soon discovered. Simpson was there all right but slumped against the side of the bridge. Then he noticed there had been no miracle; a series of large holes in the gunboat's superstructure revealed the German's aim had been good, and he did not need to look further to realise Simpson was dead.

Chapter One

Sub-Lieutenant Anderson manoeuvred his many bags through the double doors of Dover Priory Railway Station and stepped outside. It was cold, as any autumnal night had a right to be, but at least the rain had stopped. He lowered his luggage onto a small area of dry pavement under an awning and looked about. The blackout was good, but then the town was barely more than twenty miles from enemy territory although no raid was actually in progress, despite a clear moon. He could make out several walkers, mainly servicemen and apparently in no great hurry. There were also a surprising number of cars that felt their way under masked headlamps although the small taxi rank was quite empty.

Anderson glanced despondently at the pile of bags while his fellow passengers – again mainly in uniform – filed past. His journey from London in an unlit and crowded train had taken more than twice the estimated time and finished one station short of his destination. The delay had been mainly due to enemy action, several hours having been spent sheltering in tunnels to avoid two separate raids, and now he was faced with a long walk to his new base. He had no clear idea of the route and hesitated before enquiring; all the previous week he had been on leave in a city relatively unknown to him, and even fellow servicemen showed a remarkable reluctance to give strangers directions. But the road ran downhill, which must be some guide as to where the harbour would be found, and he reached down to collect the first of his luggage.

"Can I give you a hand there?"

The voice came from behind and Anderson turned in the act of swinging a duffel bag across his shoulders to see another naval officer bending to collect one of his suitcases.

"It's kind of you; there don't seem to be any taxis. Do you know where I might catch a bus?"

"You won't find any, not in the town." The man's greatcoat epaulettes bore the twin straight bars of a regular Royal Navy lieutenant; in contrast, Anderson's could only offer a single wavy stripe to distinguish him as a sub-lieutenant in the Royal Naval

Volunteer Reserve. The difference in both rank and status was significant – many established officers gave little regard to civilian entries such as Anderson although he was quick to notice no obvious prejudice. "If you're bound for *Lynx* it's no distance," the officer added. "I can see you that far."

"Actually I'm heading for *Wasp*," Anderson admitted.

"Better still, that's where I'm bound," the stranger grinned. "It's a bit of a hike but mainly downhill – we'll make it together."

"You're sure you don't mind?" Anderson asked. He was carrying one suitcase, a grip and the duffel on his back while the stranger had the other suitcases and a small bag of his own.

"Not a bit, I'm back from local leave myself so travelling light."

"You're with Coastal Forces?" Anderson chanced.

"Indeed, MGBs. Name's Chapman – Dave Chapman."

"Ian Anderson," the other replied, and each nodded to the other. The streets were dark but there was moon enough to show their features. Chapman was well built with a strong jaw and dark hair that barely showed beneath his black cap.

"So why no busses?" Anderson asked as they rounded a corner. He was slightly shorter, mildly plump and, though barely into his middle twenties, aware that the receding hairline was starting to become noticeable.

"Oh there are some, in the daytime," Chapman conceded. "You can usually get into Folkestone or Hythe if you've a mind, though they rarely run in the town itself." They were passing a row of bomb-damaged houses and he sighed. "This is Dover, they call it Hellfire Corner and for good reason."

Anderson had spent the last week in London which had truly taken a pounding during the Blitz and was still receiving regular raids; he doubted any mere town could be as badly off but sensed it might not be diplomatic to say so. "Plenty of raids I imagine," he remarked instead.

"Closest bit of England to the Hun," Chapman agreed. "But it isn't just bombs; the Germans have long-range cannon that can send fifteen-inch bricks in our direction at pretty much any time; some reach quite a way inland." He paused and shook his head. "It's a terrible sight, a town under shellfire."

"It must be," Anderson replied as he privately reconsidered his earlier assessment.

"You'll know when they start up; there's a double siren," Chapman advised, "though the first few usually arrive unannounced."

"I suppose the harbour's too good a target to ignore."

"Strangely they seem to leave that alone. Jerry still seems hell-bent on invasion, so they probably have ideas of using it themselves before long."

Anderson swallowed; it was hardly an encouraging thought, despite the other man's casual acceptance.

"Would you be for sea service?" Chapman asked.

"That's the intention."

"Often a few miles out feels like the safest place," the senior man mused. "I guess this is your first posting?"

"To Coastal Forces, yes," Anderson replied. "I was in sweepers until recently."

"Must have been fun. See much action?"

"A fair bit, I was on the East Coast," Anderson replied.

Chapman nodded respectfully. "Plenty to keep you occupied there no doubt. What about Dunkirk?"

"Oh yes." He turned to look at his companion. "You?"

"No, they spared me that one." There was an air of regret. "So, what brought you to Coastal Forces?"

"I volunteered."

"Didn't we all?"

They both laughed, then Anderson explained. "I just got tired of tidying up after Jerry; minesweeping's vital, of course, but I wanted to do something a bit more positive."

Chapman snorted. "Sometimes our work doesn't feel so very positive."

"But you do make contact with the enemy," Anderson insisted as they crossed the road to avoid more bomb damage. "I mean, get to grips as it were."

"Oh yes," Chapman confirmed. "And there have been a few successes, but they really are few. Much of the time we're like a bunch of drunks fighting in the dark. And when we do get to grips, as you put it, there's no doubting who's the stronger."

"I suppose you're talking E-boats?" Anderson asked softly.

"E-boats for certain," Chapman confirmed. "And in the main they're faster, larger and better armed than anything we have. R-boats are almost as bad though; they may be classed as minesweepers and a good deal slower, but most can outgun us with ease. And even the VPs give us a run for our money; again not fast, but armed to the teeth and solidly protected. Our tubs have never been better, though still no match for most German craft."

For a moment they walked in silence, then Chapman spoke again.

"Have you trained on launches?" he asked cautiously.

"Just back from *St Christopher*'s," Anderson assured him.

"I was there a year or so back," the older man admitted.

"Cold, dark and uncomfortable – and they make you jump about a bit," Anderson recalled.

"That's about it," Chapman agreed. "Though you won't find it much different here. Except there's slightly more chance of being killed."

* * *

The performance at the Hippodrome had been more music hall than variety with some acts verging on the burlesque. But it was just the programme for the large number of servicemen present, some of whom evidently saw the two young women, smart in their white shirts and stiff blue uniforms, as a continuation to the night's entertainment. The pair had beaten a hasty retreat at the interval and, on quitting the hall's dank fug, it was a pleasant surprise to find the rain stopped and the air crisp and clear.

"So 'ows about a wet?" Sandra, marginally the older, suggested.

Eve viewed her warily; joining the Wrens and being posted to Dover had been a major upheaval and she felt there was enough to get used to without taking too many chances – their visit to the Hippo' had been very much Sandra's choice. The pair had not known each other long and were getting on well despite obvious differences, but Eve was starting to realise her new friend tended to take risks without considering the consequences and had no intention of always being swept along in her wake.

"No, a brisk walk – it'll do us good," she declared increasing her pace.

"Hey, the pubs'll only be open 'nother hour," Sandra protested, but Eve strode purposefully around a corner. There was indeed a pub in New Bridge Road, and it was undoubtedly open, but the roar and clatter coming from behind the darkened windows was so reminiscent of the Hippodrome that Sandra let herself be led by without protest. And when they finally reached the harbour and could look out on the darkened shapes beyond, the journey seemed worthwhile.

Most of the earlier cloud had gone and, with the moon now fully risen and a sky awash with stars shining all the brighter in the blackout, much could be seen. The shipping was orderly, businesslike and easily distinguished. There was nothing to stir the heart as such, no dashing cruisers or mighty battleships, yet Eve still found herself strangely moved.

"It's turned into just the night for a raid," Sandra muttered looking up at the sky. "I suppose the rain earlier put Jerry off. Doesn't like the rain, our Jerry." She turned and, noticing her friend's attention was elsewhere, added, "Heck of a lot of boats, though I don't know what half of them are."

"Well, that's an Admiralty tanker," Eve explained, pointing towards the largest ship moored to a nearby jetty. "And that's the boom defence vessel. The tugs I'm sure you know, and that appears to be some sort of minesweeper."

"Looks more like a fishing boat to me," Sandra remarked. "You get a lot of those round Whitby – our mam came from there. We went for a sharra trip once, t'were grand."

"It probably was a fishing boat once," Eve conceded. "Over there are the pens," she said, pointing to her left. "That's where they keep the fast motor launches; torpedo boats and the like."

"The Glory Boys," Sandra stated with apparent satisfaction. "I heard about them. Prime they are. You think we'll get to meet any?"

"We might," Eve replied thoughtfully. "Most are stationed at HMS *Wasp*."

Her friend considered her. "That's not a boat, right?"

Eve sighed. "We've been here two weeks and you have to ask?"

Sandra shrugged. "But most of the time we've been stuck in *Lynx*," she protested.

"HMS *Lynx*," Eve corrected. "And that isn't a ship either, in case you hadn't noticed."

"So why call places HMS when they ain't ships?" Sandra snorted.

"The large building on the other side," Eve said, pointing to her right, "that's HMS *Wasp*."

"Looks more like a posh hotel."

"I think it was, before the war."

"So how come you knows so much?"

"We're Wrens: Women's Royal Naval Service," Eve laughed. "There, it's written on your hat – we're supposed to take an interest in such things."

"Well I'd certainly be interested in teaming up with one of them Glory Boys," Sandra grinned as her friend began to walk once more. "So what's with the prim madam?" she asked, catching up. "Come on, Evie, I know you better than that; if there's the chance of a man about you're usually as keen as any. An' we've both had the same training – they didn't mention nowt about motor launches."

"If you must know, my brother serves aboard a gunboat," Eve admitted.

"Your brother?" Sandra gasped. "What, here? In Dover?"

"That's right."

"You mean to say we've been trolling about looking for fun and you've got a real-life Glory Boy on tap and didn't think to mention it?"

"He's on leave," Eve told her flatly.

"Never mind, he must come back sometime, and I'll be ready."

"He's probably not the kind you'd like – a stoker, though really more of a mechanic," she added. "He's been messing about with engines for as long as I can remember."

"Stoker – mechanic, I'm not fussy," Sandra confirmed blithely.

"Wait till you see his nails."

"If he's four foot two, covered in oil and with claws, I'm interested; a bit of male company would make a change from typing out meaningless reports – least they're meaningless to me." The pair continued to walk as Sandra elaborated. "When I joined I thought there'd be a bit more going on, you know, entertainment. But we've been stationed here best par' o' two weeks and most evenings have been spent in caves hiding from bombs and shells. Then the one night we are allowed out we ends up in a stuffy music hall watching some naked tart on a stage covered with pigeons trained to hide her bits."

"I must say that sailor with the birdseed showed true initiative," Eve mused.

"So come on, Evie, it's getting late," Sandra pleaded. "We're due back at ten. Let's find somewhere and have us a sup."

"Oh, you fancy a pub, do you? From what we've seen of those in Dover that would certainly end the evening with a bit of excitement."

"Don't have to be a pub, there must be other places," her friend sulked. They were passing a side road and she glanced down. "Look, there's an hotel. And it's not just any hotel, it's the *Grand* Hotel. That posh enough for you?"

* * *

"Nine, eight, seven, six…" Bob Scott grinned over his wristwatch as his shipmate drained the last drops from his mug. There was a crash as the heavy glass was slammed down on the table and Sharkey glared at him.

"How'd I do?" he demanded.

"Missed it by three," Scott answered with a smirk. "I'd say you was losing your touch."

"Don't you believe it," the sailor protested, his top lip damp with foam. "There ain't no one in the fleet what comes close; I'm the best there is."

In the saloon bar, Petty Officer Price gave a private sigh. The partition that separated him from the ratings had been hurriedly thrown up a few weeks before and still lacked several panes of frosted glass; consequently, he could see much of what his shipmates were about and hear a good deal more. In action, Sharkey Ward was a capable rear gunner and, despite a somewhat belligerent attitude, there was little to fault him in most other directions. But seeing the hand now, amid the haze of cigarette smoke and alcohol and with a look on his face that spoke more of work than play, Price found it hard to believe him the best at anything.

"Over our leave I sunk more than six 'undred pints," the rating continued, and Price quietly noted the mixture of awe and incredulity Sharkey's statement caused amongst those at the corner table.

"Six hundred," Daly, the Irishman, remarked as he raised his own glass to his lips and prepared to sip. "That's quite a score."

"I calls it training," Sharkey stated with obvious pride.

"I calls it something else," Jelly countered with a smirk. Although still an ordinary seaman and yet another marked down as 'hostilities only', Jelly was settling well. But he still had much to learn and Price tensed as the lad steadily talked himself deeper into trouble.

"Well look at it this way, Shark," he continued, oblivious to the look of outright hostility on the man's face. "We got nine days leave, right?"

"Somethin' like that."

"Which works out at eight nights, and you says yourself night time's when you do your best drinking."

"So what are you saying?" Sharkey demanded, his resentment at being questioned now giving way to an element of doubt.

"What I'm saying is, you must have drunk nigh on seventy-five pints a day for over a week an' no one can have done that."

Slowly the statement and its logic permeated those at the corner table and all, bar Sharkey, began to splutter with laughter.

"An' if you could, it would take all evening and most of the night," Jelly added, encouraged by the response, "even if each were on your record!"

This brought another round of mirth and Price's concern grew. Sharkey Ward's expression was turning to something more sinister; he was positively glowering at his companions and it seemed likely all would end in a fight. The petty officer glanced back at the bar; Alf, the landlord, was watching surreptitiously from the saloon side of the partition and was the type not to tolerate trouble. If he hadn't already sent for the shore patrol, he would do so shortly.

"Seventy odd pints a day would cost a fair old wack an all," Jelly continued, oblivious to the danger he was in.

"Aye, more'n any of us earns," Daly, the boat's Irish gunner, agreed.

"So are you lot sayin' I'm lying?" Sharkey demanded and suddenly all at the table, along with most of the pub, fell silent.

"We're sayin' you're mistaken," Jelly replied more carefully.

"And it is a mistake any one of us could have made," Daly agreed hurriedly. "Especially with seventy-five pints of beer inside him. So why don't I get another round before Alf here calls time?"

"Not your trick, Pad," Jelly told him.

"Maybe not, but I've had me a bit of luck with the horses."

It was an excuse no one could dispute and Daly made his way towards the landlord while Price, on the opposite side of the partition, released a long-held breath.

In some ways the leave had come at the right time, he decided from his lonely table; the lads had been tired and, even ignoring essential repairs, their boat had needed a good deal of general maintenance. But a break at the end of a particularly bad patrol – one where a man had been killed – was never ideal. It was one thing to need replacements because of stress or injury, quite another when some poor devil had bought it.

A regular turnover of crew was not uncommon in Coastal Forces craft; even ignoring the inevitable casualties, most could take the strain for only so long. But even allowing for that, *MGB 95* seemed to get through hands like they were going out of fashion. Nearly everyone seated at Sharkey Ward's table had arrived within the last three months and Price was realistic enough to predict most would be gone in the same time again.

It was hard to give a reason for this but the most likely was Harris, their current CO. The man could undoubtedly handle a boat and, apart from the coxswain himself, was the only regular Navy type amongst them, although there was no denying, he could also be a regular tartar at times. That said, Price would rather have an abrupt captain who kept his vessel safe than some raw landlubber more frightened of his men than the enemy, but that was only his opinion.

And they were going to get another such amateur next, as a replacement for Simpson their late first lieutenant. Price knew little about the new man other than his name and had nothing against RNVR officers as such. As far as he was concerned they, and their 'hostilities only' lower deck counterparts, were needed in time of war and many seemed to be doing a sound job. Some of the more senior had even been given command of decent sized ships and were carrying on splendidly. But to Price's mind, however good their seamanship and however fast they took to their new masters, nothing could instil centuries of Royal Navy tradition into those not bred for the life. One only had to look at Simpson; a likeable enough fellow yet with no real idea of what it was to be second in command of even the smallest warship. Why, the man had been a bank clerk of all things! It would have taken years to turn him into a decent officer.

He took a sip of the beer that had been keeping him company for half an hour and would last at least as long again. But then privately Price was not altogether certain if their skipper qualified as a decent officer. Not that it was for him to judge, of course; he and Lieutenant Harris got on well enough and shared the understanding of professionals. Nevertheless, he had seen him bottle poor old Simpson on more than one occasion, and Price instinctively knew that a captain telling his second in command off in public was likely to unsettle everyone else as much as the officer concerned.

Indeed, most had been disconcerted; even temporary sailors appreciated the order of command and seemed to know how a captain should, and should not, behave. Of course, Simpson had been as much to blame; sixteen years in the Navy had taught Price that, if a man allowed himself to be intimidated, it was as much his fault as anyone's. A lot would depend on the new man and how he reacted to the skipper's dominating ways.

And despite his apparent insensitivity, Harris did generally keep them safe; the last little run-in had been unfortunate on many levels, not the least being that it marked the first fatality aboard *MGB 95* under his command. Until then the boat had been acquiring the reputation of being almost invincible; the lads had even been heard to brag about it on occasions. He glanced across at the corner table where Sharkey was bracing himself for yet another attempt at his record; Price just hoped they would feel the same for the old girl when they returned to active service, and perhaps a little better about those who commanded her.

* * *

The Grand Hotel was a definite improvement on the Hippodrome. Once they were through the double blackout curtains both Wrens found themselves in a tall and imposing hall. It was well lit by a central chandelier as well as multiple wall-mounted lamps that picked out the detailed, if slightly dusty, coving. A number of aspidistras sat in raised wicker baskets and two, slightly faded, oil paintings of Dover's white cliffs competed with each other on facing walls. Beneath their feet a thick carpet muffled any sound and a mahogany reception desk stood to one side, behind which a middle-aged woman confronted them with a starched smile.

"Would you be staying, ladies?" she asked with an ironic uplift of her eyebrow.

"Not bloomin' likely," Sandra replied and went to say more but the woman was ahead of her.

"Then meeting someone, perhaps? You should know this is a private hotel and not open to the general public," she added with emphasis.

"These ladies are not the general public." It was a strong male voice with perhaps a slight inflection and came from behind. Both turned to see a tall man with clean-cut features wearing a Stetson hat and dressed in a long raincoat. "They are members of your armed forces and should be welcomed anywhere."

"Any guest, or friend of a guest, is welcome, Mr Peale," the receptionist told him crisply. "But as you are aware, the Grand is not a place for casual recreation."

"No one could ever consider it so, Miss Withers," the man assured her in an accent that Eve decided was definitely American. "Is the bar still open?"

"Until eleven, Mr Peale," the woman confirmed with a slight nod of her head. "But it is for the exclusive use of residents and their guests."

The man stepped between the Wrens and extended his

arms through theirs. "Then perhaps we should go through?" he suggested.

"We have to be back by ten," Eve whispered once they were out of range of Miss Withers. "And it's a long walk."

"Then we have almost an hour," he told her gently while glancing at a heavy chromium-plated wristwatch. "And I will arrange for a cab to take you."

"There's really no need, Mr Peale," Eve assured him as they entered a small bar and he led them to one of only four tables.

"I insist," the American smiled smoothly, guiding them both to seats. "And it's Dale, to friends. Now, what would you like to drink?"

"I'm a port and lemon girl," Sandra replied automatically, and the elderly waiter nodded before looking to Eve.

"Oh, a lemonade, if you please."

"Martini, plenty of ice, no olive," Peale added briskly, and the man disappeared. "So tell all," he continued, turning to the girls. "Why are the two best-dressed women in Dover in its sleaziest joint?"

"I'd hardly call this sleazy," Sandra said glancing around. The room was certainly small and the cream wallpaper may once have been white, but it was pleasantly laid out with well-polished furniture and there were more aspidistras and a further supply of oil paintings.

"You should try living here," the American snorted. "A couple of days of their phoney 'if you would care to's and 'by your leave's and it would get to you."

The man spoke loudly in a clear voice and obviously cared little who overheard.

"Have you been here long?" Eve asked.

"Barely a week," he admitted. "But it looks like I'm staying a while longer, and frankly that depresses me. This place has everything you read about in Dickens except the outside johns."

"Shame you don't like England," Sandra told him primly.

"Oh, don't get me wrong, I love your country, I'd just prefer staying somewhere a little more up to date."

The waiter appeared and placed their drinks on small paper coasters; Peale signed the tab without looking at it then collected his glass.

"So what are you doing here?" Sandra asked.

"War correspondent," Peale replied after taking a deep sip. "*New York Gazette*. I write a regular piece; so far I've spent just over a month in London and a fortnight in Portsmouth, now I'm here to see what Dover has to offer."

"And you're disappointed," Sandra supposed.

"Only with the hotel," Peale assured them. "The place is just dandy and has all the feel of a frontier town, which I suppose it is, in a fashion." He beamed. "And the natives are certainly appealing."

"The natives have to be back by ten," Eve reminded him. "And, as you pointed out, are members of the armed forces."

"Oh, now I've offended you, and that really wasn't my intention." Peale leaned forward and replaced his glass on the table. "Look, don't think I'm coming on or anything, I'm just a lonely fella a long way from home who's looking for a bit of civilised conversation."

For a moment his brash exterior crumbled slightly and Eve found herself feeling sorry for the man.

"I'm not sure we can offer you that," Sandra frowned. "Neither of us are particularly well-travelled, though I'm from Yorkshire."

"That's further north, isn't it?" Peale asked.

"Somewhat," Sandra conceded. "God's own county."

Peale's eyes twinkled. "Well, I always say it's nice to have a good landlord."

"We haven't been in Dover much longer than you," Eve told him quickly.

"But those are Navy uniforms, surely?"

"Women's Royal Navy Service," Sandra confirmed.

"But we don't go to sea," Eve added.

"Never let us near boats," her friend agreed sadly. "Hardly ever see a sailor to speak to, 'cept those old enough to be our da's."

"So what do you do all day?"

"We don't ask too many questions," Sandra bristled slightly. "That sort of thing isn't encouraged."

"What do *you* do all day, Mr Peale?" Eve asked.

"Dale please, and I just walk about the place, make notes, talk to a few people – if they'll talk to me," he added glancing at Sandra. "And then I file my piece. Depending on my editor I either stay about a bit longer or move on."

"You should be careful," Sandra cautioned. "This is a restricted zone. Anyone with too many questions is likely to end up being asked a few theirselves."

Peale laughed. "You got it wrong, lady, I can speak to whoever I like. Your government seems rather keen on having my fellow countrymen on board – that's one of the reasons I'm here."

"To see America joins us in the war?" Eve asked, "Or keeps well out?"

"Oh, I'm for joining," Peale assured her. "Was before I came, and so's my paper. Mind you, there are a few who think differently. Mr Lindbergh has many followers; frankly, I'd like them all to stay awhile in your country, see more of what you're going through – that might change their minds."

"Sounds like you're doing more for the war effort than we are," Sandra sighed before sipping her drink. "With you lot on board, we'd mop up Hitler in no time."

The American shook his head. "Don't be so sure, the man's no fool and he's got a lot of support. And he's also on your doorstep, whereas we're several thousand miles away. Anyway, as I say, opinions differ."

"And do you think you'll be successful?" Eve was watching the American carefully and had yet to touch her lemonade.

"Now that I don't know," Peale admitted draining his glass. "My editor tells me the mood is changing but it'll take a lot to get the whole country behind a European war."

"So, what's your next move?" Sandra asked.

Peale shrugged. "Not certain, I'd like to see more of Dover, get the feel of the place. Seems like it's had a tough time already but everyone's very positive – a bit like London. Say, I don't suppose you gals can give me a lead? Introduce me to your CO, maybe help me write up a piece on a woman's place in a man's war?"

Sandra, who had just taken another sip, coughed. "I don't think that will go down well," she spluttered.

"This is not a man's war and never has been," Eve told him more coolly. "Women are involved as much as anyone. We might not be firing guns or driving tanks, but there's plenty of other jobs."

"Same thing happened in the last," Sandra agreed as she recovered herself. "My nan worked in a munitions factory, and probably would this time if it weren't for her leg."

"That's what I'm after," Peale confirmed enthusiastically. "And I like your spirit, it's just the sort of thing my readers will go for. Can you speak to your CO for me?"

"I suppose we could have a word with the superintendent," Sandra mused, holding her now empty glass speculatively.

"I suppose we could," Eve agreed. "But she won't be so inclined to listen if we're late back." She glanced at her watch. "I think we should walk," she added, "and I think we should start now."

"But I said I'd call you a cab," the American protested. "Stay and have another drink."

"No, really Mr Peale – Dale," Eve replied quickly. "We really must be going; thank you so much, it really has been most pleasant."

"But at least let me have your 'phone number," Peale implored, standing also.

"They don't allow outside calls at the Wrennery," Sandra explained as she rose more reluctantly.

"But we know where you are," Eve assured him.

"And will be in touch," Sandra added.

* * *

The engine room of *MGB 95* was small, cramped and boasted a deckhead some way below normal standing height. What deck space there was had almost entirely been taken up by two twenty-seven litre supercharged petrol engines. Between them ran a series of pipes, cables and hoses guaranteed to prevent normal movement in the uninitiated. But despite this, Acting Chief Motor Mechanic Carter and Leading Stoker Newman were relatively happy.

For a start, they were not at sea. They had frequently needed to carry out complex repairs to one or other engine while the boat bucked and surged amidst the chops of the Channel and often when in action, with all guns firing and an occasional shell joining them in their cramped quarters. However, now the gunboat was stationary, and not just moored but solid as a rock on a concrete slip, while her engines lay quiet and cold making normal conversation easy; a pleasant contrast to their accustomed shouting. There was also air to breathe; no one was having to share their precious oxygen with the two greedy monsters, and neither did they need to shine torches into the many awkward spaces not covered by the boat's miserly bulkhead lamps. Instead, they had solid shore power   a string of bright bulbs that lit the place like a palace at the cost of raising the temperature by several degrees. And even that was no hardship for it was pleasantly warm and not the tropical temperature they were used to. But the greatest gift of all was time. Although officially on leave, the pair had spent the past week in their usual place of work; an imposition that was totally of their own making.

As soon as the dockyard finished repairs above, they had been allowed back and there they stayed, carrying out major and minor tasks on their charges, some of which had been put off for far too long. And for the most part they did so in a companionable silence.

Leading Stoker Newman was completing one now as he moved his torque-wrench diagonally across the cylinder bolts on the port engine's inboard head. With the last one tight, the young man leant back as far as he was able and reached into his overall pocket for a rag.

"Sound is it?" the petty officer asked.

Newman did not answer immediately. Instead he wiped at his forehead with the cloth, leaving it oilier than before. "Reckon so," he grunted.

Carter returned to the valve he had been patiently lapping on the same unit's outboard head. When they started, many of the ports had been pitted and coated with carbon; if all went well the entire engine should be clean and back together by the end of the night. And that would be the second to be sorted, plus they had replaced one supercharger, both oil pumps and starter motors and a dynamo, which wasn't bad for eight days' work.

"Yardmaster says the slipping party will have her back in the water first thing," Carter continued in rare conversation.

"So I heard," Newman agreed. "We'll be done by then."

Carter nodded. They would, and with a boat far more ready to return to action. Not that anyone would notice; an efficient engine room was taken for granted by those up top – only when things started to go wrong did they become interested. He glanced at the young stoker who had been his companion for the last few days and even a couple of nights – when the starboard engine proved troublesome they had camped out in the officers' wardroom to make up time. Newman was a rum soul, barely in his twenties and hardly trained yet the lad definitely had the knack, as they say. He seemed to know by instinct what an engine was about, and where and when it needed attending to. Take that port mill, for instance; he'd been going on about the head gasket needing replacing for a while, yet every test had shown full compression. But when they finally lifted the lid there were two spots that could not have held out longer than a couple of hours.

And unlike most of his age, Newman hadn't wanted to go off on the beer but stayed at his post, solidly carrying out his duties, the ideal supporting hand. Carter grunted to himself and added a touch more pumice to the valve. If it hadn't been obvious the lad was enjoying himself, he might have felt guilty.

* * *

Two floors up from the bar where the Wrens had met Dale Peale, Lieutenant Robert Harris RN was quite alone. The room was one not regularly let out to guests but rather used by favoured members of staff or even for storage. Harris arranged to have it long term for a peppercorn rent, and it had been his home for the past three months. Since being given command of *MGB 95* in fact and, though he could have found accommodation at *Wasp*, it suited him perfectly.

Partly it was the location; the Grand was almost midway between *Wasp* and the pens where his gunboat was moored. And partly because it provided true privacy. With Dover Command fully manned, accommodation was in short supply; he might have had to share with another officer and being on-site meant he would always be available. As it was, once he entered the small bare room he could guarantee a measure of detachment.

Which was what he was currently enjoying; sitting back in a faded but comfortable armchair and resting his stockinged feet on the linoleum floor, he felt as rested as was possible in time of war. This was the first night in many he had not needed to gather with the other guests in the hotel's stuffy basement and, as he was due to return to active service the following day, was treating himself to a glass of Islay malt.

And it would be a single glass; Harris was far too conscientious an officer for more and would get his head down immediately afterwards. There was an important meeting scheduled for ten the following morning and he hoped to collect the boat during the afternoon. But this was the last night of his leave, so he almost felt obliged to mark it in some way.

The time off had been spent predictably enough. With the boat in the hands of a private dockyard near Folkestone, he had been prevented from travelling far. The first part, in Midhurst where his parents were doing great things in their community, had been mundane. His father, a dour old Scot, was an officer in the Home Guard so spent much of his time with his unit while his mother, who almost ran the local WVS, was equally active. A week was enough to satisfy both they were not neglected, and then it had been easy to blame dockyard problems for an early return. The rest of his leave went on sorting out minor concerns with the boat, although most afternoons were free for him to simply read, rest and recuperate.

MGB 95 was his first command and, when appointed, it appeared a major step in a career that began at grammar school where the headmaster had been a retired Navy commander. Under his supervision, Harris sat the necessary exams and was accepted for basic training at *Ganges*. After learning his bends and hitches he was then commissioned at *King Alfred* before being detailed to *Warspite*, a battleship launched before the Great War and one that had been present at Jutland. There he learned much but found the bulk of the ship and the size of her crew daunting, so volunteered for smaller craft. Coastal Forces had yet to be properly established in home waters, but Harris was sent to join the First Motor Torpedo Boat Flotilla in Malta where he served as second officer in a craft similar to his current command. At the outbreak of war they were ordered home and Harris' boat was one of those that survived the nightmare journey across the Mediterranean and through the canals and rivers of mainland France. Once safely back, the vessel was sent for extensive repairs and never returned to active duty, while he was transferred to act as number one in a succession of more modern gunboats until finally being promoted to lieutenant and given *MGB 95*.

And that was where his career started to fall apart, or so it appeared. With a vessel of his own it became apparent that, though he had the experience and technical skills necessary, he lacked something far more subtle but equally important; the ability to command. While serving as first officer this had not been apparent, any unpopular order or exercise could be subtly blamed on the captain and Harris had been relatively successful in melding a group of disparate men into a workable crew. But when it became his turn to lead, things turned out very differently.

He took a sip of Scotch and rested back again. Perhaps his own first lieutenants were partly to blame? Simpson was the last of three temporary RNVR officers and all tried hard enough. But one had previously practised at the bar, another used to be an estate agent and Simpson a bank clerk; how could they hope for the understanding necessary to manage a tiny warship and those who manned her? And though small in number, the crew of a fast motor launch was no push-over to control. In many cases what would have been an entire department aboard a larger vessel was reduced to one man, making a clash of personalities almost inevitable. Even the craft themselves, being powerful, sensitive and extremely vulnerable, seemed to encourage similar traits in their crew and an officer appointed to supervise needed more than just winning smiles and a fancy uniform. When dealing with men trained well in their particular field – men who required informed direction and a figure to respect – all three had failed spectacularly and, by not addressing the problem, Harris supposed he had as well.

The intention had been there, but any attempt to correct his juniors' ways only backfired and came across as bullying or intimidation – traits that hardly endeared him to the hands and only lowered morale further. The fact that *MGB 95* had survived was due more to good fortune than anything else, but now even that luck appeared to have run dry. Until the last trip there had been no major casualties and those who chose to leave did so voluntarily; now all that had changed.

Now Simpson was dead and Lawlor in hospital where he was likely to remain for some time; perhaps Harris should count himself lucky no one else had requested a transfer, although the probable loss of leave might have been an influence there. Still, when the boat was finally handed back a fifth of her crew would be new faces, while those of the old guard would surely have had their confidence severely shaken.

And Harris could only sympathise with the last point; having already gone through three first officers he wondered how many more would be allowed before a transfer was arranged for him. He must change his manner of command; the base captain had made that plain although Harris could not begin to think how such a thing might be achieved. When a subordinate does something wrong, surely he must be told? Perhaps more explanation and even guidance could have been forthcoming, but all his first officers had supposedly been trained. It was his job to captain the craft, not nursemaid a bunch of amateurs.

The thought sent a shiver down his spine and he quickly drained his glass before lowering it carefully onto the arm of the chair. In a rare moment of insight he could see that much would depend on the new man. Should he turn out experienced and capable, they might make a go of things, but if Sub-Lieutenant Anderson proved as useless as the rest, there would be problems. And it hadn't been a good start; the man was supposed to present himself that very day yet had failed to arrive by the time Harris left *Wasp* and retired to this room. Doubtless there would be a reason – or an excuse – and one likely to be the first of many if his predecessors were anything to go by. And Harris did not tolerate excuses; he expected things to be right first time. Whether or not this Anderson would be of the same opinion was yet to be seen – at least the surname sounded vaguely Scottish. Perhaps, with a fellow countryman by his side, they might form a team, one that would turn *MGB 95* around and bring her up to the standard he expected. But as he slowly rose from his chair and stretched before starting to prepare himself for bed, Harris was not optimistic.

Chapter Two

Sub-Lieutenant Anderson emerged from the officers' mess in HMS *Wasp*. Housed in the former hotel's main dining room, it was a pleasant place that boasted fine views of the Dover Strait and included much of the original highly polished furniture to make it nicer still. And he had breakfasted surprisingly well, far better than at any naval establishment in the past, with a fried shell egg and proper bacon. And the opulence stayed with him as he strode through to the entrance foyer; despite the folded-back blackout curtains, taped glass and armed sentries at the front doors, it was easy to imagine the place in its former glory. To the left of the impressive entrance an equally imposing mahogany desk spoke of old-world grandeur and a life free of austerity; even the line of smart, if notably young, naval personnel behind seemed unusually attentive. Anderson ran his eyes along them before making for the only Wren.

"Has there been any news of Lieutenant Harris?" he asked.

"He has not rung in, sir," she told him before consulting something hidden from Anderson's view. "But I see he is scheduled for a meeting at ten, so should be here shortly." She looked up and past Anderson. "In fact, I think that might be him at the gates now."

Anderson turned and, through the building's glass doors, could see a well-built officer slightly older than himself striding purposefully through the outer sentry post. Pausing only to give his thanks, Anderson hurried outside to meet him.

"Lieutenant Harris?"

The man stopped in the middle of the concrete approach and eyed Anderson cautiously.

"I'm Harris."

"Sub-Lieutenant Anderson, sir," Anderson announced, saluting.

"Took your time, didn't you?" Harris grunted as he returned the compliment. Rank aside, Harris could only have been a few years Anderson's senior, yet the attitude of a mature regular naval officer was very apparent.

"My train was delayed, sir," the younger man replied. "I arrived at nine yesterday evening and they told me you were not expected to return until morning."

"They could have 'phoned," Harris supposed.

"They could indeed, sir," Anderson agreed holding the older man's gaze. For a moment each inspected the other, then Harris seemed to relax.

"Well now you're here we'd better get on with things. The boat's in the yard and not expected to be released until this afternoon but there's plenty to do here; we've a temporary office set up on the mezzanine." He paused and scrutinised Anderson again. "Are you from the north?"

The younger man foundered for a second. "No, sir, Hampshire; Chichester actually."

"And sailing experience?"

"My father kept a yawl at Emsworth," Anderson replied doubtfully.

"So you can sail," Harris mused, "though not a Scot."

"That's right, sir."

"No matter. There's a general meeting with the flotilla SO at ten. It's not mission-specific, those are held on the day we go out, but I suppose you may as well attend." Harris glanced at his watch before continuing towards the main building with Anderson following uncertainly in his wake. "But we'll find a place for you to get settled first," he continued. "There are some returns that need sorting, AFOs to update and we're expecting further replacements later in the day; actually, you may as well skip the meeting and get straight on with that."

"As you wish, sir," Anderson replied stoically.

Harris glanced across. "Is this your first posting in Coastal Forces?"

"Yes, sir."

"I see." The senior man's voice betrayed disappointment.

"I volunteered over a year ago," Anderson added hurriedly, "and have been with the Royal Naval Patrol Service until now."

"The RNPS?" Harris glanced across at the newcomer with slightly more interest. "Minesweepers, I suppose?"

"Yes, sir."

"Where stationed?"

"East Coast."

Now respect was evident. "Dunkirk?"

"That's right, sir."

Harris paused and unbent a little. "Look we can't carry on

with this 'sir' business; I'm Robert – Bob if you must, though don't be too casual in front of the men."

Anderson smiled. "And I Ian."

"Ian?" Harris repeated lightening further. "Are you sure you're not a Scot?"

Anderson was spared a reply by the arrival of a petty officer several years older than either of them.

"Sorry to hinterrupt, gentlem'n, but there's been a message from the yard."

Harris turned to him. "What is it, Price?"

"Yardmaster says she's ready whenever. 'Parently Carter and Newman are with 'er and 'ave been most of the leave, far as I can gather."

"Well they'll just have to wait," Harris snorted. "At least until later this afternoon."

"I could collect her," Anderson found himself saying. Harris looked at him sharply.

"Could you?"

"I'm just down from *St Christopher*'s, they've most types of launch there and I tried them all."

Harris considered this, then reached a decision.

"Very well, go down and take Price with you. The returns can wait and Lord knows you'll not be missing anything in the briefing." He turned to the petty officer. "Mr Price, meet Sub-Lieutenant Anderson, our new number one." The two men saluted before awkwardly shaking hands. "Round up whoever you can," Harris continued to Price. "With luck, you'll catch the ferry."

"Very good, sar," Price saluted once more and nodded to Anderson. "I'll be back with some 'ands instantly."

"He's a good man, been with the boat longer than I have and the best coxswain in the flotilla," Harris muttered when Price had gone. Then, without thinking added, "Regular hand of course."

"I'd noticed that, sir," Anderson replied more coldly.

"Look, I didn't mean that how it sounded," Harris assured him quickly. "I've a lot of respect for you wavy types: volunteers and all that. In fact, apart from Price, our crew is totally 'hostilities only' ratings."

"Do you mean 'hostiles', sir?" Anderson asked dryly.

"Yes, that is what some call them," Harris admitted and both men smiled. "I expect you get a measure of prejudice from us straight stripers?"

"A fair bit, sir, and it's understandable."

"Oh yes?"

Anderson shrugged. "I trained as a teacher and taught geography at a prep school for three years before joining up. I'm not sure how I would have reacted to working alongside others not so qualified yet doing a similar job."

"I suppose that's it," the senior man agreed.

"But it's a job I am determined to learn," Anderson told him with obvious sincerity.

"I can see that," Harris admitted. "And am glad to have you with me."

* * *

MGB 95 was eighteen months old, which was elderly by Coastal Forces standards, and about the last to be powered by Rolls-Royce engines. Lieutenant Commander Peter Collins, the flotilla's senior officer, glanced again at the two sheets of paper before him. The dockyard's initial evaluation showed her recent damage to be extensive yet, beside it, the completion report confirmed all had been rectified, and with remarkable speed. Collins knew from experience the repairs would be adequate but no more, patches might be obvious and there were bound to be signs of previous damage, but the boat would function and that was all anyone required.

Which probably held true for her crew. Collins had been able to obtain replacements for both her casualties and was hopeful that they would do a workmanlike job. Each would have been through rapid, though thorough, training and was a volunteer. His only doubts lay with Anderson, the boat's new second in command. Men could be trained to fire a gun, take up a tow or any other physical task necessary aboard a high-speed launch reasonably quickly – it took far longer to learn the intricacies of managing people. But Anderson had been a first officer before, if in a very different type of vessel, so perhaps there was hope.

Whether he had dealt with a captain as irascible as Harris before was another matter, though. The man was a born seaman, brilliant at handling his boat and equally gifted when it came to commanding her in action, but when dealing with the men he showed serious shortcomings. In a perfect world, he would have been captain of something larger, one of the newer frigates or maybe even a destroyer; something that retained a little of the dash his temperament so needed while also giving the isolation usual for a CO. With several men to buffer him from the crew, he would undoubtedly be more popular and might easily become accepted by the ratings. But when officers and men were confined to under seventy feet of fragile hull such separation was not possible; there could be no secrets and little mystery between those who fought within such close confines. With luck, Anderson would give better support than his predecessors and Collins supposed that Harris might even have learned something from the recent action; if not he wondered if it might be better to consider him for a transfer. The navy was as short of suitable men as they were any other essential resource, and an officer who consumed manpower with such abandon was simply too expensive to keep. One of Harris' previous first lieutenants had stubbornly insisted on being returned to corvettes and was probably even now struggling in the depths of the Atlantic in an underpowered and poorly armed tub – to have chosen that as an alternative to a shore-based posting in Coastal Forces said much about the conditions aboard Harris' boat.

But Harris and Anderson would make progress, or not, without his worrying; Collins placed the two reports back into their buff card folder and reached for the next. He had six other craft and six other crews to fuss over in addition to his own. Shortly he would be holding the normal commanding officers' meeting when he would explain the general plan for the next few days. There would be no surprises, it would be the same mixture of convoy, minesweeper and minelayer support. The routine patrols might be spiced with the occasional foray into enemy waters if those at Operations took a fancy to some particular target. Whenever possible they would continue to give E-boats a wide berth, however. Not that the evil beasts could be avoided; they were one of the enemy's principal weapons and likely to be encountered on a regular basis. But despite recent improvements, even the best in his flotilla were slower, smaller and carried less weaponry while the Germans' diesel-powered engines made them far less vulnerable. If they should meet, his chaps usually accounted for themselves well enough, but the days when they willingly brought them to battle were still a long way off.

As were so many things in Peter Collins' life. He already had two children and the previous evening Miriam, his wife, had ruefully admitted a third might be on the way. It was wonderful news, of course, but not so very welcome at that moment and Collins was forced to accept the new addition would simply have to fight for attention amid his numerous other problems.

* * *

The ferry Harris had spoken of turned out to be a light Bedford truck that made a regular morning run between the local Navy bases carrying all manner of equipment and personnel as well as any less confidential despatches. As the only officer, it was assumed Anderson would ride in the cab so it was after the briefest of introductions and a cold, grinding journey of well over an hour, that he had the chance to meet his new shipmates properly.

"Should make it back in better time," Price, the coxswain, told him when he and a rating had jumped down from the lorry's tailgate.

"Should be a mite more comfortable an' all," the seaman agreed as he stretched his limbs. Anderson's seat in the cab had been no feather bed and he wondered if it might have smeared oil on his trousers, but his position would have been preferable to sitting aft amid several crates, and probably a good deal warmer.

"Sorry I had to put you through it," he told them.

"Sure, but we'd have had to come here somehows," the rating assured him casually as the three began to walk toward the small shipyard.

"Is this where the boat was built?" Anderson asked; Price shook his head.

"Na, the old girl's an early model," he replied. "Built in Hythe long before they started jobbin' work out to other yards. I've been with 'er since the RN took charge. She were 'riginally meant for some foreign navy as an MTB. When the government snatched 'er back they finished 'er as a Motor Anti-Sub Boat – a Masbe they calls 'em – before 'avin' another change of 'eart an' turning 'er into a gunboat."

Anderson had noticed neither man addressed him formally and was not sorry. It had been the same in minesweepers; in front of senior officers, salutes and the like would be automatic but at other times they were simply men working together. Such an attitude might not be approved of by some, but he had long since held that addressing a superior as "sir" did not necessarily imply esteem, and often the reverse. If a man was worthy of respect it would be shown in other ways.

"How does she handle?"

That was a more serious question and the coxswain's eyes flashed across to see if the new officer truly wanted to know.

"Well enough," he answered cautiously. "She's manageable

in calm waters, though less if you get in a bit of rough and at 'igh speed there's one 'ell of a turning circle. Port engine's slow to pick up though I dare say Mr Carter will 'ave sorted that b'now and none of them early boats manoeuvre well in 'arbour."

"No, I remember running a Masbe aground at *St Christopher*'s when reverse failed to engage."

"Is that right, sir?" Price asked, and Anderson noticed the honorific had slipped in.

"You needn't worry, it was my first time," he assured them. "I did improve."

"Well you won't be seein' many around as Masbes now," the Irishman, who Anderson remembered was called Daly, remarked. "They made most into gunboats when submarines weren't the nuisance they were expecting."

"But she still carries depth charges?" Anderson asked.

"Oh aye," Price assured him. "Though no ASDIC or the like, least not unless this character 'as done something clever."

The elderly man Price referred to was striding towards them wearing a greasy bowler and a tired blue suit that seemed too tight for his belly.

"Will you be for ninety-five?" he asked when they were close enough and turned to walk alongside when Anderson confirmed they were.

"Given us more than a few problems your boat has," the man admitted. "Mind, you saved us time by sending your chaps to sort out the motors; got her afloat at first light and running lovely they are."

"Is she fuelled?" Anderson asked. They had reached the perimeter fence and the yardmaster unlocked the gate.

"Exactly what she had when she came in," he assured them, although Anderson noticed he did not directly meet anyone's eye. "Ain't taken nothing out, ain't no more gone back. You've nigh on an 'undred an' fifty gallons which'll get you back to Dover and then some."

The possibility that a little might have found its way elsewhere was not lost on Anderson but such things were almost expected and all but impossible to prove. Besides, a little petty theft was not his concern; what was lay less than a hundred feet away moored to a small jetty.

Despite being little more than sixty feet in length – roughly the size of a gentleman's yacht – *MGB 95* looked every inch the potent fighting craft. Her sleek lines, purposeful bow and elegant curve to deck and superstructure spoke of speed and resilience while gun turrets to either side and a covered mounting aft showed she could fight as well. Other fittings and equipment packed the small amount of deck space and appeared to be in order; it was only as they drew closer that the defects began to show.

Work had obviously been carried out to her foredeck; light grey patches commonly known as tingles appeared wet and were the only spotless parts of the entire craft. Further areas aft stood out as plainly and the boat's lower hull was streaked with oil and grime. Anderson had seen worse; to the untrained eye *Anvil*, his last ship and a converted Icelandic trawler, had looked ready for the scrapyard. Like many from the Royal Naval Patrol Service, it was as if her crew delighted in an unkempt appearance, but to find a dedicated warship in such a state was less common, especially one coming straight from the care of a dockyard. However, it seemed Price saw nothing incongruous in her appearance.

"Old girl's back hon-line," he sighed with satisfaction as they mounted the small jetty.

The yardmaster cleared his throat. "If you'll forgive me, gentlemen, I need some signatures to approve the repairs."

Anderson stopped and considered the man who held a wad of papers out to him. "We'll inspect her first," he stated firmly.

Closer, the boat was more impressive. Although well-worn it was clear her equipment was indeed up to standard. The depth charge cradles looked well maintained and all winches and lockers were clear and serviceable.

"If you'll pardon me, you was right to take a look-see first," Price muttered to Anderson as they stepped aboard. "Not sayin' his lads 'ave done a bad job, but always better to check."

A figure dressed in stained overalls appeared from an after hatch and pulled himself up onto the deck in one easy motion.

"Les Carter, hactin' chief motor mechanic," Price announced as the man, probably a few years older than Anderson, stepped forward as he wiped his hands on a rag.

"Anderson, your new number one." The pair shook hands and Anderson was impressed by the firm, yet strangely gentle grip. "I understand this is a Rolls boat."

"Indeed, sir," Carter agreed readily. The light was obviously brighter than where he had come from and the mechanic shaded his eyes as he spoke. "Newman and I have given them a thorough overhaul. They're on the top line now."

"Newman?"

"My stoker," Carter explained. "He's below; you'll meet

him presently."

Anderson shrugged. The engine room was one of the most important areas of the ship and he was keen to see the Rolls; every engine encountered during training had been Hall-Scott or Packards. "Care to show me now?" he asked.

Negotiating the narrow hatch was not as easy as Carter made it appear, but he was soon in the cramped, almost claustrophobic, area that housed the engines.

"Bill must have slipped out," Carter supposed. "But I reckon these are what you want to see," he added patting the nearest engine.

It was low, sleek and clearly well maintained; in the light from dim bulkhead lamps, the bare metal positively glowed beneath the thinnest sheen of fresh oil. Anderson looked about; there were two of the monsters in the small compartment and they more than filled the place. He'd heard much about the legendary powerplants which were actually derived from the same units currently fitted to some fighters. Production of the marinized versions had long since ceased to satisfy a more immediate need in the air. But Rolls engines were still rumoured to be the best, providing they had the engineers to care for them and, in this case, Anderson sensed there was no need to worry.

"Supercharged?" he questioned.

Carter nodded. "Each produces just over a thousand horsepower."

Anderson stared about the small, cramped space; what the noise would be like when both were at maximum throttle could only be imagined, but that much power in a hull barely more than sixty feet long would be tremendous.

"I understand you have been overhauling them while the boat was laid up," Anderson remarked as he continued his inspection. Everything in the engine room was obviously well cared for; the place seemed to exude efficiency and expertise.

"Myself and Newman," Carter replied almost defensively. "They'd have done a good enough job at the yard, but we've come to know these beauties pretty well over time."

"And even better now I suppose," Anderson added with a grin that was immediately returned.

"You can get to the rest of the boat from here, sir," Carter announced. "That's if you've seen enough."

"I have and am mightily impressed," Anderson replied. He looked about at the crowded space once more, though apparently cluttered there were none of the patches of oil, rags or general dirt he had been accustomed to in *Anvil's* engine room. Even the atmosphere, though undoubtedly stuffy, seemed clean and businesslike. He turned back, raised himself as high as the deckhead would allow, and began to follow Carter as he made for a small ladder. "Tell me, there is no smell of petrol, is that usual?"

"Petrol?" Carter questioned almost absentmindedly as he paused to consider. "It's funny you should mention that, sir, petrol fumes is something we tries to discourage."

* * *

The basement canteen at HMS *Wasp* was run by the NAAFI, an organisation that catered for Navy, Army and Air Force personnel. And, like most, it was clean and well cared for even if the strong scent of damp walls betrayed how close the former hotel was to the sea. The area was divided into two unequal sections. One, the smaller, being distinguished by polished mahogany tables borrowed from the hotel's main dining room and carpet that had been scavenged when an upper room was stripped of all furnishing to make the Operations Centre. This was used by the Wrens and petty officers. The section for ratings was larger as it not only catered for those who worked in the building, but regular hands from the motor launches moored at the Camber.

The time for breakfast had passed some while before but, by using his unique mixture of charm and menace, Sharkey Ward, *MGB 95*'s Oerlikon gunner, had persuaded the staff to rustle up a couple of late portions. Now he and Bob Scott, another seaman gunner who manned the boat's port half-inch Vickers, were sitting back as they recovered from a meal of truly mammoth proportions.

"Very tasty, very sweet," Sharkey announced. "Say what you like about Naffi grub, you don't get helpings like that on the outside."

"Don't get them in most Naffi, neither," Scott snorted. "It's on account of us being active service – front line troops," he added complacently.

"Well he ain't front-line," Sharkey's comment was loud enough for the young rating at the next table to hear. "Barely out the cradle and 'as hardly seen the sea, yet gets to mix with his betters and shares their scran."

The lad, a writer in signals, could hardly have been twelve months younger than either of them but blushed deeply and kept his eyes averted as he swallowed the last of his tea.

Robbed of an argument, Sharkey turned his attention to his

friend. "Blimey I hung one on last night," he announced, dabbing at his forehead dramatically.

"Better break the habit," Scott warned. "We're back on the job tomorrow; clear head and a clean mind, that's what's needed."

"Won't have a lot of choice," his mate grumbled. "There'll be no leave now till Christmas, and hardly sure of a break then."

"Weather's worsening," Scott pointed out. "Germans don't like a chop any more than we do. There'll be less patrols and not so many missions – far more chance of a one hour call-up or total stand-down."

"Can't do much in an hour, not without booze," Sharkey seemed to consider this before adding, "or a willing bint."

"It won't be the same without Lawlor," Scott reflected. "He was always ready for a spree and were a diamond on local leave. Always found the best spots he did."

"Maybe he'll come back," Sharkey grunted. "They do sometimes."

"Not Lawlor." Scott was positive. "Messed up proper he were. Lucky if he keeps his arm. They'll send him back to Wales more'n like."

"Shame, he was all right."

"And Simpson won't be coming back."

"Simpson?" Sharkey exclaimed in surprise. "Our old Jimmy? Who'd want 'im?"

"Come on, Shark, the guy bought it."

"Best thing he ever managed," his mate continued unrepentant. "And about the only one he didn't cock-up. All that "if you please" an' stuff. Feller should have stayed at home and tended his flowers. No Lawlor's the one I'll miss, solid with a magazine he were, never let me run dry." He considered Scott. "I don't suppose you'd like to take his place?"

"Take his place?"

"Be my loader at the Oerlik'." Sharkey fixed him with deep brown eyes that suddenly seemed unusually liquid. "You'd do a grand job; we'd be a team." It was almost a proposal.

Scott's mouth opened but no reply was forthcoming. He got on with Sharkey as a shipmate, but the idea of being alongside him for all the time they were at sea was frankly appalling. Fortunately he was spared the need to answer by the arrival of two men.

One was Jelly, the boat's sparks. Although an HO rating like the rest, Jelly had taken to his craft and was hoping to be made leading telegraphist before long. That would not be enough, however; after several years of dead-end jobs, Jelly had finally found something he was good at and was privately determined to make the Navy his career.

"New shipmate for you, lads," he announced approaching the table and indicating the slight, rather placid youth walking a step behind.

"Name's Dowling," Jelly continued shoving the boy forward. "Michael Dowling."

"Glad to know you, Mikey," Scott declared, although his expression was less certain.

"Aye," Sharkey grudgingly allowed after examining the lad for slightly longer. He looked younger than any of them – younger even than the rating at the next table – and every bit as guileless. "First posting, is it?"

"Fresh from *Glendower*," Jelly confirmed.

The boy nodded. "I – I volunteered," he confessed.

"That were your first mistake," Sharkey told him.

"But one we all made," Scott added less forcefully.

"Maybe so, but it don't mean you can't make something from it," Jelly stated with authority.

"So, what's your trade?" Sharkey asked. Lawlor had been a loader but that didn't mean the lad had come to replace him; it was quite common for the gunners to change positions. If Scott wouldn't join him on the rear gun, he'd ask Daly, the Irishman.

"I'm a gunner," Dowling muttered.

"Half-inch is it?" Sharkey supposed as the doubts began to grow.

"No, twenty-millimetre," Jelly announced with a grin. "He's your new loader, Sharks – won't that be nice for you both?"

* * *

"So she was originally a Motor Anti-Submarine Boat," Anderson mused. They were yet to finish the inspection but had already seen enough to know a good job had been done. After signing her off, the pair retreated to *MGB 95*'s wheelhouse.

"That's right, a Masbe," Price agreed. "Beginnin' of the war everyone thought subs would be the problem. They 'adn't 'eard much about E-boats then."

"I suppose we've all learned a lot in the past couple of years."

"And likely to a bit more in them what's to come," Price snorted. "Forgive me for asking, but 'ave you been with Coastal Forces long?"

"First posting; I was RNPS before."

"Churchill's Pirates!" the coxswain exclaimed with glee before adding, "Then you'll know hall about E-boats."

"Oh yes, I've had my fill."

"My brother's a CPO at *Sparra's Nest*."

"Then we probably met." Anderson gave a wry grin.

"You'd remember, he usually starts by tellin' the new blokes they're gonna hate 'im, 'cause 'e hates 'em already!'"

"They're a pretty tough bunch but the training's excellent."

For a moment Price regarded the new officer and seemed pleased with what he saw. "Well there's only the bridge left, and that's behind you," he said. "Then we can get the Chief to fire 'er up and set course for 'ome."

"Very well," Anderson agreed. "Why don't I explore that myself while you talk to Mr Carter?"

Left on his own, Anderson stepped up to the bridge area which was set immediately behind and above the wheelhouse. But rather than a small open space, he was faced by two large cupolas similar to those found on the turrets of tanks. Each had been set into the wheelhouse roof and would hold one man comfortably. He stepped on the wide ledge beneath, eased himself up through the starboard opening and rested his arms comfortably on the rim. As much of the boat could be seen as from any bridge and he supposed the extra support could be useful in a chop or when manoeuvring fast. There was a central cluster of speaking tubes that could be used from either cupola, a bank of switches that must be for the firing gongs, masthead recognition lamps and the like. And, despite the voice pipes, in an emergency it would be no effort to communicate with the coxswain almost directly below, although Anderson could not ignore the restriction being inside a cupola gave. It was like standing in the mouth of a manhole, and something he would have to get used to.

"Chief is ready," Price called up from below, just as one engine started with a muffled rumble. "And, if you'll hec-scuse me, sar, it's customary to command from the port glory 'ole."

* * *

Harris passed out of the large glass doors of HMS *Wasp* and took a deep breath of damp autumnal air. It had been unusually hot in the Operations Room. And stuffy; several of the flotilla's commanding officers had chain smoked throughout and one kept trying to light a pipe. He glanced at his watch. It was nearly twelve; Anderson and the others should be returning with the boat shortly. He'd left his greatcoat inside but it was hardly cold and, after the fug he'd just endured, the slight chill was welcome.

He walked past the sentry post and on towards the viaduct that led into the town itself. It was not far to the Camber and the Ferry Dock where Anderson should be bringing the boat in. He would meet him there and it would be best if he imparted the news as soon as possible; for news it was – the meeting had not been a complete waste of time.

Naval Intelligence produced daily updates that were distributed to all senior officers. Known as Natal, they were rarely more than a single closely typed page and represented the most accurate account of both the war and the state of the nation available. Brooks, the base captain, had presented the previous five days' updates at the meeting and they had not made good reading. News of recent aerial and shipping losses had been bad enough, but the general summary showed factory output to have fallen dramatically. Harris had read through the figures with growing apprehension; he was no expert on economics but even a novice could see where the country was heading. The *Luftwaffe*'s savage onslaught on London might have slowed of late, but enough damage had already been done and, unless a miracle happened, Britain was unlikely to recover. Not that the war was over; another of the vital resources covered by Natal was public opinion and that remained behind the government while morale appeared to be surprisingly high. Nevertheless, the current demand for war materials could not be met by bombed-out factories and, however positive the population might be, they still needed to be fed.

Harris reached The Esplanade and continued to the harbour proper. To his right, he could see the assorted shipping that lay within its doubtful protection. The sight might not be as impressive as stories he had heard of Liverpool and other West Coast docks; at present there were no major trading ships, no massive freighters filled with vital supplies, only one dented Admiralty tanker and a collection of fishing boats, tugs and similar small craft. But the determination and sense of purpose obvious in their battered hulls were equal to any found in the most modern destroyer. Just as it was in the shattered line of houses to his left that faced Waterloo Crescent. Even those still standing in defiance of the regular shelling bore the mark of action, with dislodged tiles and windows boarded over. But light could be seen from behind what glass remained, smoke still issued from several chimneys and life was clearly continuing in some form or another. Harris supposed there must come a point when defeat became inevitable, but it was still some way off.

And there had also been more immediate news from the meeting. With a boat just back from the yard, Harris had been expecting to return to active service, although not quite so quickly. He still needed to get to know Anderson and, even if the fellow turned out to be competent, they had yet to work together. But Collins, the Flotilla SO, had been definite. *MGB 95* would be going out the following night.

They would be shepherding a small convoy through the Strait; not so onerous a task and something Harris, the boat and most of her crew had done several times before. The merchants would be picked up off Dungeness, seen past the Goodwins, then let go once all had rounded North Foreland. A simple enough operation, though one that would take all night leaving scant chance of making the run back in darkness. They might go unmolested; meteorological reports suggested squally showers although what he hoped for most was a decent chop – nothing too strenuous, just enough to keep the E-boats in their place. But whether wet or dry, rough or calm, he was going to have a goodly time in which to get to know his new number one. More than that, he would be depending on him as much as every man aboard *MGB 95*. In the past they had been a team; not the best admittedly, but one that had served its purpose and, by fluke or good fortune, no one had been badly hurt until that last mission. But now that team was no more, their run of luck had come to an end and Harris knew something more solid must be found to rely on if they were to survive.

* * *

Once at sea, Anderson soon forgot all about *MGB 95*'s unfamiliar bridge arrangement and was able to concentrate solely on staying in control. They quit the small harbour easily enough; as with most craft of her type, the helm was all but useless at slow speeds, although she manoeuvred easily under engines and, once in open water, the temptation to fully open her up was strong. At first he was cautious; his task had been to see the boat back to Dover and it would be foolish to take chances. But with the wind whistling through his hair and both engines burbling with obvious potential the temptation grew. And it was daylight; chances were strong the next time he had charge of the boat would be in the black of night, surely it was better to take advantage of such an opportunity? Price was at the wheel below, Carter and Newman would be in their precious engine room and Daly was relaxing aft and appeared to be reading a racing newspaper. With both gun turrets empty, it was as if he were alone on the boat; there would be no better time...

He glanced down at Price, whose head was just forward of his own knees. Sensing his eyes upon him, the coxswain looked up and back, and both men shared a grin.

"Very well, Cox'," Anderson chuckled. And then, in a much louder voice, "Open her up!"

From behind came a roaring crescendo as both supercharged engines were unleashed, the sound rose until it became positively painful while the beast surged forward, her screws biting deep into the mild waters of the Channel. Anderson found himself clutching at the sides of the cupola as the bows lifted and they went up onto the plane. Then they were positively skimming over the water with the forward third of their hull in free air. He glanced about, there was still no sign of other craft, only the dark anonymous shoreline was in sight but still he felt vaguely self-conscious. He looked back, a great wave of apparently solid water was being thrown up behind, higher – so much higher – than anything he had managed with the boats at *St Christopher's*. He bent down slightly; there was really no need for a voice pipe when you could almost touch the man you were addressing. "Starboard fifteen, steady as you go."

Price bellowed back the order as he swung the wheel around and Anderson gripped the side of the cupola once more. The boat seemed to dig into the water as she turned and, though the bows were now some distance above the waves, she rode them easily.

"Shift your rudder!" he yelled, and the boat turned back, then, "Starboard fifteen," once more.

For several minutes Anderson soaked in the sensation of speed before, after two more changes to their heading, common sense took hold. It was broad daylight and they were venturing deeper into the Channel; at any moment they could be buzzed by fighters or even something larger and the boat was completely unarmed. More than that, Dover was on the horizon; they would not only be on the radar but actually in sight.

"Port twenty, Cox': eighteen hundred revolutions." The boat slowed perceivably yet remained on the plane and, though her engines had ceased to roar, she was still racing along at a creditable rate.

Ever since he had applied for a transfer to Coastal Forces,

Anderson had been harbouring doubts. His job in *Anvil* might not have been glamorous but it was undoubtedly worthwhile and a valuable contribution to the war effort. And those he had worked alongside were mainly former fishermen; hard nuts who knew more about the sea than he ever would, yet they grudgingly respected his uniform and the authority it proclaimed. Coastal Forces was an entirely different proposition; the practices and traditions of the Royal Navy were far more in evidence and, until that moment, part of him was unsure if it had been the right move. But he did so want to bring the fight to the enemy and, with a lithe and powerful craft like this, he could do exactly that. Tatty and unkempt she may appear; from his current position the gunboat's unusually wide beam was very obvious while, even fully armed, she would be decidedly inferior to the best the enemy could offer. Yet now there was no doubt that this was a ship he could take to war, and equally one it would be all too easy to love.

Chapter Three

They left the following evening as dusk was starting to fall although, so dark had the day been, it was a subtle change. Since *MGB 95* returned the previous day everyone had been busy. The boat needed to be rearmed, her wireless and compasses set up, smoke canisters and depth charges taken on board and finally several hundred gallons of high octane petrol distributed between her tanks. The final task had taken two hours that morning and was completed with all electricity in the boat shut off. Now all aboard were tired but none more so than Anderson, who had still to get used to the crew as well as a lot of new responsibilities. These included the boat's navigation and as *MGB 95* emerged from the gloom of the eastern harbour entrance, he was already in the wheelhouse poring over a chart.

Harris, at his station in the port cupola, was aware of this, as he was the futility of the act. On leaving harbour the three boats of their patrol had taken up position to either side of the flotilla leader; they need only keep station on Collins' craft to arrive at the correct rendezvous point so why anyone should worry about waypoints and dead reckoning was beyond him. Then, and with a tinge of guilt, he remembered privately censoring Simpson for neglecting that very duty and was inwardly ashamed.

So, if Anderson wanted to exercise himself in setting a course and checking their position, it was fine by him. In fact, after the diligence and care the man had already shown when seeing to the boat's needs, he was hardly surprised. There were still some changes needed of course; his new second in command was inclined to be too analytical for his liking and had made sure the tanks were filled equally, as well as checking all ready-use ammunition was correctly stowed. Such things, though admittedly under the overall care of the executive officer, were usually left to the department responsible but, so transparent was his eagerness to see everything correct, neither Carter, in the engine room, nor any of the gunners had objected. Anderson was also inclined to question orders – not outright, that was something Harris would never have tolerated, but with a subtle look or possibly the raising of an eyebrow. Such traits were almost insignificant when compared with what had been achieved, however; never had he known a boat sorted for sea so quickly. They had everything finished with a little under four hours to spare and it was just a shame that a temporary fault with the W/T had prevented them spending a spell at sea working up before the patrol began.

Such a time would have been especially welcomed by their other new member; Harris glanced back to the Oerlikon as he remembered him. Dowling appeared a smart enough lad but at barely eighteen was the youngest aboard. And it wasn't just the boy's age that concerned him. He was more than simply fresh-faced: the lad had a sensitivity about him that was at odds with his current role. Quite how he would get on with Ward was another matter. As long as he did his duty, kept track of the gun's ammunition and was ready with a fresh magazine, Harris supposed he might do all right. The contrast between the two remained extreme however, yet they must serve the same weapon.

A flicker of tracer caught his eye, but it was red – British – and came from Collins' boat off their port bow. The patrol had settled to the regulation arrowhead formation known as quarterline, a pattern that allowed travel in close company without encountering another's wash, and each was now testing their guns. To his left, Frank Caswell's boat followed suit and Harris turned back and gave a nod to Daly at the starboard midships turret. For a couple of seconds the deep burble from *MGB 95*'s engines was partially buried by a staccato rattle as the single half-inch machine guns opened up, followed almost immediately by several lower and more positive thumps from the twenty-millimetre cannon astern. All functioned correctly; if they were heard again that night it would mean action and Harris supposed he was not alone in hoping they remained silent.

The young newcomer, Mike Dowling, was of the same opinion. Currently he was at the Oerlikon he shared with Sharkey Ward but, since arriving the morning before, his feet had hardly touched the ground. There was so much to do and, comprehensive though his training had been, the lad had been expecting slightly longer before being thrown into the turmoil of active service. Even some of the gunboat's crew remained strangers; he had met them all of course but was slow at remembering names. One was already etched on his brain, however, and he already felt he knew Sharkey Ward better than he would have perhaps liked.

"I wouldn't go worrying over them," the man was telling him now as Dowling carefully picked up the spent shell cases.

"They's no use to man nor beast, chuck 'em over the side."

"The guns we used in training had collection bags," the boy announced uncertainly.

"Yeah, well that's training for you," Sharkey grunted. "No one fires long enough to worry about jams; bag gets full an' the next thing you know your gun's useless."

Dowling looked up in the gloom; he was a tidy lad – his mother always said so – and despite Sharkey's explanation, was certain the cartridge cases would be useful to someone. He could ask the armourer when they took on fresh ammunition or take them to one of the collection sites in the town. But Sharkey Ward was a particularly rough man and one he had accidentally offended on several occasions during the short time he had been with the boat. Dowling wasn't sure how much of the gunner's verbal aggression was genuine and had no intention of finding out so, without another word, he tossed the warm shell cases over the stern.

At the helm, Price was probably the most settled of them all. He had guided *MGB 95* on every mission to date and done so under two captains prior to Harris. Their last patrol had not been particularly clever, but men had died aboard under previous commanders. There had been one occasion when the W/T room, barely feet away from his current position and where Jelly now sat, had been riddled with machine gun fire. The telegraphist fell along with their number one who had been standing just where Anderson now studied his maps; Price was still unsure how he, at the helm, had escaped. And there was another occasion when they lost their starboard gunner while the list of minor injuries was far longer. But other boats had suffered worse with a good few being destroyed in the heat of action or, more commonly, while limping back to base, so he supposed by that standard *MGB 95* was still a lucky ship. He just hoped her good fortune would stretch a little further.

* * *

"By my estimation, we should expect to sight the convoy in about fifteen minutes," Anderson announced as his head and shoulders appeared in the cupola beside Harris.

"Very good." The senior man's tone was harsh but his words were sincerely meant. Whether Anderson's estimate was in any way accurate had yet to be revealed, although the fact that he had attempted the calculation was a good sign and only went to confirm Harris' growing good opinion. The boat was travelling at regulation speed, which meant a little over twenty knots, and the engines were barely being stretched at eighteen hundred revolutions, so it was probably the right time for what he had in mind. "All right if we set a few ground rules?" he asked.

"Of course, sir," Anderson agreed, wondering slightly.

"I'm sure they taught you well at *St Christopher*'s but there are some things you need to know, most of which we've only picked up in the last few months. And the majority are a bit more important than banning smoking aft of the wheelhouse. In fact, most aren't official recommendations at all, but then not everything has to be done by the book."

Anderson nodded and Harris continued.

"First of all, we try and cross the enemy's T – it's about the only tactic that hasn't changed since Nelson's time and until the Admiralty sees sense and allows us a decent forward-facing gun, is likely to remain so. If we come across an E it will have one for certain, but just the one; further aft they carry a darn sight more. That said, don't ignore the rearward approach. I know what it says in the manual but believe me that can also work; the enemy's lookouts are invariably concentrating on what's up ahead and a carefully handled boat can creep close enough on low power if you do it right. Once you know yourself to be in range, veer to one side and leave it to the gunners. And I do mean leave it to them; we've only a small crew but each knows their job well and none will thank you for too much direction."

"So creep up behind?" Anderson asked, trying to keep the doubt from his mind.

"If you can't cross the T," Harris confirmed. "The same tactics would get you into a hell of a lot of trouble in an MTB which is probably why they don't recommend it, but I've known it work with gunboats even when the moon was up, so don't let anyone tell you otherwise."

Anderson nodded silently, conscious that the advice came from experience so was riches indeed.

"And if you have to take them from the side, remember the armament. A point five Vickers is heavy metal for most close quarter work and might be fine against aircraft, but E-boats are built of stronger stuff. Give them any distance and a half-inch will hardly scratch the surface, while a VP or anything larger will simply laugh. So bear your heaviest weapons in mind when positioning yourself and make sure they have sight of the enemy. I know it's not easy when nothing of any real size is pointing over the bows but we have to work with what we've got. And while we're talking VPs, don't be fooled by them; they might look like fishing boats and come across as an easy target that can be outpaced on one engine, but they carry heavy metal and can blow a tiddler like us out of the water without even trying."

Again Anderson remained quiet. In fact, he knew quite a bit about what the Germans called *Vorpostenboote*. He supposed the old *Anvil* and her like were not so very different: civilian craft brought in to cover a warship's duties. But then his previous boat had stuck mainly to minesweeping whereas the VPs were given proper patrol duties and could carry several eighty-eight-millimetre cannon that would make easy meat of a small wooden launch.

"My predecessor swapped a Rolls two-pounder aft for the Oerlikon, and I think it was a wise move," Harris continued. "I've requested they make it up to a double though it's anyone's guess if that will happen. And I'm not alone in wanting something similar on the foredeck. The boffins might tell you the platform isn't stable enough and they could be right, but a decent forward-facing gun would make a lot of difference. For now though, that twenty mill. is the best we have, so mind you keep it in range at all times."

Anderson glanced back to where Ward and Dowling were huddled together under the doubtful protection of the gun's splinter mattress; his training had taught him how effective the weapon could be although, as the main armament for a gunboat, it did seem light.

"Another thing: don't be afraid to use the depth charges. We've no ASDIC so engaging a sub is hardly likely and, if we did, our four cans probably wouldn't be enough. However they are effective against surface craft – again, providing you get in close. And there's a good side: even if the attack is ineffective, the splash they send up is usually enough to see you clear. But make sure you do get clear – stick around too long and the amatol will wreck your hull as easily as the enemy's."

"I understand."

"Apart from that, there are the usual standing orders posted in the wheelhouse."

"I've noticed them," Anderson confirmed. "And wondered about access to the mess deck."

"You mean no one to enter in anything above a force four?" Harris gave a wry grin.

"Yes, it seemed strange."

"You've yet to see the boat in a proper chop. Believe me, she moves about a bit; another flotilla lost a hand in just such a way."

"Lost?"

"Aye," Harris agreed more seriously. "They believe he broke a leg when being flung against a bulkhead. Couldn't get himself clear and by then they were heading home on the plane – no one heard his shouts. Poor devil spent the trip being bounced about like a bead in a rattle; there wasn't much left by the time they put in."

Anderson's mouth went suddenly dry, it seemed there was danger enough aboard a gunboat without involving the enemy.

"And never forget, we carry high octane fuel; a teacup has the same explosive power as several pounds of TNT," Harris continued as if reading his mind. "Even without Jerry shooting at us, the boat's a potential firework – we wouldn't be the first to brew up without even sighting an enemy."

He paused, as if gauging if his words were having any effect, then continued.

"And one final thought – look after yourself. The lore of the sea applies as much in war as in peace – probably more so. Chances might come to help another, be it one from our own flotilla, a merchant or even – God help us – a German. And they should be taken, as long as it can be done without endangering ourselves. There can only ever be one priority; it's no good trying to rescue some poor blighter from the drink, only to join him in it. Put anything or anyone else above the boat and you'll lose it, along with all aboard, and yourself into the bargain."

The cold words hung in the air for a moment, then the starboard gunner bellowed from his turret.

"Convoy in sight, bearing red five-fifty," he reported.

"Very good, Daly," Harris replied, his attention returning to the task in hand. Then he glanced to Anderson and granted a rare smile. "There's probably more and I'll tell you when I think of it. I'll tell you because you seem like the type who'll take notice, which will be a new experience for me. Just remember what I said; not everything is done by the book."

* * *

At the helm, Price had noticed one of the convoy escorts at the same moment as Daly and was ready to react when the signal came from the SO's boat. It had just started to rain although the wind was staying low and they had barely any chop; with a reasonable moon it would be a long and dangerous trip to Foreland, with probably a daylight run back to Dover. A whistle came from the speaking tube directly above his head although it was still quiet enough to hear the captain's order from the bridge without its assistance. After repeating the gruff instructions, he dutifully swung the boat about and brought her to station about a mile off the convoy's starboard beam. Then, and only then, did Price deign to inspect the shipping they were ordered to protect.

One appeared to be a light coaster and the second, which was slightly closer to the English coast, looked even smaller; neither would be grossing much in the way of tonnage but there were at least three other permanent escorts and what looked like an armed trawler to support them. Meanwhile, *MGB 95* was in the centre of the gunboat force that would see them through the Straits with the SO's craft about a mile forward and 'Cas' Caswell's probably the same distance behind. He turned his attention back to the convoy and, more specifically, their escorts. All, bar the trawler, were Fairmile B motor launches that would probably have been with the merchants since the start of their journey. They were larger than the MGBs but considerably slower, having two Hall-Scott engines that, combined, were barely more powerful than one of *MGB 95*'s Rolls units. The Fairmiles could maintain convoy speed well enough though, and were economic to the point of being miserly, whilst still having the power to clock twenty knots if needed. But that was half the speed of an E-boat and, though they carried a fair amount of weaponry, the lack of power alone made them vastly inferior when confronting the German beasts.

Price was aware of movement from behind but did not turn as Anderson appeared from the bridge. The officer flicked on the small, heavily shaded lamp, and began peering at his precious charts.

"We'll be keeping this station until the Goodwins, Cox'," he told him. "The tide's high and it's a light convoy, they'll be taking the inshore route but we'll keep the sands to port and be waiting to meet them when they come out the other side."

"Very good, sar," Price replied automatically. He didn't care for being referred to as Cox', the term always sounded rather rude, even to his seasoned ears. The skipper was a regular officer and always called him 'Swain: he preferred that. And there was really nothing so very unusual in the plan; they had followed similar a dozen times before when escorting shallow draft merchants. But it might be considered insolent to relay any of his thoughts to the new man; instead he set his thoughts to what lay ahead.

In peacetime, the unpredictable line of sandbanks that ran from Deal to Ramsgate was a navigational hazard, it was only when at war that some benefit could be wrung from them and they became as much a deterrent to German raiders as any minefield. Price would still have preferred to give them a wide berth, however. If the SO was sensible, he would lead the gunboats on ahead at speed and allow them an hour or two of lying cut, when they could simply drift with the current. Price was a petty officer and newly promoted at that, but he'd seen a fair bit in his sixteen years' service. To his mind lying cut was almost as good for detecting the enemy as this new-fangled radar everyone was rattling on about.

"Rain's setting in, Cox'," Anderson sighed, and Price politely agreed. The bad conditions would be with them now for the rest of the night and likely turn out more nuisance than help. But such things wouldn't be altered by worrying. Which was another thing Price had learned in his sixteen years; problems that could not be solved must be tolerated and, when faced with something as unmanageable as the weather, or RNVR officers if it came to it, you simply had to cope.

* * *

Three hours later, and after a burst of speed that left their dark home port astern for the second time that night, the boats were indeed ordered to cut their engines. The convoy, now out of sight and paradoxically protected by the natural hazard of the Goodwins, would emerge in due course, but until it did the men of *MGB 95* were enjoying relative peace as she and the other gunboats drifted in the swell. Only the sound of rain falling, the breeze in the rigging and a regular gentle slap of water against their chines broke the silence and, even though all unnecessary sound was actively discouraged, none felt like talking.

Certainly Daly, still seated in the turret that was home when they were at sea, had no need for conversation. Although powerfully built and with an equally forceful personality, Patrick John Daly had one major physical weakness and the change in motion, from thundering over the waves with two thousand horsepower behind them, to drifting helplessly at the will of wind and current, was finding him out. There was a bucket by his feet and he would feel no shame in using it; Jelly, the telegraphist, also had one in his tiny compartment forward and many of the gunboat's crew had been seasick at one time or another. The swell was relatively settled so chances remained strong Daly would not succumb that night, but still the Irishman wished something would happen; that their convoy might appear, or some minor emergency occur that meant they must return to Dover. Or even an enemy detected; practically any distraction would be welcomed if it stopped the slow, relentless roll that could yet take him over.

But further aft and temporarily free to enjoy the fresh air, Jelly was too busy to let nausea become a bother. Watched by Dowling and Sharkey, who remained closed up at their Oerlikon, the telegraphist sat with his feet dangling over the gunboat's stern. A piece of remarkably crude equipment rested on his lap and he was concentrating. The paraphernalia was partly of his own design but based on the standard hydrophone issued to all launches to detect the sound of nearby vessels. To this Jelly had added a small accumulator-powered amplifier which was connected to the conventional length of pipe that descended deep into the heaving waters below. A single plaited wire emerged from the amplifier and fed directly into Jelly's headset. As he listened, the young man's fingers constantly adjusted two Bakelite knobs on the warm casing. Ostensibly there was nothing to hear apart from water against their hull and an occasional surge as the current moved them, but once or twice Jelly thought there might be something more. A dull, regular thrumming; very much in the background yet consistent with an oncoming, slow-moving convoy. The sound came and went as if by choice, and he was uncomfortably aware it could equally be signalling the approach of traffic far more sinister. Close to where he sat – and it was strange how several boats left to drift so often stayed together – his opposite numbers aboard the other gunboats would be listening also but on more conventional rigs, and Jelly was oddly reassured by the fact that none were confident enough to report the sound, even if they had detected it.

However, now it was back and slightly louder; whatever it might be was definitely growing nearer, although that seemed to confirm it as the convoy. He sighed and glanced about, uncomfortably aware he was under the close inspection of at least two of his shipmates as well as both officers on the bridge. Returning to his task he eased the volume up until the constant sound of waves was almost painful; the strange hum was becoming regular yet still he had no idea where it came from. Then he visibly jumped as another noise broke in. This was deeper and, he realised, must have been present and growing, for some time. He glanced sideways at the bridge and, despite the rain, locked eyes with the captain.

"There's something, sir," he shouted, pulling off the headphones.

"Is it the convoy?" Harris demanded.

"I can hear the convoy," Jelly replied cautiously, "but this is different."

The captain turned away and seemed to be speaking into the voice pipes, then there was the clatter as one of the nearby gunboat's engines erupted into life. Hearing this, Jelly began to haul in his equipment and coil up the wire. The coxswain was keeping a listening watch on their radio and it could well be that one of the other boats had reported the sound; that or they were all going to act on his own single vague report. For a moment he felt a wave of doubt; supposing he had been mistaken, that the sound was nothing more than one of many underwater noises – noises those in the other boats had discounted? But Jelly quickly dismissed his concerns; no one could say what he had heard and only a fool would question it. Besides, he was another who tried to avoid worry whenever possible. And at least it was an end to the waiting.

Chapter Four

Once under power again a more regular motion took over although even Daly failed to appreciate it. Underway or at rest the same strict lookout must be maintained and, even though the rain now fell in sheets, the responsibility remained with him and Scott. The boats quickly resumed their previous patrol formation and began a slow sweep to the north-east that would flush out any enemy craft approaching from that direction. Conditions remained as bad and no one could be certain but, after fifteen minutes at regulation speed, all appeared clear. On the bridge, Harris spoke down one of the voice pipes.

"Anything to report, Tel'?"

There was no immediate answer, but Harris could hear a distorted and distant voice through the tube, then Jelly broke in more clearly.

"Message from the SO, sir. He'll be leading us round in a sweep to meet the convoy; says to keep a special lookout astern."

Anderson looked to his captain for confirmation then reached for the megaphone and relayed Collins' message to the boat in general while Harris closed the voice pipe and cursed silently. He wanted to ask more, he wanted to ask if anyone in the SO's boat had picked up what Jelly thought he'd heard, or Caswell's come to that. He gripped a gloved hand in frustration; there were more modern MGBs with R/T repeaters on the bridge – boats with proper bridges and guns that were almost a match for those the enemy carried. *MGB 95* was old by Coastal Forces' standards but that should not mean she missed out on the newer gadgets; his job was hard enough without being deprived of the right equipment.

"Convoy in sight, bearing green twenty!"

That was Scott, who had been a fraction faster than Daly in making the report. Harris peered through the rain; he could see nothing but then hadn't been staring into the dark for goodness knew how long.

"Keep your eyes behind as well," he reminded them gruffly, then looked towards Anderson in the starboard cupola. "Tel' might have been mistaken, but I get the feeling something's up."

In the half-darkness Anderson acknowledged this with a single nod; no other words were needed. The pair had already begun to develop an understanding.

* * *

The first sign that Jelly had not been mistaken came shortly afterwards and just as the first convoy escort was coming into sight. A flicker of blue light from the leading gunboat caused them all to start, and then Jelly's voice came through the speaking tube.

"SO reports movement on the port beam – wait, it sounds like he's notifying base."

Anderson swallowed and gripped the sides of the cupola more tightly.

"Yes, he's reporting E-boats," Jelly confirmed shortly afterwards, "and we're to take up action formation."

Harris glanced across to where Caswell's boat was slightly ahead and cursed once more. "Follow them in, 'Swain," he called through the wheelhouse speaking tube. "Maximum speed when you can but it looks like we're tail-end Charlie."

The engines' pitch increased slightly as Price guided the boat until she lay just to starboard of Caswell's wash, then they saw the first sign of tracer as it streaked across the rainswept night. It was red – British – and coming from the general direction of the convoy. Clearly the merchants or their escorts had seen the enemy and opened fire, which was doubly good as far as Harris was concerned. With luck, the E-boats would concentrate solely on the target before them and might not notice a trio of gunboats coming in fast off their beam. He peered through the night, Caswell's boat was drawing away but, even as he bent forward to order an increase, Price accelerated. Harris glanced across at Anderson and gave a wry grin. "Not always by the book," he bellowed.

Now they were close to maximum revs, the entire vessel was vibrating while every wave felt like a death blow as it thudded against their hull. Both officers strained to make out something solid in the rain-filled night but, apart from Caswell's boat, there was nothing definite to be seen. Then green bolts of enemy tracer were added to the red making a colourful backdrop to the dark, deadly vista. Anderson had donned a steel helmet and, noticing his captain was still wearing his black cap, reached for another and passed it across.

"Never wear them, Number One," Harris informed him.

"They make my head ache. If something's going to get you a tin hat won't stop it."

Anderson shrugged and took the helmet back, replacing it on the hook below his copular.

"Please God no one fires a starshell," Harris muttered to himself before leaning forward to the speaking tube once more. "Ready to move on my word, 'Swain," he shouted and received a muffled acknowledgement. Allowing the coxswain to lead them into column formation was one thing, but soon they would be in the heat of action and there must be no doubting who had control.

"Escort fine to starboard!" Daly yelled from his turret while pointing over the bow. Sure enough, one of the British Fairmiles could be seen – she had turned to face the attacking E-boats and was now pumping red tracer towards an unseen target.

"Friendly to starboard," Anderson announced through the megaphone.

"SO's altering course," Harris added. Caswell's boat was already playing 'follow my leader' and soon it would be their turn. "Port twenty!"

MGB 95 banked as she rode the change of direction before jolting sickeningly while passing across Caswell's wake; then a dark patch off their starboard bow burst into light and began to stream green tracer at the SO's boat.

"Perfect!" Harris shouted, reaching for the firing bell. But before he could do more, a stream of red tracer passed directly overhead from their starboard quarter.

"The bloody escort!" Anderson shouted glancing back. In an instant he could see what had happened: the SO might not have signalled their approach for fear of alerting the Germans but, whatever the reason, the nearest British Fairmile had them marked as an enemy and was engaging.

Harris' gloved hand quickly moved from firing gongs to masthead lamps and for a split second the bridge and much of *MGB 95*'s superstructure was brilliantly lit with the pattern of red and white lights that made up that night's recognition signal. The Fairmile's fire ceased immediately but their cover had been blown and any hope of surprising the Germans must surely be lost.

And so it proved; instead of predators the line of gunboats now became prey in themselves. Two starshells rose up and lit the area, their eerie light sending strange shadows across the waves while also picking out the British craft and soon green tracer began to rain overhead.

"Right standard rudder!" Harris ordered and *95* swerved

out of line. Anderson gripped the sides of the cupola as the action gongs rang about the ship. Harris had done right by separating them from the main force, but it also meant they were now heading directly into the path of the oncoming E-boats. And he could see one now, it was there, plain as day just beyond the captain's huddled figure and lit both by the starshells and its own tracer. The German was firing directly at Caswell's craft and appeared not to have noticed 95 break out of line. However, those nearby were more alert; an ear-splitting rattle came from Scott's Vickers as it began to play about the enemy's bows and was shortly joined by the more authoritative voice of the Oerlikon. For several seconds the E-boat appeared stunned, then green tracer finally found its way towards them, and Harris ordered yet another change of course.

A second E-boat appeared from the gloom, but 95 was still turning and unable to engage. Anderson could see the heavy bulk of the convoy to their right; the merchants were holding their own fire for fear of making themselves a clearer target for torpedoes but another British Fairmile was coming up to meet the E-boats.

"Damn fools should keep back!" Harris shouted also noticing this. "They've not got the speed!"

Anderson supposed he was right but could understand the escort captain's frustration; he had been given a convoy to protect and the instinct to do so must run deep. Besides, a vessel the size of a Fairmile would be safer making directly for an enemy than keeping the Germans on their beam. The E-boats might launch their deadly load at any moment and facing a torpedo head-on presented a smaller target.

"Port twenty and bring her down to eighteen hundred." Harris again, and the gunboat seemed to slump forward as her engine note dropped although Anderson knew they were still travelling at a considerable pace. "I'm heading for that squall," the captain shouted, pointing at an especially dark patch about half a mile off their starboard bow. "We'll turn back in that, then catch Jerry when he heads for home."

Again, Anderson could not fault the logic and was equally aware that ordering even a temporary retreat could take as much gumption as maintaining an engagement. They were allowed a free run, though, and just as they entered the dubious security of the squall, a massive explosion erupted off their port quarter. Something had been hit and the sheet of flame that momentarily lit the night sky was undoubtedly petrol fed. Anderson gritted his teeth; that meant either one of the escorts or a boat from their own flotilla had been hit but, now they were within the squall's dank embrace, nothing further could be seen.

As soon as they had gained relative safety the throttles were brought back and *MGB 95* came to a tentative rest. Freed from the constant scream from her engines, an uneasy calm came upon the vessel. Without power she felt far more vulnerable, despite the heavy cloud that obscured all else and must also be hiding them. Anderson strained to look out into the night, it seemed almost deceitful to be sheltering while, somewhere in the gloom, British sailors and a vessel similar to their own were fighting for their lives. And then, almost as a relief, Harris broke the mood.

"Half-speed and turn her about, 'Swain – shift your rudder!" The engines picked up immediately and once more the boat lurched into the tightest of turns before quickly regaining equilibrium on the opposing course. "And bring her up; maximum revs – give her all she's got!"

Now they were really travelling and burst out of their temporary shelter like any stalking hunter breaking cover. Ahead, the convoy was still in sight but, apart from a few darkened shapes off the starboard bow, no enemy could be made out.

"They should be heading back!" Harris shouted to Anderson. "It's what Jerry always does – hit and run."

Anderson went to reply but, before he could, something caught his eye.

"There, dead ahead!" he shouted pointing straight over their bow."

"Right hard rudder!" Harris ordered instantly adding, "And cut engines!" The boat rolled badly from the apparent mishandling and Anderson heard a crashing noise as something fell to the deck below, but Harris was fixated on the grey shape as it drew closer. "Target on the port beam," he yelled through the megaphone and immediately tracer flew from the aft twenty-millimetre and Scott's Vickers.

The range must have been less than a thousand yards though their prey was almost bow-on and heading directly for them. Anderson felt blood on his chin, he must have bitten his lip at some point but the pain had gone unnoticed. E-boats were known to carry more protection than British craft while being diesel-powered made them less vulnerable to fire. If they stayed put, *MGB 95* could easily be rammed and, if not, it would be a close-quarters fight with a superior vessel – something that could surely only end one way. But the target was coming on, despite the red tracer that seemed to be drawn towards her hull. There was no return fire: an early hit might have knocked out the German's forward armament or perhaps they had simply been stunned by the sudden attack coming from nowhere. Anderson continued to stare, mesmerised; it all seemed too easy, but then perhaps the enemy had other tactics in mind.

Now they were closer still, less than five hundred yards off; they would be on them in no time unless Harris acted. Anderson glanced across to where the captain stood, resolute yet dispassionate as if nothing more than a mildly interested spectator. And then, just as the oncoming boat was almost upon them, her hull seemed to separate, and the entire craft dissolved amid the force of a devastating explosion.

* * *

"Half ahead, starboard twenty." Harris's voice rang out even before the sudden fire had begun to die and the gunboat surged forward and round. Anderson watched him in silence; evidently Harris had no intention of checking for survivors and was turning away from both the convoy and any other British craft likely to be in the area. Then he recalled the man's earlier advice: any tactic was acceptable if it kept the boat safe. Presumably that was what the captain intended.

But on that particular night caution was not enough; another German craft had a bead on them and more green tracer began to fly in their direction.

"There's another Jerry in that squall to port," Anderson shouted over the sound of Scott's Vickers as it sprayed hopefully about the root of the fire.

"Open her up, 'Swain!" Harris shouted and the boat reared up yet again. "Starboard ten – meet her – port fifteen." Desperately they twisted through the foul night but either their enemy was inspired, or just plain lucky, and the barrage followed them.

Bullets began to rip down the edge of the gunboat's foredeck, the line of destruction ending just before the wheelhouse, while the whine of far larger shells passed overhead. Then one struck, instantly leaving the mast a tangle of twisted metal and line. The wreckage tumbled back along the aft casing before falling sideways into the racing sea. Straining on lines still securing it to the boat, the debris began to drag against their starboard side, gouging at decking and hull and forcing the coxswain to add port helm to keep them straight. Without a word Anderson pulled himself up through the cupola before resting uncertainly on the superstructure as he slowly regained his balance.

"Can you sort it, Number One?" Harris bellowed and, after receiving a nod in return, the captain ordered the throttles back. The gunboat was still travelling at speed, but the slower pace would make Anderson's job slightly easier, even if whatever had found them must surely still be close. The wreckage had to be cleared and cleared quickly, or they would be lost.

Anderson raised himself further and groped about on the aft superstructure. Several taut lines reached down to the dangling mast that flailed against the hull and he had nothing suitable to cut the metal cables. Then he noticed Jelly, the telegraphist, below him on the deck. The man must have realised what was about when his set failed.

"Cutters!" Anderson yelled, and the one word was enough; Jelly disappeared for a second only to return with a pair of electrician's pliers. He passed them across; the things hardly felt stout enough for heavy wire hawsers but were the best they had to hand. Anderson bent down to the tightest line while Jelly threw his weight on the bucking mast to hold it steady. Then the wire was in the pliers' mouth and Anderson squeezed for all he was worth. For several seconds it seemed futile before, with a snap, the wire separated, and the mast fell back, almost dragging Jelly into the water with it.

Once more the wreckage snagged on another line but this time it seemed easier; Anderson took grip on the wire and squeezed with more certainty. Again it was cut, but this time the mast hardly moved – another line was holding it, further forward, the wire stretched across the bridge. Crawling forward Anderson nodded briefly to the captain, who was trying to keep the shifting line still as it scraped along the top of the casing. Then he took grip with the pliers once more, gritted his teeth, and again the wire was broken.

Now the wreckage had fallen free of the deck and was dragging alongside. Anderson caught Jelly's eye; the man was next to the last remaining line and obviously expecting Anderson to toss the pliers in his direction. But he kept his head; they might gain several seconds that way, although there was a good chance the tool would end up over the side. Instead Anderson clambered down to the deck and carefully handed the pliers over.

Taking them, Jelly knelt to the last remaining wire and took hold. To gain a proper purchase meant leaning far over the side and Anderson placed his hand on the seaman's shoulder. It seemed to take longer but the wire was cut eventually, and the remains of the mast finally fell astern.

Jelly clambered up and made for the wheelhouse door. "That was good work," Anderson told him as he followed.

"With the set cold I had nothing else to do," the lad shrugged.

On entering the wheelhouse, Harris' voice could be heard through the coxswain's speaking tube. The boat began to accelerate and Anderson had eased himself into the relative safety of his cupola as the firing gongs sounded again.

"Starboard fifteen!" The captain was once more at the voice pipes and acknowledged Anderson's return with no more than a nod. "No point in giving away our position if we can't see what we're firing at," he explained. "Meet her – port ten," he continued to Price, and the boat veered again.

Anderson drew breath. In addition to the cut lip, the metal line had ripped into his Ursula suit and he could feel the dampness of blood soaking into the kapok lining. Without the mast, the gunboat would lack wireless communication while the damage done to her forecastle should also be investigated. No one would expect them to rejoin the convoy, although how his strange commander would view matters was yet to be seen. Then, after two more subtle changes of heading, the man himself turned fully to him and gave a tired smile. "Reckon we've done enough for one night, Number One," he said, his words shouted above the roar from the engines. "What say we make for home?"

* * *

"E-boat!" Sharkey Ward screamed with delight. "We got ourselves a soddin' E-boat!" Dover was in sight, dawn had started to break and that day's recognition signal was being flashed from the bridge; they were as good as home and, for the first time in what seemed like an age, the men of *MGB 95* had time to relax. And for at least one of the pair who manned the Oerlikon – the weapon probably responsible for such a tremendous feat – such freedom seemed almost too much. It was as if emotion had suddenly taken hold and Sharkey Ward was unable to express himself further, then Dowling cautiously raised himself up from the box of ready-use ammunition where he had been sitting.

"Did you see it Mikey boy? We got the bastard! Got him fair and square!" Sharkey beamed, turning to him. "Took him out, just as he were planning to deal with us!"

"Aye, Sharkey," Dowling agreed. He had indeed seen it all and was undeniably stunned although the scene was only one of a dozen that had impressed him deeply that night. It had been his first trip, after all, and what a beginning. Now he felt emotionally deadened as if nothing could ever shock him again, although there had also been something about the boats' destruction, so marvellous yet awful, that he knew would remain with him always.

"And it were down to you – you, almost as much as me," Sharkey continued as he placed a fatherly arm about the boy and squeezed way too tight. "I had her spot on, spot on I were, couldn't have been better. But it would have been nothing, nothing without them shells coming, and you kept me loaded like a good 'un."

Dowling blushed and tried to wriggle free, but Sharkey would have none of it. He was not usually one to admit his mistakes but had been wrong about the lad, although in his current mood would have cheerfully forgiven Hitler. Sweet and innocent he might appear, but Mikey had been rock-solid with the ammo, and the praise was sincerely meant.

"You an' me, we's a team," Sharkey informed him. "Best in the flotilla, and we're going to celebrate," he promised, giving an extra squeeze and a fat kiss on the side of the youngster's head. "Boat's fair knocked about so we're bound to get another leave, then we's off on the biggest bender ever!"

* * *

"You did well," Harris informed Anderson gruffly as *MGB 95* drew closer to the pens. It was not her normal berth, she usually moored up deeper into the network of jetties and quays that housed several flotillas of motor launches. But all aboard the gunboat knew she would require further attention before returning to active service. If sufficiently light, or there was space, this might be carried out in the Wellington Dock, Dover's official slip, otherwise they could expect another trip to one of the private yards and the sooner the better.

"Thank you," Anderson replied automatically. The praise from Harris was unexpected and welcome although at that moment all he wanted was bed and oblivion.

"Rare thing for a gunboat to sink an E, Number One," Harris continued as Price levelled them up with the quay and shut down the engines. "I'll admit we were lucky, but that doesn't change things."

"No indeed, sir." He'd noticed Harris had started calling

him 'number one', which meant more than any praise. "And it looks like we have a welcoming committee," he added.

Dawn was coming quickly now and there was no mistaking the figure of the base captain. Though in reality a commander by rank, Douglas Brooks was a veteran of Coastal Forces during the Great War when his own torpedo boat had sunk a light cruiser. Anderson had met him only briefly the previous day but knew he often saw boats in after a patrol, so shouldn't have been surprised to spot him. But then *MGB 95* was back early, and they had been unable to signal this, so surely it was odd to be met so?

"Glad to see you back, Bob." The greeting was friendly enough, although perhaps the man might be holding something back? Harris and Anderson stepped onto the jetty together as Price supervised the moorings. "See you've had a few pieces knocked away," Brooks added, nodding towards the damage caused by the wrecked mast.

"Yes, sir," Harris admitted. "Was a mite chancy for a while but we got through – thanks mainly to Number One here, who dealt with the wreckage."

Brooks nodded politely towards Anderson. "Good to hear, Sub.," he said. "First trip wasn't it?"

"It was indeed," Harris confirmed, he was also oddly elated, a fact betrayed by his unusually benign manner. "But you'd never have noticed – took to it like a duck to water. And we bagged an E-boat."

"Yes," Brooks acknowledged levelly. "I wanted to speak to you about that."

"There was no doubt," Harris insisted. "We all saw it go up, plain as day."

"I'm sure you did," the base captain agreed as he placed a fatherly hand on Harris' shoulder. "Only it wasn't an E-boat, Bob. It wasn't a German at all in fact. I'm afraid you sunk one of our Fairmiles."

Chapter Five

The room where Brooks led them was in a small building set close to the launch pens and seemed oddly civilised after the last few hours aboard *MGB 95*. There were three desks, each covered with paper and files that had been left in untidy piles, and several hard, wooden chairs; the place had the look of regularly being a centre of activity, and doubtless would be again once the working day began. But now it was mercifully empty and neither Harris nor Anderson was sorry.

"Park yourself down where you like," the base captain told them. "I'll send for coffee as soon as anyone turns up, but you might have to wait a while."

"Thank you, no," Harris said as he dropped onto one of the chairs and rested back; the idea of any kind of refreshment seemed almost repellent and he was sure Anderson would feel the same.

"You'd better tell me all about it," Brooks suggested as he took another chair, reversed it, and sat facing them, his chest and arms resting on its back.

"You probably know as much as we do," Harris admitted as Anderson settled next to him. "And of course, I'll be sending my action report as soon as…"

"Just tell me what you can," Brooks interrupted, although his tone and expression remained affable.

Harris shrugged and began a brief résumé of the night's activities ending rather hesitantly with what they had thought to be the destruction of an E-boat.

"And you had just come out of a squall?" the base captain clarified.

"That's right, the night was dark and there were several patches of particularly bad weather."

Brooks nodded, his active war may be over but the man had seen considerable service in similar conditions and clearly not forgotten.

"Did you challenge?" the question was asked softly, and Harris shook his head.

"I felt no need," he replied. "As I have said, it was dark and the conditions atrocious, but I could see them plain enough; a light hull coming straight for us. Any challenge would simply have given them a mark to aim at. Besides," he added as the thought occurred, "they did not challenge me."

"You were to the south-east, I gather?" Brooks again.

"Probably – I'm not sure; we'd manoeuvred considerably by then."

"Yes," Anderson stated gently. "The convoy was off our port bow, so I'd say we must have been roughly in that direction."

"Then what moon there was would hardly have helped," the older man mused. "Those aboard the Fairmile were unlikely to have seen any more than you." Anderson felt the chill of defeat threaten to take him over, but Harris was not to be beaten.

"They were out of station," he declared. "They should have stuck with the convoy, that's their job."

"Their job is to protect the convoy, Bob," Brooks stated softly. "There are no set parameters for such a task. And sometimes the rule book must be thrown away – you of all people must appreciate that."

"But they could see us firing at them, damn it!" Harris snapped. "That sort of thing happens all the time in such conditions; they could have flashed a friendly – or veered away. Coming straight at me, what was I supposed to think?"

"You were definitely thinking all was well aboard the Fairmile," Brooks suggested. "And clearly still are. Yet for all we know they could have been damaged; the bridge or wheelhouse might have been hit – she could have been totally out of control."

Harris sighed as he accepted this, and Anderson felt his stomach churn. There could be no argument, it was just as Brooks stated and the whole sorry affair seemed doubly foolish when related in the peace and safety of an empty office. But at the time there had been no chance to think, no chance to analyse and properly assess the situation. In the confusion of close action, they had acted instinctively and been horribly mistaken.

"So what happens now?" Harris asked finally.

"I'm not sure," the base captain admitted. "There may be a court martial, though frankly I doubt it. If there is, you'll find plenty to speak in your favour – it's not as if you'd do such a thing on purpose... And we have to wait for confirmation, of course. But for now, and for a number of reasons, I think you'd both be better away from here. It would save any unfortunate incidents if next of kin turn up."

"I'm billeted at the Grand," Harris pondered.

"Then go back there," Brooks urged. "But take fourteen days' leave and get out of Dover as soon as you can. I'll arrange the paperwork and for the boat to be taken in for repairs; someone can be detailed to keep an eye on her. Just make yourselves scarce."

"What about the men?" Harris asked thickly. "If we're in any way to blame, they might be also."

"No one will pin anything on them," Brooks spoke with calm assurance. "Worse anyone can say is they should have disobeyed orders."

"They did well," Harris now seemed to be talking from the depths of a nightmare. "All of them. Especially the tel'." He brightened slightly. "He and Number One cleared our wrecked mast and damn near saved the ship. In other circumstances..." The man's voice trailed away and he was clearly on the edge of tears.

"Go. Go now," Brooks urged. "Get some food and some sleep. Send in your report when you can but clear off, at least for a while. Let us know where you are when you get there, but I doubt if anyone will call you back. Not unless there is good reason."

"I want to come back," Harris insisted suddenly. "I want to come back, back to the boat the crew and the job. And I want this man next to me," he added, almost as an afterthought.

Anderson was taken aback by the outburst, but Brooks seemed to expect it. "Of course you do, Bob," he said. "And we will want you I am certain. Now get some rest."

* * *

Most of *MGB 95*'s regular hands had made straight for breakfast in the NAAFI, many without bothering to change out of their seagoing clothing. It was the usual procedure when returning from a patrol, after ten hours of strain the draw of food was strong as was the reassurance of seamen from other vessels, or even those with more peaceable occupations. However, that morning they stayed together and commandeered a linoleum-topped table for their exclusive use. The news had leaked out almost as soon as the boat moored and was greeted in various ways by the gunboat's crew, as well as those apparently authorised to judge them. But as the base captain had predicted, there were few accusations; those with sea time aboard fast motor launches knew only too well of the dangers, while the rest – the lucky ones – who spent their nights safely ashore, wisely kept any opinions to themselves. But even the worst that could have been said was nothing to the self-recrimination they subjected themselves to, and breakfast was a quiet and stilted affair.

"I still says it were an E," Sharkey maintained as he pushed aside his plate of half-eaten spam and powdered egg. "Saw her hull as plain as day – white, it was, like all them Jerry bastards."

"Fair few Coastal Forces hulls are white," Jelly pointed out. "Or a light colour anyways."

"But we didn't see it for long," Scott, who had been manning the port Vickers and was at least as responsible, added. "Thing were a blur most of the time and certainly moving. Faster than any Fairmile, I'd have said."

"You're right," Sharkey seized on the comment as if it had been salvation itself. "She were fair belting through the water, and it was one hell of a chop."

"One hell of a chop," Daly agreed more languidly. "And terrible weather, so it was."

"But we should have been sure," Scott supposed reluctantly. "And any boat is fast when it's heading straight at you."

Dowling said nothing, as befitted his status, but the events of the night had certainly affected him and his food remained untouched. He knew little of the whys and wherefores of what had taken place, only that his time on patrol had been a living hell. That he had survived without disgracing himself was some relief, but the doubts were not cast off on reaching solid ground. For even in his short time as gunboat crew, he had come to depend upon the solid, capable men that currently surrounded him. And, now they were showing signs of being every bit as rattled, he felt totally without support.

"Now then, lads." A strange voice came from beyond their group and several turned to see two seamen standing over them with filled plates. The first, a familiar face from another gunboat, had the ruddy skin and distinctive clothing of one recently returned from the sea, while his companion, equally well-known, was more conventionally dressed in square rig and appeared rested. Both greeted them cheerily enough. "Tucking in are you?" the first, a Yorkshireman, enquired. "Seeing there's nothing left for those who hadn't flitted early?"

"We took damage," Sharkey told them curtly. "Lost radio and were shot up bad so Skipper brought us in."

"Is that right?" the better-dressed sailor asked affably. He was a Liverpudlian who crewed an MTB and a popular figure in the base. "Mind if we joins you?"

They did, though none of the gunboat's crew felt able to object and the two men made themselves comfortable at their table.

"So what was it, normal patrol?" the Scouser asked as he helped himself to a liberal amount of brown sauce.

"Convoy escort," Scott admitted reluctantly.

"Aye, they was with our lot," the first confirmed through a mouthful of powdered egg. "And we lost a boat."

The 95's ratings tensed but their visitors continued unaware.

"That's tough," the torpedo man grunted before seeing in another large delivery of breakfast.

"Aye, Cas Caswell's," the other agreed. "Whole lot went up like a Roman candle – terrible it were an' nothing left to collect."

There was a second or two of respectful silence, then the Yorkshireman spoke again.

"An' a Fairmile's missing," he continued. "One of the regular escorts; not made it back an' there were another explosion a way off so Skip reckons they're probably done for as well."

"Fairmile B was it?" the Scouser asked and received a nod from his mate. "Them Bs are more nuisance than they're worth," he continued. "You wouldn't get me aboard one."

"How's that then?" Scott asked, and the rest of the gunboat's crew listened attentively.

"No power," the torpedo man grunted. Best they can do is twenty knots, and that's on a calm sea with the wind behind them."

"Yeah, but a touch more room, an' a bigger crew," the Yorkshireman insisted. "Hull's more 'an half as long as one of ours, so it'll be a better gun platform an' all."

"I ain't interested in gun platforms," the Scouser maintained. "Get in fast, release your fish, an' scarper; for that you needs power. 'Sides, them Bs look too much like E-boats for my liking."

"Like an E-boat?" his friend repeated in disbelief.

"Work it out," the Scouser instructed. "Hull's near the same length an' they both carry torpedoes. A lot of our boats 'ave hulls painted white an' all. Ask me it won't be long until some chump gets the two confused."

"Nay, lad," the Yorkshireman assured him as the gunboat's crew wriggled uncomfortably. "They're streets apart. Fairmile's slower, and way different up top. 'Sides, they got a bleedin' funnel! Only a berk would take one for t'other."

* * *

74

They arranged to meet some time before the disastrous patrol and Newman had considered cancelling although it was always hard to raise his sister, even when he used a base telephone. He had also managed several hours' sleep in the morning and, with no chance of going out that night or for many others, supposed there was little reason. It was also good to get away from *Wasp* and do so alone, although if any of his shipmates had known he was intending to meet with an attractive Wren, Newman would have had plenty of company whether he liked it or not.

The streets of Dover were filled with people, but few appeared to be going anywhere specific. In the two years since war was declared the town had suffered badly from enemy action; as he walked, Newman passed several piles of brick and timber that until recently had been family homes or active businesses. Some had not been dealt with quite so harshly and these were now getting the most attention with teams of workers patching up roofs or boarding over windows while the owners, their friends, or casual passers-by watched and commented. Much of the damage had been caused by air raids, an evil that affected many towns, although Dover was rare in being subject to an additional terror.

Twenty-one miles away enemy guns were in position and could send a barrage of heavy shells upon the town at any time of the night or day. The quality of ordnance ranged from pieces built to serve in the Great War to others that were the height of sophistication, but there was little difference in their deadly loads and the first warning of an attack usually came when the shells began to land.

In addition to the workers, Newman noticed several groups of feral children. With schooling suspended more than a year ago, most of Dover's young had been evacuated to foster carers in South Wales. Some had since returned, or escaped, while still more avoided exile in the first place and now spent their days in glorious rebellion and adventures that would credit a latter-day Huckleberry Finn. Shelters and camps were built amid the debris of bombed-out sites that might once have been their own homes while improvised games of football and cricket were common in the streets and annoying those attempting to clear roads or replace power lines was always a popular sport. The groups encompassed every age from toddler to teenager and had the brutal self-reliance usually only encountered amongst gangs of petty criminals, or cats.

But despite the bombing, shelling and apparent lawlessness, Dover did not feel particularly unsafe. Advice and criticism were freely offered to those making repairs, and there may have been the occasional argument in the constant queues for everyday essentials, but the spirit of the town was generally positive. And though opportunities abounded there was remarkably little looting, while the various welfare organisations ensured no one truly in need went uncared for.

Newman was nearing Market Square and could see his sister standing outside a partially boarded up café. She looked pretty and neat in the dark blue uniform; her glorious golden curls now tamed by a smart stiff hat although he was sure the kindly, yet rebellious, spirit remained as strong. As he drew closer he noticed a passing soldier make some remark that drew her attention. She turned, briefly considered the man, then gave an equally inaudible reply that sent the squaddie hurrying on his way.

"Sorry to be late, Eve," he said approaching. "It took longer coming from *Wasp* than I thought – I don't go into town much."

"That's all right," she told him. "I'm on twenty-four hour local leave."

"Shall we go inside?" he asked doubtfully, looking at the café. She shrugged.

"Can if you like. The super' doesn't approve of the place, says it's run by Italians, though I don't expect they intend poisoning us. We could always go for a walk instead?"

"That would be better," Newman agreed. He had changed his clothes and done his best with hair and hands but knew the scent of engine room still clung and, compared with his sister's crisp appearance, felt positively shabby.

"Are you going out tonight?" she asked when they were heading out of Market Square.

"Not tonight," he replied, before adding more softly, "nor for a while actually – we ran into a spot of trouble last time."

She paused slightly. "But you're okay?"

"Oh yes, though the boat's bashed about a bit – I can't say much more."

"Of course not, though I assume your engines are fine."

"Engines are on the top line," he replied automatically, then looked at her more intently. "How did you know?"

"If they weren't, you wouldn't be here," she stated. "Even now I'm surprised you are and not stuck inside that hole you call an engine room."

Newman smiled ruefully. "You know me too well," he said.

"Now that's where you're wrong." She considered him. "Sometimes I don't think I know you at all."

They were moving out of the town now and were alone on the otherwise empty path that led to the Western Heights, so it was easier to talk.

"I suppose you mean about me volunteering for active service?" he asked.

"Exactly," she confirmed. "This is the first time we've met up since, at least the first time when Mum and Dad weren't around. It's so unlike you, Billy – what were you thinking of?"

He shrugged. "I'm a mechanic, I don't carry weapons or anything, just mend engines."

"But you go into action," she insisted. "You were out last night and will be again; that's hardly in line with our creed."

"Quakers don't have a creed," Newman reminded her. "At least, not a fixed one."

"You know what I mean, our faith then."

"Maybe not," he allowed. "But then maybe it is. You've enlisted," he pointed out. "I know Wrens don't go in for any actual fighting, but they help others to, which is almost as bad."

"Currently I'm arranging welfare for the families of those lost while on duty," she told him primly. "That's hardly helping the war effort."

"But it is," he insisted. "Possibly not in an obvious way, but your actions go towards defeating Hitler just as much as mine."

"I'm not fighting," she protested. "What I do is no worse than raising money for war bonds or collecting scrap pots and pans. You might not carry a gun, but your boat goes into action; men could be killed – *you* could be killed – by your efforts."

Newman paused for a moment as he remembered the previous night; there was so much he wanted to tell her yet instead found himself caught up in this stupid argument. "But it's all the same," he declared at last. "If his family won't be cared for, the fighting man's morale is lowered, and a saucepan melted down to make a Spitfire is just as deadly as any bullet. Okay, I could have joined the Friends' Ambulance Unit, or become a fireman, but I can use my talents better where I am. War is terrible and, if they're honest, few want to fight in one, but if it is a just fight – which this undoubtedly is – we should knuckle down and get it over quickly."

"It seems strange justification," she said.

"It's an old one," he pointed out. "When the Great War broke out ten per cent of British Quakers volunteered."

"For the Ambulance Service," she agreed.

"For the infantry," he countered. "They carried guns and headed straight for the trenches, and for the same reason I'm crewing aboard a gunboat."

They walked a little way in silence before Eve spoke again. "Well, that's your choice," she decided finally. "And I know you well enough to realise I'm hardly going to change your mind. So let's talk about something a bit more cheerful. Are you free tonight?"

"Free?" he seemed surprised. "Why do you ask?"

"I've a friend and we've been asked out by an American – a journalist. I'd really rather not tag along like a gooseberry; if you came it would make things so much easier."

"How long have you been in Dover?" he asked.

Now it was her turn to be taken aback. "Nearly three weeks."

"And you've paired up with a Yank already!"

"Hardly paired up," she snorted. "I've only met the chap once, and don't think he has any romantic intentions. Poor chap is just a long way from home."

"Which gives him excuse for all the romantic intentions he can muster!"

"No really, Bill, it's not like that. Or if it is," she added as a thought occurred, "if it is, you can be there to defend me." She paused. "And Sandra..."

"Who's Sandra?"

"Ah, I thought you might ask about her," she laughed. "Yorkshire lass, we share a cabin at *Lynx*."

"So, she's a Wren an all?" he asked, considering.

"Of course she's a Wren, we work in the same office."

"Okay," he said at last. "What time?"

* * *

"No luck, mate?" the lad enquired and Daly, still holding the betting slip in one hand, shook his head.

"It isn't my day," the Irishman confirmed.

"What did you have?"

Daly consulted the piece of paper despite knowing exactly what it said. "*Bold Leader*, three o'clock," he replied.

"You was unlucky," the youth, who appeared unusually well dressed, grimaced. "Should 'ave walked it, that one."

"So maybe it did at that," Daly suggested. "Maybe that was the problem."

There were several other men in the small space that was actually nothing more than the front room of a semi-detached house. But rather than pictures, the sporting pages from various newspapers had been pinned to the wallpaper while a dusty backboard held a series of surreal names and chalked figures. And there was no comfortable furniture, instead kitchen chairs were set facing a plain wooden counter that ran along three of the walls. Most present were reading form books or peering at newspapers and the atmosphere was closely akin to that of a reference library. Daly had been there for little more than an hour and in that time had lost over a fortnight's wages. If *Bold Leader* had lived up to its name, he would just about have balanced out. As it was...

"Look, don't take on so," the youngster told him. "There's still the three-thirty to be run."

"No, that's me spent," Daly told him sadly. "Won't be no more bettin' for a week or more, an' little else either."

"That needn't be the case." The lad was almost whispering now. "I can tell you of a man what subs servicemen, always has."

"Is that right?" Daly asked, brightening slightly.

"Served in the trenches 'imself in the last lot an' got a whiff of gas into the bargain so you can trust 'im," the youth confided. "Anyone in uniform gets a tab."

"Well there's a fine thing," the Irishman beamed. "And a fine man too, by the sounds of him."

"Come with me," his new friend urged. "I'll introduce you."

* * *

"I'm afraid I'm not terribly good company," Harris admitted.

They had decided on a meal at the Grand, it being Harris' hotel and far enough from the base to be private. Not that either officer was being blamed for what had happened, but the constant barrage of "Bad show, old boy" and "Could have happened to anyone" was almost as upsetting as an outright accusation. And Anderson had also noted that some of their fellow officers were purposefully avoiding them.

"That's hardly surprising," he laughed dismissively. "It was a hell of a time, last night, even without..." It was the first time the subject had been raised, and even then the sentence was left unfinished.

"No, perhaps not," Harris agreed. "And tomorrow we have leave, so there'll be plenty of time to get over it."

Anderson nodded and glanced about the dining room of the hotel. It had only just turned six, both had spent much of the day trying to sleep but still felt in need of an early night and, out of the twenty or so tables that filled the ornate room, theirs was the only one occupied.

"But it was good of you to join me," Harris continued. "Must admit I usually prefer to eat alone, which is one of the reasons I chose to billet here, though there are those I make exceptions for."

Anderson smiled; three days ago he had not met the strange man opposite and there was much still to discover. But he already knew enough to understand a little of his nature.

"I seem to remember your mentioning being at Dunkirk," Harris continued as he played with his food.

"Actually, it was you that mentioned it," Anderson reminded him, "but yes, I was there."

The senior man's eyes flicked up from his plate. "What was it like?"

"Chaos at times." Anderson gave a tired smile. "I know the press say differently and speeches and the like have built it up. But you cannot evacuate over three hundred thousand from under the noses of your enemy without some things going awry."

"Was it really so many?" Harris abandoned the remains of his rabbit pie and sat back as he contemplated. "I was training at Fort William at the time and quite a bit's happened since."

"Apart from some big stuff on the periphery, there was little larger than a destroyer," Anderson continued his eyes growing distant. "We were in *Anvil* and making several trips a day but there always seemed to be more to take off. And some wouldn't come," he added.

"Wouldn't come?" Harris questioned.

Anderson shrugged. "Military efficiency," he replied ruefully. "The brass hats devised a schedule which was passed down the order of command and the lower it got, the more they stuck to it. We were almost prising men off towards the end."

"And those little ships everyone speaks of?"

"Oh, they were marvellous," Anderson conceded. "Though a few insisted on taking anyone they rescued straight back to England when really they would have been of more use ferrying them to destroyers or trawlers like us. And there were one or two who came once and were never seen again."

"How did you get the men off?"

"There was little in the way of jetties in our sector, so it was breakwaters and groins; other than that, we improvised."

"Improvised?"

"Trucks, lorries, tankers, anything the Army had to spare,

which was a lot as not much went back," Anderson replied. "They'd be driven into the water at low tide, six hours later the men could crawl along them and be rescued."

Harris sighed. "What a waste," he said.

"Waste indeed," Anderson agreed. "Though I don't expect anyone truly knows the half of it. And if they do, they'll be keeping it to themselves."

"So, not quite as glorious as they make out?" Harris supposed.

"Actually no, for all the faults and mistakes, it worked and did so better than anyone had a right to expect. And though by no means a victory, I'd say it was glorious indeed."

For a moment the two officers considered this, then Harris looked up. "You won't mind if we call it day?" he asked. "Stay for a pudding by all means, but I intend making an early start in the morning."

"Yes of course, are you going far?"

"Just to catch up with the folks," he muttered. "You sure you don't mind?"

"No, I'll see you when you get back," Anderson assured, half standing as his companion left. And then when he was finally totally alone in the dining room he sat back.

The memories had stirred something inside. His transfer to Coastal Forces came through over a year later but Dunkirk was what had made him decide to look for something other than minesweeping. Now he wondered if it had been the right move; at least he had been saving men's lives, which was a direct contrast to the events of last night. Harris had ordered a bottle of Empire wine and most of it remained. Anderson reached forward and poured a little more into his glass, then silently and in total isolation, finished his meal.

* * *

Bill Newman had been especially lucky. A consignment of brand new number two white shirts had been issued that day and he was wearing one as he strode along Snargate Street bound for the centre of town. And he had managed to secure a bath for a whole hour, which had given him time to pay serious attention to his hands. With the aid of pumice stone and a metal nail file, much of the ingrained oil had been removed and, though the skin was now red-raw and tender while his nails seemed abnormally short, it was undoubtedly an improvement.

He was due to meet Eve outside the former college where she and the mysterious Sandra were billeted, and he was right on schedule. Not that Newman was excited; until that point, his life had mainly revolved around engines of one sort or another with women playing only a minor role. But after hearing outlandish tales of his shipmates' previous time ashore, then remembering the two impassive twenty-seven litre lumps that had kept him company, he had been swayed and was now determined not to be left out. Indeed, as his freshly polished boots pounded on the pavement it would have taken something truly significant to delay him. Then, just as he was approaching the Red Star Club, something did.

It turned out to be three men – seamen, and two he knew instantly. The most familiar was clearly the worse for wear and appeared to have been ejected from the club. Now he stood uncertainly on the pavement in front of Newman, while one of his companions attempted to steady him.

"Let me be!" Sharkey Ward demanded, as Scott, the Vickers gunner, clung to his arms and tried to guide him towards the nearby wall.

"Trouble lads?" Newman enquired as he approached.

"This one's had more than a skin full," Scott announced, propping up the gunner's swaying body. "And even Mikey's a few seas under."

Newman's attention turned to the youngster who had joined them so very recently and now stood grinning inanely with the end of a dead cigarette resting forgotten on his lips. The change seemed incredible – he used to be such a polite and unassuming young man – and there was no doubt Scott had his hands full.

"It's all Shark's fault," his shipmate informed him. "Wouldn't let the lad be, insisted he matched him pint for pint, and now we got ourselves a problem."

"We ain't got a problem," Newman laughed as he helped steady the two bodies. "I'll see you settled but have to be off straight after."

"Help me get them to that bench," Scott agreed. "I'll take it from there."

Wrapping Sharkey's arm across his shoulder, Newman heaved the sagging gunner across the road, while Scott followed with the lighter Dowling.

"Kind of you," Sharkey told him, his feet dragging on the tarmac and face uncomfortably close. "Never believed a word they say about stokers meself. So what about a drink?"

"You've had enough for one night," Newman grinned as they drew near to the bench. "And I've better things to do with my evening."

"Better things than sharing a wet with a shipmate?" Sharkey enquired with disgust. "You grease monkeys are all the same, everyone says so."

"There, I'll leave them with you," Newman said, lowering the gunner's body onto the bench.

"Appreciate the help," Scott told him. "With a bit of luck they'll sleep it off."

"Just one little drink," Sharkey pleaded. "There must be a pub in Dover who don't mind serving sailors."

"I'm sure you'll find a stack tomorrow," Newman assured him, "but you've had enough for tonight."

"Oh, but I'm nowhere near started," Sharkey protested suddenly standing upright and magically becoming stone-cold sober. "Now are you going to drink with me or not?"

"Not tonight, chum," Newman patted him cheerfully on the shoulder. Then he looked back to check on Scott and Dowling and so missed the right hook Sharkey threw at him.

"Now what you go and do that for?" Scott asked as the three of them stared down at the fallen mechanic. "Poor bugger were only trying to help."

"That seems to be a problem right now," Sharkey confessed rubbing his hand ruefully. "I can't seem to tell friends from enemies."

* * *

He had drunk most of the wine and the now full dining room was starting to become noisy, so Anderson decided it was time to go. There would also be something of a moon, so he might have to spend part of the night in a shelter and, with only a couple of hours' sleep separating him from the horrors of the previous evening, only a fool would delay. But still he felt reluctant to move and as he reached for the last of his drink the dining room door opened especially wide, as if someone particularly important was about to enter. Noticing this, Anderson paused with the glass halfway to his lips.

A civilian in a well, but sharply, cut suit was the first to appear and Anderson instantly dismissed him as a spiv. But the two uniformed Wrens that followed were far more appealing, and the one with tight golden locks and a cute, slightly turned up nose definitely captured his attention.

"Table, sir?" a waiter asked, floating towards the newcomers. Anderson had been taking up a table of four by himself and the same pretentious member of staff had been casting covetous eyes on it for some while, which was one of the reasons he had lingered so long.

"Yes, but we won't be eating," the man informed him crisply. "We only want a drink."

"I'm afraid this is the restaurant, sir," the waiter explained carefully, as if to a child.

"So I understand, and it looks pretty full, but then your bar is a good deal fuller so, unless you want me to check out and make sure no one else from the *New York Gazette* ever bothers you again, I suggest you find a place for me and my guests."

Anderson smiled to himself as he replaced the glass. The newcomer was obviously an American and not afraid to say what he wanted; such an attitude was refreshing and might even do the staff at the Grand a bit of good.

"The only space we have is on this officer's table," the waiter explained, adding, "though I believe he may be about to leave," with special emphasis.

"There's no need to on our account, sir," the American told him as he came closer and Anderson was quick to note that, in addition to golden-hair, the Wren behind him also had fabulous eyes. "Stay and have a drink with us, you'll even up the numbers."

Anderson half rose as he indicated the three vacant chairs and was glad when the girl took the one to his right.

"So, is it Martinis all round?" the American asked, then flashed a look at the waiter before anyone could reply. Anderson grinned to himself, this might not have been the way he had planned to spend his evening, but the change was every bit as welcome as the company. And if anything could wipe away thoughts of the previous night, he might just have found it.

* * *

"But the bands don't swing!" Peale insisted. "I've been in your country over a month and have yet to hear anything decent that didn't come from the States."

"Maybe that's because it's what you're used to," the Yorkshire lass, who Anderson learned was called Sandra, suggested.

"Maybe," Peale agreed. "Though some of your home-grown stuff just doesn't cut it. Not that you get to hear much, maybe an hour late at night from some hotel that sounds as stuffy as this one. And then all they play is quicksteps or foxtrots; doesn't anyone jitterbug or jive around here?"

The Wrens stared back blankly while Anderson took a sip of his second Martini. Peale was the first American he had met face to face and he still felt unsure of the chap. But his enthusiasm couldn't be faulted.

"And Ambrose, what kind of a name is that?" the man continued. "Or Geraldo? Have you guys never heard of the Dorsey Brothers or Goodman?"

"I'm an Ellington fan myself," Anderson announced softly and immediately had the table's attention.

"Ellington, heck, now you're talking," the American told him through a grin. "How did you get hooked on the Duke?"

"Before the war we had quite a choice, there was Radio Normandy or Luxemburg. And the BBC does play some jazz and swing if you're prepared to seek it out."

"That so?" Peale remarked with a look of respect. "I guess I'll have to do some checking. So how do you feel about Basie?"

"Ellington, Basie... They both sound as daft as Ambrose," Sandra declared before draining her third Martini.

"It's *Duke* Ellington, and *Count* Basie," Peale told her firmly. "You Brits can't teach us anything about dumb names." He turned to Anderson. "Look I brought a few discs over with me if you'd care to hear them."

"You have a gramophone?" Sandra asked aghast.

"I'd go mad without one," Peale assured her. "What say we adjourn to my room and try it out?"

"We can't," Eve, the golden-haired Wren, announced. "Our leave ends at oh-six-hundred tomorrow so we really should be getting back."

"Oh, stay for a while," Peale pleaded. "I'll call a cab when it's time."

"It's time now," she said standing. "But this has been a splendid evening, and so nice to meet you, Lieutenant."

Her last words were directed at Anderson and were about the only ones she had spoken since sitting down half an hour before, while the second of her cocktails had yet to be touched.

"Well I'm staying," Sandra stated determinedly. "I want to hear this King Ellington bloke."

For a moment Eve seemed at a loss and Anderson wondered if he had been wrong about her. Until then she had come across as disdainful, preoccupied and more than a little frosty. All attempts to draw her into conversation had been politely brushed aside and he had pretty much written her off. But as she stood alone and clearly uncertain another emotion was triggered, and he rose to join her.

"Yes, I should be going as well," he announced to the table in general. Then, turning to Eve, "If you're heading for *Lynx*, I'd be glad to see you home."

Again she hesitated, then her expression melted and she finally met his eyes. "If you're sure, Lieutenant, I would appreciate that."

* * *

Once outside the hotel however, she seemed to change her mind.

"You're billeted at *Wasp*, aren't you?" Eve asked and, when Anderson admitted he was, she glanced at her watch. "Can we go there instead?"

"To *Wasp*?" he exclaimed, wondering if he had misjudged her yet again.

"Yes, we should get there by five-and-twenty past nine, and there's a ten o'clock ferry that runs back to the Wrennery, I could catch that."

"But why *Wasp*?"

She smiled. "I suppose it must sound strange and am sorry, I must have been perfectly dreadful company this evening. You see it's my brother, he's billeted there and was supposed to meet us tonight. It's so unlike him not to turn up, I'd like to make a few enquiries."

"You could 'phone," he reminded her, as she took him firmly by the arm.

"I could, but I'd so much rather walk with you," she said. And then, unbending some more, "I have to say that Yank was starting to get me down."

* * *

Almost the first person they saw on entering the base was Price, *MGB 95*'s coxswain. He was standing by the reception desk and looking concerned.

"Glad you're 'ere, sar," he said approaching and all but ignoring Eve. "Ward's been pulled in by the local rozzers. Redcaps 'ave 'im now, 'long with Scott and Dowling."

"Ward," Anderson sighed. "Why am I not surprised?"

"But that's not all," Price added. "He took a swing at Newman – Lord knows why, fella wouldn't do no one no 'arm. 'E's with the PMO."

"Newman?" Eve remarked. "*Billy* Newman?"

Price turned and seemed to see her for the first time. "That's right, miss, know 'im do ya?"

"He's my brother, whatever happened?"

"Oh, it's nothing, 'e's in the clear – just took a bash on the swede. It's the others what's in the suds."

"Look I'm sure we can sort this out," Anderson said. It had been a particularly pleasant walk from the Grand, and the last thing he wanted was to break the mood.

"Sub-Lieutenant!" The voice came from behind and belonged to Commander Brooks, the base captain, and Anderson felt nothing would surprise him further. "Glad I caught you; is Lieutenant Harris with you?"

"No, sir, he's back at his billet, I expect he can be raised by 'phone."

"Then we'll have to." The officer glanced at one of the ratings behind the desk. "Call Lieutenant Harris will you, quick as you can."

Anderson's attention returned to Price, who seemed to have taken a step back with the arrival of a senior officer. He was about to ask more about his men when Brooks spoke again.

"Actually, you may as well hear the news," the commander said and was now smiling. "We got word from the missing Fairmile. It was messed up in the action, but you had nothing to do with it."

"Really?" Now all surprise was abandoned leaving Anderson merely feeling numb.

"Really. The boat was badly shot up so had to make for shore. Radio had gone down and they were finally forced to abandon. Most were unharmed and made it to the Carleys safe enough. A sweeper picked them up off Ramsgate earlier this afternoon."

"Well, that's good news, sar!" Price spluttered, although Anderson seemed to have lost the ability to talk.

"Good news? I should say." Brooks was now positively grinning. "And it means your lot have accounted for an E-boat." His attention focused on Anderson. "So why are you looking so damned glum?"

Chapter Six

The boat was repaired well within the predicted time and returned to active service. Three weeks later she had completed eight further escort details, four with convoys and four escorting minesweepers as they carried out a duty both dangerous and largely unacknowledged, at least by the general public. In addition, there had been independent nightly patrols and one tentative venture into enemy territory which was called off due to a sudden storm. And in all, not a shot had been fired in anger. No one could be sure of the reason for this; admittedly it had been a particularly unpleasant autumn with heavy rain and an almost constant chop plus it was well known that, in line with their counterparts in the air, light German naval craft were less inclined to venture out during bad weather. But though she could not add to her trophies, neither did *MGB 95* suffer further casualties, and the period of concentrated activity did much to finally meld her crew into a workable fighting unit.

This was very much on Harris' mind as he met with Collins, the flotilla's senior officer, on board a moored *MGB 95*. It was a bright and thankfully clear morning and, subtle though it might be, Harris had been aware of the change in his command's morale for some while. He was actually intending to bring the matter up, had there not been something more concrete to bring to the flotilla SO's attention. As it was, Jelly, the boat's telegraphist, had rigged a form of R/T repeater that would allow those on the bridge to monitor spoken radio messages and such innovations had to be approved before being officially adopted.

"Of course, R/T communication is notoriously unreliable," Collins pondered.

"Indeed, sir, and even if we make R/T contact I still won't be able to talk back to you, or the other boats," Harris agreed as they stepped off the boat and onto the jetty, "but at least I'll hear what everyone's saying."

"Which will be a distinct improvement," Collins allowed. "And I must say your man's done a thorough job. Besides, being able to issue orders without anyone answering back sounds like the ideal arrangement to me."

Harris eyed his superior cautiously before realising the last remark was intended as a joke and quickly broke into a smile.

"I wish we could do more for you," Collins confessed. "A lot of boats have two-way repeaters, which gives total control over voice traffic and the radios themselves are progressing all the time."

"It's still an improvement," Harris maintained.

"And there aren't many left with your particular bridge arrangement," Collins continued, eyeing the boat, "but not much we can do about that without a total rebuild."

"It's something you get used to; I don't see it as a problem," Harris paused. "Though a double Oerlikon aft would definitely be of use."

Collins gave a brief smile. "So you've said before and it has been noted. But it would mean a powered mount and installing one is out of the question at the moment. Right now the yards have their work cut out keeping up with repairs and routine maintenance while builders seem to be putting all their efforts into the new boats."

"New boats?" Harris' ears pricked up.

Collins nodded. "We'll be getting a few at Dover shortly though probably not our flotilla."

"But we're due replacements for those that have been lost," Harris pointed out.

"And sadly are not alone in that. But Coastal Forces in general is finally being taken seriously by the Admiralty and provisions are in hand for increased production as well as new designs."

"Something that can truly match an E would be good."

"And it will happen," Collins assured him seriously, before relaxing slightly. "Though some people haven't done so badly with what they've already got."

Harris conceded this with a nod and a smile. For all his time in Coastal Forces he had dreamed of sinking an E-boat but, now he had, the magic seemed to be missing. Maybe it was something to do with the way it happened, or rather the short period afterwards: those dreadful hours when everyone thought a British vessel lost. The relief on learning otherwise was blessed indeed but hardly mitigated the horror that had gone before.

"If we did arrange for a double Oerlik', could your gunner handle it?" Collins asked softly, and both men's attention switched to Sharkey Ward who, with Dowling's help, was servicing their current weapon.

"I should think so," Harris replied. Even from a distance and allowing for the fact both ratings must know themselves under the eyes of two senior officers, they were obviously working well and together.

"Bit of an explosive character, from what I hear," Collins remarked.

"He certainly was," Harris agreed, "though strangely the E-boat kill seems to have sorted that out."

"Really?"

Harris shrugged. "There was that spot of bother immediately afterwards but since then he's been as good as gold."

Collins smiled wryly, then a thought struck him. "Oh, I meant to tell you, Miriam's expecting."

"Congratulations." Harris' reaction was automatic, but then the news seemed totally unrelated. Children and families had never mattered much to him and he had become even less interested since the outbreak of war. Others felt differently of course, and he was diplomatic enough not criticise them for it. "You must be pleased," he added. "That will make two won't it?"

Collins' eyes rose briefly. "Three actually, though who's counting? Fact is, I've been offered the chance to step down."

"Step down?" Harris exclaimed – this was of far greater importance.

"They seem to think I've caused enough problems here," Collins continued dolefully. "So are offering me the chance to show others."

"Switching to training then?"

"Aye, probably *St Christopher's*, but that's not certain; there are a couple more bases specialising in newbies. Coastal Forces has come a long way in a short time and, as I said, it seems we are finally being taken seriously."

"You'll be missed." It was true, Collins had been the flotilla SO for all of Harris' time at Dover and it was not an easy job. Brooks was good enough as the overall commander but had other flotillas to consider and naturally must be shore bound; it took special qualities to serve alongside the men you commanded.

"Well it won't be for some time," Collins continued. "We're currently awaiting my replacement and experienced officers can be as hard to find as fresh boats."

"So, you'll be carrying on as normal?" Harris confirmed.

"We all will," Collins replied. "Though I seem to remember you've had a busy few weeks."

"It's been brisk," Harris agreed.

"And you're happy to stay on the duty roster?"

"Of course. We can go out again tonight if you wish."

Collins hesitated. "Perhaps not tonight," he said. "Maybe a period of stand-down is necessary?"

"Not on my account," Harris insisted, adding, "And I'm sure I speak for all my men."

Collins considered him for a moment but made no comment. "Very well, what say I'll roster you as reserve for the next five days? That will be immediate so better summon your number one and position yourselves on the end berth. You might still see some action if we get a call during the day or if someone from an evening patrol falls out. But if all fire up correctly, you can put your chaps on one-hour standby every night, and chances are the boat will remain in harbour until Friday. Should give you the chance to spruce the old bird up a bit and get a few nights' decent sleep. How does that sound?"

"That sounds fine," Harris replied.

* * *

It was an arrangement that also suited Anderson. The period of intensive work had been good on one hand; he now knew so much more about the boat, her crew, and his place amongst them. But another aspect of his life had definitely been neglected.

And it was one that had suddenly become foolishly important. In the odd evenings when the boat remained in harbour, he and Eve had spent some free time together and there was one whole Sunday when they borrowed a car and enjoyed an entire day well away from the sea. Admittedly much of the time was apparently wasted in one air raid shelter or another, but even that hardly seemed to matter. German bombs and shells could do what they liked to wreak further devastation on the small town and, though the noise, and smell, of others seeking refuge was hardly convivial, they were together and that soon became enough.

From Anderson's point of view, he had finally found someone he could relate to, and it quickly became apparent she felt the same about him. Not even the fact that her brother was a shipmate had been a problem, for Anderson had immediately felt comfortable with Newman, *MGB 95*'s stoker.

The lad was not only skilled at his work but well liked by the others while any unpleasantness that might have resulted from the incident with Ward was soon forgotten and might even have increased his popularity. A similar maturity had been shown when confronted by his sister's apparent infatuation with his superior officer and he quietly accepted their relationship without trying to gain advantage or spread gossip.

It was equally apparent to Anderson that all aboard *MGB 95* were pulling together nicely, which was doubly pleasant as he had initially overheard a number of less than complimentary rumours about them. He supposed an E-boat kill might have helped – Ward had lost no time in marking the achievement on the Oerlikon's mount. But everyone involved in Coastal Forces' work knew a victory could never be the work of a single man. It had to be a joint effort, and it seemed the crew of *MGB 95* were now proud to be part of just such a team. And whatever the reason for their improvement in morale, Anderson was pleased and strongly suspected Harris to be also.

"Tea, sar?" Price enquired as he returned from the mess deck with two steaming mugs.

"Thanks, Cox'," Anderson said as he collected one and placed it next to his current work. There was probably more space in the wardroom but Anderson preferred the convivial atmosphere of the wheelhouse. "All straight below?"

"'Ardly straight." The coxswain gave a toothy grin. "But the lads are making a go of it."

One of the first priorities had been to obtain a fresh spirit stove to replace the one that mysteriously went missing when the boat was last on the slip. A 'safari' vacuum flask did much to keep soup drinkable for the homeward leg of a patrol, though nothing could compete with piping hot tea, or kye, the potent naval version of cocoa. And while he was at it, Anderson had also seen the enamel tin mugs replaced with heavy china versions. The former might be more durable, but all knew how they, and the standard issue mess trap, could burn the lips.

It was their second day of standby and, though dry, the chills of late autumn were starting to make themselves known, so most of the crew were employed below. And Anderson certainly had enough to keep him occupied with corrections to charts and revisions to Admiralty Fleet Orders. Meanwhile, attention was being given to sprucing up the ratings' accommodation.

"Every fire's goin' flat aat to dry the paint," the coxswain added over his drink. "It's like a Turkish bath dan there."

MGB 95 was undeniably small and facilities at *Wasp* reasonable so all were billeted ashore, but as such a large part of their lives was spent aboard, everyone had an interest in making the boat more comfortable. As a result, Scott, the port gunner, had acquired several pots of white paint and, along with Daly and Jelly, was now freshening up the boat's mess deck while Price had been polishing the wheelhouse speaking tubes along with any other brassware within reach. Newman and Carter were in their precious engine room continuing the maintenance their spoilt engines demanded. Only Dowling and Ward were on deck. They had serviced the Oerlikon the previous day and were now adding fresh canvas to the rear gun's bandstand screen; the thing did little to keep them dry in anything above a gentle swell but at least provided a modicum of shelter against wind. And all was being done in an atmosphere of companionable order, so when the captain burst in through the wheelhouse door, it took them all by surprise.

"Ready to be off, Number One?" he demanded as he erupted into their peaceful world.

"Ready whenever, sir," Anderson replied.

"We've been detailed to put out in search of downed bomber crew," Harris continued, hurriedly unbuttoning his uniform tunic. "The Raff have been looking all day and most of last night with no joy, now they're asking for help. How long before we can slip?"

"Pretty much immediately, sir." It had been one of Anderson's stipulations when agreeing to the work; the boat was on standby so nothing must be undertaken that could not be abandoned instantly. "I'll alert the Chief; tell the lads below, will you, Cox'?"

Harris stood back to allow Price past, then reached for his Ursula suit that hung behind the W/T office door. The boat was oddly warm and smelt of wet paint and burnt paraffin while the wheelhouse itself looked unusually spick. He watched as Anderson spoke briefly into the engine room speaking tube and was rewarded shortly afterwards by the rumble of their engines starting up, then Jelly appeared from below and took station at his radio. Everything was working as it should   as it had each time they put to sea in the past, whatever the urgency, Harris quickly reminded himself. But now there was something else, something he could barely identify.

The men were reacting with more purpose, perhaps? This might be due to the E-boat kill, or possibly something else, although Harris was at a loss as to what. But whatever the cause, there was no doubt the very atmosphere aboard the boat felt decidedly healthier, and he for one was glad.

Five boats from different flotillas had been detailed to the emergency and *MGB 95* was delayed as one, an MTB directly ahead of them, was unable to start her port wing engine. But once the fault was cleared and they were all on the open sea, their new R/T repeater crackled into life.

An MTB lieutenant commander had charge of the eclectic fleet and soon each boat was given separate areas to search. Harris glanced at his second in command when their sector was announced, and Anderson promptly ducked down into the wheelhouse to set a course.

"Places us about ten miles to the east of *Gris Nez*," he announced on his return.

Harris nodded. "Then we can expect shore bombardment," he grunted, "as well as aircraft and I wouldn't exclude an E-boat or two joining in so close to home."

The engines were burbling gamely as they powered them through the gentle swell at a regulation twenty knots, although both men were experienced enough to make themselves heard over the noise.

"Crew of a Wellington," Anderson recollected. "That would be six men, and you can bet your life the Raff will have checked all the likely places."

"And the safest," Harris agreed with an ironic grunt.

Both looked up and considered the weather. It was unusually clear, the sky was actually blue in places and what cloud there was, quite high.

"Seven hours of daylight," Harris muttered as he glanced at his watch. "Let's hope someone finds them soon."

* * *

By early afternoon they had reached their allotted area and were starting a standard box-pattern search. Twice formations of enemy aircraft had been spotted heading out from the French coast but on both occasions they were too high to be a nuisance and seemed more intent on a distant, and doubtless more worthwhile, target. As did the shore batteries; *MGB 95* had slowed her speed to fifteen hundred revolutions but was still too quick and small for heavy artillery to get a reliable bearing. And probably too cheap, Harris decided soberly as he stared at the nearby land. All told, the gunboat had cost a little over twenty thousand pounds to build –

or forty barrage balloons, if looked at another way. He had no idea how much an artillery shell cost, but they certainly weren't inexpensive, and it would take a fair number to hit such an elusive target.

"Getting close to the coast now, sir," Anderson's words came through the wheelhouse speaking tube. "Time to turn about and begin another run."

"Very well," Harris muttered absent-mindedly. It was good to have reached the stage when such things could be left in the hands of a competent second in command. Behind him, Scott and Daly were sweeping both sea and sky, while Ward was similarly employed at the stern along with young Dowling, who was balanced precariously on the small boat's whaleback with one hand grasping a shroud and the other a pair of binoculars.

The vessel slowed slightly, then began a turn that was almost sedate in gunboat terms, before adopting the reciprocal course. About six miles to either side and barely distinguishable from the grey water, other boats were performing the same task and all knew that, even with an excess of luck and time, their efforts would probably be wasted.

But the turn did herald some action, even if it wasn't the raft they all hoped for. With a shriek that betrayed his age, Dowling pointed excitedly at the French coast that was now gradually being left behind.

"Aircraft!" he announced gleefully adding, "German," for greater clarity and then, "over there!" to totally compound the error.

Harris raised first his eyes, then his binoculars but, as he focussed on the image, all thoughts of Dowling's sloppy enthusiasm were quickly forgotten. There were indeed German aircraft; three of them, and flying low. From that angle they appeared to be fast bombers of a type that could hold their own against fighters and were probably his worst nightmare.

"Get on to the SO, Tel'," Harris instructed down the voice pipe. "Report JU 88's heading this way and copy that to base on W/T."

With luck, the air cover that had been promised would be swift in coming, although there was bound to be a period when the launches must defend themselves. Anderson appeared at that moment and looked back at the oncoming planes.

"Too low and too few for long-distance bombers," he commented dryly. "I'd say these have been sent especially for us."

"Nothing else in sight," Harris agreed, adding, "and they're

Junkers for sure." Then he pressed a button and the firing gongs rang out throughout the boat.

Immediately both wing gunners abandoned their glasses and, donning helmets, centred their weapons on the oncoming planes while Dowling skipped down from his perch and, skidding once on the deck, took up position next to Sharkey Ward on the rear Oerlikon. Harris flipped up the cover on the engine room speaking tube.

"We've company upstairs, Chief," he announced. "I might have to ask quite a bit from you."

"Very good, sir," Carter's voice came back just as firmly. Then the captain glanced at Anderson, "I think we might be about to get some exercise, Number One," he said.

* * *

At first all aboard the gunboat thought they might be spared. Just as the planes became distinct, their camouflage and contrasting markings looking almost pretty in the clear light, they banked steadily north and became black dots once more. But it was only a temporary reprieve; for several seconds they watched as fire was exchanged with the MTB on their starboard beam, and then the trio began heading for them.

They came in low and fast, covering the distance between the two boats in a matter of seconds, then *MGB 95*'s guns began to speak. And it was very different to a night action; in the bright autumnal light, the red tracer was barely noticeable while Anderson only knew the enemy were also firing by the fountains of water that suddenly erupted to either side.

"Maximum speed," Harris roared. Then, "Starboard ten."

The boat obediently reared up and to one side, silencing her own guns and tearing up the water behind her.

"Meet her," Harris continued, and they righted. Ward was the first to catch the planes again, shells from his Oerlikon reaching up in an attempt to drag them from the sky, although his aim was off, and the shots fell well to one side.

"They'll be going on to chummy to port," Harris bellowed, and it seemed a reasonable assumption. The first run was to test out their defences; then they would return with bombs.

"Bring her back to eighteen hundred." The order was shouted down the voice pipe and the boat duly slowed. Silently they watched as the next launch in line, another MTB, similarly failed to catch an aircraft and then, for a precious few minutes, the sky was clear once more.

"You can be sure we haven't seen the last of them," Anderson muttered as he tightened the strap on his steel helmet. "Where are those fly-boys? Don't they know it's their chaps we're looking for?"

"Here they come again," Scott at the port turret announced, and once more the men of *MGB 95* prepared to meet the onslaught.

* * *

But this time they came slower and were slightly higher in the sky. All in the gunboat were sure their sister launch had not been bombed; it seemed likely they were to be the initial target. Ward's Oerlikon was the first to reach them; the tracer was no easier to follow yet Anderson sensed their shells were passing close. Two of the Germans replied but there was no return fire from the third. Instead, a stream of dots began to fall from its belly and Anderson found himself gripping the side of the copular just as Harris shouted down the voice pipe once more.

This time the boat veered to port and did so with such verve that Dowling, at the Oerlikon, was sent sprawling against the gun's bandstand screen. Spray from a line of fountains splashed against the hull and for a second it appeared impossible that they could not be hit but, as Harris corrected the trim and the guns were able to fire once more, it seemed they had been spared. And then Daly brought the news they had so recently been praying for, but now dreaded more than any other.

"Object in the water, bearing green forty-five!"

For a second no one spoke or moved. The guns had fallen silent and the bombers were no longer overhead but had turned their attention on the northernmost launch. Harris snatched up his glasses and swept the area off their starboard bow. Sure enough, there was something out there but a good way off and not necessarily the dinghy they sought. And as he looked further the doubts began to multiply; it was probably a large chunk of driftwood or some other piece of wreckage – enough debris had been created during the last few months' action to make such a thing commonplace. Or perhaps a mine had come adrift; a single one could sink a battleship, let alone his thirty-five ton launch. But there remained a chance – a small one perhaps – that the sighting was exactly what they had been sent to find. And Harris had long since discovered that, in war, every chance must be taken.

"Starboard ten and throttle back to fifteen hundred," he

ordered as the three black dots in the distance began a run on their sister launch. Then, to Jelly in the W/T office, "Report object sighted and give our position." He turned to Anderson. "The SO has his work cut out for the next few minutes, but at least those back home will be aware." Then that ironic grin returned. "And if the Raff think we've found their airmen it might even speed up some air cover..."

Robbed of its power, the boat slumped forward in the light swell and took up a more leisurely pace which slowed further after another command from Harris. Now their platform was lower the sighting was lost to all, but Harris had a good idea of the position and no intention of arriving at speed.

"Aircraft dead ahead." That was Daly in the starboard turret and he had done well to notice; despite approaching what could be anything from a rescue operation to sudden death, the Irishman was clearly keeping the far horizon properly scanned.

"They'll be British," Harris supposed. "Coming from the right direction anyway, but even if not, too far off to bother us for now."

"I have it!" Scott's voice rang out as he pointed from his turret. "Just off the port bow; it looks like we found 'em."

It did; as Harris ordered a slight turn and reduced speed still further a dull yellow dinghy came into view. It was oblong, rather than the ring he had expected, and almost comically bulbous. The thing reminded him vaguely of past family holidays on the beach; sand in the sandwiches and scratch games of cricket, although the three figures huddled inside appeared anything but jolly.

"Ward, Dowling, lend a hand there!" he called, and the two aft gunners stumbled forward with Sharkey freeing a boat hook from the aft superstructure as he went.

"Poor buggers," Harris muttered to himself. They were less than twenty yards off and heading to come within reach yet still none of the occupants had moved or even raised a hand in greeting. Noticing this he felt a moment of doubt; the weather had been inordinately fine for late autumn, but those airmen must have spent a good twelve hours in the dinghy and may have been wounded to begin with.

However, as they drew closer one did move. He watched as Ward stretched out with the boat hook, then almost reluctantly grabbed hold, and the small boat was dragged alongside.

"Looks like the SO's caught one," Daly reported dolefully and Harris' attention was torn from the rescue. A pall of black smoke hung in the middle distance and their sister boat was slowing beneath it, clearly the victim of a bomb or some lucky hit from machine gun fire.

"Report the SO's boat injured to base," Harris shouted down to Jelly.

"Enemy bombers are coming back," Daly stated, and indeed the three black dots were steadily growing larger as they bore down on them once more.

"Hurry it up there, Ward!" Harris shouted. Then, to Anderson, "I wish the bloody air cover would move themselves."

The approaching British planes were closer, but it would still be several minutes before they could interfere and in that time the Germans would have attacked. Ward had hauled one of the dark-clad survivors aboard and was reaching for another, but it was all taking far too long.

"Get down there and lend a hand, Number One," Harris ordered, "and take Jelly with you." Anderson vanished from his copular to appear seconds later outside the wheelhouse with the telegraphist in tow.

"They're coming in!" Daly warned, then lowered his binoculars and took control of his Vickers.

There was one man still to rescue: until he was safe Harris knew he could not move. And to make matters worse, Ward and Dowling were involved forward, so their Oerlikon was unmanned.

With a staccato rattle both turret guns opened up but the last airman was clearly hurt and taking longer for them recover. Harris found himself ducking slightly as the German bullets cast lines of fountains in the waters about them and the temptation to call for speed was strong. Then, just as a series of dark shapes fell from the belly of the centre plane, he heard a shout from Anderson and, even before he could give the command, the boat lurched forward under both engines.

"Full starboard rudder!" Harris yelled down to the coxswain, who'd had the initiative to set them in motion. Then he braced himself as the boat rose up and into a tight turn. "Meet her, midships!"

With a roar, the planes passed overhead and almost simultaneously a series of far larger splashes erupted off their starboard beam.

"Port ten!" By his estimation, each of the German planes must have emptied their load but there was still time for them to close for another strafing pass before the seemingly reluctant RAF intervened. He glanced forward; Anderson and Ward were holding one man down on the bucking foredeck, while Dowling, Jelly and the other two seemingly fended for themselves. "Give her everything, 'Swain!" Harris added and there was a grunt in reply but it seemed the boat was already at maximum revs.

"They're coming again!" Daly shouted, "Though this time with the British behind – they look like Hurricanes!"

Harris turned back and saw the three deadly shapes, still in formation, as they prepared for another run. They were lower so his estimation about their bomb load might have been correct, but it would mean another dose of heavy machine gun or even cannon fire was on the cards and, with British fighters following, Daly and Scott would be unable to reply.

With a double press on the firing bell, the turret gunners released their weapons and took what cover they could. The Hurricanes were coming up fast and from a great height; by Harris' estimation they would fall on the bombers just as they started their attack and he could not risk one falling to a stray shot. And he must be equally careful not to be in the way of the fighters' line of fire. A shout to Price brought another change of course and the boat was just gaining equilibrium when the German guns began to speak.

Again, the seas about them boiled in a maelstrom of foam and spray as bullets dug deep and, once more, Harris altered their speed and heading. Then there was the brief but gratifying sight of one of the German planes dropping out of formation as a Hurricane, brilliantly lit in the lowering sun, fell upon it with machine guns blazing.

"And starboard ten," Harris ordered, as the boat heeled and reared some more. The fighters were definitely in contact now and, although they only matched them in numbers, it was clear the Germans had no plans to stay longer. As he watched they began to make for the French coast, their engines screaming, with the British in full pursuit.

"Bring her down to eighteen hundred, 'Swain." The immediate danger was gone and Harris could afford to take stock. One of the airmen was presumably wounded and still lay on the foredeck with Dowling, while the others seemed to have been moved below. And they were drawing near to the SO's boat. Something had taken a chunk out of her stern, neatly removing her rear gun and the vessel was visibly lower in the water. But, amazingly, she could still move and was making for the British coast at a reasonable speed, presumably to activate her self-bailers.

"Make to the SO 'have three survivors on board'," Harris

bellowed down the W/T office speaking tube and was relieved when Jelly responded. "And ask if they need assistance," he added.

"All well, sir?" Anderson enquired, appearing in the copular next to him.

"I suppose so, Number One," Harris allowed. "Though it looks as if our fighter friends have given up the chase."

Sure enough, the three Hurricanes had turned back and were now circling above the launches.

"Blighters think they've done us a favour," Harris hissed, "but simply chasing them off won't do any good."

"They might have a reason for not following," Anderson suggested mildly.

"They might," the captain grudgingly accepted. "Though I can't help but think that lot treat this war differently to us."

Anderson said nothing; to his mind Fighter Command and Coastal Forces had much in common although it was probably not the time to say so.

"Which reminds me, how are our survivors?"

"One's wounded; not badly but they couldn't bandage him properly in the dinghy and he's lost a lot of blood. The other two are suffering from exposure."

"Then we'd better get them back without delay," Harris sighed. "Perhaps a spell aboard will give them a greater appreciation of what we do."

"I doubt that, sir," Anderson replied flatly. "They would appear to be German."

Chapter Seven

"So, you're telling me you spent all that time and trouble – all that risk – in order to rescue a bunch of Krauts?"

Anderson smiled ruefully and took a sip of his drink. He had not meant to expand so, especially to Peale who was a civilian, a foreigner and, of all things, a reporter. But it was his third Martini and the story had just slipped out.

"What of the airmen?" Eve asked. "The British bomber's crew, I mean."

"They were picked up shortly afterwards," Anderson replied. "Or at least five of them – the last is still missing."

"Would you mind if I write that up as my next piece?" Peale enquired. "It's just the sort of thing the folks back home will pick up on and can't hurt international relations any."

"I'd really rather you didn't," Anderson said. "If they think it worthy there'll be a press release through the official channels."

"Aw hell, Ian, then every damn hack will get hold of it," the American grumbled.

"Sorry, chum, but those are the rules."

Peale pulled a face although there was perhaps a glimmer of understanding in his eyes and it was something Anderson had noticed in the past. In fact, the better he got to know and like the fellow, the more he understood him. There may be a brash exterior but that was mainly for show; deep inside lurked a far more sensitive soul and one, he sensed, that could be trusted.

It was a week later and in the dining room of the Grand where they had just fought their way through a lamb casserole that had borne a greater resemblance to mutton. *MGB 95* was back on the active roster and had made two further patrols without incident before the weather changed dramatically. After a relatively calm couple of weeks, the new month had begun with an almighty storm; strong winds lashed the coast bringing up heavy seas that made even convoy work almost impossible while the low cloud and torrential rain had proved more than enough to dissuade enemy activity both at sea and in the air. Consequently, every flotilla based at *Wasp* had been stood down and all crews were enjoying a brief holiday, one the weather could only spoil by improving.

"Well, what do you say to involving me in another way?" the American persisted. "You know my views on the war, and that America should be taking a greater part in it. Some insight into what you guys get up to might help."

"You mean come out with us on patrol?" Anderson asked, incredulously.

Sandra was in the midst of taking a sip from her own drink and coughed generously but Peale ignored her.

"I guess so," he beamed. "Several have done it already; there've been US observers aboard battleships and destroyers, why not one of your Coastal Forces craft?"

"It's an idea, I suppose," Anderson pondered.

"And a rotten one if you ask me," Sandra pronounced, dabbing at her blouse with her handkerchief. "Tell him, Eve," she instructed, "tell him them boats are a liability."

"Oh no, I'm staying out of this," Eve replied quickly. With two men – a brother and what was fast becoming a suitor – aboard the same craft she felt it best to remain neutral, although it was good to hear someone else acknowledge the fears she had been hiding for so long.

"If we did anything it would have to be official," Anderson continued.

"Wouldn't want it any other way, bud," Peale assured him. "It's how *The Gazette* works – straight down the line. I'll make enquiries with my people, then see where we go from there. But once we get the all-clear, you'll be happy to take me?"

Anderson shrugged. "I'd have to run it past my CO," he replied with a subtle wink at Eve. "But guess we can win him round – providing the right moves are made, of course."

* * *

"Cats and dogs out there," Sharkey commented dolefully as he peered behind the blackout curtain.

"You there, get away from that window!" a gruff voice bellowed from behind the bar and Ward turned back.

"Ain't nothing going on, Alfie me darling," he said.

"Never you mind that," the landlord replied. "If them ARPs mark me down many more times I'll lose me licence. Then where will you be?"

"Drinking somewhere else, I shouldn't doubt." Sharkey

raised an eyebrow to his friends at the table and released the curtain. "Jerry's all tucked up warm," he added. "Or putting a few beers away, if he's got any sense."

"Just like us," Dowling, the youngster, agreed as he stubbed out a cigarette and reached for his pint. Both were newly acquired habits; the lad had changed significantly – some would say grown – in the brief time he had been a part of the gunboat's crew. He now felt truly at home and very much a man.

"Now that's where you're wrong," Sharkey told him firmly. "Your German ain't nothing like us."

"The ones we fished out of the drink were," Scott pointed out. "Weren't till we was getting the first aboard that anyone noticed the difference."

"Oh, I was knowing well afore that," Daly claimed. "The uniform gave it away, so it did."

"Well I didn't hear you say nothing," Sharkey grumbled.

"I had me own job to do. Besides, it wasn't as if they were going to give you trouble."

"Poor blighters would have been dead in a few hours," Scott agreed.

"One might still not make it," Dowling added.

"Glory be, we'll be going to visit them in the flakin' hospital next!"

"Oh come on, Shark," Scott protested. "You were as concerned as any of us, once we'd got them in the mess deck."

"Gave them each a tot, as I recall," Dowling reminded him.

"Well, you do," Sharkey agreed. "In that sort of situation. But it don't mean they ain't bastards, nor anything like us."

"I'm a bastard," Scott announced cheerfully.

"You what?" Sharkey enquired.

"Mum and Dad never bothered getting married, after a while they became quite proud of the fact."

There was a pause while all about the table digested this, then Sharkey went to pick up the thread once more, although Daly was ahead of him.

"The average German is no different," the Irishman claimed. "Most of those aboard the E-boats probably weren't sailors until recently, just like any of us."

"I'm a sailor," Scott again.

"Well make your bloody mind up," Sharkey told him.

"None of us are sailors," Daly maintained. "Not naturally. As soon as this lot's over we'll be back to our old jobs."

"So what were you doing, then," Scott asked Ward. "Before

104

you joined, I'm meaning?"

The gunner shrugged. "Four months in Pentonville, if you must know. What about you Irish?"

"General builder, so I was."

"Then how come you're not in the Army?" Dowling asked. "As an engineer or somethin'?"

"Ah, isn't that the mystery?" Daly marvelled. "But them boys we picked up, they were probably all labourers or farm hands or factory workers a while back."

"Farm hands don't fly aircraft," Sharkey pointed out.

"No, but it don't take geniuses to fire a machine gun neither – or an Oerlik' if it comes to it," Daly added slyly.

"Well I still say them's different," Sharkey persisted, totally missing the Irishman's jibe.

"The officers, they're the ones what are different," Scott suggested.

"Not even them, most of our lot aren't regular Navy men," Daly said. "It's the politicians, they're the villains."

"So they're like ours as well!" Scott exclaimed in delight.

"Are all our politicians villains then?" Dowling asked doubtfully.

"Oh yes, that's common knowledge," Daly assured him. "Only they never say so. Not when they're askin' for your vote."

* * *

By the time they finished their meal the storm had actually increased. Standing on the damp side of the hotel's double blackout curtains, Anderson looked out at the almost horizontal rain.

"I'm sorry about this," he said.

"Oh, I love it when you do that," Eve smiled.

"Do what?"

"Apologise for things out of your control. Like the weather."

"You know what I mean," Anderson sighed. "Are you sure you don't want to go back inside? We could join the others, they were going back to Dale's room."

"I don't think we'll be very popular."

"Why not? They'll only be playing records."

She pulled a serious face. "Yes of course they will, I was forgetting. Man and woman go up to a hotel room together and gramophones are bound to be involved."

"It's what they said," he protested.

"Really, Ian, sometimes you are such a fool!"

He looked at her sharply. "I'll have you know you are addressing a superior officer."

She shrugged. "Have it your own way – sometimes you're such a fool, sir!"

When they laughed together Eve often clutched at his arm – it was one of so many things that endeared her to him.

"I suppose we may as well make a run for it."

"Well you don't have to see me home," Eve remarked. "There'll be no one out on a night like this and little chance of a raid."

Maybe not, but once I'm soaked, I find I don't get any wetter," he said, "though I must admit I wished I'd worn the Ursula..."

Then he grabbed her hand and together they ran through the unlit streets, their shoes stirring up splashes from the puddle-ridden pavements that, to Anderson, seemed oddly reminiscent of something far less innocent. But though they were quick it was not quick enough, and the first shell landed to the north of the town when they were still some way short of the Wrennery.

"What the hell was that?" Anderson exclaimed, looking up at the cloud-filled sky.

"The Channel guns have started!" Eve exclaimed as the truth dawned.

"But why?" Anderson began as he wiped the rain from his face. "I mean, it's not as if the Germans can spot in these conditions. They must be firing blind."

Another shell exploded, this time slightly nearer, and was followed by the first strains of multiple air raid sirens.

"Shall we make for *Lynx*?" he bellowed. She shook her head.

"It's too far, and I wouldn't trust you amongst all those Wrens."

He looked about in desperation; another shell landed slightly further away but it was clear the town was in for a regular bombardment.

"The shelter," he said, pointing to one of several flat-roof brick structures that had been placed on opposite sides of the nearby square. Taking her hand again they set off once more, although this time with slightly more purpose. The sirens stopped, only to restart again as they tumbled through the large dripping entrance to the heavily built building. Inside it was pitch black and smelt strongly of damp and stale humanity.

"Hello?" Anderson called out.

"It seems to be empty," Eve remarked as she peered about.

"Most'll have taken shelter in the caves," Anderson supposed. "These places are mainly used in the daytime; I reckon we've got it to ourselves." There was a flash of light as he stuck a match.

"There's a lantern, or rather several." She pointed to a pile of supplies by the door.

Soon yellow light flooded the place, revealing a collection of chairs and benches, an oil heater and a small bed on which lay someone's abandoned knitting.

"I suppose we had better leave the door open, in case anyone wants to join us," she mused while replacing the blackout curtain.

"I don't see why," Anderson replied, lighting another lantern.

"But someone else might want to take shelter."

"Do you think that's likely? It didn't seem so very busy just now."

She shrugged and closed the door.

"There's no paraffin for the heater," Anderson continued, "but I can probably drain some from the other lamps – I must say it's darned cold."

"It's strange, being alone like this," Eve sighed. "And not something we've experienced much."

"That and one or two other things," he agreed, turning and drawing her closer. "It's just a shame we didn't think to bring a gramophone..."

* * *

By morning the storm had passed leaving only dank, damp streets although there was debris in differing forms from eighteen private houses, two small businesses and three bereaved families that made a more permanent record of the shelling raid. But for those at *Wasp,* there was rarely time to look back. A flotilla meeting had been called in the Operations Room and Collins was leading, along with a rather superior RN commander. Well into his forties, the opulent and slightly balding man appeared unusually elderly when compared with the young men he faced while, if his uniform were swapped for a cassock, he might easily have passed for a vicar.

But Commander Rogers was not a cleric, instead he served

ashore on the C-in-C's staff and evidently felt he had something vital to impart – something far too sensitive for *Wasp*'s own staff officer operations, to handle. But those who had been gathered together were prepared to listen, although it would be on their terms and, when the usual permission was granted for men to smoke, far more lit up than was usual.

"Our thinking is Jerry's E-boats have been kept at home for the last few days so are pretty likely to show up tonight," Rogers began when all were settled. It was a reasonable, if depressing, assumption and received no more than a polite mumble from the congregation. "Consequently, there will be no British convoys putting out. More than that, our friends to the north will not be continuing with the extension to the Declared Mine Area in the southern North Sea and most sweeping activities are also being suspended."

Now a little more interest was aroused although, to men accustomed to sleeping most of the morning, it was unquestionably early for serious thinking.

"Instead we will be targeting the enemy in their home ports and it will be a combined operation." He paused. "A combined operation, gentlemen, and I believe the largest Coastal Forces has yet undertaken." Now his expression had changed to one of expectancy, as if a special treat had been delivered and recognition was due, before turning to Collins. "But I will leave it to your SO to explain the part this flotilla will take."

A haze of smoke rose up from the crowd and Collins cleared his throat as he stepped forward. Harris and Anderson were seated towards the back of the room and both were struck by his apparent vulnerability in the defused light. It was now common knowledge that Collins was due for a transfer at any time. This would probably be his last shout and the man had given much to the flotilla. Consequently the respectful hush was made more poignant still when he regarded them all as if intending to remember the moment.

"Indeed, it will not just be our flotilla," he announced at last. "All of Dover Command will be active, as many boats as can be mustered in fact, and each will have a specific objective."

A few in the audience exchanged glances but there was no time for comment, Collins had a lot more to say.

"Our particular target will be the E-boats stationed at Boulogne," he announced. "We have seven serviceable craft and all will be going. We leave at dusk and head for Charlie Seven; for the new faces, that's a buoy moored about two miles from the harbour mouth. By the time we arrive any German craft venturing out should already have left: we intend lying cut in order to welcome them home on their return."

Now there was a definite rumble of discussion from the assembled officers and even Harris flashed a look at Anderson seated by his side.

Rogers stepped forward again and all eyes turned to him.

"And that is the nub of it, gentlemen. Obviously, you will be given more details but has anyone any specific comments so far?"

A hand was raised nearer the front and a newly promoted lieutenant spoke.

"I know the spot well, we'll be in full view of the shore."

"You will," Collins agreed. "Though the Met. Office is confident of a decent sea mist. And I don't mean a fog," he added quickly as a further rumble of comment arose. "There should be little wind and no moon to speak of, at least at the time we will be waiting."

Harris thought he noticed a slight crack in Collins' voice. The pair had not spoken since that brief conversation at the pens, indeed it was a surprise to find the man still on station. But then neither had his successor arrived, nor a replacement for Caswell's boat, and Harris supposed it simply proved the adage that your own side could be just as unpredictable as any enemy.

Another hand was raised. "And how long will we be waiting?" its owner asked.

"Well that's a difficult one," Rogers conceded, with an attempt at geniality as he recovered control of the room. "We're assuming all should be in position by nine. I suppose Jerry could show up any time between then and dawn."

This brought the loudest reaction yet. To lie cut with all senses primed and engines cold was hardly the most restful of occupations, and to do so over thirty miles from home, while under the guns of German shore batteries and within reach of armed trawlers or R-boats was doubly disconcerting. It could take up to ninety seconds for a launch's engines to fire up and full power to be delivered, time enough for their fragile craft to take a pounding.

"Can we be certain of the mist?" the original questioner asked.

"Aye," another unidentified voice agreed. "How about one of the Met. boys coming along to make sure?"

This produced a measure of laughter, but the atmosphere remained tense and expectant.

"We can be certain of nothing," Rogers announced. "Obviously if the night is clear or the enemy are in evidence the plan must be abandoned; there will be similar exercises at other major ports along with another, more concerted, effort further north that it's best you know nothing about. But basically there will be plenty of parties to join if yours falls flat. Your SO will be with you to advise of other arrangements should they be necessary although no one at Operations anticipates calling this one off. For it is an important mission, gentlemen, and not just for the results it might bring tonight."

Rogers lowered the papers in his hand and surveyed them as if unsure whether to grant absolution or damnation.

"Until now, Coastal Forces' role has been a defensive one. Some incursions into enemy territory have been made and on several occasions individual flotillas have taken the offensive with encouraging results. But never before have we launched such a concerted attack. We're hoping to give Jerry a bloody nose, and not just us; if all goes well there should be a number of similar successes along the French and Dutch coasts – something that should make the Hun think and perhaps be a little less cocky in future."

"That's all very well, sir, but we are hardly equipped." The comment came from the other side of the room and was almost an interruption. Anderson's eyes switched to the speaker and was surprised to recognise the lieutenant who had accompanied him from the station on his first night in Dover. Since then he had found Dave Chapman to be a solid CO who did his job efficiently and without fuss; this was definitely the first time he had spoken out at a briefing but, now he had, the attention did not seem to bother him one bit.

"Do you have a particular problem with your command, Lieutenant?" Rogers asked caustically, while Collins visibly stiffened. "Or perhaps the flotilla in general?"

"The boats are fine, sir, as far as they go," Chapman continued unabashed. "Never better, in fact. But none are up to meeting an E through choice."

Collins cleared his throat again and went to speak but Rogers was ahead of him.

"I say again, this will not be the only flotilla out tonight," he said. "Others will be involved in missions just as dangerous, in some cases more. Some will be facing VPs – they might not have the speed but are a far tougher opponent to disable and more heavily armed into the bargain. So do not let any of you think

110

yourselves hard done by, there will be plenty more taking similar risks if not greater."

"Other flotillas have more modern craft," Chapman countered swiftly. "Admittedly a couple of ours are relatively new but most started life as Masbes. They lack the firepower to tackle an E on equal terms and are far smaller and more vulnerable. Frankly, sir, I think we are being set up for a drubbing."

The older man's face had grown red and Collins coughed twice but it was the reaction from those around them that struck Harris and Anderson. Some were disputing what had been said, in one case quite animatedly, though the majority were more supportive. Chapman had definitely hit a tender spot and Commander Rogers RN did not like it one bit.

"Well I must say I am amazed at such a negative response," he began. "From what I hear, this flotilla has been reasonably successful and even accounted for an E-boat relatively recently."

"And in the same period we have lost two of our own," Chapman interrupted. "Such a rate of attrition cannot continue."

Now Rogers' eyes were ablaze. "It certainly must not," he said. "I hope that lessons will have been learned, and your performance improves. And it will do so with actions such as the one proposed for tonight. This is a relatively new flotilla and, as I have said, has done well, but not as new as some, and not as well as others. Fresh craft are certainly on the way and you will be provided for, but please do not confuse inexperience with poor materials. All your vessels are extremely well maintained despite the most trying of conditions and have benefitted from considerable improvements. Frankly, I am surprised not to receive more positive support for an operation of this magnitude."

There was silence now and several of those seated glared back unrepentant while others considered their nails or glanced out of the window.

"We have to move on," Rogers continued petulantly. "I have other flotillas to address and a long day ahead of me. If the first officers will stay behind, we will issue call signs, recognition codes, wireless frequencies and waypoint details. Departure will be after eighteen hundred hours; there'll be two flotillas leaving before, so you'll have to wait your turn. Until then I suggest you all return to your commands and see everything is ready. And if there's the chance, get what sleep you can. Dismiss."

Harris had never attended a briefing that ended so abruptly, or on such a sour note. He flashed a look at Anderson who had a cardboard file ready to receive the promised notes.

About him men were lighting fresh cigarettes or filling pipes and there was a little conversation although the mood was undoubtedly reflective. He glanced over to where Dave Chapman was in deep discussion with two officers from other boats. It was impossible to tell if they were criticising or praising but of one thing Harris was certain, he had made an impression.

* * *

It was dark when they passed out of the eastern dock and, at a signal from Collins in the leading boat, the gentle burble of their engines increased. Soon all were travelling at cruising speed and throwing up individual towers of water behind as they jockeyed for position.

Harris was vaguely surprised to see Anderson appear beside him in the other copular. "Have you a course for us, Number One?" he asked after they had positioned themselves at the starboard edge of the formation.

"Allowing for tides it's roughly south one-forty, east," Anderson told him flatly. "But Price is keeping station on the SO's boat." He nodded briefly to the dark mass off their port bow. "I thought it would be as well to let them lead us in."

"An eminently good idea," Harris told him.

* * *

In the wheelhouse, the arrangement suited Price as well. Not that he had any objection to following a heading but for as long as the nearest gunboat could be made out, he much preferred lying off its quarter.

"Fancy a brew, Mr Price?" Dowling enquired as he tumbled into the wheelhouse, clanging the door shut behind him.

"That'd go down a treat, Mikey," the coxswain told him. "Ward do without you, can 'e?"

"He sent me to make the tea," Dowling replied, cautiously. He'd already discovered older or senior men were inclined to tease him and the coxswain qualified on both counts. "All right to go on the mess deck?" he asked.

"Go on the mess deck?" Price asked absentmindedly.

"Captain's orders," Dowling explained. "We're banned from it in anything over a force four."

"Yes, of course," Price agreed as he stared out at the gentle waves that were barely moving in the dull still air. "Mess deck's fine, no fear of drownin' dan there."

* * *

By the time Dowling's tea had been distributed they were more than halfway to Charlie Seven and conditions were staying worryingly clear. It was dark, for sure, and there was a degree of mist, although nothing strong enough to provide the concealment they needed. And it was also patchy – too patchy, with areas lying relatively clear where bright stars shone boldly.

"Don't like the look of this, Number One," Harris muttered. "Coast is very much in sight, and so will we be shortly."

"They'll pick us up in no time," Anderson agreed. None of the boats was showing so much as a glimmer of light but as they drew closer they would still become horribly apparent. Even at regulation speed, each was throwing up a wave of fluorescent wake and if the Germans missed that they would definitely hear their engines.

"R/T from the SO," Jelly's voice announced through the voice pipe and was followed by a crackle from the repeater.

"Okay lads, I think we might have drawn a blank," Collins' voice was heavily distorted, although Harris still thought it contained an element of relief. "We'll throttle back for a spell. Then, if there's no sign of the mist thickening, turn back."

Jelly's confirmation could be heard through the speaking tube, Harris gave the appropriate orders, and the boat slumped down and continued at a slower pace.

"Can't be helped, I suppose," Anderson muttered. "If it's like this for us, you can bet the others will be similarly affected all up the coast. And when you think what the weather's been like…"

"To be honest, Number One, I'm not sorry," Harris replied. "I don't mind admitting I've rather had my fill of blasting about in constant tempests. A gentle cruise in something a little clearer makes a change."

That was certainly the case; although, even as he spoke, Harris knew his words might sound strange and certainly not what a captain of a gunboat was supposed to say. But as he glanced at Anderson the man showed no sign of surprise; if anything, he sensed understanding from his second in command. It was a pleasant reaction and, as he realised then, one he was starting to expect. If they turned back shortly, they might all manage a few hours' sleep that night, and there was surely nothing wrong in admitting the fact, although Harris was relieved for another reason.

With the storm over and the air now clear, they were probably in for some relatively fine weather; it could even be a week before conditions were suitable for another attack on the E-boats, and in that time Collins' transfer might have come through. Harris still trusted the man, even though he had been showing signs of strain of late. It might have something to do with the expected child – that or the two he had already – but something was getting the better of him and it was definitely time to go.

But then how anyone could fight a war by night and maintain some semblance of home life during the day would always be a mystery to him. It was probably easier for those detailed to ships when long deployments were balanced by spells of extended leave, but Collins' way of living was more akin to that of aircrew, where war and peace was often separated by no more than a matter of minutes. Not many could maintain such a life for long and, if Collins had reached the time to move on, he really should.

Even as Harris decided this, a whistle from the W/T speaking tube caught his attention. It was Jelly and he had news, important news. It seemed their night was not to be a total washout and, rather than a quick run home, they could expect to be in action and probably very shortly. Suddenly there was no room for abstract thoughts, and everything became extremely serious.

Chapter Eight

The word was Dover radar had picked up a slow-moving convoy seven miles to the south which, rather conveniently, was making straight for their position. Harris listened to Jelly's report then turned to Anderson. But before he could speak the repeater crackled again and this time it was Collins' voice on the R/T, although stronger than before.

"Okay chaps, that sounds like action, if not what we expected. Bob, take Mike and Phil to the west – a mile or so should do it. The rest follow me and we'll try for a scissor action. Keep your speed down, no bow waves or wash to give anything away. When you see the first starshell or any sign of action make your run. I'll aim for the rear; Bob's division take the front, and we'll try not to meet in the middle." Then there was a dull click and silence.

Harris leant towards the W/T office speaking tube, "Very well, Jelly, acknowledge that." Next he called up Price and soon the boat began what was quite a leisurely turn before straightening up and leading the two other MGBs directly away from Collins' force.

"Shame we have no MTBs," Anderson muttered.

"It's a shame we aren't carrying torpedoes ourselves," Harris added with a snort. "One twenty-millimetre and two half-inchers hardly qualifies us as a gunboat."

"Maybe that's what they meant by better craft on the way?" Anderson added and they both nodded wisely.

"This will do," Harris told Price a while later. "Start a slow one-eighty to port."

The boat began another gentle sweep while Anderson turned his attention astern.

"They've both seen us," he confirmed as their two dark shadows followed them around.

"Good," Harris grunted. "The last thing we need is someone lighting up an Aldis."

The trailing boats also mirrored their example when it came to slowing further and soon the three gunboats were drifting listlessly in the swell, their engines barely turning over.

"When they fit those tubes, they could add radar as well,"

Harris mused.

"Some have it already," Anderson replied.

"A scant few, and it will take a lot longer before we're blessed." Then, leaning forward to the wireless room speaking tube, "Anything from base, Tel'?"

"Nothing, sir," Jelly replied, and Harris pursed his lips in disgust.

"Some blighter in Dover'll be watching them on a plot no doubt; damn fool can probably see us as well but can't be bothered to keep everyone informed."

Anderson said nothing; the frustration was plain, although speech radio transmissions were not in code and could easily be intercepted. Even a ciphered Morse countdown could give a clue as to what was about to take place.

"It's just a waiting game, I guess."

"You guess?" Harris repeated in feigned disgust. "Have you been mixing with Americans, Number One?"

Anderson gave a sheepish smile. "I might have, sir," he replied.

* * *

"I think I have something," Daly announced cautiously from behind and it was a sign of his doubt that the usual reporting protocol had been abandoned.

"What is it?" Harris demanded.

"Hazy shape off the starboard bow. What do you make of it, Scotty?" The last remark was addressed to his opposite number in the port turret and all waited for the response.

"I can't see nothing," Scott admitted at last. "The mist is rising all the time."

"If we'd known this was going to happen, we might have waited for the E-boats," Harris muttered but again Anderson made no response. Mist had definitely been predicted; it was just a shame the timing was wrong. But, given the choice between facing a convoy that might be protected by anything, and a rich unadulterated dose of E-boats just for them, he knew which he preferred.

"Wait, yes – I think I've got it now," Scott added.

"Object in sight, green oh-twenty," Daly reported more formally. "And there's tracer!"

Sure enough, the flashes of red could be seen through the growing smog and were quickly joined by more numerous flakes of green that seemed to be coming from a far wider area.

"Full ahead, steer starboard fifteen!" The steady rumble from below began to increase even before Harris' words had been spoken and within seconds the boat had risen on to the plane and was heading for the distant action. Anderson glanced back. Their two followers might not have noticed the convoy but only a fool could have missed so much firing. Then as *MGB 95* bucked at a rogue wave, he noticed Mike Barton's boat pull ahead slightly, and the other, commanded by the more reclusive Shaw, settle down as back marker.

"They've formed a line astern," he shouted at Harris, who nodded in acknowledgement.

"First merchant looks to be a freighter," Daly announced from the starboard turret just as a starshell burst over the rear of the convoy. Those on the bridge could see as much and there was another shape, large but otherwise indistinguishable, close behind.

"Can't see any sign of escorts," Anderson remarked as he reached for a steel helmet and passed another across to Harris.

"With a bit of luck they'll have turned back to meet the SO's lot," Harris roared, taking the thing but resting it on the panel in front of him. "That's where the starshells are coming from," he added as another flare rose up. Then the night sky was lit by a tremendous eruption. The sudden light was off their starboard bow and positively painful to eyes accustomed to the gloom of night; several on deck turned away from the glare.

"What the hell was that?" Anderson asked.

"I'd say it was one of Collins' lot," Harris replied, his voice void of emotion.

"Well we know they were making their attack," Anderson agreed as the flat, dull noise of explosion reached them. "Probably one was just unlucky."

"At least Jerry will be directing all his attention there," Harris added, with a little more energy.

"In which case the front of the convoy might be exposed," Anderson agreed. "This could be the chance of a lifetime!"

"Get down to the depth charges, Number One," Harris snapped. "They'll be our best bet if only we can get close enough. And listen for the command from Price," he added.

For even a reserve sub-lieutenant to be under the orders of a petty officer might have sounded strange but Anderson knew the reason and was happy to defer to the coxswain who was far more experienced in such a manoeuvre. And he also understood the captain's insistence on firing the charges manually; much could go wrong and even the briefest of delay could ruin the entire exercise. He clambered down from his perch and into the relative tranquillity of the wheelhouse. The boat's motion was increasing and he was forced to grab hold, first to the chart table, then the W/T office door.

"I'll release one depth charge, 'Swain, Jelly the other," he shouted. "We'll both be waiting for your signal."

"Very good, sar," Price replied; the petty officer's weather-beaten face was set forward with his mind apparently fixed on the task ahead. Yet still he had noticed the first lieutenant address him properly and was inwardly pleased. "I'll be using the klaxon then."

Anderson was about to thump on the thin bulkhead that partitioned off the W/T room when Jelly appeared ready clad in oilskins.

"It's depth charge duty, Jelly," Anderson announced, "though you seem to have guessed that. We'll be releasing them manually," he added.

"I've done it before, sir," the telegraphist confirmed. He appeared totally prepared and was certainly dressed for the job although Anderson still sensed something amiss.

"Are you sure you're all right, Tel'?" Even in the poor light there was a distinct hint of green about the rating's face as he secured the stiff cloth about his neck.

"Don't worry about me, sir, I'll be fine. Take the port side, shall I?" he asked, then made for the far door before Anderson could reply.

"Do you think he's okay, 'Swain?" Anderson pondered when he had gone.

"What, Sparks?" the older man chuckled. "Nothing wrong with 'im – least nothing a good chuck out won't cure. But port side's best," he added. "It's to leeward, see? If my guess is right 'e'll find that comes in 'andy."

* * *

Harris felt strangely alone on the bridge without Anderson beside him. The leading freighter was becoming a more likely target for depth charge attack with every passing second, but there was still no sign of escorts and their absence was almost disconcerting. Over to starboard the sky was regularly being lit both by starshells and strands of tracer; a battle was being waged, probably by what was left of Collins' division but still it seemed the approach of their own trio of gunboats was going unnoticed. Of course the mist, rolling northwards as it was, might be hiding any number of smaller craft – he could be leading them directly into a trap; at any time they could find themselves in the crossfire from several escorts. But until one appeared there was little point in worrying; he must assume they were safe.

"Okay, 'Swain, I still have her but be prepared to take control as we get closer."

Price muttered a brief acknowledgement through the voice pipe and Harris looked about. Both turret gunners were lining up their weapons ready for the moment they came into range. Half-inch machine gun bullets would make little impact on the hull of an ocean-going freighter, but the merchant may be armed, and they should at least keep the German gunners' heads down.

And then suddenly there was fire; a stream of green tracer was issuing from the transport's stern. For a second the line weaved about in the mist like a torch seeking them out in the darkness, then it settled a little ahead of their bows. Instantly Scott and Daly's Vickers rattled out a reply and soon the air was rent with flecks of tracer. Harris lowered himself slightly in the copular and slipped on the steel helmet Anderson had given him. Usually he hated the things but in the present circumstances its small assurance was welcomed.

"Very well, 'Swain," he bellowed down the speaking tube, his voice set and determined as a man free from all doubts, "you have control!"

Standing back, Harris gritted his teeth and took stock once more; his turret gunners were intent on keeping the German freighter's decks swept and everyone else aboard the gunboat was placed far lower, so he only had his own eyes to trust. But there remained no sign of any escort and the chance of making a successful run was growing by the second. The boat bucked slightly; they were travelling at speed and closing fast but Price was starting to throttle back. The manoeuvre seemed to confuse those aboard the freighter, or perhaps they were now unable to reach them with a stern-mounted gun, but their fire held off. Harris swallowed as the last few hundred yards seemed to vanish in no time and then the dark hull was suddenly directly before them. The klaxon echoed out like a roar of defiance as Price threw the helm across. There was a pause before the boat reared up yet again as the engines were given full throttle, their roar being joined, almost unexpectedly, by the solid thump of the aft Oerlikon as Ward and

Dowling joined the battle for the first time. Then a massive explosion cut through the air and water was thrown way above the freighters bows. Harris watched it for no more than a second, before turning back to the voice pipe.

"Okay, 'Swain, well done. I have her now," he called. "Hard port rudder!" Spray and spume rained down through the mist as the gunboat's stern dug deep, her screws fighting for purchase in the dark waters. There was a metallic tapping on the aft superstructure that he later decided to be machine gun bullets – small arms fire from the freighter or perhaps the merchant had an illegal gun mounted forward. He ordered another stiff turn and saltwater was suddenly washing over all on deck. For a moment he clung to the sides of the copular, then bellowed down again. "That's it, check your swing, now right standard rudder." A movement nearby caught his attention and he turned to see Anderson returning to the bridge and taking up position next to him. "How did it go, Number One?"

"Well enough, thank you, sir," the younger man replied.

Harris nodded, then turned back to the voice pipe. "Port fifteen, 'Swain," he bellowed. "And your timing was bang on."

In the wheelhouse, Price received the news with a satisfied smile. The sound of their depth charges had certainly penetrated his dark space and, even if he could see little aft, he knew the boat had been in a perfect position; the only part that might have gone wrong was the launching of the depth charges. But the first lieutenant had seen to that, and Price knew him to be a good officer.

"Glad to hear it, sar," he replied, before looking to the compass again as another change of direction was ordered.

* * *

"Hold your fire!" Dowling yelled but Sharkey sent several more shells towards the freighter.

"Stop now, fat-head!" the younger lad demanded.

Ward glared angrily at his mate before reluctantly releasing his grip and leaning back from the weapon. "You'd never have said that a few weeks back."

"97's right behind us," Dowling explained gruffly. "They'll be going in to attack."

"Right you are then," Sharkey admitted, only mildly

crestfallen.

"Never mind," the youngster told him as he made ready with the next magazine. "Least one of us remembered."

* * *

The next attack failed, either Barton's boat was not able to get in close enough, or the depth charges had not been correctly set, but by then *MGB 95* was a good way off the freighter's starboard bow.

"We could go in again from this side," Anderson suggested. "There are still two charges left."

"No," Harris shouted back. "That might disrupt the others' attack. We'll see how Shaw does, then regroup."

"Vessel in sight, green oh-four-five!" Daly's voice cut through. "E-boat – up close an' comin' right for us!"

"Right standard rudder!" Harris bellowed while Anderson announced the new danger over the megaphone.

"And release the smoke floats!" Harris added.

Dowling leapt from the aft gun mounting, ducking only slightly as Ward emptied the last of his current magazine barely inches from his body. Then the Oerlikon fell silent as the lad struggled with the first of two containers. Each contained chlorosulphuric acid that would create a dense cloud of smoke which should grant them a modicum of cover.

"And port twenty," Harris ordered from the bridge, as the boat continued to weave, dodging the stream of blinding green tracer the E-boat spat at them.

Both turret gunners were in action but the Oerlikon was empty and must stay silent until Dowling returned. And the Germans were firing effectively; several times a line of bullets ripped into the gunboat's superstructure with disconcerting accuracy and shells were constantly passing close overhead or to either side. But Dowling was soon successful and, as he returned to his gun, grey-white smoke was already issuing from the abandoned floats.

A scream came from Scott; Harris glanced across, but the port turret seemed to have disappeared along with its gunner. Then the enemy found their mark yet again and began to dig deep into the gunboat's vitals. Sparks were raised as bullets shattered fittings, the mast was squarely hit and fell about them in a tangle of wire and steel while several shells passed easily through the frail wooden skin causing untold damage within.

"Meet her, left standard runner!" Harris bellowed. They were still travelling close to maximum speed, but it couldn't last; already the gunboat was critically wounded and showing signs of tiring as she dipped and dived in the swell. Then the Oerlikon was back in use and had sight of the enemy; despite the boat's motion, Ward was sending an unbroken stream of tracer about the bridge and bows of the E-boat, seemingly holding the predator at bay until finally it slewed to one side and bore off.

Though obviously damaged, the enemy's fire continued and even as the hull of the E-boat was being left behind, more shells hammered against the British vessel's fragile sides and burst into her superstructure while several large holes opened up on the foredeck and prow.

"There's mist!" Anderson yelled, pointing desperately to starboard.

"Right standard rudder," Harris ordered and again the boat twisted. Daly's gun released a final stream of red as the gunboat headed for the patch of particularly dense cloud, then grey smog finally enveloped them and the captain rang for cease fire.

For a moment they had found sanctuary; their own engines were spluttering but the boat continued to move forward at a reasonable speed and of the E-boat there was neither sight nor sound. A whistle from the engine room speaking tube drew the officers' attention and Harris bent forward to answer.

"We've taken damage, sir," Carter's voice was reassuringly calm. "Starboard engine's down and I'm not sure we can keep the port going much longer.

"Very well, Chief," Harris replied with equal dispassion. "We've found a bit of shelter; give us all you can – we need it for the bailers – and I'll try to keep away from further trouble." He turned to Anderson. "What think you?" he asked.

"Convoy's close by but will soon be past," Anderson replied.

"Collins' lot must be near as well, but without radio we can't contact them or the others. Better take a look around, Number One."

"Very good, sir," Anderson replied and ducked down from his copular.

Harris glanced back; if anything, the mist was thickening further and, close by or not, he could see no sign of other shipping. Even the sky, dimly visible through the haze, bore no reflection of tracer; it was as if they were suddenly alone and on a totally empty ocean. Their final engine coughed twice, seemingly recovered, before cutting out completely. For several seconds they drifted in dreadful silence, powered only by their own momentum, before power returned.

The boat straightened as Price brought them back under control. They might manage a reasonable speed on one motor, and could certainly make England, although much would depend on the state of their hull and Harris sensed that would not be good. He hoisted himself up on the copular and peered forward in the mist. The boat's foredeck was a mess of shattered wood and, as he turned his attention aft, he could dimly make out the remains of the port turret. The twisted mounting and mangled remains of the machine gun were comprehensively entwined about Scott's distorted body. He glanced across; the starboard turret was also empty so possibly Daly had been hit as well. Aft, the superstructure had taken a hammering and then he saw his starboard gunner. The Irishman had abandoned his weapon and was opening the engine room hatches allowing a cloud of what might be heat or fumes into the cold night air. And slightly further aft one of the Oerlikon gunners had been hit, he couldn't see who as the other had his back to him, as he attended to his mate.

Harris slipped down from his perch, removed his helmet and rubbed both hands over his face. They had been at rest and considering an early run home barely thirty minutes before, yet that time might now be many hours in the past.

"Anything at all from the set, Tel'?" he asked, leaning forward to the W/T office pipe.

"Mast is down and I've lost power on both R/T and W/T, sir."

"Are you all right?"

"I'm fine, though the bullets were flying rather. It looks like a transformer problem, and I can't do much about that."

"See if you can help with the damage then."

"Very good, sir, I'll do what I can."

"Engine room's in a bad way," Anderson announced as he reappeared shortly afterwards. "Water's entering through the lower hull but that's no bad thing as two of the tanks have fractured; place stinks of petrol."

"Can we reach the damage?"

"Can't even see it," Anderson replied. "Though I reckon quite a bit's coming in forward. Jelly's there now and chocking up with hammocks and bits of furniture, but it doesn't look good. Any chance of taking her in backwards?"

"Difficult on one engine," Harris grunted. "And if we try, we'll get no benefit from the self-bailers."

"I can organise others to help," Anderson suggested. "That might keep us afloat a while longer."

"Do that," Harris agreed coming to a decision. "Take Ward and Dowling, see if you can't bail out in the lazarette aft of the engine room, that's bound to be the lowest point."

"Ward's injured; Dowling's seeing to him."

"Very well, I'll go forward and join Daly, probably take Price with me; he can lock the helm. Any idea where we are, Number One?" he added as the thought occurred.

Anderson looked doubtful. "The convoy was sailing about four miles off the French coast; I'm afraid the plot's not bang up to date."

"Hardly surprising, a rough guess will do."

"Dover is to the north-west but a long way off."

"Very well," Harris replied evenly. "We shall just have to do what we can."

* * *

Two hours later *MGB 95* was still afloat, but her prospects did not seem good. The port engine was rumbling at low revs in an empty engine room, a leak having been discovered in its exhaust manifold that could not be contained with any amount of asbestos strapping. Carter and Newman were forward in what remained of the mess deck along with Daly, Price and Jelly; together they took turns in either shoring up the boat's shattered bows or manning the hand bilge pump that flushed out a heady mixture of seawater, petrol and oil. But for all their efforts everyone knew the boat would not last much longer; they would have to take to the Carley float and were still many miles from the English coast.

Anderson was further aft with Harris; together they had dealt with Scott's remains in as dignified a way as possible. There seemed little point in even the most perfunctory of public funerals, although the thought of leaving a shipmate's body to go down with the boat was oddly repugnant. Eventually the deed was done and, with their late gunner safely despatched into the dark waters, they could turn to clearing away the life raft and checking through what supplies they would need.

"Two tubes of morphine should be enough," Anderson remarked, "though if there is another in the engine room cabinet, we may as well take that too."

"Take the whole damn lot," Harris told him. "But be careful when you go down there, the place is full of gas."

"How long do you think the boat's got?"

Harris pondered. "An hour, maybe slightly more, but it makes sense to leave it as long as possible. We're not making much progress but it's a darn sight more than the Carley will manage."

Both men paused as the sound of far-off aeroplane engines came to them through the fog.

"More of our boys heading home," Anderson remarked. It was the third wave they had heard, and all were hidden by the mist that seemed to encase them in a very private world.

"May as well try another flare," Harris replied.

Anderson reached for the Very pistol, opened it briefly to check the cartridge, then looked up in vain hope of some clear sky before aiming it randomly at the thick blanket of cloud. The charge exploded with a sharp crack that was followed by a jet of light which shot high and was quickly absorbed by the mist. It was questionable if those aboard the returning bombers would see such a signal, while any subsequent rescue could only rely on luck to find them. But if nothing else, the men of *MGB 95* were announcing their existence to civilisation and, trapped as they were, the effort seemed worthwhile.

Below them and slightly further forward, Dowling and the injured Sharkey were in the wardroom. The gunner's leg wound had been cleaned, tight strapping applied and a generous dose of morphine injected from a disposable tube. It was about the extent of the boat's medical resources; now there was nothing to do but make him as comfortable as possible on one of the officers' bunks.

Sharkey slept for much of the time but the last few minutes had signalled a change; there was movement and it appeared likely he was regaining consciousness, so it was no surprise to the waiting Dowling when his friend finally spoke.

"Thought it were a dream, Mikey," Ward said with uncharacteristic tenderness. "Thought I were imagining it. Then I finds myself in the officer's digs with what feels like a five-inch hole in me leg."

"No dream, Sharkey," Dowling informed him. "But it ain't nowhere near five-inch – I seen it. Not much larger than a tanner."

"Well that's something I suppose," he muttered with a hint of disappointment.

"Do you want some more of that stuff?" the lad asked.

"Not for now," Sharkey replied. "But stick with me."

"I ain't going nowhere," Dowling assured him. "The rest is up for'ard and either pumping or trying to block them leaks. I'd rather stay here an' talk with you."

"Why they pumping by hand?" Sharkey asked and the lad shrugged.

"Beats me, but it's not doing much good. Word is we're sinking, and the fog's still thick so not much chance of a rescue."

"It's the Channel," Sharkey stated with more confidence. "Busy place, we'll be picked up in no time."

"You mean like them Germans?" Dowling asked.

"Yeah, like them Germans," Sharkey agreed. "They were all right, weren't they? Even after a good long spell they seemed none the worse." He considered this for a while. "You know I've been thinking a lot about them," he said at last.

"Is that right?" Dowling replied with little enthusiasm.

"Aye, and that E-boat."

"The one we sank?"

"The one I sank," Sharkey corrected.

"You done great, Shark," Dowling agreed. "Went up like a rocket – I reckon you must have set off one of her torpedoes – really neat!"

"I didn't feel so, not when I thought it were British."

"Course not; but it weren't – we discovered that soon enough."

"Aye, maybe," Sharkey agreed. "But them Germans we rescued weren't so very different from our lot."

"We thought they were our lot," Dowling reminded him. "Until they started talking funny."

"That's what I mean," Sharkey sighed. "So I reckons I'm done for it," he added after a pause. "At the Oerlik' I mean."

"Aye, reckon you're right there," Dowling agreed. "We'll get you back safe, then they'll send you off to some nice crisp hospital with nice crisp nurses who'll put you to rights. You could be away for months, maybe years. By the time you comes back, I'll be the gunner, though there'll be a place for you as my loading number."

"Kind of you I'm sure," he muttered, then winced with pain.

"I'll get an officer," Dowling informed him, rising. "He'll give you some more of that stuff."

"No, wait a while," Sharkey implored. "You see I ain't coming back. We volunteered ourselves into this little lot so can volunteer out of it. And I've had my fill."

"What you saying?" Dowling was half standing in the tiny room.

"I'm saying I've had enough," Sharkey told him more firmly. "No more for me, I'm finished."

"It's the stuff," Dowling stated. "Made you go soft."

"Maybe," Sharkey allowed. "But it's how I feel now. When they take me off this boat I ain't going near another, not for no one."

* * *

That time came just under two hours later when the deck was almost level with the lapping waves. There were still several hours to go before daylight and the fog was just as dense as Daly secured the float next to the gunboat's hull while Dowling and Newman carefully passed Ward's trussed-up body to willing hands.

"I should say that's about it, Number One," Harris muttered after Daly had followed the others into the float and they were the last left on deck. "Strange," he added. "I thought It would be different, having to abandon my command and all that. But really I don't feel a thing."

"We've still got to get ourselves to safety," Anderson reminded him. "You'll probably notice it once we're back on dry land; I guess we all will."

"There you go, guessing again," Harris snorted. "I'll have to meet this American friend of yours – pretty is she?"

"Not especially, sir," Anderson replied flatly. "Shall we make a move?"

"We have all the torches?"

"And medical supplies. Jelly boiled up some water for the safari jar and I've taken all the blankets. Flares are on board and what confidential books there were have been ditched."

"Then we may as well be off," Harris supposed. "You go first, Number One; we'd better do this properly."

Chapter Nine

"Come on, its oh-six-hundred hours, time to be up."

Sandra moaned once then turned over and buried her head under the sheet.

"I'm not waiting," Eve insisted. "If you're late for breakfast it's your lookout, I'm hungry." But she paused on turning to go as it was clear her friend had gone back to sleep.

"Come on, old girl," she instructed, pulling some of the blankets back. "Get yourself up or you'll fall foul of Ma Gregson."

Sandra let out a deep sigh, then heaved herself upright and winced as she placed her bare feet on the cold linoleum floor.

"What on earth is that?" Eve asked abruptly pointing at the black box that lay to the other side of Sandra's bed.

"What?"

"The thing," she replied. "It looks like some sort of medical equipment."

Sandra directed a sleep-filled head to where Eve was pointing. "It's a gramophone," she said, before slumping back sideways onto the bed.

"A gramophone? Where did you get a gramophone?"

"Dale gave it me." Sandra yawned, rose up once more, and rubbed at her eyes.

"Must have cost a bit," Eve supposed.

"No, were a present." She was stretching now. "Said it was for his special girl."

"And that's it, is it? You're now his special girl?"

"I am if he gives me gramophones."

"Well I'm not sure what Gregson will say about it; don't you have to get permission for that sort of thing?"

"Gregson can go boil her head," Sandra announced before finally rising from the bed and staggering across the small room to a chair that held an untidy pile of underwear and uniform.

"I think you might be seeing too much of that reporter," Eve told her.

"He's not a reporter, he's a war correspondent," Sandra muttered while sorting through her clothes. "Gorra white shirt, have you?"

"There's a blouse in the top drawer. But it's my last; you'll have to replace it by tomorrow morning."

Sandra grunted eloquently as she shuffled across to the chest of drawers, opened one and began rifling through its contents.

"Hey, careful, I've just ironed that lot."

"I'll replace it," her friend muttered.

"That will be a first. So why the gramophone?"

"I like music. And I like Dale."

"Because he gives you gramophones?"

She stopped to consider this. "Partly. But mostly 'cause he's an American."

"I had noticed."

"No, but they aren't at war. He's got money, a flat in New York, only he calls it an apartment and never seems to be there. And they have shows on Broadway with all sorts of famous names. And streetlights, and everyone drives about in cars an' nothing's rationed. Oh, Evie, it's a different world!" she added dreamily.

"It certainly sounds it. And you want to go there?"

Sandra paused halfway through buttoning the blouse. "I would if he asked."

"So he hasn't yet?"

"No, so far all he's done is give me a gramophone."

"And did you pay him for it?"

Sandra looked away. "How could I on our slave wages?"

"You know what I mean."

"What if I did?" She looked back. "And it's not like paying any road, more a deposit. A down payment on a better life – right now anything would be an improvement on the one I've got. And anyway," she mumbled finally, "he sung like a horse."

"Whatever do you mean, he sung like a horse?" Eve questioned before blushing suddenly. "Well you're going to have to get permission if you intend keeping it," she added hastily.

"Why? Annic Mutter's gorra wireless."

"That's not the same as a gramophone. You get news from a wireless; some might say it can aid the war effort. All a gramophone does is play music."

"Yeah, but what music!" She held her crumpled skirt against her chest in apparent ecstasy. "Oh Evie, Dale plays me the most wonderful tunes, and by people you don't hear of in England, yet in America everyone knows them. The country's got the best of everything, and if I don't go there with Dale, I'll find someone else to take me. Besides," she added, considering the more immediate problem, "who's to say gramophones can't help the war effort? We can use it on our evenings off, take it with us t'shelter – it'll cheer folk up. And you can't play Lord Haw-Haw on a gramophone."

* * *

When dawn broke in the Channel the fog was just as strong and their only clue to the sun rising was a subtle lightening of the mist. But most of the men were comfortable enough and reasonably warm as they lay huddled like animals under a tarpaulin in a deep but fitful sleep. Only Daly and Jelly were awake and separate. The float's lively and uneven motion had aroused their seasickness; both were lying at the edge of the Carley and occasionally dry retching into the nearby sea.

"Supposed to be one of the busiest shipping lanes in the world," Anderson grumbled. "You'd think someone would have picked us up by now."

"That's in peacetime," Harris corrected him. "And they would have, had it been decent weather. We've heard plenty of planes and that was surely a launch an hour or so back. If our flares could be seen, we'd be warm and dry. How many have we left by the way?"

"Plenty," Anderson told him as he tapped a tin container. "Another whole box."

"Well we'd better be a little careful," Harris cautioned. "Only use them when there's a good chance of being noticed."

"Wonder which of our boats bought it," Anderson mused.

"You mean earlier in the action?" Harris sighed. "Hard to say, but you're right, it was definitely one of ours. That was a petrol explosion."

"Then it would have been part of the SO's lot."

"Judging from the direction," Harris agreed.

"Or Collins himself."

Harris said nothing but had been thinking along similar lines. There were four boats in Collins' division, so the odds lay against it being him, but still he had an inkling about the man. It was just a shame his posting did not come earlier – a shame for him and his young family.

"Wonder what damage we did to the freighter," Anderson added.

"Probably never know," Harris mused. "Though I dare say we shook them up a bit."

"I thinks I can hear sommat, sar," Price interrupted from the opposite side of the float.

Both officers listened for a moment without success, then a faint clatter came through. It was slight, nothing more than the sound made by shrouds or halyards rattling on a moored vessel.

"What do you think, Number One, a buoy?"

"Might be, I've no way of knowing our position."

"There – in the mist." Price spoke louder this time and half stood as he pointed. "Looks like a launch or sim-lar."

Harris glanced at Anderson before they both rose up and flung their blankets away. If it was a boat of some kind it must have crept up on them in silence – far more likely to be a buoy, but still worth investigating.

Standing awkwardly, Anderson tried to make more from the dark mass; in such conditions it could have been fifteen feet away or fifty.

"Come on lads, stir yourselves," Harris ordered, pointing at the dim shape. "Get the paddles out and make for whatever that is."

It took a while before any form of momentum could be created and even then the float was impossible to steer. But eventually they were drawing near to the source of the sound.

"Cripes, it's a bleedin' sub!" Dowling muttered when what looked like a small conning tower came into view.

"If that's a sub hit's a mighty sick one," Price countered firmly. "Look at how she's buckin' abart – that'll be anchored for certain and there won't be much of an hull to talk about."

"It could be one of those ASR buoys," Anderson suggested to Harris. "Jerry's been using them for a while and I heard we've started."

"Could indeed," Harris agreed. "They're not the sort of thing we would have run across at night, unless we happened to be especially unlucky."

"Well whatever it is, we might have found a bit more shelter."

Harris turned to the men at the paddles. "Come on lads, put your backs into it!"

Within ten minutes Price had secured the float alongside. The buoy itself was shaped like an upturned mushroom and mostly yellow in colour although large red crosses could be made out on what would be the stalk, which was surrounded by a railed gallery. A tubular ladder reached down as far as the waterline.

Anderson glanced at Harris. "Would you care to lead, sir?"

Harris raised his eyes briefly before heaving himself up the ladder, which was cold to the touch with rungs that were wet and slippery. But soon he was on the outer gallery and facing a small red door.

"Be a shame to find it locked," he supposed as Anderson joined him. But the door opened outwards easily enough and Harris entered.

Inside there was nothing more than another ladder, but this led to the depths below. Exchanging a quick look with Anderson, Harris began to descend.

It was dark, what light he had came from the open door and barely penetrated but Harris reached for his torch and began to examine his surroundings. A circular chamber packed with equipment, furniture and supplies was revealed. There was a pair of tiered bunks to one side and bundles of what might be blankets or mattresses opposite. Several plain chairs surrounded a small table which was secured to the deck and there were lockers and a larger cupboard. He could see a line of kerosene lamps fixed to the low deckhead and a radio was set against one bulkhead with a bank of switches alongside.

"Comfortable place," Anderson said as he eased himself down the ladder.

"Germans obviously care about their airmen," Harris agreed. "Better have Jelly in here and see what he makes of those switches. And Ward, do you think we can get him out of the float?"

"I guess so," Anderson answered without thinking. Then, on catching Harris' expression, corrected himself: "I mean, I'm sure that will be possible, sir."

* * *

An hour later they were comfortable. Manoeuvring Ward on the ladders had not been easy but finally achieved with the help of a webbing hoist Anderson found in one of the lockers and presumably provided for such a situation. And Jelly had investigated the switchboard; electric light now lit the small room. It was powered by an accumulator which the telegraphist reckoned would be good for at least forty-eight hours.

"When I turned the lights on it seemed to activate some sort of distress beacon," Jelly reported. "I switched it off, but could change that if you wished, sir."

"No, you did right, Tel'," Harris confirmed.

"The other switches work lamps outside," he added. "While

this one looks to be some form of siren; it's marked in red."

"Then we'll leave that alone for now as well," Harris grunted.

With warmth coming from a small alcohol stove and a store of provisions that ranged from biscuits and chocolate to tinned meat, several gallons of fresh water and even a small bottle of cognac, they were certainly well provided for. But before anyone relaxed, Harris knew he must consider their next move.

"As far as I'm aware, these things are mainly positioned close to the French coast," he told Anderson. "If we can get a message to Dover Command, they'll send a launch to collect us, but first we must give a location."

"And it's possible even switching the radio on will alert the Germans," Anderson pondered. "They'll be able to reach us long before our chaps."

There was little privacy aboard a high-speed launch and, when the most junior rating was rarely more than a light wooden bulkhead away, the officers were used to sharing their thoughts and plans quite freely. But now both spoke guardedly; their next decision could mean the difference between being rescued by their own men or spending the rest of the war in a prison camp.

"What do you make of the set, Jelly?" Harris asked more loudly. The telegraphist looked up.

"It seems pretty conventional, sir," he said. "I can take it to pieces but there is no sign of any automatic beacon. And I seem to have found our location," the young man added pointing to a paper pinned to the wall.

Anderson moved across to look.

"This places us off *Cap Gris Nez*; that's further to the east than I would have thought and quite a way north."

"How far from the English coast?" Harris asked.

"I'd say a little less than twenty nautical miles – from Dover that is."

"A decent boat could do that in well under an hour."

"Yes, sir," Anderson agreed. "But then it's less than half that to Boulogne."

There was a pause while Harris considered this. All were quiet; even Ward, asleep on one of the bunks, had ceased to snore.

"We do it," he said at last. "There's no telling how often Jerry checks on these buoys; they could come knocking at any time. And no point in waiting for the weather to clear; with an exact position, we should be found, even in this damned fog." He turned to Jelly. "Go ahead, Tel'. See if you can contact Dover."

Two hours later the mist remained as thick as ever and there was no sign of visitors from either side. Jelly had made contact with Dover Command and boats were on their way; twice the sound of high-speed petrol engines had been heard but not close enough to make a flare worthwhile in the dreadful conditions.

"I suppose we might try the klaxon," Anderson pondered as he and Harris stood together on the small outer gallery.

"Be some point if we could see the buggers," Harris snorted. "As it is, you know how sound reflects in the fog and with engines in the high twenty hundreds it's hard enough to hear yourself think."

"And they might not even be looking for us," Anderson agreed.

"I bet whoever is will be cursing." Harris gave a wry smile. "Just what you need after a night out, or with one to look forward to – stooging about in the fog off an enemy coast."

"There's another," Anderson said suddenly, and both men fell silent.

"That's never petrol," Harris almost whispered.

"And not travelling fast – probably a harbour launch or some form of patrol vessel."

"Maybe coming to check on their rescue buoy..."

Again they fell silent. The sound was firm and growing; whatever it was might indeed be passing by on a totally different mission, or it could be heading directly for them.

"If it is Jerry there's no point in fighting it out," Anderson said. "Not with three Service revolvers and a handful of knives."

"No indeed," Harris agreed, although his mind was not on the conversation. Was it his imagination, or had there been a slight change in the engine note? And the sound was definitely getting closer; at any moment he expected to see a dull shape looming out of the cloud. Within minutes – seconds – they could be taken prisoner and the next time they slept would be on enemy soil.

He supposed it would hardly be a disaster; goodness knew, there were few enough on land to miss him. His parents might make great play about their son being a captured hero, though he doubted they would really feel any loss. But Harris did not want to be a prisoner. He wanted to get home, back to the base. Maybe to commission a new boat and return to the job that, he suddenly realised, had become terribly important to him.

The sound grew louder and changed pitch yet again – the

mystery vessel was definitely slowing. Then the cloud parted, and something the shape of a small trawler was revealed.

"A VP!" Anderson gasped as both men ducked down. As soon as it appeared, the vision vanished, but it had probably been less than fifty yards away.

"Might have been a VP," Harris agreed. "But then it might also have been a normal fishing trawler," he added rising slightly. "That's how most of them start out, after all. It's only when they add eighty-eight-millimetre cannon and several tons of concrete they become a nuisance."

"Well whatever it is, they must have seen the buoy," Anderson remarked.

"And if it's a VP, we can expect them to come closer for an inspection."

"And if a trawler, they'll probably keep well away."

Again they waited, each secretly expecting the engine pitch to change yet again. Then it finally rose, the vessel increased speed, and gradually the sound dwindled as it was entirely swallowed up in the mist.

* * *

By noon, Daly and Jelly had changed places with their officers on the buoy's outer gallery. Although the motion was less than on the Carley float, neither had been able to fully conquer their seasickness and preferred the crisp air outside, even if they lacked a comforting horizon to stare at. Besides, Price had appointed himself cook and was currently making some form of stew in the poorly ventilated cabin below and, though both had empty bellies and were starting to come to terms with their condition, the idea of lukewarm tinned meat did not appeal.

"So the way I sees it, it's even money," Daly remarked as he leant against the rails. "Both sides will be looking for us, it's just a question of who gets here first."

"It's nice to be wanted," Jelly supposed.

"Well, there's no sign of the weather clearing, and not a breath of wind. As long we're in the fog, I reckon we'll stay hidden."

Jelly nodded wisely; there could be no doubting the Irishman's logic. "But then some boats have radar," he suggested as the thought occurred. "They might send one of them."

"Precious few in Coastal Forces."

"No, but destroyers have it, and a few corvettes."

Daly chuckled. "You won't find them sending a destroyer

this close to the enemy shore, not just to pick up a bunch of hostiles, and one of them a Paddy."

"I didn't tell them we had a Mick with us."

The Irishman acknowledged this with a good-natured nod. "That's probably as well though, if they knew, they might think to bring a few potatoes with them."

"I could murder a baked spud right now," Jelly declared.

"Aye, piping hot with lard and pepper," Daly agreed, warming to the subject. "Maybe we're getting better? Though I'll have to go a pace further afore facing one of Pricy's stews."

"What's that?" Jelly exclaimed suddenly, touching the Irishman's shoulder.

"Can't say I hear anything meself."

"No, listen..."

They did and gradually the intense roar of high-speed engines became louder.

"They're petrol, or I'm a Dutchman," Jelly hissed.

"Aye, but coming at full speed; hardly likely in this fog."

"Unless they have radar," Jelly grinned. "Paddy me old mate, I think we've been found!"

* * *

"It was really a question of speed over accuracy," Lieutenant Commander Conway told Harris and Anderson in the comfort of his wardroom. "My boat's got eyes but little actual grunt; best we can make is twenty-five knots, and that's downhill. But we've been testing one of the new radar sets for the last three weeks. It's pretty basic, only works dead ahead so you have to constantly alter course for a full sweep but effective enough. Found your lot anyway."

"And we're most grateful," Anderson assured him as he sipped his drink, a mixture of kye and sherry which the lieutenant commander was particularly proud of.

"Should be, the Germans check those raft affairs pretty regular; I'd say that fog was your saviour."

"So you're based at Dover?" Harris asked.

"Only transferred a few days ago; this is still experimental stuff, not for official issue, though I doubt it will be long."

"Do you have any news of our flotilla?"

"Well strangely, yes," Conway beamed. "I was at school with your old SO, Pete Collins – we trained together. He's going to be missed."

"Missed?" Harris felt his spirits drop as his hunch was confirmed.

"Yes, heading north or so it seems," Conway sighed. "Best place for him and all that. I only hope they appreciate his talents."

"North?"

"Fort William, I understand he's being sent to *St Christopher*'s to teach the new blokes how not to make the same gaffs we did. Due to go off tonight, as far as I know. Couldn't be better for him, what with another child on the way; I hear Miriam's moving up as well. Capital thing for them all, goodness knows the old blighter's done enough of the shot and shell stuff."

"Yes," Harris agreed as he considered. "I suppose he has."

"But yours wasn't the only boat lost last night," Conway continued. "Another went down, though, on the plus side, two merchants were badly damaged. Jerry had to tow them to harbour. And we're pretty sure an E-boat was messed about a bit as well."

"Who else?" Harris asked. So convinced was he that Collins' boat had exploded, his thoughts had not travelled further.

"Don't know the number, I'm afraid. Fellow by the name of Chapman, Dave Chapman. Straight striper and been at *Wasp* a good while I understand. Boat blew up with all hands, terrible it must have been. Did you know him?" Conway asked.

"A fellow CO – how could I not?" Harris grunted. "I seem to remember him making a fuss at yesterday's briefing."

"As well he might," Conway sighed. "Whole operation was a cock-up; Met. boys got the weather wrong and our boats simply aren't up to an all-out assault. It's given Operations something to think about and the DNC; I dare say we might get something a bit more suitable before long. But that won't help the chap you lost, nor Dave Chapman and his lot."

"What's the matter, Number One?" Harris asked abruptly as he noticed a change in Anderson's expression.

"Nothing, sir," he replied. "I was just thinking how futile it all seems. Caswell gone, Scott gone, and I doubt Ward will be back for a while. And now Dave Chapman and another entire gunboat's crew, just to get those in authority to believe what we've been telling them for ages."

"Can't argue with that," Harris grunted. "I had no idea you knew Chapman."

"Not as well as you, perhaps," Anderson assured him. "But still it seems a waste."

Chapter Ten

"You're getting a new boat," Brooks told Harris almost as soon as he sat down. "And this one will be a bit different."

"Indeed, sir, in what way?"

"Larger, greater power and better armed, though the main difference is possibly more subtle; she's a Yank job," the base captain told him. "Made in Connecticut, I understand. Though a Scott-Paine project, and he was instrumental in her design. That's the British Powerboat chappie responsible for your last. The engineer's one of us as well."

"I'd heard Scott-Paine had gone to the States," Harris confirmed settling back in his chair. It was devilishly cold outside and the base captain's office was heated by a two-bar electric fire that would probably be permanently glowing now for the next six months.

"Can't blame the fellow for hightailing it off," the commander agreed. "Admiralty appears partial to the Vospers, and the two companies were deadly rivals. Besides, if Lend Lease continues it can only be for the good."

"Of course." Harris was pleased to hear Brooks' news, especially as his next command sounded reasonably up to date, although memories of their last escapade were still strong.

For losing men was a relatively new experience. Of course, there had been Simpson and he still felt a slight chill when thinking of the young man and how he came to die. But that being so, Harris had naïvely considered himself immune to further pain. Such hopes had been revealed as wishful thinking and, despite his recent survivors' leave, that terrible image of Scott in his wrecked turret remained with him.

"Anyway, we can talk more about the boat later," the base captain continued. "You're getting the last of twelve; the rest went to flotillas at Lowestoft, but we pleaded poverty and the Admiralty took pity. Currently she's being fitted out to RN standards at Hythe – I expect they'll be putting the helm on the correct side, that sort of thing." Brooks smiled to show he had cracked a joke and Harris dutifully reciprocated. "But I have more to tell you and may as well let it out all at once. You're getting an extra half stripe into the bargain."

That was indeed news, and probably more important than any fresh boat for the latter had never been in doubt; no seasoned officer would be left without a vessel for very long but his elevation to lieutenant commander had come very much out of the blue.

"Obviously it is deserved, otherwise I wouldn't have recommended you, but I'm pleased for another reason." Brooks' expression now became more reflective. "The powers that be are waking their ideas up, certainly as far as the RNVR is concerned. Between you and me, the wavy chaps haven't turned out as badly as we feared. But now they've found their feet it's good to see the old guard are not being ignored. None of us knows how long this war will last but, when it's finally done, you'll still be part of the Royal Navy. Therefore, your rank will be retained, even when the Sunday sailors have gone back to playing golf and swanning about the City; I hope you appreciate that."

"I do indeed, sir."

"And having you as a two-and-a-half striper is convenient in another way; officially we're still awaiting a permanent flotilla senior officer. I'm not saying the post is definitely yours but you can have it for now at least and, providing you put on a good enough show, it could be permanent."

Revelation upon revelation; that was not just an advance in rank but also responsibility. Harris supposed he should have expected the move when Brooks announced his promotion and could hardly blame the chap for being careful.

"Collins is gone and already making waves up at Fort William, or so I hear. You can start when you like and go out with any of the other boats before yours is ready. But that will be up to you, as will a lot from now on." He sat back and paused for a moment. "I have to be honest with you, Bob, if Dave Chapman hadn't bought it, I may well be talking to him right now. You are a fine commander with a good track record both in action and for keeping your crew safe – it was just the one fatality before, as I recall?"

"Just the one," Harris agreed as the unwelcome spectre of Simpson briefly joined that of Scott.

"On the other hand, I think it fair to say relations between you and your men have not always been ideal – until lately, that is."

Both points were undoubtedly true and Harris knew where the credit lay.

"But things have improved, and I have to say your last command was gaining an enviable reputation."

"Thank you, sir."

"I don't need thanks; I think we both know the change was not entirely down to yourself." Brooks smiled and for a moment a glimpse of the young officer from the last war was revealed. "Command is a difficult thing, Bob, and almost always a combination of personalities. I don't think any of the great leaders in the past could have done much without reliable support, and we're certainly no different. Anderson did well in his last posting, indeed if he'd remained where he was the fellow would probably have two stripes and his own command by now. So we're giving him the promotion at least; he has all the experience expected of an RNVR lieutenant and will rise to it I'm sure."

Anderson a full lieutenant; Harris felt genuinely pleased and the emotion surprised him as much as anything else the base captain had told him that morning. But Brooks had more to say.

"Frankly, the pair of you have all the makings of a winning team, and all I want is for that to continue."

Harris smiled. "That's all I want as well, sir."

* * *

Daly came away from the anonymous house in Pencester Gardens with mixed feelings. It was the last day of his two-week survivors' leave and much of the time had been spent travelling to and from what to outward appearances was a respectable home. But the net curtains concealed far more than was usual; the place was yet another unofficial betting shop and run by a weedy individual by the name of Remer. It was a slick organisation and mainly manned by several younger, and fitter, assistants, including his son, the lad who had originally introduced him. As far as holidays were concerned, Daly supposed it had not been everyone's choice but, despite still living in the barrack room at *Wasp* and taking his meals in the NAAFI, the Irishman had been able to sink into a completely different world. And, in general, it was a better one; far away from enemy craft, passing shells or the sight of strong men with set expressions removing what was left of his opposite number from the port turret. Instead, he had been able to immerse himself in what he knew as 'The Racing'; reading papers, analysing results, studying form followed by that all-important trip to Pencester Gardens to place his bets.

It was a trip that was truly unnecessary; Remer's boy would

have met him outside the base and taken his money just as easily. But somehow Daly felt the journey to be part of the process and, in making it, he was doing the job properly.

The end results did not always confirm this, however; apart from one memorable afternoon early in the leave when three successive wins had brought his losses back to something close to manageable, his liabilities had grown steadily and, after the previous day's disastrous turnout, he was now deeply in debt.

But that morning old man Remer had been as unconcerned and positive as ever. As far as he was concerned, Daly was in employment; it might not be the most stable of jobs but, providing he stayed alive, they could both be certain of treasury money every two weeks. Consequently, he was happy for their arrangement to continue a while longer – Remer even gave the impression some sort of civic duty was being performed and another three pounds' credit had been allowed for future stakes.

Daly had thought nothing about spending it all there and then and, though he had chosen quickly, it was the result of a lifetime's experience – a passion almost. He could be reasonably sure at least one of the three horses selected would bring home the bacon and cover the others if they lost. But if two of them won he would be in the money and all three coming in must make some impression on his previous losses. So really all he had to do was continue, and his obligations would be settled. Realising this, Daly began to cheer up and, as he walked down the narrow, paved street, there was really quite a spring in his step.

* * *

"So you're dead set against coming back?" Dowling asked. "When your leg's better, I mean."

"Dead set," Sharkey confirmed as he heaved himself up in the bed. "They reckons it'll be a month or more before I'm walking properly, and even then I might not be as solid. So it's an easy life for me – shore-based, probably in some home gaff with a host of commissioned lovelies wandering around making sure I get all I wants."

"Or they could ship you out somewhere," Dowling mused as he glanced around the room. It was a rum old hospital; more like a massive house really. Pleasant enough, though, and not far from Dover with loads of grounds for anyone who wanted a bit of fresh air. But somehow it didn't feel right; the nurses in their long skirts and starched aprons seemed out of place, while all the patients – grown men in identical pyjamas and bright blue dressing gowns – looked like children sent to bed early. Even the ward was oddly posh, with carved oak panelling and a massive chandelier. "I hear there's lots going on in Malta and liable to get a sight worse," he added. "Plenty of work for a gunner there."

"Yeah, well we'll see about that," Sharkey grunted. "You set up with a new boat yet?"

"Comin' at the end of the week; Skipper and Jimmy are going down to take a look but the word is it's all tickety-boo. And Scotty's replacement arrived yesterday."

"You'll need a replacement for me an' all," Sharkey reminded him. "If you can finds one."

"Already sorted," Dowling confirmed with a grin. "I went out on Calder's boat last week. It were a practice run and I was officially on leave but we shot up a few seagulls and the gunnery lieutenant from *Wasp* says I got the eye. All my papers from training are in order, so I'll be in charge of the new piece; we're just waiting for my loading number to arrive."

"So you're replacing me at Betty?" Sharkey questioned, settling himself lower in the sheets.

"Only I might not call the next one Betty," Dowling pondered. "Word is they're fitting a double, and Betty sounds a bit lame for that much punch."

"Double Oerlik'." Sharkey whistled. "Can the boat take the weight? Can you, come to that?"

"It'll be a powered mount," Dowling announced with pride. "And the boat's one of them new Yank jobs. Triple Packards and a darn sight more stable than we was used to."

"Double Oerlik'," Sharkey repeated to himself. "And a boat made in America – I suppose we've just got to hope they put the wheel on the right side..."

"Yeah, there's been a few who've said that," Dowling sighed. "We was down *The Red Lion* last night to see Scotty's replacement in. Straight bloke, name of Bishop, though there's nothing holy 'bout him. We had a rare old time, this has been the best leave ever, Shark, you'd have loved it."

"Yeah, can't beat *The Red Lion* – Old Alf still as miserable, is he?"

"Alf's all right," Dowling confirmed as one who knows. "You just got to know how to treat him. Never said a word when we had a crack at your record."

"My record?" Sharkey asked. "Anyone get close?"

"Most were rubbish," Dowling sighed.

"Always were," the gunner agreed.

"Then I beat it by two seconds."

"Two seconds?" Sharkey repeated, half to himself. It was impossible; barely a couple of months ago the confident seaman beside him had been a mere boy who wouldn't have said boo to a goose. Now he planned to take over his gun, his position, and already had his record.

"But I mustn't keep you," Dowling added as he began to wriggle in his seat. "I have to get back to base. No idea when my new man's due but I'd like to be around to check the kid out."

"Kid..." Sharkey whispered.

"Anything else I can do for you?" Dowling added, standing.

"No, I got all I wants here," Sharkey assured him.

"I heard the grub's all right." The young man's eyes travelled across to one of the nurses. "An' you can't grumble at the company."

"Company's fine," Sharkey agreed as inspiration struck. "Nothing to match it at *Wasp*. You see that dark-haired bint over there?"

Dowling's glance travelled to a nurse at the end of the room and he nodded with appreciation.

"Well they're worried about bedsores, see? So every so often she, or one of her pretty little friends, comes along and gives me a good sound rub on the bum." He grinned slyly. "Know what, Mikey? I reckons I got it made!"

* * *

"Well, I'd say you'd got it made!" Peale exclaimed with delight. "Promotion, bigger boat – American built, by the way – and the sweetest Wren in Dover on your arm. I tell you, bud, it doesn't get much better."

Anderson nodded and took another sip of his Martini. "But she's not the only Wren in Dover," he pointed out.

"You mean Sandy?" Peale laughed. "Sure, I was forgetting."

It was early evening and the bar in the Grand Hotel was quiet. The two men sat at a table with their drinks but both were keeping watch on the door where their respective partners were due to enter at any moment.

"So, are the pair of you serious?" Anderson asked.

"I'd say so," Peale agreed, replacing his glass. "At least as serious as it is possible to be in a place like Dover. One thing's for sure, she knows how to show a guy a good time."

Anderson cocked his head slightly and the American elaborated.

"You'll have to excuse me if I'm direct at times – it's being in a foreign country and the middle of a war, I guess. I know you boys think you see all the action, but that isn't altogether true." He paused. "Only the other day I was in the town when they were bringing bodies out of a wrecked building. And they weren't soldiers or airmen, but a young girl and her baby. I tell you, bud, it brought me up short. There's no way you can plan for the future with such things going on; you just have to grab every slice of happiness that comes your way."

"I suppose so," Anderson allowed. "But then you don't have to be here."

"Oh, but I do," Peale corrected. "This is the most important job I've ever done, and probably ever will. Ignoring my commitment to the paper, I could no more walk away from this than cut off my right arm. I knew the US played a part in the European war before I came, but never realised quite how vital it was, nor how much you boys are relying on us. It's fortunate *The Gazette* is anti-isolationist, otherwise I would have had to change papers fast. But as it is, we're doing a lot to sway public opinion."

"Which is?"

Peale shrugged. "Still divided I guess, at the present anyway. A lot of folk are on the British side but quite a few of those can't see you surviving much longer. And why should you when so many countries have already fallen under Adolf's jackboot?"

"And they might be right," Anderson added gloomily.

"Well that isn't the angle I'll be portraying," Peale declared. "But in some ways what places like London and Dover are going through is exactly what they should be hearing about."

"That we're undergoing constant air raids and regular long-range shelling?"

"No, that you're surviving it. You Brits aren't the only ones who love an underdog; if I can show you're not beaten and, with a little encouragement, are ready to bite back, it might make a difference."

"I see what you mean," Anderson mused. "Lend Lease has been a Godsend."

"It's a miracle the act was even passed. There may be support in the States but some are against as well; they would be happy enough with Germany controlling Europe. And others simply want a peaceful life and don't give a damn for what happens several thousand miles away. Granting Lend Lease was a major breakthrough, however careful they may be to keep to the letter of the law, sending you guys boats, planes and materials has threatened both our neutrality and the political stability of the government; the next step, coming across and physically joining in, can't be that far away."

"Well, you'll be welcome to join in whenever you feel like it."

"Good to hear. So how's about I start right away?"

Anderson looked his confusion.

"Come on, we've discussed this in the past. Let me aboard your gunboat; take me into action so I can tell the folks back home where their hard-earned bucks are being spent. And there's more reason than ever now; you guys are getting one of our boats!"

"I've no objection, but you will have to go through the proper channels."

"The okay from you is the first hurdle; I'll use that when I talk to your top brass. Expect to hear more, and soon."

Anderson raised his eyebrows and sipped the Martini. Peale had the air of someone who got what he wanted – probably an essential attitude in a job like his. The door opened and two Wrens entered. He smiled at Eve who returned his look pleasantly enough, but there was something far more earnest and pleading in Sandra's face.

"Dale, I've missed you so much," she announced, breaking away from her friend to embrace the man.

"Me too, kid," Peale assured her briskly. "Think about you all the time. Now what are you ladies having to drink?"

* * *

"We've removed the Dewandre turrets and replaced them with Mark Vs," the armourer told them. "A pair of Vickers' point fives either side should give you a bit of clout and your boys will appreciate those power mounts. They're designed and built by a sports car manufacturer," he added slightly wistfully. "Amazing what changes a war can bring."

"We only had single Vickers before," Anderson volunteered.

"Then you'll notice the difference," the lieutenant assured them. "Sadly we couldn't do as much aft; it would have been nice to double up on the Oerlikon. It's something we've been testing for a while but they're not for general issue yet. She seems a tough old bird though and I'm sure will take the weight so we could talk about it in the future."

Harris pulled at his chin; it was a shame, but then they had managed well enough with the single gun in the old boat. Besides, adding a twin twenty-millimetre cannon would have been something else to get used to when Dowling had only just stepped up as their gunlayer and the new loader was a totally unknown quantity.

"No chance of something larger forward-facing I suppose?" Harris chanced and the young man smiled.

"The idea has been mooted," he admitted, "and there are short boat hulls in development that would definitely handle the strain. I cannot say more, though suspect you might be pleasantly surprised before long."

That was encouraging at least. "But only two depth charges," Anderson remarked.

"That is so," the officer confirmed. The young officer was attentive, polite and clearly knew his stuff, though both sensed there were more important matters that needed his attention.

"Very well, you won't mind if we jump aboard and take a look round?" Anderson asked.

"Help yourselves," the armourer replied, already turning to go. "They're moving her off the slip this afternoon and I'm pretty sure the yardmaster will be ready to sign her over shortly afterwards. She'll be yours then and hopefully for a long time to come so you'd better get used to her."

"What do you think, Number One?" Harris asked once they were alone.

Anderson regarded the chocked-up craft before them. "I think she looks fine," he said. The boat was barely seven feet longer than 95 yet looked far larger and, with a fresh coat of paint and so much new equipment, very much smarter. But under the protection of the yard's camouflaged shelter, she also seemed too vulnerable for the chops of the Channel, let alone any of the ferocious close action they could expect to meet there. "Had a bit of damage in the past," he added, looking pointedly at an obvious tingle on her starboard side that had been solidly, but not invisibly, fixed to her hull.

"I noticed that on my first inspection," Harris agreed. "Seems this is an experimental hull and there was a good deal of testing in the States before they sent it over. Yard's done a good job though, and I must say I never liked those Dewandre turrets. They coop up their gunner like something out of a bomber and can't be as efficient."

146

Anderson said nothing; Harris may well be right but at least an element of protection was offered. The new turrets, being mounted further forward and to either side of the bridge, would have a greater angle of fire, however, and be better able to concentrate on an enemy directly ahead.

"So come on, then," Harris suggested, "let's take a proper look."

* * *

Once they had both heaved themselves up the ladder, the boat was even more impressive. Much of the superstructure was obviously new as were the fittings. They had two Kent clear-view screens as well as what appeared to be a fixed tannoy, which would be far more convenient than any portable megaphone.

"They would keep referring to this as the pilot house," Harris complained as he opened the door to the wheelhouse and stepped inside. "And the bridge as the cockpit, but I think we'll stick to the British way."

"Absolutely," Anderson agreed following. Many of his RNVR contemporaries referred to a gunboat's bridge as 'the dustbin' but he would never expect a straight striper like Harris to lower himself so.

The wheelhouse was plain and functional with all that was necessary, and nothing missed out. Most of the engine gauges were larger than he was used to, but that might be an illusion, although the heavily chromed throttle quadrant was undoubtedly weighty and would have looked equally at home aboard a far bigger vessel. That or a Cadillac.

"Good to see it actually has a wheel down here," Harris remarked, fingering the chrome-plated rim. "They're missing them out below in a lot of the new Vospers as most prefer helming from the bridge, but somehow a wheelhouse isn't a wheelhouse without one."

"I suppose there is an axillary steering position aft?" Anderson added.

"Bound to be," Harris agreed as he continued to look around. "There's more storage space and the W/T office's a mite bigger," he added, opening a small door and peering inside. "And you seem to have a larger chart table; other than that, I suppose it's very much what we're used to."

Anderson could only agree, except the general standard of finish was also markedly better than that of their last boat. And he had heard good things about Elco boats' performance, although that would only be confirmed when they got her on the water.

"Bridge is up here," Harris announced pointing to the narrowest of passageways, and when Anderson had followed him up, the differences were even greater.

For it was a real bridge; not as large as that of a destroyer for sure, but definitely an improvement on the twin cupolas they had been confined to in the past. Harris was beaming at him from the port side.

"This is so much better," he announced, now gently rocking the second wheel.

"But no instruments, apart from the compass," Anderson noted.

"No, but there's a window down to the wheelhouse." Harris tapped at a pane of Perspex just forward of the wheel. "Anyone at the helm can see to those below."

Which would explain the larger instruments, Anderson supposed, privately pleased with himself. Apart from the wheel there were three throttles that this time had been finished in a matt black lacquer, what looked like a proper two-way R/T repeater with a handset, a telegraph and a tannoy mike while the two chrome-plated loudspeakers that sat to either side looked powerful enough to address other boats. And there would be none of the scrambling about they were used to; they had space, the chance to move: it was a distinct improvement.

"I checked out the engines the day before yesterday," Harris informed him. "They look fine, less than seventy hours each."

The recommended service life of a fast motor launch engine was five hundred hours; many might exceed this and a good few be replaced before, but there still should be no need for extensive repairs for some time.

"I expect Carter and Newman will want to look them over," Anderson remarked.

"I expect they will, and doubtless a Packard won't have the kudos of a Rolls, but they're supposed to be first rate mills and we have three of them."

"Fast as well."

"They reckon up to forty-five knots in the right conditions," Harris agreed. "Quick enough to catch an E anyway."

"I wonder if we will," Anderson mused. "I mean, another."

"Not impossible," Harris was now looking around the grounded craft with something approaching proprietorship. "In fact, with a boat like this, I'd say it was quite likely."

* * *

"Well the place is a sight larger, but then it needs to be," Carter exclaimed on descending into his new home and regarding the three gleaming V12 engines. They were set in a triangle with the centre unit at the apex and, though it must be possible to reach all the important areas, some would doubtless prove a challenge.

It was the following day and he and Newman had spent the past seven hours travelling by train to Southampton, a journey that proved more difficult than anyone had expected. And now they were there the captain, who had driven down by car with Price, Jelly and the first lieutenant, was keen to be off. But Carter was not one to be rushed, especially where machinery was involved, and had decided to have a good look at his new charges before getting underway. Besides, they were still waiting for the additional stoker.

An extra man would certainly be needed if they were to attend to three engines and, again, Carter would have preferred some time to get acquainted with the fellow. But despite the late hour, Ordinary Stoker Pickering had yet to show his face and neither Carter nor Newman relished the prospect of managing three unfamiliar engines on their own.

"Well, there are a lot of similarities to the old Merlins," Newman muttered as he examined the nearest unit.

"Same designer was involved," Carter told him. "And they have the same superchargers and magneto ignition."

"Water jackets look similar as well," Newman confirmed.

"Aye, stainless steel and no gaskets between cylinders and valve housings."

"Cooling?" the stoker asked.

"Closed-circuit," Carter replied. "There are thermostats, saltwater scoops and heat exchangers to play with – and a dry sump, of course," he added.

"What will they do?"

"Twelve hundred horsepower at twenty-four hundred revs, thirteen-fifty at twenty-five."

"Impressive," Newman nodded.

"Direct connected reverse gear, double cone type clutch and positive forward drive," the petty officer concluded. "I'd say we had our work cut out."

"Well the new bloke was due at twelve," Newman remarked following his superior's train of thought. "But if he had the same problems we did, it might be midnight before he shows up."

149

"Skipper won't want to wait that long. We're travelling back effectively unarmed as it is."

"Maybe he'll be happy on two engines?"

Carter shrugged. "Can't see it myself, but what say we start up the vents?" So saying he flicked a series of switches and a low humming began to emanate throughout the engine room. "Boat was fuelled yesterday, but I haven't had the chance to check every union."

"How long's the warm up?" Newman asked.

"There isn't one as such," Carter replied. "Manual says it's the fastest way to oil up the plugs. Soon as we get the green light we go. Skipper's supposed to keep the revs down until we give the all-clear, but I can't see that neither."

The sound of a commotion outside filtered down and both men looked to the forward door, so it was a double surprise when a figure in white overalls descended through the aft hatch, appearing, as if by magic, between the two wing engines.

"Well you took your time," Carter told him in a tone unusually harsh to hide his astonishment.

Pickering excused himself with an apology and a winning smile. "I've been travelling all day and half the night," he explained in a light north country accent.

"Never mind, you're here now and only just ahead of us," Carter told him. "We're waiting for the off; soon as it comes we'll all be learning together."

"Skipper will give us a moment to get acquainted though, surely?" Newman questioned.

"Don't you believe it," Carter snorted. "He'll have seen Pickering here step aboard and know we've got a full team; penny to a pound we'll get the off in the next five minutes."

As he spoke there came a whistle from the voice pipe and the motor mechanic raised his eyes before removing the stopper.

"Right, you heard," he said a few seconds later. "I'll take the centre, you two grab a wing each. Now, ignition off and two revolutions from everyone."

The lights dimmed slightly as each of the massive engines were turned over, then Carter spoke again.

"Cocks and plugs to go, manifold covers and air cleaners off, seawater pumps on and scoops opened."

All three worked in concert as if they had been practising for an age but, so intent was he on the job in hand, Carter hardly noticed.

"Gear in neutral, throttle check and fuel values open.

Wobble pump pressure?"

After a series of checks from his stokers and a private nod to himself, Carter continued. "Primer pump – just a couple of squeezes, and open throttles."

This was the time he dreaded the most. Until that point it was doubtful if any on the bridge guessed things were happening below but, as soon as the starters rumbled, they would be expecting miracles.

"Okay, magnetos to full retard, starter line switches closed and bring your booster coils into operation. Then let's see what we get..."

There was a dull rumble from each engine, Carter's own fired first, followed closely by Newman's with Pickering's not far behind. For a moment they luxuriated in the growl of machinery running in perfect order, a sound every bit as fundamental to them as a steady wind to seafarers from an earlier age, then Carter's voice cut through the roar.

"Check pressures!"

Again his two stokers replied in confirmation and Carter consulted his own engine's oil gauge which showed positive well within the ten second period required. He glanced down at the 'water out' temperature as it climbed rapidly towards 110 degrees with 'oil in' almost keeping pace and then stepped back and treated his men to a grim smile.

"Once all temperatures are right, I'd say we was ready," he announced.

* * *

"Do you know of a man named Peale?" Harris demanded by way of a greeting when Anderson came aboard the following morning. It hadn't been the best of journeys back; the boat performed well enough but there was only the gentlest of breezes and the rolling mist had been a nightmare. Rain set in when they were off Brighton and continued for the rest of the trip. Then, to cap it all, they were forced to wait outside the harbour for nearly an hour until all evening patrols had left. And when they did finally secure *MGB 194* to her mooring, a dozen interested faces showed up to inspect the new acquisition and, as these were exclusively of senior rank, it would have been churlish not to broach their meagre wardroom bar and toast the new ship.

But now, with a dozen and one things to do that could not be put off, and the prospect of a week of intensive working up that would stretch boat and crew to the limit, Harris was bothering him with a foolish question. And worse, it involved Dale Peale.

"I know him," Anderson admitted. "Yank reporter, is he being a nuisance?"

"I'd say," Harris confirmed as he held up a piece of buff paper. "Just had this from Dover Command. We are to take War Correspondent Dale Peale on board and demonstrate the workings of an MGB together with its place in the flotilla."

Anderson shook his head. "We've enough to do with sea trials for the boat and group exercising," he groaned.

"This isn't for working up," Harris snorted. "They want him to go out on a job."

"Active service?" It seemed incredible.

"Your friend is to accompany us on our next official patrol, and we are to give every assistance to enable him to accurately report the work of light Coastal Forces."

"This is nothing to do with me, sir," Anderson declared. "I know the fellow for sure, but the last thing I want is someone poking around the boat on our first trip out."

"You and me both," Harris agreed, throwing the paper down. "I don't like reporters and foreign ones most of all – they learn our secrets then publish them to the enemy."

"I get the impression Mr Peale is pro-British," Anderson remarked more gently. "And right now any friends we have are worth cultivating."

"Maybe so," Harris grunted. "But we've fresh hands to settle in and a new boat to get used to, yet the first time we test them for real there'll be some hack writing everything down and flashing a bloody camera."

"We can't allow a camera," Anderson assured him. "Not even Dover Command would countenance that."

"Why not? After all, this is an American boat," Harris reminded him. "If there are secrets to reveal they probably put them there in the first place!"

"I suppose you can see the point." The younger man scratched at his head as his mind ran on. "Lend Lease has made a world of difference – without it, we wouldn't have a boat at all, nor engines and spares for the others. And a good report from Peale might ease the wheels in Washington. His work is syndicated across the States, or so I understand."

Harris puffed. "Well you'll just have to look after him, Number One," he said. "I'm not going to let that delay our working up. Has the new gunner arrived?"

"At *Wasp* now," Anderson confirmed. He really should

have grown accustomed to his captain's rapid changes of subject, but they still caught him out on occasion. "I was arranging his accommodation. Cockney lad, seems the right sort; Jelly and Daly are bringing him down."

"Fine, well let's hope he settles in. And what about the stores?"

"Ammunition due this morning, then Ordnance are coming to regulate the Oerlik' and Vickers tomorrow afternoon; we can have a run out for a test fire then but there's nothing to stop us trying some heavy weather work today, the wind's picking up a bit."

"Then it's a shame we can't take your American out for a taster," Harris mused, and Anderson noticed a sly look appear on his captain's face.

"Today?" he asked innocently.

"Yes, give him a feel for what's to come," Harris added more cheerfully. "With a bit of luck we'll find a bit of chop and he'll spend so long chucking up it'll put him off making an appearance for the real shout."

Chapter Eleven

The Met. report for the night of *MGB 194*'s first patrol actually spoke of low cloud and intermittent showers but, by the time Harris was preparing to lead his flotilla out into the Strait, rain was falling like stair rods. Their sea trials had gone reasonably well with the new men settling in better than anyone could have expected. Besides Pickering in the engine room, a Londoner named Cook was now Dowling's loader. He looked every bit as young as his senior, but the pair handled their Oerlikon as if they had been born to it and were clearly melding as a team. Then Bishop, a hefty, yet quietly spoken, Black Country man had replaced Scott as their port gunner and was also acclimatising well. In truth, the gunnery practice had probably been the most successful of all exercises. Dowling and Cook worked together seamlessly throughout and though Bishop might have been initially reticent in speech he was positively eloquent with a twin point-five Vickers. He manhandled the thing as if it were part of him; Harris had rarely seen such good shooting. The more powerful weapon had obviously disconcerted Daly at the outset but soon he was also hitting his targets regularly and the Irishman seemed totally in charge by the end of working up.

And there was no doubting their new boat's capabilities; in addition to the surge of raw power that could lift them onto the plane almost instantly, she also turned smoothly and could engage reverse in less than half the time of their previous vessel. Having a slightly longer hull also gave more stability and brought Harris' thoughts back to his conversation with the armourer. Foredeck mounted cannon must soon be sanctioned, and the time could not come quickly enough for him. Now he had a craft that could comfortably match an E-boat for speed he wanted to at least equal them in firepower.

There would always be one significant disadvantage, of course; however close they came to beating German boats in other areas, the British still relied on petrol engines. The power-to-pound ratio may favour them in this, but any advantage was quickly wiped out by their fuel's vulnerability. High octane petrol was simply too volatile for fragile craft and, when carried in the quantities needed to satisfy three thirsty engines, turned them into potential death traps.

But Harris was not thinking of his vessel's shortcomings, and neither did he worry about the rain; there was more than enough to concern him that night without looking for further problems. And then he saw yet one more heading for them along the sodden jetty.

He was in company with a rating who looked anything but cheerful and both were half running through the deluge. But the seaman, clad in serviceable oilskins and seaboots, was purposeful and determined whereas the man, kicking up the tails of his fashionable raincoat as he went, merely looked ridiculous. One hand was holding down a Stetson hat, while the other clutched an umbrella close to his chest and, of all things, a gas mask bounced merrily from his shoulder.

"Looks like your friend, Number One," the captain grunted as he and Anderson watched from the bridge. Harris had already met the American on two occasions, both of them brief and it was fair to say neither had been particularly impressed by the other.

"I'd better go and meet him," Anderson suggested.

"Do that," Harris agreed. "And while you're about it, find him a tin hat and some more suitable clothing. We wouldn't want one of our colonial cousins catching a cold."

* * *

It was dark by the time they left harbour and the rain had clearly set in yet, despite this, the gunboat's crew were closed up at their posts and would remain so until they returned. For any stationed below this was no hardship and even those in turrets or on the bridge had a modicum of protection but for the two lads at the Oerlikon it was a definite nuisance. Their only shield from the rain above and a fast-moving sea beneath were the few low-set strips of canvas and a square or two of crash matting. There was regular debate over whether the latter would absorb light calibre machine gun fire or not, but it was plainly useless against any form of water and barely minutes after leaving the Ferry Dock, both rating's outer clothing was comprehensively soaked. They had only recently met but already a strong rapport had developed and was strengthening further from their shared discomfort.

"Word is we're due a load of underwear from the WI," Cook, the newcomer, announced. "Knitted woollen stuff, all warm

155

and lov-er-ly."

"I heard the same," Dowling agreed. "Supposed to be the best but there ain't never been none in Comforts, and I've bin here months. When I were a loader my gunner used to swear by a pair of women's stockings under his goon suit," the lad continued with the air of one who knows. "Said they kept him warm and dry whatever the weather."

"That's not why he wore 'em," Cook insisted with equal authority.

"Maybe not," Dowling accepted after a pause. "But I could do with a few extra layers right now."

"It ain't the cold so much, it's the wet," Cook agreed. "Be different if we had a heater or something."

"A heater?" Dowling seemed strangely appalled by the concept.

"They're fitting them on some cruisers," Cook maintained.

"Go on, someone's been winding you up," Dowling scoffed.

"Straight up," the loader vowed. "Outside gunnery positions is getting heaters – in bigger ships anyway."

"Well, we ain't got 'em on Coastal Forces nor never likely to have. I never heard of such bilge."

"Not as daft as wearing women's underwear," Cook added mildly.

* * *

"So what's the plan for tonight, Captain?" Peale asked. He was on the bridge and a strange one-piece suit had been found for him as well as sea boots and a steel helmet which he felt slightly embarrassed about wearing. The captain still sported a black officers' cap and had given his headwear a sneering look. But Anderson wore one and Peale decided he would as well, if only to keep his head dry.

"No plan as such," Harris replied guardedly. "We're patrolling an area of the Strait."

"And is a British convoy expected?" the American persisted. On top of the suit, which zipped up at the front like something you might wrap a baby in, he was also wearing a heavy pullover and a reefer jacket, yet still the cold seemed to be eating into his bones.

"Nothing is scheduled," Harris admitted. "But that doesn't mean the enemy won't turn up."

"And what about German convoys? Will you go looking for

them?"

"We will if Dover Command advises us of one."

Peale nodded and for a moment forgot the cold. "That's interesting, Captain, so I guess the English know more about shipping movements in the Channel than the Germans?"

Price, at the helm, cleared his throat and Harris eyed the American cautiously. "What do you mean?"

"Well you said yourself, the enemy may still come, so are clearly unaware if your side are sending a convoy or not, whereas you seem to know for sure when and where the Germans are active."

"Look, I think we should see anything you decide to write," Harris stated firmly.

"Oh, you shall, at least your Admiralty shall," Peale confirmed. "Every story has to be stamped and cleared before I can file it."

"That's probably just as well, though I'd prefer it if you avoided asking direct questions; you're here to observe, just stick to that will you?"

"Certainly, Captain."

"And I notice you're not taking any notes," Harris continued.

"I rarely do," the American agreed. "Notes slow me down; I'd rather keep my eyes open and remember the important stuff."

"And what if there isn't any important stuff?"

"That's when I have to use my imagination," Peale admitted with a grin.

"You mean you make things up?"

"Not as such." Now it was Peale's turn to speak carefully. "But every story is researched thoroughly beforehand. I've already learned a good deal about what you guys have gotten up to in the past; it doesn't take much to include a couple of those incidents, then maybe use a little creativity to pad the whole thing out."

"That's what I meant by making things up," Harris told him, and for a moment there was no sound other than an occasional sniff from Price and the rumble of their engines.

"Well, I fear you might have to use that imagination tonight," Harris finally continued in a tone void of sympathy. "I get the feeling Jerry will be staying at home."

"You mean it's too rough?"

"No, not too rough; this is hardly a chop. It's more intuition than anything, although the enemy's small craft usually stay put in bad weather, unless there is a very good reason to be out that is."

157

"So you think this particular patrol might be a waste of time?"

"Now there you go again, Mr Peale," Harris told him crossly. "I did ask you to avoid direct questions and definitely won't have words put into my mouth."

At that moment there was a sound from below and Anderson thrust his way up onto the bridge.

"We should stay on this course for another hour, then turn red oh-seven-five degrees for a further forty minutes," he announced.

"Excellent, Number One," Harris told him although it was hard to tell what had pleased him the most: Anderson's information or simply his appearance.

"Now hold on there, did he just tell you where to go?" Peale interrupted.

"Lieutenant Anderson is the ship's navigating officer," Harris snapped. "He is responsible for our position as well as that of the flotilla in general. And yes, I listen to him when it comes to position and direction; that's part of his job."

"Sounds like an important one," Peale replied with an ironic nod towards his friend.

"And one he performs extremely well," Harris agreed sharply. "Although perhaps not perfectly as I understand he sometimes needs to make the occasional note."

"I'm sorry, have I missed something?" Anderson asked innocently.

"No, you have missed nothing, Number One, you rarely do," Harris grunted. "But I think we are proving a disappointment to Mr Peale."

"No disappointment, Captain," Peale assured him. "I guess I was just trying to find out a bit more about what you do."

"Well, as you can see, we do very little, other than stumble about on dark wet nights looking for an enemy that isn't there."

"Look, why don't I show Mr Peale about the boat?" Anderson suggested.

"Yes, why don't you?" Harris agreed quickly. "I'm sure there'll be something that will amuse him. And, if not, perhaps you might make something up?"

* * *

From his position in the port turret, Bishop had been aware of some disquiet on the bridge. Not that there had been any raised voices – in his experience, the better officers only shouted to make themselves heard and rarely for emphasis or in anger. But an atmosphere had descended as soon as the American came on board and, surprisingly, Bishop had picked up on it.

For usually he lacked even the smallest degree of empathy, and neither was he in any way superstitious. If his betters and their foreign friends wanted to argue the toss amongst themselves it was no concern of his and, though some might hold that civilian passengers aboard warships brought bad luck, he had little time for such nonsense. Bishop had a physique that could have graced anything from a steelworker to an all-in wrestler and would be the last to admit to any form of sensitivity. That said, there was one area where he had a particular understanding; his previous posting had been as the loading number on a Rolls two-pounder and, though his duties rarely let him fire the thing, that did little to lessen the satisfaction he felt when handling it or any form of weapon.

And it had been a lifelong affair; his first love was an airgun, a break-barrel BSA given to him at the age of ten and even less accurate than the catapult which preceded it. But no one could deny the weapon's power, which could easily send a lead pellet through a tin can if the range was right. The gun had led to a succession of rifles that ended with the superb German hunting piece he still used to bag rabbits on his trips home. And it wasn't just firing the things that gave him a thrill; their very shape filled him with awe and amazement while no music, sport, drink or woman could provide the sheer joy of a target dissolving – or an animal falling – from the steady pressure of his finger on a trigger.

Something of his passion had been recognised soon after call-up and, on completing his twelve-week seamanship course, Bishop exchanged the lightweight toys he had been used to for far more manly affairs with gunnery training at HMS *Excellent*. To his mind, naval weapons were not only the best but usually the biggest, although strangely it wasn't the massive fourteen-inchers that caught his attention. They had their place, of course, and the prospect of throwing a colossal shell the best part of twenty miles with accuracy that verged on the supernatural moved him greatly. But any weapon that took a team to aim, load and fire lacked both simplicity and the personal touch Bishop craved. The lighter pieces seemed to provide this and he had been reasonably happy as a loader, though still yearned for full autonomy. It was something he had achieved by applying to Coastal Forces; now he had charge of the matched pair of half-inch machine guns before him and, though smaller and with a shorter range than anything he had been allowed to that point, Bishop could not have been happier.

For they were truly a work of art; though designed only slightly after the end of the last war, the Mark III Vickers was all he could wish for in sophistication. Each of the twin barrels sent out seven hundred rounds a minute while the powered mount meant his open turret could transverse a full one-eighty degrees in less than three seconds simply by moving a finger. And he had no need of a loader; this was truly a personal affair with absolute control over the weapon and whatever mischief it might create.

Not that he wanted to kill exactly; Bishop had few emotions in that direction. But his passion for weapons in general was now fully energised and if any who currently threatened his country were to fall from his actions, it would hardly trouble him greatly.

* * *

"I don't know what I said to upset the old boy," Peale told Anderson in the relative privacy of the wheelhouse.

"Neither do I," Anderson admitted, "although it usually doesn't take much."

"But you seem to get on will him."

"I do now, but it wasn't always the case. It would seem you have to win Lieutenant Commander Harris' trust."

"You mean he doesn't suffer fools – is that the right expression?" Peale asked.

"I guess you've got it in one," Anderson agreed.

"So this is the wheelhouse," Peale said, looking around, adding, "and, if I'm not mistaken, that must be the wheel."

Both men considered the large chromed object as it moved, apparently of its own accord.

"Yes, Petty Officer Price is our coxswain and currently at the helm."

"Fellow might want to put on a bit of weight," Peale suggested.

"He's steering from the bridge," Anderson explained. "There's a much better view."

"So, when given the choice, he would rather be out in the rain with your captain, than down here in a nice, bright, cosy little room by himself?"

"It may be dryer, but if the coxswain was helming from here, it wouldn't be so light," Anderson pointed to the windows that were heavily shuttered.

"I take your point," Peale allowed. "Though still think I'd prefer to be away from your boss."

"And through here is the W/T office," Anderson announced quickly as he moved across the wheelhouse and opened a small door. Inside, Jelly was obviously listening intently through headphones and jumped slightly at the sudden interruption. At the sight of a stranger he swiftly closed the black book that lay open on his desk.

"This is Dale Peale, Jelly," Anderson explained as the rating slipped the code book into a draw and rose slightly. "He's from America, so make sure you speak nice and slowly."

"Pleased to meet you, Mr Jelly," Peale said as they shook hands. "Hey, that's one hell of a surname you've got there!"

"It's Scandinavian, sir," Jelly explained shyly.

"Is that so?" Peale replied. "Well, I must say you don't look it."

Jelly's jaw dropped momentarily, and he was about to respond when a high-pitched sound from the headphones called him back to his set. Snatching a pencil, he began to scribble across a sheet of brown paper, all thoughts of his visitors forgotten.

"Don't quote me on this," Anderson muttered softly. "But I think we might just have found ourselves some excitement."

* * *

The three gunboats were travelling at an astonishing speed. Even standing still on the bridge was an exercise that caused Peale to grip the side rail until his knuckles felt they would shortly snap. And every breath seemed to be coming in snatches, with each needing to be grabbed from the stream of pebble-dashed air that blasted past him. Looking back, he could make out the two boats following steadily on either quarter despite the rain that continued to fall in a solid torrent. Each produced a bow wave that began a third of the way down their planing hulls. The great cascades of water seemed to hold iridescent energy of their own which was repeated in the tremendous plume of wash being thrown behind as they thundered through the dismal night.

"We should be in position in eighteen minutes," Anderson

had to shout above the roar of their engines and was addressing Harris as well as the man at the helm. Sensing action, Peale had come up from the wheelhouse but, due to the captain's presence, quickly relegated himself to the far side of the bridge. Indeed, so cramped were they in the tiny space, the American was considering retreating below just to get out of everyone's way. Then his friend turned back, caught his eye, and drew closer.

"The group we're looking for are just off Calais," he bellowed, and Peale nodded to show he understood, although that was perhaps a slight exaggeration. He had quickly picked up on the fact that the gunboats were being sent to rescue a couple of fast minelayers; vessels which had been taking advantage of the filthy weather to sow their deadly seeds. They were under attack and it seemed one of their escorts had already been hit, which was the reason for reinforcements being called for.

That was all fine and dandy but, fast though they might be, the craft in Harris' flotilla were surely much too frail to deal with such a situation. Sending such tiny boats to stand up to an enemy of any size, especially one bound to be anticipating their arrival, seemed foolish in the extreme. Peale had been in sticky situations in the past and there were more than a few times when he had known his life to be at risk. But never before had he charged towards danger at such speed, or in a vessel so blatantly unsuitable for the purpose. Anderson had more to say, though, and he bent forward to listen.

"Are you happy to stay up top?"

Peale blinked at the question; happy was not the word he would have used. Nowhere could be safe aboard the frail craft; few compartments he had visited so far appeared to be built with more solidity than a well-made garden shed and hardly any could be impervious to the lightest shell an enemy might fire at them.

And soon they would be in action, he had expected that – almost hoped for it in fact when considering the possibility on land. Even when cruising at regulation speed he had felt no more than a mild adrenaline rush; something that was stimulating but not actually dangerous. It was only after the engines were fully released that his doubts began to multiply.

But now he could fully appreciate the gunboat's amazing power, he could equally appreciate its vulnerability. There was absolutely no solidity and if the boat felt delicate when travelling at such outlandish speed, how could it possibly survive the rigours of combat?

"I'll stay," he said at last, knowing there was very little

choice and Anderson gave him that buddy look men exchange when about to share in some particularly hairbrained scheme. But Peale did not feel brave, or reckless or even that much of a friend; instead, and for the first time in his life, he was undeniably afraid.

* * *

On the opposite side of the bridge Harris was far more content. Despite a few misgivings and the unseemly haste in which *MGB 194* had been put into service, he was very happy with the boat. She had performed well on her working up exercises having more speed and weight than his previous command; the only area in which she was at all lacking was firepower. But even that was an improvement and almost made up for by what appeared to be a crack team of gunners. And the rest of the men had taken to her well; the new hands were still an unknown quantity of course, but those he had served with for some time had simply picked up the traces and carried on. In the past, there could never have been such a smooth transition and he freely acknowledged Anderson was partly responsible for the improvement. But then he hoped he had made a few changes himself, and definitely felt better about his manner of command. Indeed, such was the improvement in morale, it might even exceed the physical advantages of the new vessel. And it struck him then that no ship could ever be more than the sum of her parts; what made it effective – what truly made it live – were the men who sailed her.

Some evidence of the minelayers should be noticeable before long; they were being escorted by MGBs from his station but obviously the entire mission had been kept under wraps, presumably in the interests of security. Harris readily accepted the exclusion although it was slightly galling to have been kept in the dark until his assistance was needed. But now they were being called upon, he was eager to join the fray. *MGB 194* had already proved her worth; he was sure she wouldn't let him down, and he felt exactly the same about the crew, which probably meant a whole lot more.

"Your friend doesn't look too comfortable." Their heads were almost touching but still he had to shout at Anderson.

The younger man glanced quickly at Peale, currently staring over their starboard bow, and flashed a smile in return.

"First action," he said by way of explanation.

That was true, Harris allowed; most of those aboard the gunboat had been blooded some while back, only young Cook, at the Oerlikon, was a true newbie. But even he had a job to do and would be fully employed shortly whereas the American had only come along for the ride. And what a ride this was turning out to be; it looked as if he was about to be provided with more than enough to fill his story. This was definitely turning into one trip when an imagination would not be required.

* * *

In reality, Cook had very few qualms about going into action. With the inherent confidence of youth, and in the company of a lad almost his own age who seemed pathologically phlegmatic, he was actually enjoying himself. To one who rarely travelled in motor vehicles and whose main sensation of speed had been three trips by train and the odd fairground ride, this was exhilaration indeed. Being positioned as they were, above and only slightly aft of three massive engines – engines that powered them through the water at such a speed – was breathtaking indeed while the thrill was only heightened by two equally powerful craft following on either quarter. And there was more; his training had been fast but thorough so he now knew more about the Oerlikon twenty-millimetre cannon than probably any other subject and appreciated in detail the damage it could do. As a result, his sole wish was to inflict the same on an unseen enemy; something he knew he could do well as a dozen instructors had convinced him of the fact. So it was probably an advantage that he understood little, if anything, about the enemy's weapons, and what they might do to him in return.

"Can you see anything yet?" Dowling asked.

"Not yet," Cook shouted back. By hanging off the gun's surround he could peer past the forward superstructure and get some view of the sea ahead. The rain was easing slightly and there was no mist, so the black mass of French coastline was almost clear.

Dowling shrugged. "Ought to be something in sight shortly," he announced with the wisdom of several months' experience.

"What's that?" Cook shouted, pointing off their starboard beam where the dark night was suddenly lit by a dozen strands of green, red and white.

"That's tracer," Dowling told him. "Better hold on, we'll be turning."

So vivid were the colours that they reflected against the sky, creating a heavenly aura over the evil that was undoubtedly taking place below.

"Yes, that'll be for us!" Dowling declared with elaborate unconcern as the boat tipped violently into the turn.

This was better than any fairground ride and, as he gripped on to the bandstand stanchion, Cook shared his friend's thoughts totally and could not help but grin.

* * *

At the helm, Price had noticed the tracer as quickly as Daly, who announced it from the starboard turret, and had been preparing for the turn long before the captain ordered it. Being on the bridge was so much better than stuck below when all he could see to either side was through the smallest of casements. Now there was a proper view and he could accurately control the craft; from now on a depth charge attack was going to be a pushover. Okay, it might rain a bit and doubtless get a lot colder when winter hit but a coxswain's job was to man the helm, and that was his priority.

"Drop down to half speed," the skipper ordered, and Price eased the throttles back. There were no voice pipes to worry about either, he could both see and hear his captain and had direct control over three massive engines which was also to the good.

The boat settled slightly as the engines ceased to roar and all around seemed to breathe a shared sigh.

"How far off would you say, Number One?" the skipper asked as they all stared out at the dim cluster of shapes. Judging distances at sea in the dark was the hardest job in the world, although Price had already made up his mind.

"I'd say about a mile and a half," the lieutenant replied, and the coxswain gave a subtle nod of approval.

"Very well, make to the others to follow me in – line ahead."

Anderson collected the Aldis lamp and, with a few quick flutters of the shutter, the message was conveyed to the trailing boats. They continued at a bare twenty knots which felt like a walking pace after their recent sprint. The gunboats behind quickly took up station and soon Price felt that he was not only helming a boat but an entire flotilla. Then, as the lines of tracer drew closer still and the black shapes became actual vessels, the captain spoke again.

"Bring her up, 'Swain, but gently."

Price muttered a response as his gloved hand brought the three levers gently forward. Gradually the boat began to rise further as she gathered power and more detail became apparent. Off the port bow was what must be one of the British minelayers, Price decided; probably converted from a trawler. Just beyond it was a gunboat and both were exchanging fire with several less definable shapes to starboard.

"We'll start a slow turn and catch them on their tails; carry on bringing the speed up," the captain instructed, and Price duly brought the helm to starboard slightly as the revolutions continued to increase. Then, just as they were back to full throttle and the mystery images were resolving into a column of three E-boats, the skipper pressed the action gongs and the entire boat came to life.

* * *

In the port gun turret, Bishop heard the bells and fingered his joystick with breathless expectation. His gun's powered mount conveyed the most subtle of movements perfectly using very little effort on his part. With no loader to complicate matters and fifty seconds of ammunition in each magazine, he would shortly become a one-man fighting machine, which was totally in line with his temperament. He licked his lips and peered out into the cold, wet night, one hand hovering over the trigger. The enemy was out of range at present but as soon as one came within reach he would be ready for it.

* * *

Peale was now too fascinated to be frightened. The moments spent approaching the action had knocked away much of his apprehension. Barely minutes before, he had worried about being in the thick of things aboard a boat barely strong enough for ocean travel yet, as they drew closer and at a steadily increasing rate, his mind was slowly dismissing their own vulnerability and focussing instead on the enemy before them.

The Germans were also moving but only to keep up with the plodding minelayer and nowhere near as fast as he was in this splendid machine. The distance between the first of the enemy craft was visibly diminishing until it could only be seconds before they were upon them. Harris was clearly aiming to catch them and pass close, very close. A dozen tiny bells were ringing throughout the boat; Peale held his breath, waiting for the first shots and felt strangely disappointed when both turret gunners remained silent.

Then, as if to a silent signal, they opened up together and the rattle of machine gun fire joined the din of racing engines.

In all the jobs he had covered, never had the American known such a cacophony. The nearest E-boat must have been taken by surprise as they continued to concentrate their fire on the minelayer, and all the time *MGB 194* was growing nearer whilst sending bright red bolts of light digging deep into the enemy's hull. It could not last forever, before long the German must react to the new threat, although now bullets from the gunboat were playing about the back of the E-boat's bridge and must surely be causing significant damage. Then, before he was fully aware of what had happened, the German appeared to shy away. She must have either throttled back or lost power, and both *194*'s forward gunners abandoned her to the less than tender mercies of their own rear cannon as well as the two gunboats following close behind. But the next target was already in range, with another just ahead, and these would be far harder nuts to crack. They must have seen their comrade fall and will have recognised the threat, so both were bound to be ready for them as they approached.

Peale heard the captain issue a command and suddenly the boat was turning again. Desperately he gripped the rail as the entire vessel tipped so violently he knew it must surely capsize. But almost as soon as they reached that point, the list corrected and then he was hanging on for fear of sliding down the bridge grating towards the others; that or being thrown out altogether. The boat righted, then throttled back and Peale gathered himself to look out once more.

He felt like a child deceived by a cheap trick but, impossible though it might seem, they were now cutting between the next two enemy craft while their guns played merry hell with both E-boats' hulls. The Germans were not quite so naïve as him, however. As the gunboat passed the bows of one and the stern of another, dazzling green and white lines began to fly towards them. Peale sensed the damage rather than seeing it. Shells were striking low at their hull yet strangely he did not feel in danger; it was simply something else to note, like the fact that the rain had stopped, or the nearby minelayer appeared to be on fire. He glanced across to where Anderson and the captain stood next to the man at the helm and reassured himself that each seemed equally unconcerned.

Then, suddenly, they were free of the crossfire, their own weapons had ceased to speak and the boat itself was heading to pass behind the stricken minelayer. He glanced back; one of their two shadowing gunboats followed while the third appeared to have broken away and must be engaging the second E-boat on her right side. The engine pitch dropped and *194* began to wallow slightly as power died away. Peale caught Anderson's eye and the Brit took pity on him.

"We arrived after Jerry made their attack," he explained. It was quieter now, but still the man shouted and Peale was not sorry. His brain felt numb from what had just taken place while the ringing in his ears was so loud he wondered if he would ever hear normally again. "Now we've turned up they'll head for home."

"Aren't you going to chase them?" Peale demanded, and his friend gave a grin.

"No, a surprise attack is one thing, we'd rather not fight a pitched battle and neither would the Germans."

"What about the one you hit?"

"We'll be going back to look at him in a moment, but first we have to check round – there were supposed to have been two minelayers – we can only see one and there may be survivors from the first gunboat reported lost."

At that moment a bell rang, and the captain picked up what appeared to be a telephone and began speaking – it was a remarkably domestic act in the circumstances.

"Sounds as if our Tel' has made contact with the minelayer, that or the gunboats' senior officer," Anderson explained, and Peale could tell his friend was straining to be off.

"You'd better go and see what's about, I guess there'll be plenty to do," Peale told him.

"I need to check the boat," Anderson agreed. "You're all right?"

"I'm fine, and have seen heaps," the American assured him.

"Glad to hear it," Anderson returned the grin. "We wouldn't want you to be bored."

Chapter Twelve

"Well, all I can say is, my preconceptions were shattered," Peale confessed when he had finished relating their story.

"But what happened to the Germans?" Sandra demanded. It was late and, apart from the four at their table, the dining room at the Grand was empty. It was a situation probably caused by that day's set meal; the Woolton Pie had been dry, tasteless and universally abandoned.

"Mike Barton got in a few potshots at one," Anderson replied, "but took a good deal more in return and we had to tow him in. Most of the others escaped, though they'd done considerable damage before we turned up."

"But the one you hit?" Sandra insisted.

"Ah yes..." Anderson paused. "The two behind us carried on where we left off and I'm afraid she sank."

"Afraid? But they were Germans!" She stretched the out last word until it sounded somehow dirty.

"German or English, it's never good to see a vessel go down," Anderson told her quietly. "Phil Shaw pulled seven from the water but there should have been more."

Sandra was clearly dissatisfied and pulled a face to demonstrate the fact. Then Eve, who had been quiet throughout the account, finally spoke up.

"What damage did the E-boats do?" she asked, and Anderson squirmed slightly.

"They sank a minelayer," he conceded softly. "As well as another gunboat – both happened before we arrived."

"Put like that I guess it wasn't such a victory," Peale conceded.

"We rescued a few from the minelayer," Anderson continued, "but again not enough."

"And the British gunboat, the one that was hit before you turned up?" Eve asked coldly.

"I'm afraid she exploded," Anderson admitted.

"I guess that's the nature of the beast." Peale sat back in his chair seemingly unaware the atmosphere at their table had suddenly grown cold. "American made or not, your boats are so full of gas it's not a question of if they'll blow, but when."

Eve swallowed and considered the remains of her meal and Anderson cleared his throat.

"Though it has sure given me an insight into what you boys get up to," Peale continued. "There was no mention of any of this on the BBC."

"There may not be," Anderson replied. "For a start, it wasn't exactly a significant action and we didn't get off particularly well. Besides, it's questionable if the minelayers should even have been there in the first place."

"How do you mean?" Peale asked, suddenly alert.

"This is strictly off the record," Anderson said pointedly.

"It can be," Peale agreed and for a second the two men held the other's glance.

"That location is outside the British declared mined area," he admitted at last.

"Never knew there was such a thing," Peale shrugged.

"Hague Convention," Anderson continued. "The use of mines has to be declared and approximate locations given; our nearest pitch is supposed to be off Harwich."

"And where's the closest German?" Peale asked.

"Even further away, by the coast of Holland."

"Yet I've heard of German mines being used in the Strait," the American pondered. "Hell, the entrance to Dover Harbour's been targeted several times while I've been here!"

"Oh yes, they spread their eggs pretty liberally; drop them from planes, E-boats can carry a few and R-boats are made for the task. Sometimes you can't move for the darn things – literally. And those new 'influence' types are the very devil."

"So where's the problem?"

"I suppose minelaying is the sort of thing the enemy does, but not your own side; the general public dislikes their use every bit as much as naval men; a bit like they used to view submarines."

"You mean 'simply not British'?" Peale asked with a snort.

"Something like that," Anderson agreed. "I'd chance whoever arranged that lay did so off their own bat and without official sanction. Somewhere there'll be at least one red-faced officer without a job."

"So what's going to happen to your story, Dale?" Eve asked quietly. "Assuming, of course, you've written one."

"Oh, it's written; written and ready to be filed," Peale assured them. "Though I can always rework and leave out any mention of minelayers."

"That might be prudent," Anderson agreed.

"And how will it be received?" Eve again.

"Well, of that I can't be certain. You see, being a foreign correspondent has its drawbacks, you get to know a lot about what's happening elsewhere, but little of your own country."

"So you don't know the current mood in America?" Anderson asked.

"I know what I hear back from my editor," Peale temporised.

"Don't you have any family back home?" This time Sandra asked the question and seemed particularly interested in his answer.

"Both parents are dead," the American stated coldly. "Influenza – during the 'thirties. Brother's in the Army Air Corps but stationed well away in Hawaii; that's about it."

"And what about friends?" Sandra again and, again, clearly in earnest.

"Couple I knew at high school, but we've not much in common now," he shrugged. "That's another disadvantage of the job; they say there's no place like home and I guess in my case it's spot on. Best buddy is Ted Landers, my sub-editor. We've been together a while now and you learn a lot about a guy when he's checking your copy."

"Where were you before this?" Eve asked and the American grew more serious.

"In the last few years I've spent time in Spain, Germany and France, oh and a brief spell in Switzerland to have my tonsils removed."

"So, you have little idea of public opinion in America," Anderson clarified.

"Maybe not in detail, but from what I hear it seems to be heading your way," Peale replied. "Shouldn't be long before we're coming over here in force. Christmas is not far off, let our guys send a few photos of the starving British stomping through snow-covered bomb sites and you won't be able to move for Yanks."

"In uniform?" Anderson asked and now it was his turn to look interested.

"Sure, in uniform. You can say what you like about the US of A, but when we invest in a project, we go the whole way. There'll be tanks, aircraft, ships – as well as a bunch of guys ready to use them."

"That will definitely take the pressure from us," Anderson

conceded.

"It won't be a question of taking the pressure off, the only way to silence that Nazi clown is to take the battle to him, and that's what we'll do."

Anderson stirred the remains of his meal thoughtfully. Peale might have the right idea and he had to admit his respect for the man had grown after that last patrol. Yet still it seemed strange that a nation so far away should want to come to Britain's aid.

"Say, do you guys want to hang around for dessert?" Peale asked, "Or shall we call it a day?"

"It's supposed to be a suet pudding," Eve remarked. "Only I expect they'll be using grated potato for lard."

"Then count me out," Sandra told them.

"So why don't we go back to my room and listen to a few records?" Peale suggested.

Anderson was about to reply when he realised the offer was limited to one. Instead, he rose and caught Eve's eye. "Perhaps I could see you home?" he said.

* * *

Outside it was no longer raining but the streets were still wet and mildly slippery and the air chilly. "So, do you think they're serious?" he asked.

"Dale and Sandra?" Eve seemed surprised by the question. "Well, I think she is." They began to walk. "Maybe I didn't at first, but now – now definitely. And what about him?"

Anderson laughed. "Do we have to be experts on our own gender?" he asked but did consider for a while. There was no moon at that time and the blackout was holding well; nevertheless, enough stars shone through the light cloud to light their way. "On balance, probably yes, but there are still a few things I'd like to know about Mr Peale to be certain."

"I don't think he's like every American," she grinned.

"I don't think he could be. Though I've not met many."

"The only ones I've come across are film stars, and he's definitely not like one of them."

"Except Cagney, perhaps?" Anderson suggested, and they both laughed. A car drove slowly past, groping its way under shaded lights and then they were alone once more.

"What he was saying, about the patrol," she began again but more hesitantly, "was it true?"

"In the main," Anderson replied. "Though some of it was a

bit enhanced."

"And Billy was on board?"

"Your brother?" he answered blithely. "Yes, he was in the engine room throughout."

Now it was her time to be silent and Anderson got the impression she would remain so until he said something more. "Does that make a difference?"

"Not really, though I spoke to him earlier and he said things had been very quiet."

"I'm not surprised," Anderson told her. "Coastal Forces is a private world, you're either in on it, or you're not."

"But I'm a Wren!" she protested. "It's the same service!"

"Makes no difference, you're not a Wren in Coastal Forces. Your brother might try and explain but you wouldn't understand – how could you? Between ourselves, I think what Peale saw came as a shock, and he's a seasoned journalist."

"You have Wrens in Coastal Forces, would they understand?"

He considered this for a moment. "Probably a little more, though obviously they're not allowed out on the boats. But they do see some who make it back."

"The wounded you mean?"

"Yes, and not all injuries are physical," he added awkwardly.

"Some suffer emotionally then?"

Anderson shrugged; this was not the conversation he had been hoping for that evening. "Let's just say a few fall by the wayside."

"I see." She swallowed. "And is that common?"

"It's getting more so," he admitted. "Though I doubt Coastal Forces is unique in that aspect." They were drawing near to the spacious grounds of the old Dover College building that now housed HMS *Lynx* and he felt strangely eager for the evening not to end. He slowed his step and she followed until they were both standing quite still on the dark pavement.

"Ian, there's something I've been considering for a while, and tonight has made me decide to do it."

He waited.

"I'm applying for a transfer."

He made to protest but she stopped him.

"No, it isn't very far away, less than two miles as I understand. The Y Station at Abbot's Cliff House."

"Sound mirrors?" he asked, surprised.

"Hardly!" she laughed. "They haven't been used in years. No, but it's still a listening station where German radio messages are monitored. The Morse is mainly in code and sent up to Bletchley Park, the speech probably comes to you eventually as part of regular intel."

"You mean R/T transmissions?"

"Yes. I've made a few enquires and it seems E-boat crews spend a lot of time chatting."

He snorted. "We hardly use our sets; a well-placed Aldis lamp is far more private, and reliable."

"Well the Germans think differently, and we learn a lot from what they say."

"And you'd like to get involved?" he asked.

"It would be a little more constructive than caring for Service families," she replied. "Oh, I know such things are important, and I always said I wouldn't directly help the war effort. But, let's just say I've changed my mind."

"Because of Billy?"

"Billy, and you. In fact you most of all. To be honest, the two most important men in my life seem to be keeping secrets from me, and I don't want that to continue."

"Can you speak German?"

"I wouldn't be much use if I couldn't!"

He shrugged.

"My parents are Quakers," she continued. "They're firmly against the war and anything connected with it but, long before everything kicked off, they were involved in getting folk out of Germany."

"Really?" he was impressed.

"Oh, it wasn't on a large scale; just a succession of Jews who wanted to leave and father was able to use his contacts to bring them to England. They came across ostensibly as servants – cooks and the like – but usually knew next to nothing of their duties. My mother had been in domestic service before the first war and gave lessons in our house. When they knew enough, they'd move on, take up a job somewhere and another two or three would come in their place. I used to help as much as I could and got to know the language – I'm really quite good," she added with a grin.

"If you're serious, I'm sure such a talent would be welcomed, but it would hardly make you a part of Coastal Forces."

"Maybe not, but I'd feel a little closer." It was still quite dark but there seemed to be an inner light in her eyes. "And right now, Ian, that's what I want most of all."

* * *

MGB 194 had been holed several times but little significant damage was done and her repairs could be handled easily enough by Dover's Wellington Dock. She was expected to return to active service by the end of the week and Daly, for one, was glad of the break. He had no money and it was a situation unlikely to change for several months, but he had known worse times and at least his position in Coastal Forces meant he was being fed and watered. Besides, the time would soon pass and there was one thing in favour of his current line of work; he was rarely bored.

And he definitely had no need for excitement that afternoon; even the thought of a mild flutter – had such a thing been possible – left him cold. A gentle walk would do; maybe explore a bit of countryside beyond the town. Daly liked walking and it was also pleasant to be on his own. Not that he had anything against his mates, but any group that shared your life for each and every day grew tiresome after a while. He passed through the sentry point at *Wasp* and began to pace, his mind set on spending a good couple of hours stretching his legs. There should be countryside within easy reach, perhaps even horses and, as he walked, he began to long for the smell of grass and a chance to size up the local livestock.

But his plans were brought to a halt when a familiar face came into view. It was the Remer boy he had first met at the bookie's a while back. The youth was waiting for him at the end of the viaduct and had his usual expectant, slightly cocky, expression firmly in place.

"Not me, not today," Daly told him genially as he went to pass by.

"Don't say that, Irish," the boy exclaimed. "There's a bit of business we has to sort out."

"I told yer, I'm not in a bettin' mood," Daly replied more forcibly.

"Well maybe we ain't talking wagers," Remer suggested. "I said it were business, and that's what it is."

"And what kind of business would that be?" the Irishman asked as he slowed.

"There's a small matter of your tab, Irish, or had you forgotten?" Daly had noticed how the boy had become more familiar as his debt increased and now was on the verge of insolence.

"I haven't forgotten, and neither has your da', I'm

thinking," the seaman told him. Family concern or not – it did no harm to remind the child he was effectively an employee. Daly was coming to regret ever getting involved with him, or his enigmatic father; once this debt was settled he would take his custom elsewhere.

"Well my Pa wants to talk about that," Remer junior persisted. "He'd like to see you this afternoon and I'm to see you turns up."

"And what if I said no?" Daly asked. He was taller, older and several stone heavier than the boy.

"Then we'll find you later," Remer shrugged. "Me and some of the lads, only you won't know when or where and they sure ain't lads."

Daly paused and considered. Anyone who threatened a member of the armed forces was taking a risk; there were plenty who would support him in a fight, and he could probably get hold of small arms. The kid was right, though; he wouldn't know the time or place and Remer's family was smart enough to choose both carefully.

"Come on, Irish, don't mess me ab-art," the boy protested. "It'll only take a couple of minutes; you'll have the rest of the day to yourself. And I think Pa has something you'll find of interest."

"And what will that be then?" Daly asked suspiciously.

"Not for me to say, but it concerns your tab."

"I'm tellin' you, that will be paid."

"Oh, we don't doubt that," Remer assured him. "You're an honourable bloke and doing an honourable job; we trusts you. And it may be we could be of assistance," the lad continued. "Perhaps even ease things a little, you get my meaning?"

"What are you sayin'?"

"Not for me to say nothin'," Remer protested. "That's me dad's job; it's him you'll have to speak to."

Daly considered a while longer then sighed. "Come on then," he said.

* * *

"I won't be going far," Eve announced as she began to make her bed. "And it probably won't be for a while, you know how long these things take."

"They do when Wrens are involved," Sandra snorted. "Though I expect things'll be speeded up for one of their own. When did you apply?"

"I spoke to Madam Fish-face before breakfast."

"I bet she were delighted, losing one of her best girls."

"No, she was fine." Eve paused in the midst of straightening a sheet. "Actually she seemed very understanding; maybe we've misjudged the old bag?"

Sandra pulled a face and flopped back on her own bed, which was still unmade.

"Anyway, we can keep in touch," Eve continued. "New place is only a short bike ride away."

"I don't plan on riding no push bikes, thank you very much," Sandra replied primly. "'Sides, we'll probably be on different watches, so it won't be so easy."

"It might not be easy, but definitely possible," Eve assured her. "Most things are, if you put your mind to it."

Her friend sighed. "I wish I could think like that."

Eve paused and considered her. "Bit in the dumps, are we?"

"A bit," Sandra shrugged. "But then I'm probably moving on an' all."

"I see. Are you applying for a transfer, or getting out altogether?"

"Getting out," Sandra stated with an air of achievement. "Had enough of lisle stockings and pusser's knickers, I'm a woman and want to look like one. Be attractive, while I still can," her voice trailed off.

Eve shrugged. "You look like a woman to me, and Dale certainly thinks you're attractive."

"Ah, Dale," Sandra mused.

"Something the matter between you two?"

There was a pause, then Sandra came back to reality.

"Oh, it's nowt. Nowt at all. Couldn't be better really."

"Then what?" Eve had finished making her bed and sat down on the result.

"He's mentioned taking us back to America."

"Has he?" There was a note of caution in her voice that was not lost on Sandra.

"You mean you don't think he will?" she asked.

"Oh, he might have every intention," Eve told her thoughtfully. "Though when it comes to honouring his commitments, I'm not so sure."

"You mean he can't be trusted?" Her eyes were desperate.

"I mean he is a maverick," Eve corrected. "You heard what he said the other night, there's nothing for him in America, his life lies a long way away. In places like Dover, I suppose, and even then, only for a while."

"So you think he'll move on?" she asked quietly.

"I wouldn't like to say," Eve sighed. "Just don't pin all your hopes on him, that's all."

"But we're gerrin wed," Sandra protested just as softly.

"Married? Oh, Sandra, that's wonderful." She stood up quickly. "Look, don't listen to me, I don't know what I'm talking about and frankly my knowledge of human nature is pretty poor. Married? Well, of course, you'll have to leave the Wrens – I think it's pretty much compulsory. Have you set a date?"

"Not yet," Sandra replied flatly. "But I guess it will be soon."

"And where? In America, or over here? Have you told your folks yet? Why they haven't even met the fellow!"

"No idea where, and no idea when," Sandra snapped. "And as for Mam and Dad, they'll have to wait their turn; there's umpteen folk who don't know."

"Of course," Eve agreed, the doubts forming. "Who else have you got to tell?"

"Well, Dale for one."

"Okay, I see," Eve said slowly. "And you think he's going to marry you?"

Sandra looked up sharply. "He'd bloody better!"

* * *

With work being needed to the boat's hull, Newman had been effectively banned from the engine room and, for probably the first time since being posted to Dover and Coastal Forces, was at a loose end. It was a dull but dry day, and that about described his mood; the town had missed out on a raid the previous night and, as the German long-distance guns were also unusually quiet, everywhere had become a hive of activity. Teams of tough, determined men were shoring up those buildings that could be saved or adding the final death blows to the many that could not, while others rigged fresh powerlines and telephone cables and the WVS supported with mobile kitchens supplying tea, sandwiches and encouragement. Newman sauntered out through *Wasp*'s sentry post and made for the viaduct that would take him to the town proper. The duties of a stoker gave little chance for exercise and, in a similar way to Daly, it was his intention to spend as much time as he could simply walking. There were vague stories of the sights from Dover's cliffs and, though he truly had little use for fresh air or the countryside, a few hours spent in the open might be beneficial, even if it merely convinced him such things were overrated. But even as he strolled along, his mind still focused on the engine room of *MGB 194* and, more specifically, her starboard supercharger.

No matter how the thing was adjusted, it refused to cut in at the same time as the rest. The delay was hardly critical, probably less than a second, but such an abnormality upset Newman's ordered mind, especially when no cure was obvious. He was even at the point of suggesting delaying the other two units to create harmony although that, he fully acknowledged, might be considered defeat. But as he deliberately drew deep breaths while insisting to himself the change was beneficial, his unconscious mind was definitely elsewhere. So it was probably significant that the only distraction that could actually reach him turned out to be mechanical.

It was the sound of an engine approaching from behind. It had six cylinders, that much was obvious without looking and, equally clearly, petrol powered. It was also running irregularly – hardly out of time, as such, but as if under strain, although not overloaded. Then, as the sound drew closer still, the reason became obvious and, even before Newman had turned back to confirm, he knew the beast was overheating.

The car was an Armstrong Siddeley, he noted. And the 14/6 1938 model sedan – two very similar examples had made regular appearances at the garage he had been apprenticed to before the war. The engine would be a 1.7 in line and quite a useful lump as he recalled; free-revving and more than capable of forty-eight horsepower. That this one was overheating was confirmed by the cloud of steam issuing from either side of the bonnet and its identity as a Navy staff vehicle only registered after the more important information had been digested. Then, and only then, did he look towards the driver and recognise the ginger-haired Wren at the wheel.

She was one of several he had noticed in the NAAFI at *Wasp.* Wrens were spared the ordeal of dining with male ratings, yet the same faces were often seen going to or from the canteen, and the pretty ones became the target of unspoken admiration from many seamen. But there was little attractive in the woman now as she brought the car to a sudden halt just short of Newman and clambered out, slamming the door behind her.

"Overheated," Newman advised.

"I can see that!" she snapped, turning a chromed handle and lifting the nearside bonnet flap. The act released a cloud of dense, scalding steam that forced her to step back and onto Newman's steel-capped right boot. "Oh, get out of the way, will you?" she hissed.

Newman retreated a few paces but stayed close by, attracted as much by an engine defect as the appealing, yet hostile, woman.

"If you leave it, it will cool," he added.

"Well, I know that as well," she declared. "But there isn't time – I have to be back at *Wasp* by four." She paused and relaxed slightly. "Actually, I'm not supposed to be out at all, but that's another story."

"Okay, well let's make sure you're home in time," he suggested. She looked at him suspiciously as he continued. "First we have to identify the problem, then set about fixing it."

"It's not any of the hoses," she said, reluctantly standing back as Newman moved in to inspect.

"So I see, and the rad.'s fine, fan belt's intact, though I'm not so sure about the water pump."

"Oh brilliant," she sighed. "I could probably bodge anything else."

"A water pump can be bodged as well if you know what you're doing," he said without looking up.

"So, what are you, some sort of a mechanic?" she asked.

"Some sort," Newman agreed. "But I thought they trained you lot up?"

"Oh, I can change a spark plug and set up points and timing – even took a head off once during training, but that's about it."

He glanced back and gave a nod of approval; she seemed more relaxed now and close up her face, with its sharp and slightly pointed nose, was really incredibly attractive.

"Don't burn yourself," she warned as he began to delve deeper into the engine.

"Asbestos hands," he grinned while heaving against the pump. "They come as standard in my job."

"I've heard you can fix leaks with eggs," she suggested vaguely. "But that's stupid, where can you get eggs in a place like Dover?"

"Could try at the Naffi I suppose, but pepper's meant to be as good."

"Pepper? That's almost as rare as eggs!"

He straightened up. "Well it's the gasket that's gone; if you can get the stuff, a dash of pepper will probably seal it long enough to see you back to base. Mind, you'll have to give the whole thing a thorough flush out afterwards."

She pursed her lips in thought. "Okay, so where do we get pepper?"

"Grocers on Market Square; if they haven't any pepper, porridge oats will probably do as well, though I think they're on points."

"Porridge oats?" the Wren questioned while regarding him with amused confusion, although the effect was lost on Newman who had an engine to think about.

"That's right," he confirmed. "While you're doing that I'll knock on some doors and see if we can't borrow a couple of buckets of water. By the time we're both back the lump should have cooled and we can sort it out. That suit you?"

"That suits me fine," she said.

* * *

It was war, total bloody war, Peale realised as he held the wire in his hand. There had been some vague reports on the radio although the BBC were being cautious of course; it was customary for them to hold back on important news to give the morning papers a chance, but he had been expecting something for a while. And now this, a brief but succinct message from Ted in New York. And there was one advantage in having a sub-editor who could write; more had been said in those scant forty words than most could convey in a thousand.

He stumbled up the stairs still holding the piece of yellow paper. Inside, his room was still a mess; he'd slept in and the maid had yet to tidy up. The gramophone lay on the floor surrounded by records Sandy had been sorting through. Carefully treading past, he hurled himself backwards onto the bed and exhaled a deep sigh. Japan had attacked; a good chunk of the US Pacific Fleet was either sunk or out of action; over three hundred aircraft damaged or destroyed, and massive casualties... He swallowed remembering, not for the first time, that his brother Chuck might figure amongst those statistics and for a moment blind panic took over. He'd have to contact the American embassy – go to London if need be, find out exactly what was going on. Then he forced himself to relax. Ted was a good friend and had worked in the field himself; he knew all about Chuck and must be chasing things up in New York even now.

But the ramifications went far deeper than simply war with Japan and the prospect of losing the Pacific. The two nations had been wary of each other for many years and conflict of some sort was almost inevitable. There had already been one minor economic war that threatened to escalate – and would have done if Roosevelt had called a halt to oil exports earlier. In effect, Japan had been behaving a lot like the Germans, with the Dutch East Indies taking the place of Poland, although at least they had appeared slightly more amenable to negotiation. All thoughts of compromise must surely be forgotten now though; war had broken out and there would be little talking from either side for a while to come.

Of course, with so little information, he could only guess what would happen in Europe. With a powerful foe of their own to fight, this might spell the end of support for the British. Or it could be the beginning; the Japanese had attacked Hawaii, were they to turn on Britain as well or, more specifically, their holdings in Malaya, Singapore and Hong Kong, his original assessment might prove correct – truly total war.

He breathed out as the thoughts swirled about his head and, robbed of any real information, they naturally became personal. With America now actively fighting he might be recalled, sent to Hawaii or some Godforsaken place he'd yet to hear of. Or he might be retained here as part of what would become a far greater press presence. Chances were strong he'd wind up leading it, he had the experience after all. But that didn't sort out a far more intimate concern.

Sitting up slightly he surveyed the room, which was very much as Sandy had left it last night, or was it early that morning? The records were in piles; for some reason she delighted in categorising his music and had begun to organise him in other ways, commenting on such intimate things as his dress and hair oil. None of these did he particularly resent, but for someone who had lived alone and by his wits for so long, it took a while to acclimatise to another taking a hand in his affairs. Such a thing was probably inevitable, even to a loner like him and, if he was honest, even the thought of marriage was not totally abhorrent. But whether the hand he took in marriage would belong to Sandy was still very much in doubt.

* * *

The engine was still warm to the touch when Newman and the Wren met up again, but the pressure had dropped, and its radiator cap opened without drama.

"Never seen the chap before yet he said I could have as

much pepper as I wanted," she marvelled, handing the packet over. Newman took in her face once more and was hardly surprised.

"To be honest, I'm not sure how much to use," he confessed. "But if you promise to flush it out later…"

She nodded eagerly and Newman could not help but notice her ginger freckles.

The packet opened easily, and he tapped a fair amount into the radiator. "Now just a dash more water," he continued and they both watched as he carefully topped up the coolant from his bucket. "Right start her up."

The girl clambered back into the driver's seat and there was a deep rumble before the beast came to life. Newman bent forward, found the throttle linkage and revved the engine. For several seconds there was no result other than a cloud of smoke from the exhaust, then a small jet of steam spurted out from the water pump housing.

"No good," she said, disappointed.

"Give it time," Newman assured her. "The stuff has to get around the system."

They stood in silence while the steam continued to build, and Newman was starting to have doubts himself when it finally began to slow. She drew closer, almost touching him, and they both watched as the discharge gradually faded leaving the engine running as normal.

"Oh, that's fantastic," she said, smiling into his eyes. "I can't thank you enough – my guardian angel!"

"There's no need for that," he told her, blushing slightly. "But best if you head straight back. You'll make it easy enough and probably a few miles more, but see that block is well flushed out at the first opportunity. Oh, and mind you fit a new gasket!" he added.

"Can't I give you a lift?" she asked. "I've broken enough rules today, one more wouldn't make much difference."

"No, I'm off for a walk," he told her firmly.

"But your hands, they're filthy!" she protested.

"Nothing new there," he beamed.

"You're from *Wasp* aren't you?"

"That's right."

"I thought I'd noticed you around."

Newman nodded. "I've noticed you as well," he said.

Chapter Thirteen

The repairs were carried out, *MGB 194* returned to active service, and regular duties resumed with little outward evidence of how the crew had developed, although Harris knew for certain progress was being made. The men were working together as a team; more than that, they appeared to think as one while, for his part, responsibility had never rested so lightly upon his shoulders. And he was no longer just a gunboat captain but flotilla senior officer; the post had yet to be confirmed of course, but once more instinct told him it was his. Should he be proved correct it would be the end of individual command; at one time or another he would go out with every vessel under his charge and someone else would get the permanent captaincy of *194*. Consequently, he felt justified in using his newfound skills to meld the flotilla into a unit every bit as effective as his own craft.

Not all of his commanding officers were proving amenable, however. There had been several minor clashes during their regular exercises when he was forced to criticise or censure some, but he was starting to realise such action need not be taken from a great height; sometimes a gentle word was enough. Other lessons were not so easily learned, though; Harris still found it hard to adopt the relaxed yet efficient attitude most RNVR officers seemed born to and neither could he equal them in their innate camaraderie. But at least he no longer need worry about incompetence. It would never do to admit the fact openly, but he was privately certain every CO under him had as good an understanding of the job as himself.

There were still some areas in which they could not compete, of course. However bright and inspired they might be, none of the youngsters – he used the term loosely, some were less than three years his junior – had spent all their adult lives under naval discipline. That must make a difference, or so he stubbornly maintained, even if there were times when he privately questioned the value of such a distinction. But he seemed to have finally succeeded as a captain and had every reason to think he would do so as flotilla SO. Changes would have to be made of course, and he hoped he was becoming flexible enough to accept some must be in him. But with support from Anderson, the other commanders' cooperation and a little more effort from himself, Harris was confident they might all succeed.

And an ideal chance to prove this came shortly after they returned to the duty roster. Their first detail was a convoy duty; reinforcing the escorts through the most treacherous part of their journey up the Channel. Harris was in charge of four other gunboats in addition to *194*. After successfully meeting up at the agreed time they had kept two miles to seaward of the small collection of coasters and their permanent bodyguards as they plodded steadily through the dangerous waters of the Strait. The regular escorts consisted of three Fairmile Bs along with an armed trawler and the merchants they protected numbered four elderly three-island freighters.

And this time, Harris decided, his force would be staying with them; there would be no thundering off into the night in order to lie cut and wait for their charges to catch up. The tide was falling while the merchants were too heavy to risk negotiating their way inside the Goodwins so must take the deeper route. And they had received notice of what might be E-boats slightly to the north; Dover radar picked them up and had been tracking for some while before all trace mysteriously faded. The Germans might have slunk away to their own or another base and present no further risk, though could just as easily be waiting in the lee of a dozen wreck buoys or one of the few navigation marks that remained and Harris was not intending to take any chances.

"At least they are keeping together," Anderson remarked as they maintained the unbearably slow pace. In his days with the RNPS he had seen countless East Coast convoys make their way up the East Anglian coast; most had been far larger affairs made up of twenty or more merchants escorted by corvettes at the very least and often warships a great deal larger. But the wide expanse of the North Sea was a very different proposition to twenty-odd miles of their own troubled waters. Passage had to be made by night, and in small groups, for fear of the long-range artillery on the nearby French coast, and even then the brief time spent reaching the Estuary was usually far more dangerous than any later journey north.

"Potter's boat is out of station," Harris remarked. Anderson looked back; the moon was rising now and, by its light, their backmarker could indeed be seen to be wide and straggling. But what interested him more was the captain's formal use of the gunboat commander's name. Lieutenant David Potter RNVR was usually Dave or 'Pots' to any officer and 'Potty' – in private – to the ratings. Since his promotion, Harris had relaxed a good deal but still tended to be formal when referring to the captains under him.

"Not so easy at this pace," Anderson replied with elaborate unconcern; hard chine hulls only came into their own at speeds above twenty knots; below that the vessel would wallow and roll in any sort of sea and be that much harder to control.

"We're all travelling at the same speed, Number One," Harris pointed out and, though his tone appeared as gruff as ever, there might also have been a slight uncertainty in it.

"Yes, of course, sir," Anderson agreed.

"He always strikes me as a bit of a wild card," the captain continued. "Ever since that incident with the depth charge..."

Anderson knew exactly what was being referred to; a few days back Potter had 'accidentally' dropped a depth charge during one of their flotilla exercises. It had never been explained how the thing had been set to fire although the vast amount of hake and cod stunned by the explosion provided a feast that was welcomed by all. Anderson supposed it was just the sort of prank a regular straight striper like Harris would never understand, although that did not mean the man was totally without hope.

"I think you have to make allowances, sir," he suggested gently.

"Allowances?" Harris repeated the word as if it was somehow out of place, like laughter at a funeral or smoking in the bath.

"You might look on it as high spirits, I suppose," Anderson added.

Harris glowered and turned away; clearly high spirits fell into a very similar category. But he did not continue the conversation and neither was Potter instructed to keep better station.

And as the night wore on, Anderson took to pondering over the incident, which had demonstrated one of many subtle changes in his captain's demeanour and all were improvements. On several occasions, a degree of humanity and even humour had shown through; a slight chink in the armour when something of the inner person had been revealed. Despite what had been mooted at their first meeting, neither felt comfortable addressing the other by their first names, yet he felt he had come to understand Robert Harris a little better and appreciate how much of his apparently stern disposition was authentic and how much façade. And as he stood beside him on the gently vibrating deck, he decided he had come to like him a good deal more into the bargain. But then the doubts began; perhaps the change had not just come in Harris, perhaps he himself had altered slightly as well?

He remembered, almost reluctantly, sporadic mess inspections in the past aboard *Anvil*; how he would rush through the token efforts from his rag-tag crew of former fishermen with barely a look or comment. Now he was far stricter; discrepancies in kit or equipment amongst *MGB 194*'s men were pounced upon and, though anything was allowed at sea, on land the ratings knew they must be properly dressed and presentable. Perhaps it was being at war, or simply serving in the Navy, but Anderson knew when he finally returned to a peaceful world and normal life, he would be a very different person.

A peaceful world and normal life; he felt oddly guilty even considering such concepts although, with America joining the fight, they might soon be within reach. Things were bound to continue as they were for a while longer of course, but at least there was a hint of light ahead; hope, if not for tomorrow, then for a more distant future. As he considered the future his thoughts naturally turned to Eve and suddenly normality and the end of fighting seemed desperately important. And it was at that moment Anderson knew he simply wanted to survive, to see the thing through and come out the other side, even if he was changed in the process.

* * *

Jelly was seated in the W/T office and feeling relatively content. There had been a small amount of R/T traffic from within the convoy but, now they were nearing the danger area, that had mercifully stopped. The set itself was a far better unit than the one he had been used to and having a two-way repeater to the bridge took a lot of the worry out of transmitting verbal messages to the captain. There had been little on W/T as well, nothing beyond the occasional radio check, in fact; it was just this slow place that caused him any disquiet and made the bucket wedged between his feet necessary.

But at least he was warm, he told himself. With the flimsy door to the W/T cabin tightly shut, heat from the equipment made his small chamber extremely cosy. He carried out another quick sweep across the German R/T channels and winced slightly as the unexpected and penetrating sound of Morse came through, but it was a repeating phrase, so probably of little concern. There was also the usual chatter from the enemy, who did not seem particularly close and neither were they threatening. Rather than the purposeful planning of an attack, it sounded more like gossip.

When he had first picked up German broadcasts they had startled him; listening to the voices of those nearby whose sole intention must be to kill him was disconcerting in the extreme. Now, though, it had simply become another of the many shipboard sounds that surrounded them all. And, like seasickness, something he was able to tolerate, providing it came in small enough measures.

* * *

"Pregnant?" Dale repeated. "Sandy, are you for real?"

It was late, they had been in his room for several hours, yet neither had felt like doing anything other than playing records until Sandra dropped her bombshell.

"It's not something a woman jokes about," she told him coldly.

"I guess not," Peale allowed. "It's just so...unexpected."

That wasn't the word he was looking for, his writer's sixth sense told him there was a far better one. He had known the risks they were taking and should be man enough to accept the result. But in some ways, the word fitted perfectly. For a while he had been waiting for word of Chuck: Ted, at the office, was making enquiries and he was trying so hard to be patient. The news of Pearl Harbour seemed general now and, even though some fine details had not been released to the public, Peale guessed thousands would be enquiring about family members. And then this English woman had come along and launched her own brand of surprise attack.

"So what do you want to do?" he asked vaguely.

"What I want ain't the point," Sandra told him candidly. "I'm going to have a baby – your baby. What do *you* want?"

He shook his head. "I don't know, whatever it takes, I suppose."

"Whatever it takes?" she gasped. "What sorra answer is that?"

"I'm sorry, I don't know what else to say. Look, I guess anything you want you can have, does that suit?"

"Anything?" she asked cautiously.

"Sure, name it," he challenged. "You want money, I'll give you money. You want medical attention, I'll provide that as well."

The current record had come to a close and for a moment the only sound was a repetitive click of the needle as it played about the centre of the disc.

"I want more than that," she told him slowly.

"How can you want more when neither of us has named a price?" he demanded.

"A price? You think this is all down to money?"

"Most things are, what else did you have in mind?"

She paused. "I want a husband," she told him slowly. "I want a father for my baby. I want you."

"Me?" he was surprised as much as anything. "Sandy, do you know what I'm really like?"

"I know enough," she assured him.

"Pardon me, lady, but I don't think you do. I'm my own man – no home – no country when it comes down to it. I spend my time living out of suitcases and going to the worst places in the world. I just ain't the father type."

"And I don't care," she insisted. "You *are* the father, and I'll make sure everyone knows it."

He blushed. "Look, that didn't come out right," he said. "I'm not myself at the moment, there's waiting to hear about my brother an all that. Yes, of course I'm the father, I won't deny it. And I'll stand by you whatever you want."

"Including marriage?"

"Sure, if you're so dead set, including marriage," he agreed. "It's just not the way I expected it to happen."

"You can still be a reporter," she pointed out.

"I guess so," he agreed with a sigh. "Maybe in some small town; run a local paper, comment on the local garage sales and list the mourners at funerals."

"No, I mean do what you want to, go abroad if you like, just give me a home."

"Look, you're going to have to let me think this over," he said. "And I'm sorry for my reaction, but it's news to me. I'll stand by what I've done though, and what I said: yes, we'll get married, and yes, I'll provide a home. Money shouldn't be a problem if I can stay on at *The Gazette*, and you'll be safe in the States – both of you," he added, smiling again.

"Oh Dale, that's all I wanted," she assured him. "And I'm sorry, really I am."

"Hey, there were two of us playing the game," he reminded her. "No one says it's your fault, if anything I'm the one to blame."

"No, I meant I'm sorry you're being forced into it."

He shrugged. "With a fellow like me, sometimes you have to use force."

A loud knock came at the door.

"Aw heck, I guess that will be Dragon Lady coming to complain about the noise," he sighed, rising.

But rather than the formidable Miss Withers, a young man stood outside. And he was wearing a uniform, although not a military one; it was more like the sort of thing a kid would wear to a party, or on the stage. Peale registered this while his mind continued to reel from Sandra's news. But as the boy passed the small brown packet across, all thoughts of the baby and marriage were quickly dismissed. For even as he took the thing he knew the significance, and exactly what it would contain.

* * *

The whistle from the voice pipe was almost inaudible despite their engines barely puttering but, so attuned were those on the bridge to its noise, all reacted immediately.

"Go ahead, Tel'," Harris instructed.

"It's coded W/T from base," Jelly announced. "'Enemy expected north of our area'," he said.

"Nip down and add it to the plot," Harris told Anderson and he was about to move when a shout from Daly on the starboard turret stopped him.

"Vessels off the starboard bow, an' likely comin' our way, so they are..."

Anderson winced at the sloppy report, but Harris had not apparently noticed. Instead, he raised his binoculars and swore. Daly's message had been accompanied by a series of blue flashes from the leading British boats; obviously, those ahead had made the sighting at the same time. The dim lights momentarily disturbed his night vision but were soon finished and, in the smallest patch of clear weather, he was able to catch a glimpse of several low hulls speeding through the water.

"I'd say they're Es," he announced softly after a moment.

"I think you're right, sir," Anderson agreed, watching through a pair of far plainer Admiralty issue glasses.

The enemy boats were motoring in slowly from the east as if they knew exactly where and when the convoy would arrive; it was simply good luck that a freak break in the weather had revealed them.

"Blighters will be getting into position," Harris grumbled.

"Lying cut until the convoy comes up, then blast in under full power to attack."

"Indeed, sir," Anderson agreed obediently although he almost had to hide a smile; rather than the wickedly unfair plot Harris seemed to suggest, the tactics were identical to those of British MTBs. "Should we report them to base?"

"No," Harris replied, he was still searching the dark horizon even though the images of the enemy had disappeared. "Get down and give Jelly the coordinates from the plot; he can send them through as soon as we go into action. But not before – I don't want anything going out that might warn the Hun they've been spotted. And come straight back," he added. "I'll be needing you here."

* * *

Five minutes later the situation had developed. Harris had equally not dared signal to the convoy itself; from the current angle he might have done so in relative secrecy using a shaded Aldis, but it would only have taken one fool aboard a merchant to reply and their presence would have been revealed. And neither did he wish to use R/T, for even a short-range transmission might be overheard by the Germans. Instead, he had gently accelerated *MGB 194* up to the next gunboat in line and, passing wide to starboard, continued at just under half speed. At that rate, they were barely on the plane and made far less disturbance in the torpid water. Those behind were summoned to follow by the discreet use of a shaded lamp and, as he steadily overtook the final craft, he collected the entire flotilla. There was no change in the rain, which continued to fall as before although, if anything, the conditions were growing worse as the moon had found a particularly large patch of cloud to hide behind. But still the convoy was being left in their wake and those in the gunboats knew themselves to be closing on a particularly dangerous enemy.

Harris glanced at the two turret gunners who were studying the clouded horizon. It would be a disaster too horrible to contemplate were they to pass ahead of the enemy boats, then charge on into the night leaving the convoy effectively abandoned. But both men were being careful to sweep their entire sectors rather than remaining set on where they thought the E-boats should be. To his right Anderson had returned and wanted his attention – he was offering him a steel helmet. Harris shook his head; maybe later but for now he needed to think. Then the voice pipe whistled again, and he flipped the lid open.

"R/T message from Convoy Commodore asking where we're going," Jelly reported stoically.

"Very good, Tel'," Harris replied. "We can ignore that for now. But be sure to send our location as soon as you hear the firing gongs."

Snapping the lid closed, he glanced across at Anderson once more. They were leading a very ragged column with each boat less than a hundred yards behind and slightly to one side of the next; it was the ideal attack formation and one they had practised at far higher speeds. But the knowledge they were heading for a group of E-boats raised the stakes and when a sudden shout cut through the air, they all jumped slightly. Yet again it was from Daly.

"There's sometin', sir!" the Irishman cried out; all official procedure completely forgotten in his excitement. "They're E-boats to be sure!"

The sighting had come just as the moon broke through again and Harris knew that, even if the enemy had not seen him already, they would do so at any moment.

"Send the challenge," he commanded. Then, to Price at the helm, "Full speed, 'Swain!"

The boat rose up further as her screws bit deep and soon a veritable torrent of luminescent water was flying past the bridge.

"No reply from Jerry," Anderson reported stoically. The enemy craft were now in plain sight and appeared stationary but must know for certain they were under attack.

"How far, how far?" Harris muttered to himself. Judging distances at night was more art than science; the vague outlines might lie two thousand feet off their bows or considerably less than half that but, with the entire flotilla now blasting through the water at two-thirds of a mile a minute, they must soon be within range. Then his gloved hand hit the firing bell and all hell broke loose.

Bishop's gun was the first to speak and was followed a second later by Daly's. Both lines of tracer fell short of the enemy and there was a pause of several seconds before they fired again – once more, nearly together. Then a German boat was in plain sight; there was movement from its stern and, even as they watched, the craft began to surge forward. But no movement could be quick enough to dodge the line of charging gunboats and soon red tracer was licking about its superstructure.

"Prepare to bring us to port," Harris yelled and Price, at the helm, acknowledged with a nod as one hand reached for the throttles.

"Left standard rudder!" the captain's voice rang out and the boat reacted almost instantly, her stern digging into the dark seas as she forced her way around. Now the rear Oerlikon had sight and was sending a steady 'punch', 'punch', 'punch' into another boat while Daly continued to play his weapon on the first. And then they finally received what could only ever have been postponed; the Germans returned fire.

It came in a stream of green bolts that began from the stern of the first craft and was quickly joined by another. At first, the lines fell short before passing overhead and then, despite, Harris turning quickly to cross the vessel's bow, began to cut deep into their hull.

All on the bridge felt the blows as if receiving them personally; each bit into the mahogany hull, breaking through the dry hardwood and spreading mischief inside. With a judder, one of the gunboat's engines cut out and was quickly followed by the remaining two. Price swore silently as he hauled the boat back onto a straight course. The compass lamp had gone out as had the lights on the wheelhouse gauges.

"No power!" he announced pointlessly – the sudden lack of noise from the engines was obvious to all, besides no one appeared to be listening. Daly and Bishop were struggling with weapons that had suddenly become heavy and lifeless and, as the boat flopped onto the water, only the rear cannon continued to send out a steady stream of shells toward the departing enemy.

"Cease fire!" Harris yelled through cupped hands, after pressing the useless firing bell. Without power they were as good as dead; their only hope of survival lay in being unnoticed. The turn had done its job however, no more than two seconds of gunfire had been endured and the enemy that wounded them so was now concentrating on the remaining British craft.

"Damage report, Number One!" Harris called but Anderson was already moving towards the voice pipes.

"How is it Chief?" he asked when Carter finally answered.

"Fuel lines have been hit and we've problems with the electrics."

"Do what you can and let me know if you need help," Anderson told him briefly – the man had enough on his plate without talking to him.

"On it now," Carter snapped and was gone. Anderson glanced at Harris.

"Better take a tour," the captain told him. "Check all are okay and make sure no one shows any form of light."

"Very good, sir," Anderson replied as he slipped down to the wheelhouse.

Harris watched him go then looked about. Behind them, the rest of the flotilla had reached the Germans and the entire battle now appeared to be heading eastwards with tracer flying in all directions. As senior officer, the obvious place for him was amongst the fray, yet he could do nothing but hope to remain unobserved. The feeling of vulnerability was intense, and it hardly helped knowing their fuel lines had been fractured. Images of high octane petrol flowing freely over hot machinery came unbidden and he swallowed dryly. No doubt they had all been in tighter scrapes in the past, but at that moment he could not remember one.

Chapter Fourteen

In fact, the fuel lines proved only a part of their problem. They were fractured to be sure; a twenty-millimetre shell had struck the main matrix before travelling the width of the engine room and embedding itself in the port wing engine's exhaust manifold. And high octane petrol was indeed gushing out with the force of a torn artery, dousing everything in sight including the three men that took up much of the spare space in the cramped compartment. But of possibly equal importance, the main switchboard had been hit, leaving the boat bereft of electrical power.

By the yellow light of their torches, Carter, Pickering and Newman surveyed the damage. Newman was the first to spot the fractured feed and began to assess the problem. Which was not insoluble; they had spare piping and unions and should be able to rig some sort of feed before long. Pickering made for the stop tap and stemmed the flow, but not before several gallons of fuel had flooded the engine room and soaked into their overalls. He and Newman used mops to encourage the spilt petrol into their bilges but, without power, every ventilator fan was silent, and the air hung thick with the heady fumes.

"Right, nothing that could create a spark, do you understand?" Carter's tone was sharp, as it had been with the first lieutenant.

"I could open the hatch," Pickering suggested.

"No, even torchlight might give us away, just be careful." All in the engine room were accustomed to wearing rubber-soled shoes, but that hardly meant the chance of a spark was low. "So, what's causing the lack of power?"

"Switchboard's hit," Newman replied, shining his torch on the tangled web of wires, fuses, junction boxes and gauges.

Carter squeezed his way across and added his light. A second shell must have struck them, and the damage was extensive. "We'll have to rig something temporary," he muttered. "It'll need cable, clips and tape."

"Can you fix it?" Pickering enquired artlessly.

"I'll tell you later," the motor mechanic snorted. "Bill, you address the fuel line. Geoff can help me; cut some yard lengths of braided three core and rouse out a drum of fifteen-amp. But first everyone had better ditch their overalls; the air's bad enough as it is but we must stink like a refinery."

* * *

"Don't know what Carter and his lot are playing at down there," Harris grunted to Price. The action had moved sufficiently to grant them a measure of security, and the boat had turned almost fully about in the current. Ahead he could see evidence of the running battle taking place a mile or so off and the urge to plough back, guns blazing to take up command, was strong. There was a movement from the wheelhouse and Anderson appeared next to him on the bridge.

"Mr Carter's doing all he can. Fuel lines are being addressed but they're awash with petrol and the switchboard's a mess," he said. "I've sent Jelly to see if he can help."

"Any idea how long?" Harris asked.

"They're hard at work, but it won't be immediate." Anderson shrugged. "Chief promised to restore each circuit as he goes."

"And the engines?"

"They'll probably be a while longer; they're having to rig fresh fuel lines."

"Very well," Harris sighed. "What about the rest of the boat?"

"No one's hurt; I've explained the position and there won't be anyone lighting up."

"Glad to hear it." Since hearing of the fuel leak Harris had been conscious of the smell of petrol, although that might be nothing more than heightened imagination.

A sudden flurry of tracer caught his attention. One of the British boats – one of his boats – was engaging a German some way off their starboard bow; the pair were exchanging fire as they powered through the water apparently abreast. And all he could do was watch.

* * *

"I've got the compass lamp back," Price exclaimed with rare excitement, "an' the lights is on in the wheelhouse!"

"Progress," Anderson muttered. The tannoy was making a buzzing sound; he reached for the handset that was swinging by its lead and replaced it in the cradle.

"I don't suppose it will do any good going down," Harris

196

mused.

"I think we'd only get in the way," Anderson replied. "They know the situation we're in."

There was a whistle from the radio cabin's speaking tube and Jelly's voice came through.

"Mr Carter's sent me back," he announced. "Set has power now and is up and running. And the ventilators are working. He reckons the engines won't be far behind. Do you want to send any messages, sir?"

Harris went to reply when a deep rumble told him one of the engines was indeed starting up. "I'll let you know, Tel'," he shouted quickly before turning to Price. "Make for the action, 'Swain."

The boat picked up slowly but soon gathered speed. Then the starboard wing engine joined the centre and they rose onto the plane. To one side Daly was moving his gun on its mount freely and Bishop appeared to be sighting on some unseen target. The third engine joined in but it was only a matter of seconds before it cut out once more. Harris pressed the firing gongs and the bells began ringing just as Carter came through on the engine room voice pipe.

"That's the best I can do, sir," the motor mechanic reported. "Port engines showing low oil pressure, I don't want to trust it. Starboard has a leaking Purolator but I think she'll hold."

"Very good, Chief," Harris told him. "I think we've done enough. He paused before closing the voice pipe, then turned to Anderson. "Reckon we got off lightly there, Number One," he said.

* * *

As they drew nearer, the action became more defined and was indeed spreading eastwards. Ahead they could see one of the E-boats had been badly hit and was being left behind. Anderson eyed it with interest but guessed Harris would be determined to catch up with the rest of the flotilla. And they were making reasonable progress on two engines, although it seemed the enemy was fighting a running battle and travelling that much faster. Mercifully the rain had stopped and just off their port bow they could make out several large dim images which must be the convoy. With luck, the Fairmile escorts would have been diverted and might even be mixing it with the E-boats but that was probably asking for too much. The merchants were old and tired but any one was worth a dozen gunboats, both in monetary value and by the essential goods they could transport. And for all anyone knew there could be another E-boat pack on the water, so leaving charges unprotected in order to save a handful of motor launches belied the purpose of a convoy.

They were passing the damaged E-boat and the crew were definitely taking to life rafts and what looked like a small rowing boat. In a perfect world, they would have stopped to collect survivors and maybe take the enemy craft in tow but with the flotilla in action, Harris gave it little more than a passing glance. They were up on the plane still and finally seemed to be gaining on the distant flecks of gunfire but if *194* had been capable of twice the speed it would hardly have been enough. Then the rattle of their port Vickers caught the officers' attention; Daly's guns were also firing and, following the lines of tracer, they could all see the side of a speeding E-boat as they bore down on it.

"Right standard rudder!" Harris shouted, and Price brought the boat around just as the German vessel directed a barrage of fire that landed off their port beam, exactly where they would have been without the turn. "Meet her, midships." Price straightened them out and the aft cannon began to speak but the enemy was turning sharply to port and soon began heading to the east and safety. Harris watched her go for a moment; they might have followed although an E-boat's main armament was set aft and, even with three functioning engines, he wouldn't have relished the prospect of a stern chase.

"There's one of ours!" Anderson shouted, and Harris looked forward once more. Sure enough, in the middle distance, he could see a gunboat heading to rejoin the convoy and beyond it the vague shape of several other hulls.

Harris bent forward to the speaking tubes and called down to Jelly. "See if you can get me R/T to the flotilla, Tel'."

It took probably thirty seconds before Jelly came back.

"I seem to have a patch, sir, but not sure how long it will last." Then Potter's voice came through on the repeater and it was good news.

"We accounted for one, sir; she fell back, and Phil thinks we might have sunk her."

"I'm darned certain," Shaw's elated voice interrupted.

"I saw it an' all," another confirmed.

"Enough of that," Harris cut in sharply. "This signal might not hold for long; give me a report, Potter,"

"We saw them off, sir, but did not give chase," the man, who Harris remembered had been an assistant librarian in an earlier life, replied more soberly. "That seemed the wisest move considering some had been hit, and frankly we didn't know what had happened to you."

"What's the damage?"

"My boat's holed though the self-bailers are keeping her afloat," Potter replied. "As long as I don't stop, that is," he added with a chuckle.

"And the rest?" Harris demanded. "Tell me in pennant number order, Mike Barton first." Then they all listened while each of the commanding officers gave a brief description of their boat's injuries. None were critical and it seemed the only physical casualty was a stoker who had burned himself on an exhaust manifold but even that sounded minor.

"It really was quite a scrap," Potter remarked when they had finished; his voice sounded strained but there was also an obvious air of achievement. "Shame you couldn't have taken more of a part, sir."

"We've been damaged as well," Harris told them briskly. "What's your current position?"

"We're together and making for the convoy," Potter confirmed.

"I think I see you, that's me coming up behind."

There was a pause, then several single dull blue flashes came from the distant hulls.

"I see you, leader," Potter reported.

"Are the rest of you fit to continue escort duty?"

There was a chorus of affirmations from the other craft.

"Then you may as well carry on; Mike, you take charge. North Foreland's not far." Harris glanced at Anderson who gave a nod of confirmation. "But you can head home now, Dave; I'll follow."

"Shall we travel in company, sir?"

"No, I'm down to two engines and one of those is dodgy; Get yourself back and on the slip, I'll be along later."

"Righto, sir. And I'll ask them to keep your bacon on hold, shall I?"

Harris hesitated and Anderson could sense his confusion, then he appeared to come to a decision and spoke more positively into the handset.

"I'll have you know I am the flotilla senior officer," he announced curtly. There was a pause and it was obvious every captain was listening intently. "So it might interest you all to know SOs don't just get bacon, but sausages, kidneys," Harris continued, "and a black pudding at Christmas."

The remark brought a chorus of laughter and ribald comments that owed as much to relief as humour, but when Harris replaced the handset and turned to Anderson he seemed strangely triumphant.

"Very well, Number One," he said. "Set a course for home."

* * *

Peale lay on his back in his anonymous hotel room and stared up at the cracked ceiling. He had been there, and alone, for most of the night. Ever since eating, in fact, which was an equally solitary affair. And he had been drinking. He glanced at the bottle next to him; it was no more than a quarter full although he felt as sober as when the cork was first pulled several hours before. He reached across and splashed a little more into and over the tooth glass. The Grand Hotel did not encourage guests to drink in their rooms, not when their money could be spent on the inflated prices downstairs. But Peale was not thinking of saving cash and neither was he concerned about wasting gin. He'd heard from Ted that morning; a wire, not unlike the one that told him of Chuck's death but bearing better news.

Ted would be heading over along with several junior hacks and, together, they were going to set up a proper agency in the UK. Peale was pleased, Ted had been a friend for some while; they had worked together before and understood each other well. He paused and let his mind run on; it was even possible the hard-bitten journalist understood him better than the woman currently carrying his child. Peale had immediately written a long letter explaining his situation and detailing his plans for the future, but Ted would probably have left before receiving it. That didn't matter though, writing was Peale's medium and, once the thing was posted, he had felt something close to relief after getting his thoughts on paper. And it really didn't matter if his friend did not receive it, at least for a while, for nothing he proposed needed to be acted upon immediately; the only thing he really should do was contact Sandy and tell her exactly where she stood.

Remembering this, he raised himself up and swung his feet onto the floor. He needed to walk, to stretch his legs and take in some of that famous seaside air Dover was so proud of. There had been no air raid warning that evening, at least nothing had penetrated his own private world, and even the prospect of rain, which had been falling steadily since early afternoon, failed to deter him. His coat was hanging on the door and his shoes lay nearby. He slipped both on and reached for the ornate brass handle then stepped out and onto the dimly lit corridor.

It was strange but the stone-cold sobriety he had credited himself with while in his room vanished as soon as he walked along the worn carpet and he staggered slightly at the top of the stairs. He made it down safely enough but, when he passed through the lobby and was faced with the first of two immense blackout curtains, very nearly turned back.

"There's a raid on, sir," the hall porter warned him from his sheltered chair.

"Is there?" Peale asked, although he continued to walk. "I heard no warning."

"It were some hours ago," the old man agreed. "An' there ain't been nothing since. I expect the all-clear will sound any moment."

Peale gave a preoccupied nod and swept the first curtain aside, before stepping through. Sandy would be in her room by now or one of the shelters if there really was a raid. But he didn't need to see her; he didn't need to see anyone, so the idea of damp deserted streets was oddly attractive. And he wouldn't be gone long, just an hour or so to clear his head and get the fine details sorted. Then, when Ted came, he would be able to tell him everything face to face, although he really should fill Sandy in long before that.

* * *

194 had only travelled a few miles when Bishop came through with a report.

"Object off the port bow," he announced, his Midlands accent sounding unusually flat in the dark night. "I'd say it were a vessel of some sort, pr'aps that E-boat we saw earlier."

Harris was on the bridge and started slightly when the hated word was mentioned. Anderson quickly appeared from the wheelhouse where he had been trying to plot a course. But it soon seemed there was little threat; as the gunboat drew nearer the stationary craft appeared asleep and, on approaching further, it became obvious she had been abandoned.

"It's the same one," Anderson confirmed soberly. "I remember that direct hit to the bridge."

In the moonlight the damage was indeed obvious and there was more. Holes from light calibre shells pockmarked her hull, one of the stern-mounted guns had been knocked clean away and the rubber dinghies usually carried aft were definitely missing. But even in such a state, and so obviously beaten, the off-white hull exuded an air of menace and what might have been evil to men accustomed to fighting such craft.

"Stand-off, fifty yards," Harris muttered.

"Standing off, sar," Price duly repeated as he throttled back and brought the gunboat round until she lay almost parallel.

"What think you, Number One?" the captain asked. "Care for a closer look?"

"She appears deserted," Anderson mused. "Though that isn't to say something nasty hasn't been left behind with us in mind."

"We could take her under tow. Only have the two engines but Dover can't be so very far."

"About twenty-five miles," Anderson replied absentmindedly as he continued to study the vessel. The thing seemed to grow more sinister as he looked. When a child, he had been taken to the Natural History Museum in London and remembered staring in horror at the body of a tarantula. It was dead, pinned to a card and firmly encased behind plate glass so represented no physical threat yet still carried the same menace as the derelict boat opposite.

Or perhaps that was not strictly true; the E-boat could easily remain lethal in some way.

"Well, if she's booby-trapped, it's likely to be below," Harris remarked, and Anderson smiled to himself; though they were so very different, the pair of them had been sharing the same thought. "Scuttling charges may well have been set, or at least the seacocks opened."

"But the bridge was hit," Anderson pointed out as his eyes travelled back to the carnage that had so recently housed the vessel's officers. "With their captain dead, the rest might simply have given up."

"It's a possibility, but not one I'd care to stake my life on. Remember, E-boats carry larger crews than us, and not all those in command need have been on the bridge."

Anderson tore his eyes away from the sight and considered his captain. "If so, they haven't gone off," he pointed out, adding, "Besides, we need not go below."

Harris nodded but said nothing.

"Attach a tow and leave a decent length of line," Anderson continued. "Once we raise Dover, we can request a tug to come out to us."

"A captured E-boat would be welcomed," Harris mused. "There'll be things to learn for sure, even if all the confidential books have been destroyed."

For several seconds there was silence then Harris spoke again.

"It's your choice, Ian. If you're prepared to go across, I'll support you."

"Can I ask for a volunteer to accompany me?"

"Of course, but as soon as you smell a rat, I want you both off there sharpish."

"I can promise you that," Anderson sighed as he regarded the enemy boat once more. "There's no way I'll be staying any longer than I have to."

Chapter Fifteen

Jelly was to go with him; the telegraphist was the obvious choice as all gunners would be needed as lookouts and for defence, the mechanics had their engines to attend to and Price was far too valuable at the helm. And though the lad was by no means the strongest or heaviest of the gunboat's crew, Anderson still felt comfortable with him by his side.

There was a reasonable chop and as Price edged the gunboat closer, Anderson eyed the dwindling distance warily. They would have to jump, only a rare error from the coxswain would allow the hulls to touch. And even when they were less than five feet apart the two vessels were rising and falling as if on totally different stretches of sea.

"I'll go first, Jelly," he announced. "Once I'm secure you'll get the nod."

It was the only way when an officer and a rating faced the same challenge, but as Anderson braced himself for the leap, he could have wished it otherwise.

Nevertheless, due to Price's innate skill, the distance he needed to cover was less than three feet and easily crossed; as soon as he landed against the E-boat's canvas-covered rails he began to clamber over and quickly settled himself on the enemy's deck.

And though the German boat rocked from side to side, she was certainly more stable laterally, Anderson decided as he glanced about. But then she was slimmer than most British motor launches and a good deal longer, while the decks were much less cluttered. A quick wave and Jelly hurled himself off before landing equally squarely.

"This is quite a thing," the telegraphist remarked as he swung himself over the rails, and Anderson could only agree. Almost next to them was a torpedo; it looked dark, menacing and stark in the cold moonlight. He knew that would be one of the reloads, the launch tubes being internal and set further forward. But as he looked in that direction his attention was caught by the damaged bridge.

Rather than one heavy shell, the area had obviously suffered from sustained hits from something lighter; perhaps a twenty-millimetre cannon, possibly with additional heavy machine gun fire but the nett result was utter carnage. He had heard rumours of E-boats providing superior protection for both officers and men, but what he saw belied this. The twisted metal and splintered wood had crumbled under prolonged accurate fire; it would surely be impossible for anyone to emerge alive from such devastation and, as he looked further, there was grisly evidence to support this.

"Come on, Jelly," Anderson urged, tearing his eyes from the sight. "We'd better get for'ard."

Both men had armed themselves with Service revolvers and drawn them after boarding but, as they clambered up to the launch's raised foredeck, they automatically holstered the weapons. For there was surely little threat aboard the enemy craft, only an overwhelming feeling of sadness. As they passed the ruins of the bridge, strange homely objects swam unbidden into sight; a china mug missing its handle, the remains of a bar of chocolate and a woollen glove, clearly handmade though no longer required by its owner. But soon they were past and standing on the E-boat's streamlined foredeck.

"There's protection," Jelly commented as he glanced towards the prow. A twenty-millimetre cannon was housed there, it's mounting set deep into the deck itself and the barrel rising only slightly proud. Those manning the weapon would be sheltered by little more than hardwood and light sheet metal but the feeling of security must be far superior to that of British gun positions. A faint putter caught their attention and Anderson looked up to see Price manoeuvring the gunboat to stand off their starboard bow. And there was young Cook at the stern; the lad's grin could be made out in the pale light while his mate swung a length of hawser above both their heads and it was hard to think of them as seamen and not children playing at cowboys. Ideally, there should have been a lighter lead line and on the first two attempts the wire fell short but, eventually, Jelly was able to catch hold and secure the tow to the samson post.

"What do you want to do, Number One?" The captain's voice came over the ship's tannoy and sounded as familiar and reassuring as that of any parent. "We can leave you there or bring you back; your decision."

Anderson glanced at Jelly; was there truly a choice? If they stayed, he supposed they would be able to release the tow should it become necessary, but that would only condemn them to being cast adrift aboard an enemy boat and one that may well still prove lethal. Really there was no option and if this was yet another example of his captain's burgeoning sense of humour, Anderson wasn't sure he liked it.

"Thank you, sir," he bellowed in reply. "But if it's all the same to you, we'll come back."

* * *

They had been travelling for three hours when the first glimmer of dawn began to make itself known. Both forward gunners were in their turrets as they had been since the boat set off the previous evening. Throughout that time they seemed to have been constantly searching the dim horizon, with only brief periods of intense action to break the monotony, and now both were fit to drop. But if Bishop had heard correctly, there was still a considerable way to go, so clearly the final stage of their journey was to be made in daylight.

Which might not be so bad, he decided. Early morning was not necessarily the time when enemy planes came looking, especially as they would surely be granted air support. The reason they would be cared for, and the fact it had taken longer to return from patrol, was plain and would grow plainer still when the sun finally did lift above the horizon. Even now he could make out the ghostly shape of the E-boat as it clung defiantly to their tail. And he was not the only one to view it with suspicion; Dowling had been thoughtfully covering its prow with his Oerlikon throughout.

Having what was usually such an elusive and deadly enemy in constant sight was disconcerting in the extreme and Bishop totally sympathised with the young gunner's concern. But their skipper was determined to bring his trophy home and, though part of him accepted this must surely be more than a simple spoil of war, he was a long way from being convinced.

The thing was bound to be of use to the boffins who did their fighting in dry, heated offices, but at that moment Bishop, in his draughty turret, cared little for what could be learned. Instead, he longed for one of the NAAFI's mammoth breakfasts; that and a decent sleep which, again, was little more than his due. And though he was usually comfortable in his turret and needed nothing more than the company of his beloved Vickers, Bishop was becoming decidedly fidgety. Let those who spent their nights cosy do what they wished with the vile thing that tagged behind, slowing them down and making the gunboat the perfect target for one of its brothers. If he had his way, he would punch a few more holes in its hateful hull and send it straight to the bottom.

And those in the engine room were just as weary. Carter sat back in the small corner that had long since been adopted as his and assessed the situation. Almost as soon as the gunboat took on the extra load, the starboard engine had started to overheat. Then oil began to flow from around the filter and no amount of bodging or cursing had been enough to cure either problem. Consequently, they were now down to the centre engine alone, something that accounted for their speed which, even at eighteen hundred revolutions, was painfully slow. They might accelerate of course; the Packards were rated up to the high twenty hundreds but holding the engine back was a precaution he had recommended and, to his credit, something the captain was quick to accept. Were it not important to keep the unit cool, Carter would probably have throttled back even further, as their remaining engine actually provided more than just propulsion. The hydraulic feed to both forward gun mounts relied on the centre unit; should it fail, they would not only be without power, but their entire defence must rest with the Oerlikon cannon alone. If dawn found them alone and adrift, the enemy was likely to as well and, after such a night, the prospect of an poorly defended attack by air or sea was hardly attractive.

To his right Pickering dozed gently, his head resting against a fuel tank that held upwards of five hundred gallons of high octane petrol, while Newman was carrying out yet another inspection of their remaining engine. The bilges were almost dry but still the smell of gasoline percolated from below and, with the switchboard looking more like an abandoned cat's cradle, Carter felt his usually ordered world was in tatters. But they had survived so far, and were it not for the dead weight holding them back, everyone would have been home and safe some hours ago. He, probably more than Bishop, could appreciate the reason for bringing their prize back and already sensed himself amid a story that, one day, would make fine telling in front of a cosy fire. But given the choice, he would have gladly skipped any future recollections and cast the tow off hours ago.

* * *

"I suppose you think I'm mad," Harris told Anderson when the younger man came up from the wheelhouse. "Taking all this trouble over seeing one Hun launch back to Dover."

"No, sir," Anderson replied with transparent honesty. "Our eggheads will definitely learn a lot from it."

"Probably, but it's more than that," the captain insisted as he rested against the dodger. "So much of what we do is shrouded in mystery; we shoot at ill-defined targets and take fire ourselves from dim shapes we can barely recognise and, on the few occasions we have a success, it has to be confirmed and will doubtless be disputed by the Germans later. But this is real, a true kill; no one can deny it. And even though we can't be sure which boat caused the damage, it was certainly the flotilla – my flotilla, if you like – but that's not the reason either."

Anderson was quiet; even when they had lost the second engine, he had been in favour of retaining the prize and, though there was still some way to go and further hurdles to jump, his feelings had not changed. But now there was time to consider the matter fully he realised there were indeed more reasons to see the German craft back. As Harris had said, it was tangible proof of the private battle that they had all been waging for so long. And by proof he didn't mean a definite tick on a balance sheet or some crudely drawn swastika to show their worth. This was confirmation for the whole of Coastal Forces; validation that what they were doing really did have a reason and could produce results.

And they would be doing more than simply proving it to themselves. The town that accommodated them must see the E-boat – see it and know the daily shelling and nightly air raids it endured were not going unanswered, that there was some point in having a Coastal Forces base within its midst, despite all the unwelcome attention such neighbours attracted.

"Do you know, I'm too damn tired to explain," Harris admitted eventually, and Anderson could only nod in empathy.

"That's all right, sir," he replied. "I think I understand."

* * *

"Dover Command confirms they've sent out the *Lady Duncannon* in company with three MGBs," Anderson said as he emerged once more from the wheelhouse.

"So Jelly has just informed me," Harris confirmed, stretching. "You're sure of our position?"

"As I can be," Anderson shrugged. "It's hard enough dead reckoning on three engines when a difference of fifty revs can mean an entire knot, but running on the centre alone, and towing probably a hundred tons of E-boat..."

"I'm sure you did your best, Number One," the captain soothed. "And don't suppose for a moment you have a rough estimate for our arrival at Dover..."

Anderson gave a tired smile. "I'd say we'll have it in sight within two hours, though whether I'm right or not is yet to be seen."

"It'll be getting light."

"Actually, it will have been so for an hour."

"Well, our rescuers might have found us by then," Harris supposed. "Them or the Germans."

* * *

As it turned out, the honour was shared. They had been towing the E-boat for more than seven hours, with the last being covered in growing daylight, when first the smoke, then the superstructure of a tug came into view. Jelly had been attempting to draw their rescuer in for some while but, though remarkably accurate in the circumstances, Anderson's dead reckoning proved a little astray and it took assistance from three Hurricanes also searching for them to finally pair the two up. But even as the *Lady Duncannon* steamed nearer, and her three MGB escorts excitedly rushed on ahead to greet their brother, the first German planes were spotted.

There were nine of them in the end and they came at high speed and at a startlingly low level; three 109 fighters in the van leading a force of six Junkers fighter bombers. No one could tell if they had been drawn by R/T transmissions between gunboat and tug or were purely on a speculative mission that struck lucky, and no one particularly cared. The fact was they were about to face a concerted attack from a far superior force and that was enough to dispel all curiosity.

"Cast off the tow!" To utter such words after so long an ordeal almost caused physical pain but Harris had no hesitation and sensed support from all on board. Under their single engine and without encumbrances the gunboat might make fifteen knots, perhaps more, but tied to the German prize they could barely see five. And once freed, the gunboat would be able to manoeuvre so, despite a top speed that still fell far short of her true potential, must present a far harder target.

The first wave of enemy planes was upon them as the hawser flopped down into the sea, and Price firmly brought up the single throttle, letting the boat leap forward as if in relief. But the fighters were approaching from their stern and, despite Harris ordering them hard a port, the gunboat was hammered by a dose of machine gun fire. *194* replied and Daly was reasonably sure he caught the back of one departing plane, but it took intervention from the Hurricanes to finally see the fighters off. And the RAF were still engaged in their own individual dogfights when the first of the bombers came in.

To some extent having a captured E-boat was an advantage. It was obvious the Germans regarded her destruction with as much importance as that of the British launches, *194* having been joined by her colleagues by this point. And though the fit and powerful new arrivals circled both their wounded associate and the drifting wreck while sending up an impressive barrage of fire, the bombs released were not aimed at them but their prize. One still fell close enough to drench *194*'s bridge and turret gunners, although Dowling at the Oerlikon redressed the balance by scoring a definite hit on the starboard engine of a German plane. Wounded, the enemy quickly broke away and began heading for France followed by a trail of smoke and two of the Hurricanes. Then, after one more indecisive pass, the remaining enemy aircraft also departed leaving them in peace.

But the damage had already been done. Harris and Anderson stood together on the bridge and watched in silence. The captured and stationary E-boat had been an easy target; she had been strafed twice and now a small fire burned merrily on her rising stern. But the main damage was further forward; one of her own countryman's bombs had removed much of the prow and, in the fresh light of morning, she made a sorry sight. Her hull quickly filled with water and as their prize finally dipped below the grey waters it was almost a sacred moment.

"You did your best, sir," Anderson muttered finally.

"Yes, but it wasn't enough," Harris sighed. "And no seaman likes to see a boat go down," he added. "Any boat."

Chapter Sixteen

"What do you mean, you can't find him?" Eve asked.

"He's gone," Sandra snapped as she shook off her coat. "Not at t'otel, not anywhere as far as I can gather. We'd set to meet at seven-thirty, he said he had something important to tell us." She gave her friend a significant look. "You know, *important.*"

"When did you arrange this?" Eve questioned from her bed. She had been reading a German language primer and expecting an early night so the sudden flurry of activity had taken her by surprise.

"Monday evenin'; we were going to meet but he called me, said he had sommat he needed to write and would be busy."

"Well, maybe he's still writing?" Eve placed the book on her bedside table and considered her friend more carefully. "Come on, the chap's just lost his brother. And what with your news I don't suppose he'll be thinking straight."

"I spoke to Dragon Lady at t'otel, she said he hadn't been seen at breakfast," Sandra continued. "Oh, Evie, I think he might have done a flit."

"A what?"

"A flit. You know, moved on."

"Well, even if he has, he can't have gone far," Eve stated firmly.

"I'd say America's far enough."

"I wouldn't. You know who he works for, remember?"

"And?"

"And you have every reason to believe he's the father of your child," Eve reminded her. "America's coming into the war now and on our side, even if his paper won't tell you where he is, I'm sure we can trace him. There are official channels and you're still a member of His Majesty's Armed Forces."

Sandra shook her head, "But he wouldn't just take off like that, not Dale."

"Like I said, he's had a few shocks, probably just needs time to sort himself out."

"So what should I do?"

"You could try the hotel again. Call them if you don't want to go down."

"No, I'll go down; there's no raid on."

"Not yet, but it's a clear night."

"I'm going anyway," she said. "Try and speak to someone other than Dragon Lady, the porter's a nice old boy, he might know more."

"In that case, I'm coming with you," Eve announced leaping off the bed.

"What if there's a raid?"

"Like you said, there isn't one at the moment. And we can't go on living our lives to suit the Germans."

* * *

"The boat will be on the slip at least a week," Harris told Anderson. "Which will almost take us up to Christmas. There's not normally a lot going on at that time so if you've got anywhere to go, you may as well head off. I'll mark you down for leave if you like; no one can say you haven't earned it."

Anderson considered this for a moment. Whether he deserved it or not, he felt no inclination to leave Dover. For a start he wanted to see *194* through her repairs; mention had been made of replacing one of the Packards and he'd heard rumours that Elco boats could indeed support twin Oerlikons; if there was a chance they could double their aft firepower he didn't want to miss out. But the main reason was far more personal; his last leave had been spent in London, seemingly the ideal place for a single man with parents many miles away. But now he had something else, something far more special, and that something was in Dover.

"What do you intend doing, sir?" he asked, prevaricating.

"I'm staying put," Harris told him firmly. "As flotilla SO I don't need a boat; actually it would be good to go out with some of the others, see how they do things, and maybe drop a hint or two – subtly of course."

Anderson gave a private smile; Harris might still be an old salt horse, but he was definitely mellowing.

"Then I'll probably stay as well," he said.

"Really?" the man seemed genuinely pleased.

"Let's just say I have made a few friends in Dover."

"You could be useful," Harris mused. "Yard said they might even get things sorted earlier, and there's a spare engine just waiting to be installed."

"I expect Carter and his mob will be supervising that," Anderson laughed, "but yes, I'll keep an eye on her."

"And you could come out with me and the other lads."

Anderson noticed Harris had referred to his commanders as lads, and again was pleased. "That wouldn't ruffle any feathers?" he asked.

"Definitely not, it's customary for the SO to bring his number one, and you're a full two striper now," Harris reminded him.

"Then it's decided," he said. "Thanks for the offer, but you can consider my leave deferred."

* * *

The Red Lion was full, warm and as welcoming as ever, while around him were ratings from *194*; men he knew well and liked a lot, but still Daly felt ill at ease. For a start, he could not drink. He wanted to, but his lack of funds was starting to bite and must surely have been noticed by those about him. Some would be short also, as their fortnightly pay was not due for several days, but those already spent up had borrowed in order to make that night a good one. There were usually one or two shipmates open to a loan. Price, the coxswain for one; despite his somewhat severe nature and apparent dislike of 'hostiles', the old sweat was good for a light touch now and then, and Carter, their motor mechanic, had also proved amenable in the past. But Daly was already in hock by over fifty guineas to Remer and had no intention of compounding the problem by borrowing from his shipmates. Instead, he had invented a bilious attack; something that was readily accepted by those sharing the same NAAFI diet. The subterfuge worked well and Daly had been pleased although now was not so sure. While everyone quaffed pints of Kentish ale and were growing steadily more mellow, he was left morose and staring at the same solitary glass of milk.

But there was no avoiding the situation, and no one else to blame but himself. The money he owed Remer would take an age to pay off, yet, unless he was blessed with a sudden transfer, that's what he must do. The alternative, the one the old man had offered before their last patrol, was simply too dreadful to contemplate.

As an Irishman, Daly lacked any official stake in the war but equally held no illusions as to the outcome should England be invaded. Despite what some of his countrymen might claim, once that happened it must only be a question of time before Ireland was also under the Nazi jackboot. Such a fate had even been signalled; when Dublin and, more specifically, the president's official residence, were visited by German bombers, over thirty civilians had been killed. And his government seemed strangely eager to dismiss such outrages by accepting limp claims of mistakes in navigation. But many considered it otherwise, especially when Lord Haw-Haw – himself supposedly an Irishman – cited the raids as punishment for the help given to Britain during the Belfast blitz.

Nevertheless, Daly didn't owe Britain much, and the information Remer required – a few notes on patrol arrangements and flotilla strength – would not be so very arduous. And neither could it do a great deal of damage; from what the old man intimated he would be telling them little that could not be learned by a careful observer. But Daly was suspicious and wily enough to know that, once he let himself be drawn into becoming an informer, a good deal more would be required. As a seaman gunner, his professional knowledge was limited to the pair of half-inch Vickers he regularly tended but guessed they would soon start asking about the condition of the boat itself, intended movements of the flotilla, or maybe even more complex matters that truly were none of his concern. And though he might assure himself that revealing even the most sensitive information would not affect his own country, it would certainly damage that of his friends; the men he served alongside and was sitting with now at the crowded table.

"Smoke, Irish?" Dowling asked cheerfully as he proffered a packet of Players.

"Thank you no, I've been told I really should not," Daly lied, while his eyes rested on the small tubes of pleasure with longing. "Doctor's orders."

"I thought it were your Mary playing up," Jelly, the telegraphist, remarked.

"If fags are affecting your stomach you ain't smokin' 'em right," Bishop advised.

"Maybe he ain't smokin' 'em at all?" Pickering, the stoker, suggested. "Maybe that's his problem."

"Is that it, Pad?" Jelly enquired. "You ain't got a belly-ache, just been eating too many cigarettes?"

They all laughed, and Daly was glad to join in. He liked the men and knew they liked him however some might behave at times.

"So what does the quack say?" the lad Dowling asked. "Is the belly bad enough to leave off active service?"

"Paddy can leave whenever he wants," Bishop cut in. "Irishmen don't have to fight, he does it 'cause he wants to, ain't that the case?"

"Now there you're wrong," Daly corrected. "No matter what my government says, I'm a British subject."

"But you could get a discharge," Bishop insisted, "if you wanted."

"Aye, maybe I could an' that," Daly agreed, his mind running on. "But it's not something I'm looking for."

"Why not?" Dowling gasped after draining the last of his beer. "Give me a chance to get out of this lot and I'll bite your hand off."

"Is that a fact?" Daly asked. One advantage of remaining sober was the ability to think more clearly than anyone else. "You're telling me you'd walk away and leave your friends?"

Dowling shrugged. "I don't know, maybe not."

"Sometimes I think it's one of the best things about the job," Jelly sighed and all turned to him.

"How'd you mean, Wobbler?" Pickering asked.

"Friendship," the telegraphist explained. "I know you'll say I've gone soft, but it's important, to me at least."

They were unusually quiet for a moment as all considered this.

"We work together, play together," Jelly continued as the sentiment continued to flow. "Know each other well and know where to look to for support if we needs it."

That was true, if mildly embarrassing to have it pointed out, although the majority were at the stage when a little sentimentality was quite welcome.

"I mean, if Paddy here were in trouble, we'd want to help, ain't that the case?" Jelly continued, eyeing the Irishman thoughtfully.

Again, they nodded and this time it was Daly's turn to feel embarrassed.

"So why are we sitting here watching him drink milk when we all know his stomach's as healthy as any of ours?"

Pickering wriggled uncomfortably in his seat. "Man says he's got a dodgy tum, it ain't for us to examine the blighter."

"Oh come on, look at the evidence," Jelly insisted. "Pad's been short of money for weeks, given up the fags and don't drink more than a nun at Easter. Just because he ain't chipping us for a rubber, don't mean there's not a problem."

"That right, Irish?" Bishop asked. "Bit skint, are you?"

"I've known better times," Daly admitted.

"Right, well it's my round," Bishop announced rising. "And it will be a full one, you can stick that cow juice, Paddy, I'm getting you a pint."

There were grunts of agreement from others at the table.

"And when I comes back you're going tell us all exactly what the problem is," he added looking specifically at Daly, then the rest of the seamen. "And we're going to fix it, right?"

* * *

Dragon Lady had actually been quite helpful at the hotel but could shed no further light on Peale's disappearance. Only when the aged hall porter was consulted did they discover anything new, and that was hardly encouraging. The elderly man spent most of his waking hours, and many of the rest, snug in a heavily upholstered chair off the front lobby. He had definitely seen the American leave earlier that morning, but not return.

"The ARP," Eve stated decisively on hearing this. "There's a post on Snargate Street, we can enquire there."

"Enquire for what?" Sandra whined. "See if he's been killed in an air raid?"

"See if he's been seen," her friend corrected. "Anyone walking about Dover at that time of night must surely be spotted; someone might have spoken with him, or just made a note. And besides, if he's injured you'll want to know about it won't you?"

"But Jerry came early last night," Sandra protested. "There weren't nothing after eight o'clock."

"Then you haven't anything to worry about," Eve countered.

"Oh, but there was more," the porter interrupted with sudden importance. "Unexploded bomb in Council House Street. I hear they had to evacuate all from Pencester Road right down to Saxon Street."

"That's just the sort of thing that would have caught his eye," Sandra sighed. "Bloody journalist."

"Yes, but unexploded," Eve insisted.

"Only it didn't stay that way," the old man snorted. "Took out seven houses in the end, it did," he added sadly. "Think of it, seven 'ouses – all them folk 'omeless..."

* * *

216

Repairs had already been started on the boat and their new Packard was due to be installed the following morning; until that happened, there was little for him to do. So, with the evening to himself, Newman had set off to find his sister at HMS *Lynx*. Yet when he enquired at the Wrennery, she was not to be found. Most of the other ratings would be in *The Red Lion*, but the idea of filling himself with beer did not appeal. And neither did the damp streets of Dover, so Newman had rather dejectedly turned away and set off back to *Wasp* and an early bed.

The rain returned as he was heading down Snargate Street and the driver of a passing car slowed as if about to offer him a lift. But as soon as he looked up, the thing sped off, splashing him slightly as it went. As a result, when he finally arrived back at *Wasp*, he was in a hurry to get to his room, throw off his damp clothes and hit the sack. Tomorrow would be a long day; with luck, they would get the new mill installed and make a start on sorting the other two, while a sparks should be arriving in the afternoon to see to the electrics. He passed the sentry post with a nod to the man who had checked him out not forty minutes before and was making for the rear entrance – ratings not being permitted through the front doors – when a coarse whistle attracted his attention. He stopped and looked about but no one was in sight, then went to walk on when the sound was repeated. And it was at that point he noticed the neat figure standing next to a staff car.

"Is there a problem?" he asked, approaching cautiously.

"Not anymore," a feminine voice replied. "My engine was overheating, but you sorted that."

Newman grinned; starlight caught her face although the trace of ginger hair peeping under her hat was enough.

"I thought it was you in Snargate Street but didn't want to take a chance – there are such strange people about these days."

"And not all of them in cars," he agreed.

"Absolutely, and I have to take some papers to Folkestone. It's part of the Defence Area, so someone riding shotgun might come in handy."

"I wouldn't be allowed," Newman laughed.

"No one will know, and you're in uniform, so neither will they question," the girl countered. "Besides, I need my guardian angel protecting me, and you might come in handy if the car packs up."

"You did drain it out properly?" he insisted, suddenly serious.

"Yes, I drained it out," she sighed. "And flushed it through with clean water before fitting a brand-new water pump. Did it all by myself as well, you'd have been so proud!"

"And a new gasket?" he checked.

"Of course a new gasket," she confirmed. "Now are you coming or not?"

* * *

"Well if what you say is right, I don't see a problem," Bishop declared, but Jelly was not so certain.

"We're still taking a chance," he said. "There has to be another way."

"I still says take 'em on," Dowling added, flexing his young and slight frame. "There are us lot, and whoever else we can round up from the base. One old man and his son wouldn't stand a chance."

"There's more than just the two of them," Daly admitted. "I seen several at different times at his house. And they're tough nuts."

"Besides, we hit them and they'll only regroup, come back and hit us a good deal harder," Jelly added softly. "None of us will be able to walk about in Dover unless we're mob-handed."

"So why don't we just report them to the authorities?" Cook asked. "What they're doing is illegal, even without trying to touch Paddy for information."

"Yes, and see our mate put in jankers," Dowling mocked. "And the debt would still be there."

"Then it's what I said," Bishop again. "We all go and place our bets. When the horse comes in, we pay off what Paddy owes and all will be sorted."

"But you're assuming it will win," Jelly was starting to get frustrated. "Forgive me Pad, but if you're such a brilliant judge of horseflesh, you wouldn't be in this mess to begin with."

"No, it can't lose," Daly insisted. "I got a tip from my cousin from Killarney; if my credit was good with Remer, I would be betting on it anyway."

"Can't lose?" Jelly questioned. "But you said yourself, it was a steeplechase; I'm no expert on the horses but have seen enough Grand Nationals to know there's no such thing as a certainty."

"Last time I bet on the National my horse got shot," Dowling grumbled quietly but Daly remained definite.

"Believe me, it can't lose," he said.

"So, how do we play it?" Bishop asked. "We can put our money down with your pal Remer – he gives a slate to servicemen, you say?"

"Yes, and if Pad's horse comes in last we'll all be in the same position he is," Jelly pointed out.

"And he'll smell a rat," Dowling added.

"And probably alter the odds, so he will," Daly agreed.

"So we divides," Bishop decided, taking control again. "There are a dozen places in Dover that will take a bet; we each go to a different one at the same time. Paddy needs to clear fifty guineas and if it's going to be nine to one, we each have to raise thirty shillings for our stake."

"That'll pay out a sight more than fifty guineas," Jelly told them.

"So we go on a spree afterwards," Bishop shrugged as if it were the logical conclusion. "Come on, we can all find thirty bob. And if it's to help a mate..."

Put like that they could only agree, although Jelly at least still had doubts.

* * *

Buckland Hospital was only in Union Road; they found it easily and within half an hour of being referred to the main Bridge Street ARP Depot, the girls were sitting on metal chairs in a sterile corridor. Both were in uniform but neither felt particularly smart and Sandra was having to control a regular sob that had been plaguing her since they heard the news.

"If only I'd known," she repeated. "I've had such terrible thoughts, and all the time Dale were lyin' in t'ospital."

Eve made no reply; there appeared to be nothing she could say that Sandra would accept and now felt it better not to bother. Instead, her mind began to wander as she took in her surroundings. The walls of the corridor were painted dull green and yellow, with a thick band of brown dividing the two at waist height. There were no pictures, no flowers, nothing to dilute the sense of austere efficiency that prevailed throughout. Even the nurses, bustling to and fro with set expressions and tired eyes, seemed wholly fixated on their current task, with none of the banter and chit-chat she was used to in her work. Christmas was fast approaching yet there were no signs of decorations; the impression of dedicated competence was almost daunting, and she felt quite humbled.

"Miss Duncan?" a man in a white coat had approached, unnoticed, and now stood over them. Eve jumped and Sandra rose slightly in her seat.

"I'm her," she said.

"You're here about this morning's casualty?" he confirmed.

"Dale," she agreed weakly.

"My name's Johnston, I'm the junior registrar," he announced. "I've been looking after him for most of the day. Actually, we're grateful; until you came we weren't sure exactly who he was – we could find no identification."

"Dale Peale," she said. "He's an American; a reporter."

"I see, and you are a friend, perhaps?"

"She's his fiancée," Eve announced when Sandra hesitated.

"Very well, and I suppose you want to know how he is." The doctor sat down next to them as two nurses wheeled a patient past on a trolley. "I'm sorry we have to talk out here; there really is no space. We've been at full capacity for well over a year now; ever since the raids began."

Eve noticed the man appeared quite young, hardly older than Billy in fact. He had fair hair that was clean but hadn't been combed in ages. And nice eyes; the left one twitched slightly when he talked.

"Mr Peale has serious head injuries," he continued. "We're not sure how extensive at the moment but are very concerned."

"But he's going to be all right," Sandra stated.

"That we cannot say, not at the moment. He's very ill and," he paused, "and frankly Miss Duncan, even if he pulls through, things may not be quite the same. You have to prepare yourself for that."

"I understand," she said slowly. "I understand and I don't mind." Her eyes sought the doctor's, imploring. "I'll take him back however he is. Just make him better."

Chapter Seventeen

"Brooks wants us out in an MTB, Number One," Harris told him. It was several days later and they had already been on three patrols with vessels from their own flotilla. All were completed without any real incident, but Anderson still learned a lot as, he suspected, did Harris. And there was no doubt all three crews now knew, and possibly understood, their senior officer a little better.

"An MTB?" Anderson repeated. He had trained and exercised aboard torpedo boats while at *St Christopher*'s but couldn't remember setting foot aboard one since.

"They've just taken delivery of the first two with radar," Harris continued. "Brooks wants all flotilla SOs to get acquainted with the new technology in case we're ever similarly blessed."

"I see, well, that sound fine, when can we go?"

"Tonight, if you're up for it." Harris gave a rare smile. "There's an assignment scheduled; briefing in Ops in twenty minutes."

"Wouldn't miss it, sir," Anderson confirmed. His only commitment that night was to visiting Peale in the hospital with Eve, but she was bound to understand and Peale, still being unconscious, wouldn't know any better.

"Fine, then we may as well get along there now."

"I need to make a telephone call first," Anderson said.

"Then I'll see you later. But don't be late – I get the impression we'll be going after Jerry in a big way."

"And it'll be a change to be carrying torpedoes," Anderson mused before realising Harris was looking at him sternly.

"Oh, don't get me wrong," he added quickly. "I'm a firm believer in gunboats. But a torpedo is definitely a step up; they're weapons that can really make a difference."

* * *

And despite Harris' reaction, once he surveyed the boat that was to carry them Anderson knew he was right. It was one of the latest Vospers, though fitted with the same three Packard engines that powered *194* and, being very slightly longer, would probably not be quite as fast. The guns she carried were less substantial as well;

a turret of Vickers point fives amidships and two single Browning 303s set to either side of the bridge. But what really counted, what made all the difference in the world, were the twin twenty-one-inch torpedoes she carried; their presence placed the tiny craft into the true ship-killing category.

They lay amidships, one to either side of the superstructure, and were a work of art in themselves. Anderson's mind ran back to his training; each would be powered by a four-cylinder radial engine fed by compressed air and would be capable of running at speeds of over forty knots. Only the previous month it had taken a single hit from a similar weapon to sink the twenty-two thousand ton *Ark Royal*, and the forty ton boat he was about to board was equipped with two.

"I believe we have met before," the lieutenant commander announced when he was shown up to the bridge. Harris was already there and standing next to the officer who did indeed look familiar, although Anderson could not quite place him.

"Conway," the man announced taking pity on him and extending a hand. "Picked you up from that German rescue buoy a while back – radar found you in the fog."

"Of course, sir," Anderson hurriedly agreed.

"We were only testing our little toy then, of course, but now they've given me a set of my own, and a new boat to use it on."

"And it looks very impressive. One of the new Vospers, I believe?"

"Only a foot or so longer than *194*," Harris interrupted. "But I'm amazed at what they've been able to pack in."

Anderson could only agree; from the little he had seen on his way up, the wheelhouse was almost a third bigger while the bridge where they currently stood might have graced a small destroyer.

"But the beauty of it is the radar," Conway explained proudly. "We've got the 286, which I think will become standard. Once you've experienced it you'll wonder how you ever got anywhere without one. You'll be shadowing my number one," he added directly to Anderson. "And if you're not screaming out for a set of your own by the end of the night, I'll be amazed."

"I'm looking forward to it," Anderson assured him although inside he wondered if that were really the case. It was one thing being shown something that made your life easier; quite another to be told you couldn't have one of your own.

"Boat has a complement of eleven ratings," Harris was obviously already enamoured with the craft and had no reservations.

"And all are necessary," Conway confirmed. "Fewer dedicated gunners than you, of course, but we need torpedo chappies instead and there's a PO to look after the set. Why don't we go down and I'll introduce you? I expect we'll come across my number one as well; he knows almost as much and can give you the low down: I know you'll be impressed."

* * *

"So how do you find Lieutenant Commander Conway?" Anderson asked the first officer a little later. They were in the wheelhouse and had been examining the radar, which truly was an impressive piece of equipment. And Anderson had immediately taken to Stidwell; he was of his own age and rank, and yet another RNVR officer. The two had a lot in common, in fact, including serving under captains from the regular navy.

"Well enough," he said after considering for a moment. The petty officer who usually looked after the set was visiting the heads so they were alone and could speak in relative privacy. "The initial impression might be all RN and pusser, but he isn't quite as stuffy, not when you get to know him." He chuckled briefly. "Sometimes I think the old boy might even be mellowing."

"Must be hard for the regulars," Anderson mused. "They look after the Navy throughout the quiet times then, when war breaks out, a bunch of amateurs come along and take over."

"I wouldn't exactly say take over, but we must outnumber them."

"By quite a long way," Anderson agreed. "Certainly in Coastal Forces."

"And how is it with Harris?" Stidwell asked and now it was Anderson's turn to smile.

"Roughly the same," he said. "At first I thought we'd never get on, but somehow he seems to have grown on me."

* * *

It was a novel experience for Harris to find himself aboard a boat on active service yet effectively unemployed and, he had to admit, not an unpleasant one. And, after his recent experiences, equally fascinating to watch how Conway organised his flotilla. The man was older and undoubtedly more experienced than him, and decidedly relaxed in the way he handled the other commanding officers, yet from what he could judge after overhearing conversations on the R/T repeater, each gave back just as much respect as they would a positive tyrant, and possibly a good deal more.

One of the boats had been forced to turn back when they were no more than a mile out. It was, as Conway explained, a persistent problem and one that could be blamed on the Vospers originally being intended for very different engines. The design had been altered to allow them to carry American Packards, but it was not a happy union and knowing that made Harris feel a little better about his own craft. *194* might be smaller in both size and crew and, however powerful her gunnery, would never compete with torpedoes – weapons that could deliver high explosives deep into the very heart of an enemy, yet Elco boats were proving extremely reliable, it being rare for them to fail for any reason other than enemy action. The mission was continuing with four boats, which meant there were still eight torpedoes to hurl at any unsuspecting German, and Harris was unashamedly looking forward to the experience.

Their target was a convoy; Dover Command had tracked it throughout the previous night and, when last recorded, the small cluster of shipping had taken refuge in Boulogne. But the three merchants and seven escorts were expected to continue their northward journey that evening and the four remaining MTBs had plans to meet it.

At first, seven escorts had seemed a reasonable number for the small force to take on, before Harris remembered they were not gunboats; MTBs carried considerably less than half the firepower he was used to with nothing approaching a twenty-millimetre cannon – to his mind the very minimum needed to challenge an E-boat. But then there would be no necessity to move in close; MTB tactics were very different to those of a gunboat. A torpedo could run for more than seven thousand yards and, though its effective range was considerably less, tonight would be nothing like the close-quarter fighting he was used to. And it occurred to him then that there must be some mileage in combining the two classes of launch; if gunboats were involved, perhaps to confront the escorts and create a diversion – something to allow the MTBs to take up position in relative safety – it would surely make for a more efficient attack. There may be reasons why such tactics were impractical of course, and doubtless the next few hours would tell him more, but it was definitely something to think about.

"I notice the Met. Office got it wrong again," Conway commented from his side of the bridge, "but it's good to have a spell of dry weather." Indeed, the rain that had been forecast was holding off and it was relatively warm for a December night. The moon had yet to rise but there were enough stars alight to give reasonable visibility.

"How long to rendezvous?" Harris asked and Conway gave a self-satisfied smirk.

"No idea," he admitted. "And with radar on board I have little need to find out. My number one will doubtless tell me in due course and the information will be far more up to date than anything we used to get from Dover. In fact, I think that's him now."

So saying he turned as Stidwell clambered up from the wheelhouse with Anderson close behind.

"We have the convoy on the set, sir; they're about five miles to the south-east and heading our way at just under ten knots."

"How far from the coast are they?" Conway asked with obvious pride.

"I'd say three miles, and we're about double that."

"There you are Captain, the wonders of radar," Conway announced, and Harris could not help but be impressed.

"And it's more than that," Anderson told him softly as Conway began to talk with his first officer. "This isn't a bad night and we might have had no difficulty in finding Jerry in the normal way. But think what could be done in a storm."

"Even then, would it be possible to dig them out?" Harris asked.

"Oh yes," Anderson confirmed. "I'm told the jigs show up on the set as plain as day even in heavy weather."

"The what?"

"Jigs," Anderson repeated innocently. "It's what they call identifying marks on the radar screen." Harris continued to look mildly disgusted, but Anderson continued unabashed. "If this were a gunboat action in the midst of a thunderstorm, we could still come right up and just start firing. And unless they were using radar as well, no one would be expecting us."

"And what about tonight?"

"Tonight it will be roughly the same but, being a torpedo attack, we need not come anything like as close. As far as I can see, we'll still be appearing from out of the darkness and should vanish just as easily."

"While at all times keeping track of our own boats," Harris

remarked, his mind running on.

"Exactly. If radar is being issued to small craft, we simply have to get it; even a set aboard one boat in the flotilla would make all the difference."

"It's all right, Number One," Harris snorted. "I'm convinced."

* * *

An hour later the four MTBs were lying cut about three hundred yards apart and in an increasingly ragged line abreast. Harris and Conway were still on the bridge and the convoy was in sight but barely visible in the rising moon. They were off the starboard bow but too distant for a torpedo to reach with any hope of accuracy, although just seeing the vague outlines made their target somehow more real. Beneath them, in the wheelhouse, Anderson and Stidwell would have a far better view on the radar's glowing screen. Conway leaned forward and spoke down one of the brass voice pipes.

"Start up and engage the Ford, Chief," he said before turning to Harris. "We've a V8 that can be coupled to our main drive," he explained. "Won't give much more than six knots but it's pretty near silent and just what we need in situations like this."

Harris nodded; such a thing would be of more use in an MTB and could hardly have fitted in *194*'s cramped engine room, yet still he felt undeniable pangs of jealousy.

"Make to the other boats, Tel'," Conway was at the voice pipes again. "Follow me under auxiliary power."

"You're not worried about Jerry intercepting your R/T?" Harris checked.

"Why should I?" Conway asked with a disarming smile. "They have no idea where we are, and if a couple of escorts are sent to investigate, we'll be out of here before you can say 'abort attack'."

That also made sense, although Harris was able to take some consolation; such an attitude would never suit a gunboat commander.

"Twenty-one-inch torpedoes are a lot more expensive than the old eighteens," Conway expanded further. "One costs as much as a Rolls-Royce motor car and is about as complex; such things cannot be wasted."

Again, Harris reminded himself it was a constraint that hardly affected him. He had never gone into action with any consideration to the financial aspect, even if the expense of

Conway's weapons momentarily shocked him. But he quickly rationalised the latter; whatever their price, and even if it took two torpedoes to sink a small coaster, the merchant would be worth many times more, so they might even be considered economical. A movement from below caught his attention and Anderson could be seen clambering up the short ladder.

"Enemy are continuing as before," he announced, then glanced across their starboard bow. "But I guess you can see that."

"I guess we can, Mr Anderson," Conway agreed with a wry smile.

"You'll have to excuse my first officer," Harris snorted. "He mixes a lot with Americans."

All three laughed politely but in Anderson's case it was slightly forced. Being reminded of Peale brought on a pang of guilt. It was past the time when he and Eve had intended to visit. When last seen the American had looked far from well and Anderson secretly doubted he would make any form of recovery.

"Auxiliary engine, Number One," Harris explained, cocking his ear to the faint rumble from below. "That will be another for your wish list."

"Sits between the wing engines, or so I understand," Anderson agreed. "I doubt we'd have the space."

"They'll be giving boats of this size to you boys shortly," Conway assured them. "And they'll be able to carry heavier guns along with something decent forward-facing. Believe me, you'll never want to go back to your old seventy-footer."

Harris and Anderson exchanged glances; they had expected to learn a lot from the night's activities but not become quite so disheartened.

* * *

Considerably less than an hour later all was in place. The four boats had crept forward and were now a scant two miles from the projected path of their enemy — something that had been far easier to calculate using the marvels of radar, as Conway had gone to great lengths to explain. For the rain was finally falling and the German convoy, though now considerably closer, was slowly dissolving into a series of faint smudges that could barely be made out amid a sea topped with low lying cloud.

"Couldn't ask for more!" the MTB captain exclaimed, smacking his hands together as if a lifetime's ambition had been fulfilled. "We'll drop our fish and be off before the Hun even know anyone's about!"

"One of the enemy escorts is altering course, sir!" the rating by the starboard Browning announced just as a whistle came from the wheelhouse voice pipe.

"Very well, Number One, I am aware," Conway sighed as he spoke into the tube. "Ask Tel' to signal the others to follow my lead; I'd like to get just a little closer if possible." He moved across to the second speaking tube. "Crash start, Chief," he said, "and prepare to give us maximum revs."

The scream of three starter motors was followed by a hesitant cough from the MTB's main engines and the entire boat began to vibrate.

"Torpedoes are best launched at a speed of twelve knots," Conway declared over the row. "Any faster, or slower, and they take a while to settle to their optimum depth. My chaps will spread out and get as close as they can, that way it shouldn't mean we all go for the same target. As soon as everyone's in range, we'll cut back to a thousand rpm. Then, once our fish are in the water and running, turn about, still at low speed, before packing everything on and high-tailing it out of here."

Harris nodded; the plan sounded reasonable – impressive even, as had everything heard so far that night.

"Open her up, 'Swain," Conway ordered as he pressed the firing bell, and the petty officer at the helm obediently brought the throttles forward. But something was wrong, Harris sensed it, even before the coxswain turned to his captain.

"Beggin' your pardon, sir, we only got the two motors," the petty officer reported.

"Two?" Conway questioned, while firmly presenting his back to his visitors.

"Centre and starboard are fine, but not getting anything from the port; it just didn't pick up."

Conway seethed slightly. "Never mind," he said looking up but still not turning around. "The rest seem to be taking the lead."

That was indeed the case; the other MTBs – two to port and one to starboard – were fast disappearing into the night and, even at its lesser speed, the German convoy was coming into clearer view from Conway's craft.

"Do your men need permission to fire?" Harris asked, and Conway jumped slightly as if surprised at being addressed.

"There's not the need," he answered quickly. "My COs are experienced and know exactly where to place their fish. And I suppose it is possible we won't get the chance to follow them."

Harris noticed the man glancing longingly at the engine room speaking tube, clearly desperate to speak to his motor mechanic. But those below would be aware of the stalled engine and must be doing all they could to start it – having their captain interrupt for an explanation would hardly help matters.

"E-boat closing on the starboard bow!" the same lookout reported suddenly as he shouldered his weapon. Harris drew breath; the range of a 303 Browning was less than five hundred yards and, even if it were to reach, little impact would be made on a speeding E-boat.

"Very well, we'll have to drop out from the attack," Conway spat before leaning forward to the W/T office speaking tube. "Tell the others to carry on without us, Tel', we're having to turn back." Then, to the petty officer at the helm, "Take her about 'Swain."

The boat heeled dramatically as she was brought round and both Harris and Anderson were soaked by a sudden deluge of spray.

"What of the others?" Harris shouted.

"They'll do all right without us," Conway was almost sulking now.

"Will they engage the E-boats?"

"They shouldn't, MTBs don't have the firepower. But with all engines running, and in this filthy weather, it ought to be easy enough to give them the slip."

That was reasonable, although the sudden turn had not deterred their own inquisitive German. The E-boat had settled on their tail and was definitely gaining. A flurry of green tracer passed overhead and was followed by the staccato rattle of the torpedo boat's aft-mounted Vickers. Fire from the half-inch machine gun might silence the German gunners for a moment, but the enemy craft must be doing more than forty knots, whereas Harris guessed they could only be touching twenty-five. He looked at Anderson in concern; what had begun as a demonstration of an advanced craft packed with the very latest technology was quickly turning into something highly dangerous.

"Prepare smoke floats!" Conway's voice on the tannoy echoed about the small craft and two torpedo ratings made their way aft to the CSA canisters. There was a clatter as the firing bell sounded again, this time to stop any further action from the gunners and then, at a wave from the captain, both floats were dropped over the stern.

Harris was watching Conway carefully; he knew the instinctive reaction was to turn as soon as the grey-white smoke began issuing from the canisters, but for the subterfuge to work properly a little patience was called for and he hoped the torpedo boat's captain knew this. Fortunately it seemed Conway did; they kept to the same heading until the cloud of smoke had grown considerably and was roughly equidistant between them and the pursuing enemy.

"Very well, right standard rudder!" The boat turned and picked up speed but, before she had truly settled, Conway ordered her round to port and in an even sharper turn. And it was then, as they straightened out and most were looking back at the dense cloud that now totally hid the enemy, that the third engine finally rumbled into life.

"Thank the Lord for that," the coxswain muttered as he adjusted the throttle and the boat surged forward under the extra power.

"Well you might not have seen us at our best," Conway admitted as he regarded his two visitors once more.

"Engine trouble would seem to be a major issue," Harris commented.

"It is a problem with the mounting – amongst other things," Conway grimaced. "Vospers were designed around the Hall-Scott engine. Everyone's been working on modifications and things are improving, though a few teething problems remain."

Harris nodded: he understood entirely. The M4-2500 Packard was a splendid engine but, in the rush to get the craft operational, corners may have been cut. And rather than ensuring the boats and their power units were thoroughly matched, it seemed they were being sent straight into action. He thought back to his own flotilla; most of the craft were British Powerboat seventy footers which had also been designed specifically for the American engine. In the last eight patrols there had only been one instance of failure and that was swiftly rectified.

He caught Anderson's eye and the two exchanged a private smile; whatever the advantages of radar, torpedoes and the larger hull that carried them, they would be pleased to return to *194*. And the sooner the better.

Chapter Eighteen

The time actually came faster than either of them could have hoped for. Two days earlier than expected, and still more than a week before Christmas, *MGB 194* was released from the dockyard and returned to active service.

"New engine seems fine, sir," Carter reported as he wiped his hands on an equally oily rag. "It's barely run in."

"And the switchboard?" Harris questioned, bending low in the engine room's cramped space. The motor mechanic shrugged.

"All up and running," he replied, then grinned. "That's the thing about electrics, mostly they're working or they're not."

Harris nodded in return; he probably should have expected such an answer from a mechanical engineer. "Fine, well we'll be taking her out for her sea trials shortly, I expect to know a bit more then."

"I guess so, sir," Carter agreed cheerfully, only wondering slightly why the captain appeared to react oddly to his words.

"Dockyard seems to have got rid of the smell of petrol," Anderson interjected quickly, and Carter turned to him.

"Yes, that's all gone now," he agreed. "Though me and Newman gave the bilges a final flush through with detergent, just to be sure."

"Newman does quite a lot," Anderson remarked.

"He does indeed, sir," Carter agreed. "I'd be lost without him. Geoff Pickering as well, of course, but Bill especially."

"He's a leading stoker now," the captain mused. "Not much I can do in recommending him for promotion, unless he were to transfer, of course."

"That might be best for him – for his career, I mean," Carter clarified. "Though I'd be sorry to see him go. And I think he's happy here."

Harris scratched at his head. Though there had undoubtedly been changes in the past few months, it still came almost as a shock to hear any man was actually happy under his command.

"And I know he wouldn't want to move from Dover," Carter added.

"Made friends around here has he?" Anderson asked.

"Not friends as such," the motor mechanic gave a knowing smile. "Actually just the one, but I gather it's serious."

* * *

"Tomorrow?" the girl, whose name was Sophie, exclaimed. "But I thought you'd be off at least until the weekend."

Newman shrugged. "Boat's back in commission so all leave ends," he said. "We're due to start sea trials; nothing I can do about it."

"But I've barely seen you!" she protested, and Newman noted how her eyes screwed up delightfully when mildly cross.

"We've had some good times," he reminded her.

"When you weren't tending your bloody boat," Sophie replied with a pout that was equally attractive. "I don't know why they bothered sending her to the dockyard, you could have sorted everything out on your own, given the chance."

They were in the Italian Tea Rooms off Market Square; it had become their favourite haunt and the owners, who seemed as British as anyone, had quickly taken to them and usually found something special for the couple's regular visits.

"I haven't just been on the boat," Newman claimed. "We've come here enough times, and there was that walk along the cliffs. And I sorted out the heater in your car. Besides, you've mainly been on duty yourself so there wasn't much else for me to do."

"I know, but I've got forty-eight hours off from tomorrow," she sighed. "I was looking forward to spending them with you."

"There'll be other times," he assured her, while secretly sharing the disappointment. "What about Christmas?"

"Do they give you lot Christmas off then?" she asked, her face brightening.

He laughed. "Not exactly, but I doubt there'll be any convoys running – so nothing to protect. And I get the impression the Germans like a bit of a knees-up as much as we do."

"Well I didn't put in for leave as such; there didn't seem any point, not until now. But I can change that – I'll get as much time off as I can, and we'll get together then."

"Only a week or so away," he agreed, pleased beyond measure that he had already gained importance in her life.

"So, will you be going out again?" Sophie asked more

cautiously.

"How do you mean?"

"On patrol, or whatever you call it," her voice was lower now and he tensed slightly. In the short time they had known each other neither had asked much about their respective jobs. He understood she was a driver and carried most of the senior officers at *Wasp*, and she obviously knew him to be gunboat crew, but that was all.

"Active service means active service," he replied enigmatically.

"And you don't know where, or when?"

Now he was definitely worried. Even without the warnings about keeping mum, Newman never discussed his work in detail with anyone, even Eve. And however he felt about Sophie, he had no intention of spilling any beans to her.

"Why are you asking?" his voice was suddenly hard and she looked away.

"It's not what you think," she replied. "I don't want to know, not really. I just heard something."

"Something?"

"In the car," she looked back and her eyes were troubled. "It was this morning. A lot of the officers talk when they're in the back; they don't think about their driver – sometimes I wonder if they even know they have one."

"And what did you hear?" Newman asked, before realising he was starting to sound a bit dubious himself.

The middle-aged woman who did all the cooking swept past their table and surreptitiously dropped a warm scone onto Sophie's plate before bustling away. Both automatically looked up in wonder and thanks, and Sophie immediately cut it in two and handed a piece, still steaming, across.

"There's only a dab of jam and no butter, would you like some marge?"

Newman shook his head; the thing was glorious enough on its own.

"You were going to tell me what you heard," he reminded her when they finished.

"I was not!" she replied, firmly, then softened slightly. "But it wasn't good, Bill. I'm not sure what's happening at Christmas, but something big looks likely to blow up before. And if you're going straight back to active service, it sounds like you're going to be involved."

"We've sea trials first," he assured her. "After repairs

233

they're customary; it would have to be something massive to interrupt them."

But Sophie wasn't convinced. "I think it might be," she said. "And you should be careful."

* * *

Soon it became clear that others were not being quite so cautious with their news. By that evening, when *194*'s ratings were preparing for the following day's sea trials, there was quite a buzz going around the room they shared.

"Word is the Germans are planning a big push," Bishop claimed as he lay back on his metal-framed bed. "An' I say, let 'em come."

Wasp was one of the best billets any of them had been in; the room contained ten beds but, because their coxswain and motor mechanic were petty officers and there were only seven actual seamen, they had far more space for themselves. The heads were also only next door and, though a wireless was not allowed, there was music; some boffin had rigged up speakers in all the ratings' accommodation through which records were played until lights out. Most were old – the last three had been Lew Stone's band and featured Al Bowlly, whose star had been on the wane even before the singer was killed in an air raid earlier in the year. But music of any kind made the place more homely and they were quite satisfied.

"What, do you mean an invasion?" Cook asked.

"Hardly likely," Jelly assured them from his bed. "All that's behind us now the Yanks are coming into the war."

"They didn't think Force Z would be destroyed, but the Japs still got 'em," Bishop sniffed. "Only good the Yanks have done so far is to land us with another enemy."

"I still don't think the Germans are coming," the telegraphist replied coolly as he turned the page in his novel. "Even Hitler's not that stupid."

"What then, heavier air raids?" Bishop again.

"Wouldn't affect us much." Pickering this time. The stoker had spent most of the day tuning up the new engine and had just returned from scrubbing at his fingers, which now looked more raw than clean. "Most times they come at night and we're usually at sea."

"Aye, safest place," Jelly agreed with a wry look.

"Well, shelling then?"

Bishop was doubtful. "Can't see that stirring up the top brass, and them's the ones what seem most concerned."

"Where did you hear all this?" Newman asked. Of all present, he probably had the most reason.

"Base captain's called for a senior officers' meeting tomorrow morning," Bishop told him.

"Nothing unusual in that."

"No, but it's for every flotilla," the seaman gunner insisted. "Whatever they're planning's going to call for all the boats we got. And we all know how quickly ours was rushed off the slip."

"We've yet to do our sea trials," Jelly pointed out.

"Hardly likely to now, neither," Bishop countered.

"An' there was me hoping we wouldn't be going out again this side of Christmas," Pickering sighed.

"Maybe we won't," Jelly suggested. "They might just be sorting stuff out for the new year."

"No, there's more to it than that." Bishop was positive. "There's been more cars comin' an' going the last day or so than we usually see in a week. It's like Churchill was making another visit."

"Maybe he is an' all," Cook suggested.

"Give it a rest," Pickering hissed. "We've not got over the last time."

"Well, at least we got the bets on. We 'ave, 'aven't we?"

There was a series of grunts to Dowling's question and Pickering looked around.

"What bets will they be?" he asked.

"We got a consortium," Dowling announced importantly. "*Noted Fox*, in Saturday's 2.30."

"First I heard of it," the stoker grumbled, glancing over to Newman who also shook his head. "Stokers not included then?"

"It's not as it sounds, Picky," Jelly claimed. "We decided when your lot were working on the boat. Paddy's got himself into an 'ole, so we're digging him out."

"Got a tip for the meeting at Killarney," Bishop added. "Should bring in enough to sort matters and give us a decent wet after."

"Aye, all betting on the same horse at the same time," Dowling added knowingly. "That way we keeps the odds high."

"It would have been nice to be included," Pickering muttered as he picked up an old copy of *The Daily Mail*."

"Still can," Bishop supposed. "Nothing to stop you joining in. As Mikey says, once Pad's paid off we're pooling the rest for a proper bender."

"And you're assuming it will win," Newman pointed out as he stood up; it was his turn to do battle with the grease and the job had taken on far greater importance since Sophie entered his life.

"Oh, it will win," Daly assured them. "There can't be any doubt about that."

* * *

Peale was alone when he died and many miles from the place he loosely referred to as home, but that was not to say his passing caused no ripples. Sandra was the first to hear; at Eve's insistence she had registered herself as his next of kin and a message arrived in the small office where she worked at HMS *Lynx*. She took the news surprisingly well, even to the extent of finishing her watch, and some of the other girls hardly guessed at the enormity of what had happened.

But then neither did she fully comprehend the news. All of Dover Command had descended into what was customarily referred to as a flap; the number of coded messages to and from Bletchley Park doubled and a stream of high ranking officers descended from the recently opened Coastal Forces HQ at London's Wendover Court. The sudden increase in work even affected writers in the welfare department; Eve, who was still awaiting news of her application to the nearby Y Station, was suddenly in demand for her German language skills and relocated to a dusty office in *Wasp*. There she was placed under the command of a severe middle-aged chief officer who viewed her good looks and obvious abilities with suspicion and allocated a series of mundane duties that bore no reference to the latter.

Robbed of her friend and with an increased workload, Sandra was able to throw herself into the job and it was only later, when she finally met up with Eve in the institutionalised domesticity of their shared room, that she began to crumble. But even then her tears were dry and restrained and, though distraught, some control was retained, even if she was obviously in a highly dangerous state.

"Look, I can get hold of the PMO," Eve suggested.

"He'll be off b'now," Sandra mumbled. Though fully clothed she was in bed and lying on one side, knees to chin and a thumb pressed firmly into her mouth. "Anyways, I don't want to see no doctor – they couldn't do nuthin' for Dale."

"But they might help you," Eve insisted sitting next to her. "Maybe find something to ease the pain a bit – there are some wonderful pills nowadays."

"I don't need owt, or anyone," her friend declared. "Never have and never will."

"Well that's fine, but you aren't just thinking for yourself now." Even as she spoke Eve realised her words might be misconstrued, but Sandra seemed to take them at face value.

"A few tears won't hurt my bairn," she mumbled defiantly. "Probably best it gets used to me blubbin' a bit. Won't be the last time, not judging by the life it's going to have."

"That will do," Eve told her firmly. "I can't begin to imagine what you're going through but know for certain thinking that way won't help."

"But I'm pregnant," Sandra wailed, turning to look at her. "And him what done it has pegged out."

"Yes, and it is terrible. But you're not alone: I'm with you and will stick by whatever. And you're still a Wren – that is the case isn't it?"

Sandra nodded silently, turned back and replaced the thumb.

"So you have the Royal Navy behind you, and they look after their own."

"They won't want me, not when they know I've got a bun in the oven."

"Whatever happens you won't be abandoned; I'll see to that."

The words seemed to have some effect and the thumb was removed once more. Eve watched her carefully but with a degree of dispassion. For what she said was true, she could not imagine her pain but then neither could she understand the attraction of living in America, nor how a sensible girl like Sandra could have let herself get into such a predicament in the first place. But this was not the time to be a prude or start wagging admonishing fingers; the problem was clear and, empathy or not, she would help her to a solution. Though despite her resolution, she remained slightly surprised at one aspect of Sandra's reaction; there appeared no real remorse at losing the man himself.

* * *

The rumours continued to circulate throughout the base and opinions varied between a German invasion to Dover Command being expanded, amalgamated or even demobilised, but all was explained the following morning at the flotilla senior officers' meeting. Unusually this did not take place in the Ops Room at *Wasp*, instead a far smaller area had been made available at the Camber, near where their boats were moored, and those attending found themselves seated on a selection of swivel chairs that had obviously been borrowed for the occasion.

"You must forgive the arrangements," Brooks explained after he had called the meeting to order and given permission to smoke. He looked strained and preoccupied, but Harris was relieved to note the man was alone, with no brass hat from the Admiralty to confuse matters. "What we are about to discuss is of the utmost secrecy, consequently this building has been cleared. So you can rest assured no Wren writer will be missing her seat."

This was greeted by the expected laughter and a few ribald comments but when Brooks held up his hand for silence it came instantly.

"Some of you may have heard stories that the entire station is about to be placed on standby duty, and one reason I have called you here is to confirm that is indeed the case, as well as explain the reason. I shall not expect anything to be discussed with your men for the moment; even your COs and first officers must remain in the dark a while longer. When they are informed all outside 'phone lines and sentry posts will be closed down; in effect, no one will be allowed to leave here or *Wasp* and there will be no communicating with the outside world. Your first officers and men will be brought here by ferry; until then, I regret you are all my prisoners."

Again, there was a little light laughter, although no one felt the need to comment.

"First of all, I should assure you we are not expecting an invasion. Jerry has already been defeated in the air; for as long as we maintain control of our skies such a thing simply cannot happen. Besides, neither does he have the resources; the landing craft previously prepared have in the main been destroyed – something I believe a few faces present are partially responsible for. Put simply, we do not think he will try again for a considerable time. But that isn't to say he is not active."

Brooks cleared his throat and referred to a small piece of paper, but no one stirred and neither did they whisper; he had them totally.

"Currently there are capital ships in western French ports

that have been concerning us for some time. After causing a hell of a nuisance in the Atlantic, *Scharnhorst* and *Gneisenau* arrived in Brest back in March. They were followed by *Prinz Eugen* in early June – that was after she lost her chum, *Bismarck* – then *Seydlitz*, *Prinz Eugen*'s sister, joined them a few weeks later. Obviously, the Raff have been paying them attention and considerable damage has already been caused. I realise not all of us view our cousins in the air with any great affection, but I may say that, were it not for their intervention, both battlecruisers would have been able to join with *Bismarck*, and she would probably still be afloat. But that need not concern us for now; the main point is they are maintaining the pressure. Raids are set to continue on a nightly basis and it is understood at least two of them are unable to sail for the foreseeable future. Of the third we are not so sure but can be relatively certain the *Seydlitz* remains undamaged."

Disabling three ships out of four was not bad considering they were sheltering in one of the best defended and most densely camouflaged ports in occupied France, but it still meant a heavy cruiser was free to roam the oceans, which was hardly a pleasant prospect.

"Obviously the Germans will want her to remain safe and, with the current intensity of bombing, the best way of ensuring that is for her to move. And she may well go back into the Atlantic, although intel suggests a more northerly route is on Jerry's mind."

He paused, regarded them again, then drew breath.

"Consequently, all Coastal Forces bases are being brought up to a state of maximum alert and should be prepared to react instantly. The moment movement is detected from Brest we must prepare to sail and do battle. I don't need to tell you it would take little more than twelve hours for a heavy cruiser and her escorts to reach us here in Dover, so that is all the warning we are likely to get. And if they give our intelligence the slip and put out undetected, it might be a good deal sooner."

With the news delivered the tension had dropped slightly although there was still not a sound in the room.

"So that's about it," Brooks concluded. "Your target is a heavy cruiser – true David and Goliath stuff. Although I should point out that such a contest has been won in the past, and I'm not talking Bible stories!"

At this there was a ripple of restrained laughter; Brook's own exploits in the previous war were well known and he was universally respected for them. But what they had heard was still too shocking for anyone to be distracted for long.

"I assume there will be questions," the base captain added, and Harris noted his expression might almost be one of relief. An officer near the front raised his hand.

"Can I ask, sir, are we certain the *Seydlitz* will be heading our way? Surely another foray into the Atlantic is more likely?"

Brooks acknowledged this with a nod. "I'll not say such a thing is impossible," he allowed. "But we have good reason to think otherwise. At the moment it seems Hitler is more concerned with protecting Norway from invasion and we suspect he intends withdrawing all four ships to that station. I may add that it is partly to encourage such thoughts that much of our home fleet is currently at Scapa Flow, but that is neither here nor there. Obviously the fastest route to move such a force northwards is through the Channel, so there would be every point in making a dummy run, as it were, with a single vessel."

The answer was greeted in near silence as all individually digested the information and then, before many had finished, another man raised his hand.

"Will we be supported by any capital ships?"

This time it was the question that brought comment and Brooks sighed.

"As I mentioned, our home forces are mainly stationed at the Flow. In addition to the Norway question, they are there to defend against any appearance from *Tirpitz* as most of you know. And you should also be aware that *Tirpitz* is every bit as large as her late sister *Bismarck* and probably more up to date, so you can appreciate our concern. Our main forces may well become involved if *Seydlitz* makes it through to the North Sea but that is someone else's headache; we have to focus on the Strait. I should point out this is primarily an RAF and Fleet Air Arm show; the naval aspect will be minimal."

Now there was definite comment, and even a few raised voices but Brooks' rose above them.

"We will have destroyers, of course, and possibly something slightly larger, but they will be spread over a wide area. And as far as the Dover sector is concerned, it's down to you chaps."

The muttering continued even after a lieutenant commander raised his hand. It belonged to Conway, the officer who had so recently taken them on an MTB sortie.

"Is this expected to be a night operation, Commander?"

Apparently a fair question although one with an obvious answer that came without too much consideration.

"No," Brooks replied quickly. "We expect Jerry to leave in darkness, so if they are allowed to reach the Strait, it will be daytime when he arrives and you will be able to see him quite plainly."

"And he us," someone called from the back but there was no laughter.

Another hand was raised. "And what enemy escorts can we expect?"

Again, there was an obvious reply to this, but Brooks gave the question full weight.

"We should expect destroyers aplenty, plus E- and R-boats as well as anything else the Germans can rustle up."

He paused and considered them; there was silence and it was clear no more questions would be forthcoming.

"I must make it clear, gentlemen," Brooks continued, "we are not expecting miracles. But If *Seydlitz* is allowed to pass through unhindered, it will open the door for the others to follow. And should four capital ships be allowed to combine with the *Tirpitz*, it would be a force far larger than that faced when we took on the *Bismarck*. Consequently, I will be combining flotillas; you will all be given details but basically MGBs will be paired with MTBs, with the SO being the one with the greater seniority. If any of you can get close enough to launch an attack on *Seydlitz* herself, so much the better but, as I have said, we are not expecting miracles. Even a couple of escorts damaged would make an impression and possibly change Jerry's mind should it come to the others making a run for it.

"We will be directing operations from here as far as possible, but much will be up to you; on the front line, as it were. Be aware of aircraft; you can be certain the Germans will have extensive air cover, but our own planes will also be up. Again we will do our best to warn of individual raids, but some might come unannounced and it is essential your gunners are prepared, and able to tell friend from foe. And there will be shelling. Enemy batteries on the French coast are bound to lob a few bricks over their own ships in an attempt to wake us up, and we will be replying; so make sure you keep your heads down."

Now the laughter was more general and seemed almost relaxed, but then the concept of avoiding a fifteen-inch shell by ducking could never be taken seriously.

"If there is nothing more, my secretary will see all are given their appropriate pairings and you can repair to your boats. I would expect crews and first officers to be joining you shortly. We will ensure everyone is fed and watered, though I think you must prepare yourselves for something of a wait. But do bear in mind that Christmas is only around the corner and, when this little lot is over, I trust we can enjoy a peaceful one."

Chapter Nineteen

Anderson duly joined Harris an hour later and the rest followed shortly afterwards. None of them were strangers to standby duty, but neither did they welcome it. They were together and on board, yet the gunboat was not putting to sea, nor might she for several days, so no one was at their action stations. The engine room lay empty and almost cold, the only sound being the generator's gentle putter and with all guns under cover their crews had joined the rest in what was suddenly an unusually crowded mess deck. Anderson and Harris quickly took refuge in the wardroom where one tried to doze and the other read, while Price and Carter settled themselves in the wheelhouse and began what soon became a marathon chess tournament. With oil heaters hissing throughout it was warm enough although condensation quickly began to gather and, by the time their first meal was delivered, the deckheads were running with sweat. Then slowly the scent of burning paraffin combined with that of cigarette smoke and stored humanity to make a heavy fug that seemed at once comforting and utterly repugnant.

Certainly this was the case further forward where the seamen gunners mingled awkwardly with stokers in a space that was usually relatively empty. Jelly, being the only man present with no immediate colleagues, felt decidedly out of place although all found the conditions unsettling. At least when on standby duty in the past the weather had been fine but, with heavy rain ruling out any possibility of going on deck, no obvious way of entertaining themselves below and the prospect of a particularly nasty mission ahead, all were uneasy.

Their first meal had consisted of a pork pie salad followed by Chinese wedding cake – a glutinous mixture of rice, milk and raisins that was popular, if only on account of its ease of serving. All had been shared out fairly enough and eaten at a folding table placed between the twin couches that ran to either side of their space. But, with the food consumed, no one felt like clearing up nor making the obligatory mugs of tea. Instead the plates lay scattered in untidy heaps until Dowling, Cook and Bishop began a game of brag, when they were dumped unceremoniously onto the sole and, though there was a series of several less than subtle gasping noises and a number of eyes travelled to the small spirit stove, the kettle lay cold and unattended.

"Could do with a spot of music," Dowling muttered over his cards. "Any chance of the wireless, Wobbler?"

"No BBC I'm afraid," Jelly informed them from his place next to the door.

"But it's *Workers' Playtime!*" Dowling complained, glancing at his watch.

"Sorry, them's the rules," Jelly told him.

"Well can we not have that row turned off?" Cook asked, his eyes darting to the small speaker set in the deckhead above them. The only noise it gave out was a gentle hiss, with the occasional squawk to show all was not dead but even that, in such confined conditions, was beginning to annoy.

"Can't do that neither," Jelly sighed, and returned to reading his novel.

"Don't know why they're keepin' us in the dark so," Daly grumbled. He had curled up on the only bit of couch that was free but even then his stockinged feet pressed against Bishop's thigh. "It ain't as if we can do anything stuck out here."

"What do you think's happened?" asked Cook.

"Maybe the Krauts are invading?" Bishop suggested hopefully.

"Krauts are never invading." Pickering spoke with rare authority. "They're never coming, not now they knows what's waiting for 'em."

"What then?" Dowling this time.

"Just some sort of scare." Pickering again.

"We was 'aving them all the time in Pompey," Bishop added. "Confined to barracks, that sort of thing; played hell with leaves."

From his place next to Jelly, Newman's mind was running on similar lines. He was not due any time off and Sophie was bound to know what was going on so should hardly be expecting to hear from him. Yet he felt unusually cut off and almost guilty for not keeping in touch.

"Well we're not likely to get any papers," Daly supposed.

Bishop shrugged. "It don't seem so."

"Why d'ya want a paper?" Cook asked innocently.

"T' horses," Daly replied succinctly.

"Race ain't till tomorrow, Paddy," Pickering reminded him. "An' it's running in Ireland, so there might not be any report till the day after."

"Right," Cook agreed firmly in an effort to reassert himself.

"So it'll probably be Monday before we know; that's three days away. But if we had the wireless, we'd find out a lot sooner."

"No wireless," Jelly told them flatly without looking up and no one felt inclined to argue.

"Three days shut in this hole," Bishop grumbled after a while. "Hope they don't keep feeding us growlers."

"Aye, pork pie ain't the most sociable of meals," Newman agreed. "Not in the circumstances."

"Kicks up the wind something terrible, so it does," Daly observed.

"Not sure my stomach can take it," Pickering murmured, before sighing deeply.

"Not sure any of us can," Jelly added with feeling.

* * *

In the wardroom the atmosphere was slightly less overpowering, though no more optimistic.

"When are we able to tell the men?" Anderson asked from his position on the rarely used bunk. He had only recently discovered the reason for their enforced confinement and felt almost desperate to share it, if only to see how others would react.

"Blowed if I knows," Harris admitted from the small, hard couch. "Keeping the lower deck in the dark isn't exactly customary but then I suppose they don't want them dwelling on it. After all, what we're going to face will hardly be a pushover."

"If we are going to face it," Anderson pointed out. "I know what Brooks said, but there's still no guarantee Jerry will come our way."

"True enough," Harris agreed, glancing around the small cabin. The place seemed unusually dark and cramped and he had been wondering vaguely about taking a brisk walk. But rain continued to batter against the thin walls, and the entire boat constantly jerked against her mooring wires in the strong wind. "In which case all this hanging around will have been wasted," he added lamely.

Anderson nodded, closed his eyes once more, and tried to return to sleep. "Well, if they do change their mind, I won't hold it against them," he muttered softly.

"But even if not, it might not be as bad as Brooks made out," Harris pondered, more to himself than Anderson. "The sector they've given us is hardly large; Jerry will be gone before anyone knows it."

"And with air cover, we might not even get a look in," Anderson agreed distantly. "Besides, I still can't see gunboats doing much against a heavy cruiser."

"But we're there to support the torpedo boys," Harris pointed out.

"I guess so," the younger man began before waking slightly and correcting himself. "I mean, I'm sure you're right. And Conway's lot won't stand by and watch while such a target passes them by."

Conway, yes, Harris contemplated, that was another part of the equation. The man had several months' seniority over him so would be in overall command of both flotillas. Of course, the MGBs remained Harris' concern, but responsibility for the entire force lay elsewhere. And though Conway could hardly have been blamed for the engine trouble on their last show, Harris was not sure he entirely approved of the man's reaction to it, nor his attitude in general.

Voicing his concerns was not possible, however; it never did to discuss any officer with a junior man. Then it occurred to him that Anderson was also RNVR – what he used to consider an amateur sailor. The fact made little difference now though; he trusted his second in command more than any of his predecessors – more than most regular officers if it came to it. The thought that a former school teacher might achieve such a position would have been laughable a few months back. And there was something greater than trust; in a strange way, he respected the younger man.

For Harris was not blind to the way he appeared to others; his approach was undeniably direct, but it was a style that had been drummed into him during training as well as on his various deployments with other regular men. Now he supposed the attitude was as much a part of his personality as an ability to set a course by sight or shave in the dark, although that didn't make it easier to deal with. Yet Anderson had succeeded, and done so well enough to make his current command the happy ship she had become. And there was more, he now found he genuinely liked the fellow. Many of his methods might not be standard RN practice, and he would keep dropping those absurd American expressions into his conversation, but there was no denying his methods worked. And at times like this, when they were waiting to face what could be an invincible enemy, Harris sensed the warmth he felt was fully reciprocated.

"We've yet to complete our sea trials," Anderson muttered softly; the enforced idleness was finally taking effect and he was starting to fall asleep.

"Complete?" Harris laughed quickly. "We barely started! What was it, a quick run out to sight the guns in and see she's not taking in water!"

"All seemed smooth enough, though."

"Aye, all seemed smooth enough," Harris sighed. "And the crew did well. I reckon we've a good bunch."

"I guess so," Anderson agreed.

* * *

The afternoon slowly merged into a gloomy December evening then, seamlessly, a dark and troubled night. The gunners took up places in the bunks and hammocks rigged in the forecastle while Carter and Price chose the PO's mess. This was an area hardly bigger than a cupboard and indeed generally used for storage – they needed to remove several boxes and a drum of paraffin oil before moving into the airless space – and others chose less conventional places to rest. Both stokers decided to bed down in the engine room; an area more like home to them. Even the generator's gentle humming seemed fitting and soporific while the scent of engine oil and machinery was definitely preferable to that of the general ratings. And Jelly, too, chose his place of work. It would probably have been acceptable to use the adjoining wheelhouse as there was no space to lie flat in his tiny compartment. But Jelly could sleep in a chair as easily as any bed and the valves of his radio gave a warmth far cleaner than any from an oil stove. It would probably have been acceptable to turn the set off – they were in harbour, should an emergency arise it could be signalled in many other ways – yet he still felt more comfortable listening to the distant hiss of static through his headset, and it was while doing so that he gently dozed off. In fact, all slept well, even Harris, who had more reason than most to worry about forthcoming events. Only Anderson remained awake for any length of time although, following his afternoon nap, this was in no way an imposition.

For he was quite content; the bunk was small, even for his short frame, and there was barely room to turn without rubbing against the hard metal edge, but he was perfectly snug. And though his mind did occasionally stray to what the next day or two might bring, and some time was definitely spent on the loss of Peale, a man he had come to both like and respect, it was thoughts of Eve that filled most of his waking hours. For this was probably his first chance to take stock and properly consider their relationship and it came as a shock to realise they had known each other for so short a time. Only a matter of months in fact, although the rigours of war made it seem longer, and already he was starting to assume they would always be together.

Such a concept had not appealed before; Anderson could never have been considered a ladies' man: there had been other relationships in the past of course but none that matched the intensity he now felt for Eve. And, though he might have privately hoped to one day marry, never had the prospect assumed such importance or, as he now saw it, necessity. The expectation of taking a small, volatile and ultimately vulnerable wooden boat to meet the might of a heavy cruiser was, of course, daunting, but no more so than many encounters he had already survived, for a twenty-millimetre shell might account for him as easily as one far larger. And even if he survived the next few days – and Anderson was still youthful enough to make this an apparent certainty – there would be plenty more opportunities for the enemy to deal with him if that was to be his fate.

But in the early hours of the morning, in a cramped bed and with Harris snoring softly nearby, the young man had no thoughts for death, his outlook was far more optimistic.

* * *

They rose early as no one wished to remain abed in such dismal circumstances but, by the time dawn crept up on them, their conditions had already improved significantly. The changes were instigated by Anderson, although Price saw most of them through while thinking of a few more of his own along the way. All bedding was stowed along with bunks and hammocks, condensation was mopped up and as much fresh air as possible encouraged through the various vents and hatches. A rota was also drawn up for providing refreshments, washing crockery and distributing food as well as the less popular tasks of cleaning the heads, emptying waste buckets and topping up with paraffin and fresh water. And when the catering van arrived from *Wasp*, the scratch breakfast of porridge, bacon and bread almost brought a holiday atmosphere to the gunboat.

This was heightened by an equally agreeable change in the weather; during the night all traces of rain had disappeared and, in place of dark heavy cloud, a bright, if ineffectual, sun now shone amid a crisp blue sky. Encouraged by this, several crews from adjoining boats had gathered on the shingle shore. When joined by most from *194*, an improvised game of football began involving two unequal sides each containing ridiculously high numbers and, on occasions, two balls. By eleven, all had returned to the boat ready for the slabs of bread pudding the truck then delivered which were washed down by vast quantities of tea, necessitating an early filling of their freshwater tank. But once that was done, and with no prospect of entertainment until their next meal, a sense of unease broke out. Some began to fidget and there was almost an argument between stokers and seamen – a dormant threat in vessels of any size. Noticing this, Anderson spoke with Price.

"I'd like to keep everyone busy, but not obviously so," he explained quietly, and the petty officer nodded in understanding.

"We could 'ave another 'og out," he pondered, "give the old barge a bit of a birthday. 'Ave to be up top though, we've already seen to below an' no one takes kindly to the same task twice in a day."

"It's an idea," Anderson supposed. "Any others?"

The coxswain shrugged. "While we's on standby there ain't much else, not without desertin' the boat."

"What about some sort of quiz?"

"Might work within a mess," Price replied, uncertain. "Get a bunch of lads together what do the same job an' it's a dream. But what we got is specialists; gunners are about the only ones with the same abilities, them and the stokers, and there are only two of them."

"Seamanship skills then?" Anderson sighed.

"Still wouldn't work for the grease monkeys." He shook his head sadly. "They'll last a bit longer as they is, an' there's a meal due in an 'our or so, what will take up some time. Other than that, we can set the gunners to maintenance work; at least while this good weather lasts. Stokers can look after theirselves – stokers usually do..."

Anderson pursed his lips, that wasn't ideal, he would have preferred to have found them something more recreational, especially as they might be in action within a couple of hours. They were standing on the otherwise empty bridge. In the winter sunshine it was a pleasant place to be and for a while both had been vaguely conscious of movement ashore. A motorcycle had drawn up by the Camber buildings; probably a despatch rider from *Wasp* or maybe Dover Command itself, and those stalwarts still playing football on the hard were pestering the poor man for information. But instead he strode boldly on to one of the jetties and approached the first boat in another flotilla. Noticing this, Price turned to Anderson and gave a toothy grin.

"Though if you asks me, there's going to be movement enough presently, and no one'll be bored for long."

* * *

And Price was soon proved correct; Anderson had returned to the wardroom and was reporting what he had seen when there came a tap at the door.

"Tower's signalling us to stand to, sir," Jelly announced. "And there's been a load of other traffic on W/T, though none for us."

"What are they saying, Tel'?" Harris asked.

"Orders for departure," Jelly replied. "They're taking the early numbers and giving out places; I'd better get back and keep a check."

"Do that," Anderson agreed as there was further movement from outside, then Price pushed past the departing telegraphist with a thick Manilla envelope.

"This were just delivered from SOO, sir," he announced, holding the package out.

Harris took and opened it, then, after reading for no more than a few seconds, looked up and caught Anderson's eye. "Very well," he said. "I think it's time I addressed the men." He glanced at the petty officer. "Call them together will you 'Swain?"

Price touched his forehead briefly then left as well; Anderson looked to Harris.

"Shall I come?" he asked.

"No, Number One, I'd like to do this on my own," Harris told him. "Don't think I don't appreciate what you've done; we have a good crew and that's mainly down to your efforts in managing them."

"It's a first lieutenant's duty, sir," Anderson commented softly.

"Maybe so, but you've carried it out well, and frankly I'm glad of the chance to say so. But telling the men what they are about to face is a captain's job, and I think I should do it on my own."

* * *

Price duly called them to the mess deck on the tannoy and, when all had assembled, Harris appeared and took up position. He had yet to change into his seagoing rig so, in regular uniform and with one hand reaching up to the deckhead above, made an imposing figure as he surveyed his men. Most were not so smart but returned his glance readily enough and, for a moment, there was silence.

"These are orders for action," he told them finally, holding up the envelope in his other hand. "We'll be going out in a while, so it'll be a daytime job. And you can forget merchant convoys, either protecting them or attacking, we will be facing big guns; proper naval combat."

A few glances were exchanged, but no one felt the need to comment and Harris was struck by how accommodating they were when compared to those at the senior officers' briefing the day before. The men seemed ready to accept anything he said and act upon it, almost without question, which was especially strange considering he may be condemning some, or all, to their deaths.

"A German heavy cruiser is in the Channel and heading this way," he continued while considering each man's face individually and apparently impressing it upon his brain. "Last reports place her about eighty miles off, so we're going to have to move quickly. All serviceable Coastal Forces craft will be in action, both from this station and all along the South Coast, but we have a defined sector, so can ignore the rest at least in the initial stages. Our flotilla has been detailed to support MTBs and will be under orders from their SO although we may also be acting independently at my command. If the torpedo chaps can gain a favourable position, they will try for the capital ship, otherwise it'll be one of the escorts and we are going to react accordingly. There is expected to be heavy air cover, both from our own planes and the enemy's, and possibly a torpedo attack from either Bomber Command or the Fleet Air Arm, so gunners must be especially careful what they're aiming at." His eyes now found Dowling, Cook, Daly and Bishop.

"Only fire if you are sure of your target, I don't want any mistakes," he continued. "Those flyboys will have a hard enough job without us making it worse."

Now his attention switched to Pickering, Newman and Carter.

"And engine room staff must also be on their toes; we shall be controlling from the bridge but that may break down so keep an eye on the telegraph. It's my guess there will be a good deal of manoeuvring; if you are slow, it might mean an eight-inch brick hits you first."

There was no laughter, he had not expected any; this was far too serious for humour. Yet the reaction was good – it could not have been better in fact. The men seemed stunned but nothing more; there were no looks of panic or distress: the closest he could detect was surprise.

"I'll keep you informed as much as possible but wanted to give an outline," he promised finally. "Now, if there are no questions, we'll go to stations for leaving harbour."

Harris' gaze swept around the sea of faces once more and no one looked in need of further guidance. Then, turning swiftly, he was gone, leaving behind a stunned silence that soon dissolved into a dozen muttered comments.

"You 'eard what the captain said," Price growled, stepping forward. "Stations for leavin' harbour so get yourselves changed and movin'." He also glanced about at the assembled men; the good the bad, some popular, others less so, but all he knew well and most for longer than any officer. The captain had said nothing about the odds they would be facing, but all must understand what was being asked of them and had reacted in just the way he would have hoped – just the way he would have expected. "And good luck, everyone," he added.

* * *

MGB 194 led her flotilla out and, once clear of the harbour, quickly joined with Conway's force.

"I'd like us in an arrowhead formation," the lieutenant commander's voice came over their R/T repeater. "Bob, group your boats to starboard of me."

"Make to flotilla; 'form up in quarterline, station to starboard'," Harris ordered, and the Aldis began to click. He could have used R/T to signal but it was more convenient to keep that channel open for anything else Conway had to say. And besides, Harris didn't care to have his orders overheard by all and sundry.

"SO's setting a fair old pace," Anderson shouted shortly afterwards. As soon as the boats were organised Conway, in *MTB 115*, had taken off at speed forcing Harris to order maximum revs early to catch up. But *MGB 194* was the slightly faster boat and a reduction was soon possible, although the engines remained running in the high twenty hundreds.

"I suppose he'll be trusting on his little toy," Harris bellowed in reply. "Though I can't see it will be much good on a day like today."

That was certainly the case, after so much rain, the weather was clear and still. An unaccustomed sun shone out of an all but cloudless sky and was positively painful to men used to squinting in the dark. But the fine conditions were not welcomed and the captain had been correct, radar must surely be of little value when individual buildings could so easily be picked out on the looming French coast.

"One of his toys seems to have broken already," Anderson remarked, pointing over their port beam.

Harris turned to look and, sure enough, what had been a line of five evenly spaced boats on the opposite flank now showed an unsightly gap. The reason could be seen further back; one of the MTBs had clearly suffered an engine failure. The cause might be a fuel or electrical fault, or even some more complex reason, but she had lost her main motive power and was wallowing in the gentle sea while her colleagues powered on ahead.

"A new Vosper," Harris commented. "They really don't get on with the Packards."

Anderson nodded. His right hand was resting on the bridge's mahogany frame. Through it, he sensed the regular beat of their own engines and could only feel grateful.

"Smoke off the starboard bow," Daly reported and both officers turned to look.

"I think that might be our friends," Anderson remarked while Harris focussed his glasses.

"Well it's smoke right enough," he said. Then the R/T repeater crackled, and Conway's excited voice burst through.

"Smoke reported green..."

Harris glanced at Anderson, before bending forward to the voice pipes. "What's up with the set, Tel'?" he asked.

"Nothing our end, sir," Jelly reported. "Everything's on the top line as far as I can see; must be the SO's."

"All we need is for the R/T to go down," Harris fumed. "Flash him a signal, will you?"

Anderson duly collected the Aldis lamp; if they lost reliable radio communication it would indeed be a nuisance, but at least the clear day meant signalling by light would not give away their position.

"There's aircraft as well," the captain added, still staring out to starboard. Anderson raised his own glasses and looked. Yes, aircraft indeed; rarely had he seen so many. They were some distance off and the enemy vessels remained below the horizon, yet those small flecks of grey meant substantial air cover. The distance was too great to tell British from German, but any battle in the sky looked like being as fierce as that on the surface.

"Flotilla leader's turnin', sir," Price called out and both officers brought their attention back to the boat.

"Follow him round, 'Swain," Harris grunted. Conway had altered course a couple of points to starboard; it was not enough to risk taking them out of their sector, although Anderson wished they could cut the speed down slightly; they must soon be drawing level with the oncoming Germans.

"And now 'e's slowin', sir!" Price grumbled, while his hand reached out to the throttles.

"Very good, bring her down to match."

Behind them, the four trailing gunboats also began to decelerate. Each was commanded by men they had sailed with on active service and exercise, and Anderson was confident all would perform well. But the MTBs that trailed to port were a totally unknown quantity. On that one sortie when Conway's boat experienced engine trouble, the rest had gone on to perform well enough; a freighter had been badly damaged to the point that she needed to put in for repairs. But Conway's flotilla did not have an impressive record in general and would shortly be facing an enemy that must test them to the limit.

"Enemy to starboard!" Bishop's shout revealed much about the man's heightened state of mind, but Harris raised his glasses without comment. Besides, Bishop was undoubtedly right, the first dim shapes of the German force could now be seen on the horizon and it was clear they were moving at speed.

"How far are we from the next sector, Number One?" Harris asked.

"Dobson's lot were given the patch between Folkestone and Dungeness," Anderson replied. "They left first, quite a long time before us."

"So they'll probably be engaging about now," Harris supposed.

"I guess so, sir," Anderson agreed.

As he spoke, and before Harris could correct his grammar, a brief flash lit up the horizon. Something large had exploded. From that distance it was impossible to say what; possibly a torpedo strike or, judging from the nature, more likely one of the

British launches had been hit and instantly turned into a charred memory. Evidently there was action indeed, and not so very far away.

"Well, it looks like they're busy," Harris muttered. "And it will be our turn soon."

Chapter Twenty

"I never known nothing like it – a bloody armada!" Cook exclaimed as if his slender years held so much more than a few weeks' combat experience. "And there's more kites up than I ever thought we 'ad."

"But not all of them are ours," Dowling told him with the authority of one several months his senior. "'Fact, most of them aren't," he added.

"Way out of range, probably don't even know we're 'ere," Cook mused. "Do you think they'll bother us?"

"I'll bother them if they do," the older lad promised.

Both had abandoned their gun and were seated on the smoke floats to *194*'s stern. From that position they could view the oncoming German force relatively easily; there were several small craft in plain sight off their starboard bow and something large, grey and looming was gradually gaining shape beyond. Now the British gunboats had slowed it was getting easier to see, while the engines that had been making such a racket were suddenly content to give out little more than a gentle rumble and normal speech was possible.

"Them lot is ours," Dowling added as a group of aircraft flew low overhead. They had come from the west, so been missed as both lads were focussing elsewhere, although neither felt in any way guilty.

"Hurricanes," Cook agreed, watching them go. "Be off to join the fight."

"So we're going to have to be pretty smart," Dowling cautioned. "With that lot mixing it with the Germans, it'll be hard to tell the two apart."

"Doesn't bother me in the slightest," Cook told him, and Dowling gave a quizzical look. "I only have to load the thing," the lad explained, "it's up to you who we fire at."

In the W/T office, Jelly was equally confident and casually fingering the dials on his equipment. Since the last communication breakdown he had been unable to raise the flotilla SO, or any of the MTBs on R/T although the other gunboats were still in touch and his brief W/T test transmission had been received and acknowledged by Dover Command. But he continued to maintain a watch on all home frequencies while occasionally allowing himself quick dips into the enemy's R/T wavelengths.

He knew little German as such but had picked up a few words in the course of his work and sometimes the same voices were heard so often they became quite recognisable. These were radio operators aboard E-boats or other escorts; vessels they had encountered in the past and, though he would have laughed out loud at the thought, there was something vaguely comforting in their familiarity. But all he now heard were unknown and very different in their delivery. There was none of the informality he was used to, no gossip or chit-chat – nicknames and occasional laughter. The enemy they now faced was far more professional and whoever had charge was organising his vessels with cold efficiently. But there was something else in the clipped words and concise instructions that his alert senses could detect; the force they were heading to meet was undoubtedly more powerful but, whoever his counterparts were aboard the enemy vessels, not all appeared confident. And some sounded decidedly apprehensive.

In the starboard turret, Daly lowered his glasses and took a crafty glance at his watch. The enemy was drawing closer by the second. He had already identified and reported two Z17 class destroyers, several M-class minesweepers and a handful of smaller stuff in addition to the heavy cruiser that seemed to be gaining strength and size as she drew steadily nearer. All was interesting enough and would doubtless be causing those with a mind for such things great consternation. His opposite number in the port turret definitely appeared tense, but not Daly. As far as he was concerned, his responsibilities ended with the twin half-inch machine guns he controlled and, despite the mounting odds, part of his mind was considering a very different subject.

Somewhere, many miles away and in a place where they referred to global war as 'The Emergency', a horse race should just be finishing, and Daly was thinking of that as much as any impending combat. And even then, his thoughts were contemplating something other than the result, for that was a relative certainty in the Irishman's mind. At that moment what fascinated him more was how one country could be at war while another, so very close, at peace. It was even hard to accept the green turf and gaiety of such meetings could be part of the same earth that also held the towering monster they were setting out to fight. Or that those equipped with identical bodies could harness similar emotions to fight and play. It was ostensibly confusing, yet he felt there would be a logic to it, if only enough thought were applied.

But at that moment he didn't care to trouble himself; the sun was up and, though December, this was as fine a day as he could hope for. And even if there were truly no doubt in his mind, he would still have liked to know exactly how that race had turned out.

* * *

As the German force drew closer, Conway's boat reduced speed further until, in response to frantic signalling, Harris ordered *MGB 194* alongside.

"I want you chaps to lay a smoke screen!" Conway's voice came over his boat's tannoy and, even so distorted, the man sounded under strain. "Close as you can, and off the cruiser's port bow. We'll be following you in, so keep out of our way as you leave."

Harris had been expecting something along those lines and repeated the instructions before clicking off their own tannoy and catching Anderson's eye.

"I suppose the wind is light enough," he said. Both men turned to look. The Germans were in clear sight now; to the centre lay the grey bulk of *Seydlitz* and surrounding her a number of smaller craft. These consisted of E- and R-boats and were mainly grouped towards the cruiser's stern; what caught their attention were the destroyers and, specifically, one nearest to them riding off the big ship's port bow. And it was not alone; close to and also in the enemy's van were a pair of minesweepers, although neither were similar to Anderson's previous ship. Rather than converted trawlers, the M-class vessels were purpose-built and armed with guns as big as some destroyers'. The cluster of British MTBs and gunboats were easily within range of all forward escorts as well as the warship they protected, but such a target would be hard to hit with a single shell and might even be considered unprofitable. Whether they would remain so when the boats moved in to attack was uncertain, but both men sensed they were about to find out.

"Very well, we'll crank up to full speed and make for the enemy," Harris announced. "I propose to come as close as I can to the cruiser's bows, the escorts may prove a problem of course, but we'll just have to risk it. With a bit of luck, the bomber boys will see what we're up to and stage their run at the same time, that way we might share out some of the secondary armament. But whatever, we'll start laying smoke from the stern of the line to give

Conway's boys the best chance to come in unobserved. That means ours will be the last; is that clear, Number One?"

Is that clear? Anderson very nearly took a step back. They were about to head hell for leather into the very teeth of an enemy force, the smallest of which was probably ten times their own size and power – to his mind nothing could be clearer.

"Yes, sir."

"Then have Jelly send it off on R/T, if anyone fails to respond, see it repeated by semaphore."

"Very good, sir." For a moment he met his captain's eyes and the two men exchanged a glance, then Anderson left the bridge and Harris turned his attention to directing Price at the helm.

* * *

Now they were really motoring; Harris didn't know if Carter had pulled out something special, or the nearest enemy escorts were to blame. Both destroyer and minesweeper were targeting them and few things increase the illusion of speed better than being under fire. But whatever the reason, he didn't think *194* had ever travelled so fast. And, despite Price throwing the helm about as if determined to send them under, the German gunners were making good practice; already the bridge had been soaked from the spray of three near misses. The shells they currently faced must also be larger than anything the gunboat had met in the past; a single hit would probably signal their end, even if it failed to explode. Their one consolation lay in the cruiser herself being relatively quiet. The *Seydlitz* remained a good two miles off their starboard bow but, at the speed the enemy squadron was making, such a distance would soon be covered. The cruiser's main armament would be of little value against small, fast-moving targets but she carried sufficient secondary weapons to sink them with ease. His earlier wish had been granted, however; an air attack was in progress. Overhead several light bombers were making a tentative approach while both country's fighters gave battle above and the *Seydlitz*'s lighter guns were also firing in that direction.

He glanced back, the other boats in his flotilla were close behind and keeping good station – as well they might, he told himself, since *194* was at their head and attracting most of the enemy's attention. His gaze returned to the cruiser; she would be in optimum torpedo range shortly so it was time to start making smoke and, almost instinctively, he turned to his right. But Anderson had not returned to the bridge, instead, he was next to the Oerlikon where he obviously intended supervising the release of their own smoke floats.

Which was the best place for him, Harris told himself firmly. To have come so far and not distribute the CSA correctly would be more than a waste of time, they would have placed themselves in peril for no reason. But as he ordered the start of the smoke screen, he still missed the younger man's presence.

* * *

"That'll do!" Anderson shouted as he and Cook heaved the second CSA canister over the side. "Get back to your gun, we'll be turning at any time."

Glad to have performed well in front of an officer yet keen to do some true fighting, the lad quickly obeyed, leaving Anderson alone at the gunboat's stern. He looked back; Potter's vessel was immediately behind and had dropped her floats some while ago: now she was turning for home, but beyond he could see very little. For their screen seemed to be holding well; the grey-white smoke was already forming into a thick low cloud, if the gentle breeze remained as it was, it should roll it down towards the enemy shipping and be even more of an asset. A heavy shell passed overhead, missing them perhaps by twenty feet and he steadied himself on the Oerlikon's depression rail as Price began a full speed turn.

Soon they were heading west once more with the thick wall of cloud to port. He peered past the gunboat's superstructure and could just make out the rest of the flotilla as they, too, headed for safety. All had turned about as soon as their floats were released; Potter's boat was the nearest but was already settled on course and drawing away. Meanwhile, off the starboard bow, Conway could be seen leading his force of MTBs in to attack. Anderson watched as they powered towards him on their deadly mission, keeping to the safe side of both the smoke and the fleeing MGBs. All were travelling flat out and the two flotillas passed each other at over ninety miles an hour; in no time the torpedo boats were gone, and he drew breath. A few shells were still being lobbed over or through the smoke and some landed nearby but *194* had been hidden and in relative safety for several minutes. The enemy must be firing

260

with no regard to direction and it was at that point he wondered if they might even have been spared. He would return to Harris on the bridge and together they could see the sortie out to its end. Maybe the cruiser would be hit by one of Conway's torpedoes but, whatever happened, they had surely done their bit.

But as he began to clamber his way forward it seemed they were still very much in action. To that point those at the Oerlikon had been robbed of the chance to fire, first by *194*'s position, then the smoke screen she had helped lay. But the air above was clear and both lads had finally found an unobscured target and were making up for lost time.

The British bombers were gone now, chased off by a swarm of German fighters that still buzzed busily overhead and it was these that had caught Cook and Dowling's attention. All were 109s and, when silhouetted against the bright sky, their stark wing profile was so different to any British plane there could be no concerns about hitting one of their own. And the Germans were under strict restraints: fear of further air attacks was forcing them to conserve both height and ammunition while the need to remain close to their charge meant they could not stray far. As a result, each banked steeply as they turned and hung, apparently stationary, in the air above the gunboat, making a prime target for a twenty-millimetre cannon and two eager boys.

"Fish in a barrel!" Dowling exclaimed as the third aircraft fell to his fire. Cook inserted a fresh magazine; soon a further sixty rounds would be ready to account for yet another and both had never felt so fulfilled or elated. But while the younger lad worked, and before Dowling could return its slender barrel to the killing position, the Oerlikon itself was struck.

In many ways it was a lucky hit, or rather a succession of them. The tight trail of shots that rained down on the gunboat's stern were relatively light, and possibly came from a cannon remarkably similar to the one they destroyed. The barrage could have originated from one of the larger escorts' secondary armament, or maybe an E-boat had felt the need to contribute. But, robbed of a plainer target, some frustrated hand must have aimed blindly into the smoke and, by fortune good or bad, neatly raked *194*.

And fortune was definitely involved; if just one shell from a larger weapon had found its mark, the gunboat would have ceased to exist. Instead, a series of holes were punched into her deck, neatly encompassing the Oerlikon and finally ending just short of the bridge. The cluster of shots was not the only danger, however; of almost equal menace was the cloud of twisted metal their impact created. Even Bishop, many feet forward in the port turret, was struck by a razor-sharp splinter and glanced down in mild astonishment as blood began to flow beneath a gloved hand. But all luck had ended for those beside the cannon and, in the innocent beauty of a bright winter's afternoon, they became the first aboard *194* to die.

Chapter Twenty-One

Harris felt, rather than heard, the shells hit. *MGB 194* was travelling at close to her maximum speed and supposedly fleeing from danger, so he had been allowing himself a moment of relief. That they remained vulnerable became immediately apparent however and it was equally clear his command had sustained major damage.

He instantly took in the casualties by the Oerlikon but experience combined with the certain knowledge he could do nothing for them banished the details from his mind. Of more immediate concern was that their principle gun had been destroyed. But there was more physical damage to consider; the gunboat's entire aft section lay strewn with bent stanchions, battered ventilators and other assorted debris while the gun platform itself was now only fit for firewood. Quite what harm had been caused within the engine room he could not tell; some shells must surely have penetrated but all three engines were running and, while they did, he was content to let them.

"Do you have control?" he snapped at Price who gave the wheel a cautious turn.

"Steering's responding normal, sar," the coxswain confirmed, his voice as level as ever. Harris nodded; that was a relief at least though it would probably be better to check on Carter and his lot.

"Then take her into the smoke," he ordered. "We don't want any chance of being hit again."

Price dutifully guided them to port and soon they were totally enveloped in the thick, chemical haze. Harris coughed twice before bending forward to the engine room voice pipe and had actually flipped the lid open when something made him stop. It was memories of Conway's reaction when an engine failed aboard his MTB; if Carter had anything to report he would be in contact, otherwise it must be better to leave the man alone – he may have other matters to attend to. Harris straightened up and closed the flap; usually he would have sent his second in command to take a look, and it was then he realised Anderson was missing and, almost simultaneously, the man had last been seen next to the destroyed Oerlikon.

A cold feeling of dread ran through the captain's body; he looked aft but could now see little other than the damned fog. Instinct had prevented him from inspecting the twisted bodies too carefully and for a moment desperation took hold. He had to physically fight back the urge to shout out loud, but even then there were other demands on his attention.

"Starboard engine's down!" Price reported briskly, and the boat veered slightly in that direction before being pulled back to her correct course. They were still in the midst of the smoke but it surely couldn't be long before all would begin to clear.

"Centre's feeling dodgy an all!" the coxswain added. Harris drew closer and peered at the revolution counters in the wheelhouse below. Port was holding up and showing well above twenty-five hundred, but the centre engine had dipped below fifteen and continued to fall further as he watched. The loss of power had brought them off the plane and soon they would be running out of the smoke's protection.

"Very well, 'Swain," he muttered, and it took effort to make his tone sound like anything approaching normal. "Hold her as she is for now, there's still a measure of screen left; all we need is for Mr Carter to perform one of his miracles."

Price pursed his lips. "Aye, sar. Anytime 'e likes – can't be too soon for me!"

* * *

At the port turret, Bishop first removed his glove and then the minute shard of metal that had caused the cut. He sucked at the wound absentmindedly while peering forward into the smog. For as long as the smoke lasted, there could be nothing required of him and he was glad. Without a target or the chance of one, he had no call to fire his Vickers, while the dense smoke ruled out lookout duties leaving him free to consider matters. The injury, small as it was, had brought on a change far greater than any physical harm. It was as if the tiny gash was demonstrating something much larger, something he had never fully comprehended before.

Men were regularly wounded and often killed doing his job, that fact had never been in doubt – how could it when his very presence was due to another's death? But while supposedly accepting this it had taken a half-inch cut to physically demonstrate he was made of the same stuff and might also become a casualty.

The smoke was holding out and no more German shells

had come near for some time, so he should be safe. But that was surely an illusion; they had not seen the vessel that delivered their most recent punishment and might not the next; for as long as he remained aboard the gunboat he would be in danger.

He eased the glove back and made a fist noticing, as if in passing, that both hands were shaking slightly. Which was foolish, the wound was surely nothing more than a scratch; it would only bleed for a while. But even as he assured himself all was well, Bishop knew otherwise and that a small splinter of metal had actually caused an injury far deeper than he could imagine. The matched pair of weapons before him caught his eye and he regarded them, as if for the first time. And, also for the first time, found no beauty there.

* * *

Harris was right, Carter had more than enough to keep him occupied. Several shells had entered his domain with one landing squarely on the port engine block where it did little damage other than send shards of razor-sharp metal ripping through the crowded space. But the others achieved more; one embedded itself in the starboard engine's exhaust manifold while another shattered the same engine's water jacket, sending jets of superheated steam over the nearest stoker, and a fourth embedded itself deep into the inner workings of the centre engine.

Scalded and screaming, Pickering spun round, his hands clutching hopelessly at the raw mess that had so recently been his neck and shoulders.

"Steady there, steady!" Carter soothed almost tenderly as he drew the man away while blood flowed freely from a slice across his own cheek. The stoker's screams slowly dwindled to sobbing and Carter laid him gently down on the engine room sole.

For there was no time to do more; the damage to their machinery must take priority and had yet to be assessed. All but two bulkhead lamps remained alight and the three Packards were running, but the boat was obviously within range of the enemy.

"Starboard's exhaust is shot through," Newman reported solidly from that engine.

"Guessed as much from the stink," Carter snapped back. "And she's losing water by the gallon - shut her down and get that hatch opened." As he spoke his eyes travelled to the centre engine and what he saw there was enough to turn his blood cold.

High octane petrol was flowing freely over the warm block;

how the whole lot had not ignited was beyond him. He crouched down and looked closer, rather than the fuel line it was the pump itself that had been shattered. Petrol was still being fed into the thirsty engine, but far more flooded out through the cracked dome.

"Centre fuel pumps done for," he called out to Newman, who was now checking the port engine.

"Can you fix it?" the stoker asked.

"Not a chance," Carter replied, his voice intentionally flat. "I'm shutting her down too."

"But it's the centre!" Newman protested and Carter stopped. He was right; other equipment relied on that engine running, yet they were already bathing in petrol and the merest spark would account for them all.

"I'll reduce revs then," he said at last. So far he was the only one who knew the full extent of the problem and it was probably better that way. And at least the port engine seemed unaffected; with that at maximum revs and the centre merely idling they could make some progress. He only hoped it would be enough, and that nothing caused a spark.

* * *

Minutes later they were almost clear of the screen and heading for clearer air so there seemed little point in continuing through the fading smog.

"All right, 'Swain," Harris muttered, take her to starboard and let's see what's about."

Price muttered something through the scarf he'd pulled up over his mouth and turned the wheel slightly; soon they were emerging into full daylight and the bright, crisp sunshine almost hurt. Harris immediately looked back; enough of the smokescreen remained to obscure his vision directly aft and he supposed Conway's lot must be doing their deadly business on the other side of it. Then he realised the enemy cruiser was actually in sight, and not where he had expected to see her. She had turned sharply to starboard and lay almost stern on, presumably to avoid Conway's torpedoes. But there was no sign of the MTB flotilla, except what appeared to be a single hull abandoned and burning roughly where they might have launched their attack.

But though the cruiser had been forced to divert there remained a cluster of E-boats stationed off her port quarter. They could be no more than a mile or so away and one may even have been responsible for their current damage. Whatever the case, they must surely spot a solitary wounded gunboat limping out from the smokescreen's cover.

Ahead were the distant images of his own flotilla heading for home at full speed. They were a good way off but then none had suffered any loss of power. Harris cursed under his breath; the time spent under cover of the screen had been wasted. He should have contacted the others immediately; warned them they had engine problems and called some back to cover him. Anderson might have thought of doing so, but Anderson was not present.

"We're losing support at the guns, sir!" This was Daly in the nearby starboard turret; presumably the Irishman felt his captain didn't have enough to worry about. But Harris immediately saw the point; both turret-mounted Vickers relied on hydraulic power for their control. This was generated by the centre engine and the low revolutions were making the weapons hard to manage; were it to fade entirely they would be almost impossible to train properly, leaving the boat totally defenceless. He leant forward to the W/T office voice pipe and forced himself to speak normally.

"Call up Potter, Tel', along with anyone else you can raise. Tell them we've engine problems and get them back here sharpish."

Without waiting for a reply Harris snapped the lid shut, then looked longingly at the engine room pipe once more. The temptation was strong but, if a man like Conway could resist, he could as well. Whatever was going on down there, Carter was best left to deal with it without interruption. Then Price cursed out loud and the centre engine failed completely.

* * *

In the starboard turret, Daly was wrestling with his guns. Despite the loss of power, he could still elevate the weapon to some extent although lateral movement was almost impossible. By pressing down hard in his seat he might wrench the entire assembly slightly, but there was no chance of accurate fire. He glanced across at Bishop to port, but his oppo had already abandoned his weapon and Daly had never known the man miss any chance of firing. So the problem was obviously general, and their guns were effectively redundant. Which was a shame, as there were two E-boats coming up on their stern and one had already opened fire.

* * *

Never had the atmosphere in the engine room been so intense. The idea formed as soon as Newman realised the centre engine's problem and he began work without announcing his intentions. But Carter soon picked up on the plan and even Pickering raised himself and, whimpering slightly as he moved, began handing out tools and advice wherever they were needed.

Carter had been forced to shut down the centre engine and was now crouching over it as he stripped away the remains of its damaged fuel pump while Newman fought to remove the same unit from the starboard. And the whole performance was made just that little bit harder knowing a single slip – one scrape of a tool against another metal object or anything that created the smallest of sparks – and they would be incinerated.

Speed alone could not avert the risk; if anything, rushing the job would make an explosion more likely. Instead they must work cautiously and with thought even if the lack of a centre engine was making the boat extremely vulnerable. So neither could they afford to dawdle; there must be just the right amount of care and haste, and not a fraction too much of either.

* * *

Harris had also noticed the E-boats. They were now passing what was left of the smoke screen and coming up on the gunboat's port quarter and one was currently releasing a stream of tracer in their direction. But the shots were going wild and wide; the Germans would have to close the range if they wanted to cause serious damage.

Which was happening as he watched, he reckoned *194* was making maybe fourteen knots on her remaining engine; reasonable by anyone's standards, but not good enough to avoid the pair of larger enemy craft approaching at almost three times the speed. He watched as they drew closer. German designers did not rely on hard chine hulls so even flat out the long sleek vessels hardly rose in the water; it was as if he were being pursued by two massive torpedoes. And they were closing fast; in no time both would open fire again and then the shots would surely tell. Harris had already lost two men for certain with one seemingly missing, but for all he knew the engine room was full of corpses. No, that couldn't be the case, he assured himself. Someone was working below; he could tell that from the changes in engine speed that had not been ordered from the helm. But whoever it was, and whatever they were doing, he wished they'd get a move on. He glanced forward and was relieved to see three shapes heading in his direction. That must be Potter and a couple of the others; Jelly had reported them acknowledging his signal, although quite what good they would do at such a distance was anyone's guess.

So what were his options? Grey flecks of aircraft still filled the sky toward the north-east; *Seydlitz* had resumed her previous course and the party was moving on up the Strait with both sides taking their air cover with it. A couple of fighters might spot their predicament and decide to keep the Hun at bay, although that might be hoping for too much. With the cruiser apparently undamaged, little thought could be given to a single wounded launch and the oncoming E-boats would shortly start to knock his command to pieces.

Should he surrender now; get Jelly to try and contact the Germans on R/T? But how would that work when a larger British force was also bearing down? No, surrender was impractical and fighting back impossible: the only thing he could do was sit tight and await the inevitable.

* * *

"Pump's free!" Newman exclaimed as he eased the warm device away from its seating.

"I'm struggling," Carter admitted from the centre unit. He had shut off and detached the fuel feed, and removed most of the shattered pump assembly, but the base itself was distorted and had wedged itself firmly into the engine block.

"Have you tried a wrench?" Pickering asked.

"I've tried everything," Carter sighed. "Apart from a Manchester screwdriver."

"Hammer won't fix it," Pickering winced as he collected the working pump from Newman and passed it across.

"I'm not trying to fix it," Carter snapped. His face was smeared with grease and oil which mixed oddly with blood from his torn cheek. "I just want the damned thing off."

"Okay," Newman said. "Let's think about this logically; a hammer actually might be of use."

Carter regarded him quizzically.

"The thing's out of shape," Newman explained, "if we can knock it back square it will probably come free."

"Bend it straight, you mean?" Carter snorted. "It's a thought but try doing that without raising a spark."

"We need a hide mallet, but there isn't one on board," the

stoker agreed. "Maybe we could improvise with a cloth?"

"Maybe," Carter allowed. Newman's face was almost as filthy while Pickering's bare shoulders and neck were quickly taking on the appearance of a peeled pomegranate. "Providing we can find one that isn't soaked in fuel," he added.

Newman shrugged. "This seems reasonably clean," he said, passing a rag across. "There's a touch of petrol but, if you don't make a spark, it shouldn't matter."

"And if you do, nothing will..." Pickering grunted.

Carter wrapped the cloth about the remains of the pump before collecting a two-pound engineer's hammer. Then, after resting its face against the shrouded unit for a second, he tapped once, quite hard, and then again. The cloth was removed to be replaced by a wrench and, gripping the base firmly, he tried to prize it free.

After half a minute of intense effort, the motor mechanic stopped. "It's not coming," he gasped.

"Better try it without the cloth," Newman suggested.

"I was thinking the same myself," Carter agreed. "Though it could well make a spark."

"Ain't going to shift it otherwise," Newman predicted gloomily.

"Are you two behind me in this?" the petty officer's question was almost formal.

"I'm game," Pickering declared, and Newman nodded his head in silence. Then Carter picked up his hammer and once more addressed the seized petrol pump.

* * *

Now green tracer was flying again; several short bursts had been fired but they passed overhead. All the Germans needed to do was lower their sights and take a firm bead on the gunboat as it weaved desperately in their path. Bishop's turret remained strangely silent, but Daly was doing his best to return fire. Either luck or effort had allowed the Irishman to raise the twin barrels and point them aft sufficiently while Price, at the wheel, was steering to allow the shots to sweep across the E-boats' bows like a poorly directed hose. As a method of aiming it was not particularly accurate though did seem to be keeping the German gunners quiet. But then they had no need to fire further; they were closing rapidly on their stricken quarry and, as each E-boat boasted a crew of twenty or more, it should be possible to capture, board and begin towing *194* away, under the very noses of the British.

And then, just as such a fate became inevitable, and Harris was almost resigning himself to it, there came a rumble from aft.

"We got the centre back!" Price cried out in delight as he eased the middle throttle forward.

Sure enough, the gunboat quickly rose on to the plane and, though her speed was still slower than the pursuing enemy's, at least it would buy them time. And there were other advantages; with two motors to play with Price could lead the Germans a merry dance. The delay in their fellow launches reaching them was also being made shorter, although the major benefit must lie in the return of their Vickers turrets. Now energy had been restored to the hydraulics they were working properly, and the Germans could be paid proper attention.

But it was hardly a reprieve. Though not as quickly, the E-boats continued to gain and, suspecting they were to be cheated of their prize, were once more firing in earnest. Several shots passed close and one hit the gunboat's mast, sending the thing crashing down on the afterdeck in a tangle of wire and twisted metal. But the next salvo was harsher still, and ripped across her stern, digging deep into the hull and lodging within the aft lazarette. And then the Germans raised their sights and sent a barrage where it could do the most damage.

* * *

It landed on the aft superstructure, taking in much of the bridge as well as the port gun turret. A lethal combination of shells and bullets that streamed down causing devastation and injury and an onslaught that must surely spell defeat.

Although amazingly Bishop was not hit. Heavy calibre machine gun rounds did strike his turret and some burst through the light plating, although each missed his body, in some cases by barely an inch. But though he was conscious of the miracle, the gunner did not benefit from it. Instead, he slumped sideways in his seat with both hands wrapped firmly about a body that was now shaking uncontrollably.

The earlier scratch had been the start and, combined with such a close shave, proved more than enough. If only he'd been struck mildly, a glancing blow, something that would raise a bit of blood and give him a decent way out. But, honourable or not, Bishop knew this was the end; his time in gunboats was over as suddenly and emphatically as his interest in weapons. When Daly's guns returned fire he had not followed suit and, as the ungoverned mount rocked the twin Vickers back against him, he brushed the hateful things away.

But nearby Harris and Price were not so lucky. Both were struck and crumbled to the deck while, robbed of a steady hand at her helm, *194* began to weave and stagger before settling on an extended turn to port. Then, as the hard won engine revolutions fell away and her pursuers drew steadily closer, it was as if the boat herself had acknowledged defeat and was throwing herself into their path and onto their mercy.

Chapter Twenty-Two

Anderson had not been struck by enemy fire; ironically it was a lifebelt that caused his main injury. When the earlier shots that accounted for Dowling and Cook landed, he had been heading for the bridge and just gained relative shelter to starboard of the aft superstructure. He instinctively ducked as the shells rained around him and, though some passed close and a cloud of debris was thrown up, nothing hit him directly. But as he crouched, the heavy cork ring was torn from its bracket and smacked him squarely in the face, bruising bone and releasing blood from his nose, while knocking him back to crack his bare head against the deck.

That was all he could remember and even those recollections were vague but, as Anderson recovered consciousness, personal injuries were not his first consideration. He felt giddy and mildly disoriented although that could be controlled; *194*'s current situation was of far greater importance.

For the boat was in trouble; rather than the definite lunges to either side that Price had been directing, she was now turning steadily to port. And more than that, the engines had died to little more than a rumble while her hull had come off the plane and was settling fast. But what was probably of greater concern, the enemy were now so confident of victory that, yet again, they were holding their fire.

He rose uncertainly and, grasping the side of the superstructure, stared over. The E-boats were horribly close; well within range and *194*'s strange heading would soon be bringing them closer still. It was clear the helm was unattended so manning it must be his priority. He eased himself carefully towards the wheelhouse door but felt the entire vessel jerk slightly on reaching it; then the engines' note began to increase and, as if by an ethereal hand, the gunboat was gently guided back to her previous course.

He clambered through the entrance as the power rose further and almost knocked into Jelly standing uncertainly at the wheel. The man must have realised what was about and taken over the helm; now he was adjusting the throttles with one hand while holding the boat on course with the other.

"Can you manage?" Anderson asked. Jelly glanced at him

briefly.

"Not sure I know exactly where to go," he shouted back, "but think I can keep us out of trouble – this really isn't as hard as Pricy makes it look."

Anderson felt a sudden stab of pain and put a hand to his head; the spinning sensation had returned and he knew he must not surrender to it. Under Jelly's guidance, the boat's course had changed dramatically; ahead he could see the oncoming British MGBs, and they were so much clearer now – almost within reach.

"Something's amiss on the bridge," the telegraphist continued. "It must be, else they'd have control from up there."

Yes, that should be the next place to investigate although Anderson was strangely reluctant to leave the wheelhouse. But with limited vision aft, he could not tell how far the E-boats lay from their tail; he must discover that, as well as the fate of the captain and coxswain and, bracing himself for bad news on every front, he made for the short ladder.

Once level with the grating, however, all hesitancy left him as he noticed Price slumped beneath his precious helm. Harris lay to the other side and seemed conscious. Anderson approached the captain only to be waved away.

"Look to Price," Harris directed. "He's bleeding badly."

Anderson turned to the Coxswain who had been wounded just above the elbow; the man tried to raise himself but fell back, exhausted.

"I'm going to try a tourniquet," he told him after briefly examining the wound. Price had a faint pallor to his face and nodded weakly. Glancing about, Anderson snatched at the tannoy mike, ripping it from its housing. The lead, roughly a yard of plaited, cloth-covered cable, would suffice and, bending down to the still recumbent petty officer, he threaded it twice about the arm before tying it tight. The blood continued to seep – more pressure was needed. A hefty splinter of wood lay nearby, one of many fragments from the smashed woodwork. Grabbing hold, Anderson eased it under the binding and gave a firm twist. Price let out a brief moan, but the blood ceased to flow.

"I'll secure this," Anderson told him, but the petty officer shook his head.

"There's no need, son, I can 'old it," he muttered.

"You're sure?"

"I'm sure," Price confirmed, taking hold of the splinter and giving it an extra twist. "What about the 'elm?" he demanded.

"The helm's manned; Jelly's controlling from the

wheelhouse and doing fine."

The man nodded once then rested back and closed his eyes. But his hand remained set and the tourniquet tight, and Anderson sensed neither would change.

"That was well done," Harris told him also trying to rise. A steel helmet was set crookedly on his head; as he moved it clattered to the deck.

"Take it easy, sir," Anderson advised.

"I'm all right. What about you, 'Swain?" he added.

"Never better, sar," Price mumbled from his position on the grating.

Harris snorted slightly, then turned to Anderson. "What's the situation, Number One?"

"Potter's lot are heading our way."

"Potter?" the captain mumbled while half-raising himself; Anderson placed an arm about his body and helped him the rest of the way.

"They should be with us shortly," he declared.

"And what of the Hun?" Harris continued while being gently guided onto the flag locker.

Anderson felt a pang of guilt; while helping Price and Harris he had all but forgotten about the E-boats. He straightened himself and peered aft; both remained in range although neither were firing. In fact, one was in the process of turning away while the other had clearly throttled back. Then he noticed several dark shapes beyond them; the rest of Conway's MTBs were returning from their attack and, with Potter's boats also bearing down, the Germans were in danger of being trapped themselves. Then the second E-boat shied off, and Anderson returned to his captain.

"They're making a run for it," he sighed, wiping blood from his face with his sleeve. "Conway's lot are behind; they'll sort them out."

Harris gave a snort. "If they don't break down first."

"What of you, sir?" Anderson enquired.

"Something got me on the back of the head," Harris replied, feeling carefully at his scalp. "It wasn't a shell else I wouldn't be here. Probably just a lump of shrapnel."

"Shall I see to it?"

"No, it's a bump, no more. But will you take a look at that?" So saying he pointed at his helmet now lying on the grating near to Price. Anderson collected the thing; a deep dent had been made across the back.

"I guess you'll need a new one," Anderson told him flatly.

"I wouldn't have been wearing the darn thing," Harris huffed, "except some fool of a geography teacher made me feel as if I should."

"Then it's a shame I didn't take my own advice," Anderson grunted, feeling at his own face. "I might have kept my looks a little longer."

"Seems we've both learned something from the other," the older man sighed. "But not always the right things."

"Are you sure you're okay?" Anderson checked and it was obvious that he was in earnest.

"Oh yes." The captain gave a weak smile. "I guess you could say I'm fine."

* * *

"My name's Ted Landers, Miss Duncan. I was a friend of Dale's." The man had fair wavy hair and a moustache and looked slightly older than Dale but the similarity in accent was astonishing. "We've never met, but I feel I already know you; please sit down."

She supposed it reasonable for Landers to have invited her to the Grand; he was obviously staying there, and a stranger newly arrived in a foreign country could be expected to remain at his hotel. But being in the bar again was horribly comforting, even the smell of the place brought back memories.

When the message came through to her cabin at the Wrennery she had thought twice about turning up, then considered taking Eve with her. But this current fix was entirely of her own making and, if there were loose ends to tie up, she really should see to them herself. A waiter approached and the American glanced at her.

"Dale said you're partial to a dry Martini," he announced. "Shall I order us a couple?"

"No," she said firmly. "I'd prefer something lighter – an orange cordial."

"Guess one of us must have got that wrong," Landers shrugged and turned to the waiter. "Make that two orange cordials and go heavy on the ice."

The man slipped away and for a moment they stared at each other.

"This isn't easy," Landers admitted at last. "For both of us, I guess. But I did want to speak to you personally, and really appreciate your agreeing to meet up."

She nodded but said nothing; staying quiet was becoming

a habit of late.

"Dale said a lot about you, though I may have got some of it confused," he gave a quick smile. "And it's rare for a fellow who writes for a living to spend too much time on correspondence. But you clearly knocked him flat, Miss Duncan and, if I may say so, I can see why."

"It's Sandra," she told him, and he repeated the name.

"His last letter was a long one; it came just as I was heading for the airport – I managed to bag a flight on military transport, and only by chance did it reach me. But I had plenty of time to read on the way over, that and think about the ramifications."

"You mean my baby?" she asked coldly.

"I mean yours and Dale's baby," he corrected gently. "Look, I won't beat about the bush, Sandra, I'm speaking to you now on behalf of my paper. We know nothing about what's been going on here apart from what we've heard from Dale. And I dare say a lot could be done with private investigators and the like, but that isn't the way *The Gazette* works. Nor me, come to that, and certainly not Dale. You say it's his kid, that was good enough for him and it's good enough for us. He would have supported you and so will we, it's as simple as that."

The statement made Sandra shiver slightly and, noticing this, Landers instinctively put a hand out before withdrawing it as quickly.

"Don't think we're trying to muscle in," he added. "I just want to make it clear we're behind you – behind you in anything you want to do."

"I want to keep the baby," she stated firmly.

"As did Dale," he confirmed.

"He did?" she was near to tears now.

"That was made very clear. Hell, I've never heard a man go on so – talking about train sets and baseball. The chance of it being a girl never seemed to enter his head."

"I didn't know," she said.

"Then you do now."

Their drinks arrived and she glanced about the room as they were placed down.

"So," Landers continued when the waiter had gone. "Do you have any ideas?"

"I – we: we were going to live in America," she said slowly.

"That's still possible," Landers agreed. "And something Dale also mentioned; even asked if there'd be an internal posting for him."

"I thought he wanted to stay abroad."

Landers gave a short laugh. "Not with a wife and family at home he didn't. I haven't been able to check up fully, but there'll surely be a way to get you to the US. And if it helps, I've family in New Jersey. I'm an only child and never likely to be married; Mom's been despairing of me ever providing her with a grandchild. My folks have a spot near the sea, I know she'll welcome you."

Sandra nodded quietly but said nothing.

"And you needn't worry about money," he continued. "Dale's only provisions were made in the name of his brother, and sadly he's no longer with us. But whatever the situation, *The Gazette* won't see you go short. Our overseas correspondents are covered to the hilt and we're a big enough customer for the insurance company not to mess around."

Still she stayed quiet.

"But I don't want to press you to a decision now," Landers added. "I'm going to be here for a while, we're setting up a bureau in Dover as well as London, so will be on hand to see you have everything you need, you'll only have to ask."

"Thank you," Sandra said finally. "Thank you for everything, I do appreciate it. And what you say sounds grand, just what I want, or what I thought I wanted."

Landers gave an inquiring glance and she continued.

"What I thought I wanted when Dale was alive," she clarified. "But now he's gone I've changed my mind. You see I realise now that all I really wanted was him."

* * *

They removed the bodies first; several ambulances were waiting on the quay when the gunboat came in and Dowling and Cook were taken away in the first. They were bound for Noah's Ark Road where the former Isolation Hospital had been converted into a mortuary. Pickering and Carter had a more hopeful destination and left in the second with Price and Harris following in yet another. And Bishop had also gone; initially Anderson had considered him unhurt and just a little shaken but the medics recognised something else and led his dazed body away without question, placing him in an ambulance by himself. Anderson remained though; his wounds would require attention eventually, but the bleeding had mainly stopped and, in Harris' absence, he wanted to see the boat secured. In this he was helped by Jelly, Daly and Newman; between them they saw their fuel drained and what remained of the ready-use ammunition removed. Surprisingly the hull had held up well, although extensive repairs would be needed to the stern and a good portion of decking, to say nothing of at least two of the engines.

Anderson was returning from inspecting the latter when he noticed Commander Brooks boarding.

"Good to see you, Lieutenant," the base captain told him. "I understand you had a lively time of it."

Anderson shook the proffered hand. It must have been a particularly busy operation and he wondered slightly that the man should have made a special journey to meet them.

"Yes, sir. We've lost two men and have several wounded, including Lieutenant Commander Harris."

"I realise that and have asked to be kept informed. You don't look too chipper yourself."

"I shall be fine," Anderson assured him.

"Very well, finish up here and then get that nose seen to," the commander growled. "As an SO's boat, _194_'ll probably be one of the first on the slip, though I doubt she'll be back in service until well into the new year. But then you did superbly, all of you."

"Thank you, sir. Can I ask how the operation went?" Anderson chanced.

"No reason why not," Brooks replied, "all is due to be announced shortly anyway. We didn't get the _Seydlitz_."

"That's a shame." Anderson's reply was automatic; he was too shaken to feel any real regret.

"Frankly we weren't expecting to. Cruisers aren't the easiest of prey. Oh, I know I bagged one myself, but it's a different matter catching your prey asleep in harbour to meeting it on the open seas with all guns manned and a fleet of escorts in support. We put up a good show, though; Conway's lot sunk a destroyer, and that'll definitely make the Germans sit up and take notice."

"Excellent." Again Anderson's response was instinctive. His head was starting to spin again, and he had a sudden vision of the shell of that MTB as it lay abandoned and burning; their victory had come at a cost.

"Of course, I don't know the exact details," Brooks continued. "There'll be a pile of action reports to read, but I thought I'd drop by and check on you chaps first."

"I appreciate that, sir," Anderson replied. "We're just about ready to be slipped."

"Well, see that done, then get yourself attended to. As I say, little will be required of anyone for a while. Go find your sweetheart and explain where your good looks have gone."

Anderson grinned. "Actually, I can see her now," he said, looking past the commander and at the small neat figure waiting patiently on the jetty.

Brooks glanced around. "Of the two of us, I'd say she's the prettier," he grunted, "so I'll be on my way. And well done, once again. It was a good show."

* * *

There were still two more days before Christmas, but Daly didn't want to leave it any longer. He had actually been looking forward to the task for some time and would enjoy the celebrations all the more knowing it done. Not done entirely, of course; they had been unable to cash in Dowling and Cook's stake, and Bishop seemed to have totally disappeared. The fellow was in hospital, that much was certain, and apparently being well cared for, but they couldn't find out where and the chiseller in Cable Street refused point-blank to pay up on his account. But *Noted Fox* had come in at good odds and they had more than enough to pay Remer and leave a bit for a decent craic over Christmas. The Irishman had rather more than his share in his pocket but exactly enough to pay his debts. And, though he was not so foolish as to think he would never have another punt, Daly was darned if any more would be going in that particular direction.

He rounded the corner and entered Remer's street but slowed almost immediately. Something was up, there were barriers across the road and a temporary sentry post had been erected. He approached, his hand resting protectively around the wad of notes in his pocket, then spotted an ARP warden.

"Problem is there, mister?" Daly asked.

"Not for some," the older man sighed. He looked tired and had a light coating of dust over his face and overcoat. "Jerry took out most of the street last night."

"What of number thirty-nine?" Daly asked.

"Got that one an all," the warden confirmed. "They're using these new bombs, see; bloody things are tied together so they fall in a tight pack; devilish they are. Anyone you know in there?"

"Father and son, name of Remer."

The man picked up a small board. "We pulled out four from thirty-nine, all men. Yet to be identified but I reckon they'll be among them. I'll make a note, father and son, you say. Any first names?"

"Are they dead?" Daly snapped.

"Aye, all dead," the warden replied after considering Daly for a moment. "Friends of yours, were they?"

"I knew them," the Irishman muttered, his hand still resting on the money. "But they were no friends of mine – or yours if you did but know it. We should be happy they're gone."

The older man nodded seriously although he had a faint twinkle in his eye. "That's not the reaction we usually gets," he said.

"Well these weren't your usual casualties," Daly sniffed. "Good riddance to bad rubbish."

"You have a good Christmas," the warden told him.

"Oh, I will," Daly confirmed turning away and still fingering the money. "We all will, don't you worry about that."

Author's Notes

MGB 95 is fictitious, the number was never used. She is based loosely on earlier craft produced by the British Powerboat Company and specifically numbers 40-45 which featured Rolls-Royce engines. Many of these were originally commissioned by foreign navies and requisitioned at the start of hostilities. Due to the nature of their production, the range of engines and armament available at time of building and future modifications it was rare for two vessels to share the same exact specification. The unconventional cockpit arrangement described was not popular and quickly discontinued.

MGB 194 is equally not an actual boat but depicts one of twelve PTCs built in Groton, Connecticut and, after being transferred under the Lend Lease Act, allocated to the 5th and 7th Flotilla during 1941.

The initial teething problems encountered when Packard engines were fitted to the first Vospers could partly be blamed on poor installation design by both builders and the RN contractors. Overheating in the oil heat exchangers was temporarily cured by forcing the thermostats open using fishing line before a more permanent solution was found. In the same way, water leaks from the welded seams of cylinder water jackets were regularly addressed with a series of jubilee clips, often at sea while the engine was hot and leaking steam.

Throughout the book I have referred to 'radar' when RDF (Range and Direction Finding) would probably have been a more familiar term in England at the time. I am, however, aware that other countries translate the acronym as Radio Direction Finder so have introduced the more familiar expression slightly early to avoid confusion.

Air Sea Rescue Buoys were used by both sides, the German version being known as a *Rettungsboje*. Both were anchored in relatively shallow coastal waters and contained provisions sufficient to keep a group of men alive for several days, as well as medical supplies and communication equipment.

What became known as the 'Channel Dash' actually took place a few weeks after the fictitious action depicted. In reality, sister battleships *Scharnhorst* and *Gneisenau,* accompanied by the heavy cruiser *Prinz Eugen* and a variety of escorts, left Brest at 9.14 pm on 12th February 1942. Their departure went unnoticed for more than twelve hours and it was not until the squadron approached the Straits of Dover that British forces were mobilised. Attacks by the RAF, the Fleet Air Arm, the Royal Navy as well as coastal artillery were generally inconclusive; it was only when both battleships struck mines in the North Sea that they were significantly damaged. Two days later all three vessels were secure in German ports. The Admiral Hipper-class heavy cruiser *Seydlitz* (sister to *Prinz Eugen*) was laid down at the end of 1936 and launched just over two years later but never completed.

At the start of hostilities, the civilian population of Dover was slightly over forty-one thousand. Many left at the outbreak of war and, when the air raids and shelling were at their worst, there were less than fifteen thousand. But due to an error in administration, the alcohol allowance remained for the full population and Dover was possibly one of the few places in England where drink could be easily obtained.

And on the subject of evacuation, many of Dover's children were sent to foster families in South Wales, while older folk were allocated places in the West Country. The occupants of an entire retirement home were rehomed in this way and, due to another clerical error, admitted to a mental hospital where they were regarded as patients. All protests were ignored and only after one was able to escape and notify the authorities was the mistake corrected.

Alaric Bond
Herstmonceux 2020

Selected Glossary

AFO	Admiralty Fleet Orders. Routine instructions issued to all vessels and establishments for information, guidance and action. They were constantly updated.
Aldis	A form of signalling lamp.
ARP	Air Raid Precautions (originally Civil Defence Corps). A predominately voluntary service providing support to civilians during air raids.
Bob	*(Slang)* A shilling (twelve pennies). A tanner was sixpence, florin two shillings and a quid was (and still is) one pound.
Berk	*(Slang)* A fool. This is actually rhyming slang (but don't investigate further).
Bint	*(Slang)* A female.
Boffin	*(Slang)* A scientist or, more usually, anyone who knows slightly more than yourself.
Bottle	*(Slang)* A reprimand.
Buzz	*(Slang)* A rumour.
Camber	The Camber; an area of the eastern docks where the motor launches were berthed in pens.
Carley float	An invertible life raft issued mainly to warships. Designed by American inventor Horace Carley *(1838-1918)*.
Chine	The change in angle on a hull. A "hard" chine hull has sharp steep sides. A vessel so designed has a flat underside that creates hydrodynamic lift allowing it to rise up on to the plane at speed.
Chiseller	*(Slang)* A cheat.

CO	Commanding officer.
CSA	Chlorosulphuric acid; a smoke float would 'burn' for approximately ten minutes.
Defence area	An area designated especially at risk of invasion. Anti-tank, minefields and other defensive measures were increased and casual visitors banned.
Depression rail	A guard against a vessel's armament hitting its own superstructure.
DNC	Director of Naval Construction based at Bath (so often known as simply 'Bath').
Empire wine	With the fall of France and turmoil in other European countries, wine had to be imported from further afield; the result was always expensive and often disappointing.
Flit	*(Slang)* To move, usually quickly, quietly and nefariously.
Force Z	A naval squadron consisting of *Prince of Wales* and *Repulse*, supported by destroyers. The principle ships were sunk by Japanese forces on 8th December 1941 – the first capital ships to be destroyed solely by enemy aircraft while underway.
Friends' Ambulance Unit	The FAU was committed to relief work in areas under military control. It was founded by members of the British Religious Society of Friends (Quakers) and staffed by registered conscientious objectors.
Goon suit	*(Slang)* A kapok-lined one-piece suit similar to a boiler or flying suit. See Ursula.
Growler	*(Slang)* A pork pie.
HMS *Excellent*	Naval gunnery training school on Whale Island, Portsmouth.

HMS *Glendower*	A naval training establishment near the Welsh town of Pwllheli. After the war it returned to being a holiday camp run by Billy Butlin.
HMS *King Alfred*	Initial training base for RNVR officers at Hove, Sussex.
Heads	Toilets.
Hog Out	*(Slang)* Clean up.
Hostiles	*(Slang)* 'Hostilities Only'; ratings called up for the duration of the war.
Hove	See HMS *King Alfred*.
Jankers	*(Slang)* Military punishment.
Jimmy (the One)	*(Slang)* The first lieutenant.
Kye	*(Slang)* A drink made from shavings of chocolate mixed with boiling water and usually heavily sweetened.
Lord Haw-Haw	Initially the nickname referred to several announcers who regularly broadcast German propaganda in English to the United Kingdom. William Joyce *(1906-1946)* became the most prolific and soon took over the sobriquet. Despite strong rumours of being Irish, Joyce was actually born in Brooklyn but brought up in Ireland. During the Irish War of Independence he worked as an informer on IRA movements for the British government. His broadcasts, initially from Berlin, were viewed with suspicion by most civilians yet still attracted an audience of up to eighteen million. He was captured at the end of hostilities and, despite his country of birth and having adopted German citizenship, tried for treason, it being argued that he also held a British passport and had voted in United Kingdom elections. He was found guilty and hanged.

MGB	Motor Gun Boat.
Manchester screwdriver	*(Slang)* Hammer.
Mary	*(Slang)* Stomach.
MASB (pronounced Masbe)	Motor Anti-Submarine Boat.
ML	Motor Launch.
MTB	Motor Torpedo Boat.
NAAFI (pronounced Naffi)	The acronym for Navy, Army and Air Force Institutes, an organisation set up in 1920 to cater for servicemen and their families.
Old Sweat	*(Slang)* Seaman or marine of considerable experience.
Pentonville	A prison in North London.
PMO	Principal medical officer.
Purolator	A brand of oil filter.
Pusser	*(Slang)* Originally a casual term for the purser, it has since become associated with all things 'Old Navy'.
PO	Petty officer.
Points	In addition to many specific foodstuffs being rationed, points were allocated to allow the purchase of other items including dried fruit, cereals, biscuits and tinned goods. This was later extended to incorporate clothing.
Pompey	*(Slang)* Portsmouth.
Rozzers	*(Slang)* Police.
RNPS	Royal Naval Patrol Service, a branch of the Royal Navy that operated small auxiliary vessels for anti-submarine, minesweeping and escort purposes.
RNVR	Royal Naval Volunteer Reserve, formed from the Royal Naval Volunteer Supplementary Reserve.
R/T	Radio Telegraphy (voice).
Rubber	*(Slang)* A loan.
Safari jar	Large vacuum flask for soup or other liquids that can be kept hot for several hours.

Saint Christopher's	Coastal Forces training base in Fort William Scotland.
Salt horse	*(Slang)* A regular sea officer without specific training in a technical field, and often taken to mean one with an old-fashioned (usually pre WW1) approach.
Scouser	*(Slang)* Liverpudlian; scouse being the slang for stew which those from Liverpool were presumed to eat a lot of.
Scran	*(Slang)* Food.
Sharra	Short for charabanc, an early form of bus often used for day trips.
SO	Senior officer.
SOO	Staff officer operations; the officer responsible for issuing orders transmitted from the commander-in-chief's office to an operational base.
Sound mirrors	An early form of aircraft detection on Britain's South Coast. Initially giant dishes were cut into the chalk cliffs and later more permanent concrete structures erected to catch and magnify the sound of approaching aircraft. They worked to some extent but were swiftly replaced by RDF (radar) as being a more reliable method of detection.
Spiv	*(Slang)* One who deals in black market goods.
Sparks	*(Slang)* Electrician or telegraphist.
Sparrow's Nest	HMS *Europa*, the training camp for RNPS personnel in Lowestoft.
Straight striper	*(Slang)* A regular RN officer. Due to the stripes denoting rank being straight (rather than 'wavy' for RNVR officers).
Tingle	A wooden or metal patch used to repair the hull.

Ursula suit	Heavy, waxed cotton clothing derived originally from motorcycle racing wear.
VP	*Vorpostenboote*. German patrol boats usually converted from fishery, or similar, vessels. Heavily armed with medium to light calibre weapons (usually 88, 40 and 20mm) which could be used against aircraft or shipping. Crewed by up to seventy men and with gun emplacements often reinforced with concrete, they were a formidable, if slow, opponent to Coastal Forces' craft.
Wavy (Wavy Navy)	RNVR officers' stripes denoting rank were wavy, (rather than straight for regular officers).
W/T	Wireless telegraphy (Morse code).
Woolton Pie	A pastry dish of vegetables named after Lord Woolton *(1883-1964)*, the Minister of Food until 1943. Under his direction food rationing was implemented so well that it was reckoned the average civilian was far healthier after six years of war than before. The Woolton Pie was probably his only failure, being universally unpopular.
Workers' Playtime	A BBC radio programme broadcast at lunchtime from canteens throughout the country.
WVS	Women's Voluntary Services; founded in 1938 the WVS recruited women to assist in air raid precautions and with general civilian support. It was noted for having no hierarchy; all members being considered of equal rank and value.

About the Author

Alaric Bond has had a varied career, writing for various periodicals, television, radio comedy as well as the stage. He now focuses on historical nautical fiction with sixteen published novels, thirteen of which are in his acclaimed 'Fighting Sail' series.

Set in 'Nelson's Navy' of the Revolutionary and Napoleonic wars, these have no central hero but feature characters from all ranks and stations; an innovative approach that gives an exciting and realistic impression of life aboard a warship of the period.

Hellfire Corner is the first in an intended new series and marks a change in emphasis, although future 'Fighting Sail' instalments are planned.

www.alaricbond.com

About Old Salt Press

Old Salt Press is an independent press catering to those who love books about ships and the sea. We are an association of writers working together to produce the very best of nautical and maritime fiction and non-fiction. We invite you to join us as we go down to the sea in books.

Visit the website for details of all Old Salt Press books:
www.oldsaltpress.com

The Latest Great Reading from Old Salt Press

Linda Collison

Rhode Island Rendezvous

Book Three, The Patricia MacPherson Nautical Adventures.
Newport Rhode Island: 1765. The Seven Years War is over but unrest in the American colonies is just heating up... Maintaining her disguise as a young man, Patricia is finding success as Patrick MacPherson. Formerly a surgeon's mate in His Majesty's Navy, Patrick has lately been employed aboard the colonial merchant schooner *Andromeda*, smuggling foreign molasses into Rhode Island. Late October, amidst riots against the newly imposed Stamp Act, she leaves Newport bound for the West Indies on her first run as *Andromeda's* master. In Havana a chance meeting with a former enemy presents unexpected opportunities while an encounter with a British frigate and an old lover threatens her liberty – and her life.

Joan Druett

Finale

The year is 1905, and the heyday of Thames, in the goldfields of New Zealand. Back in 1867, Captain Jake Dexter, a flamboyant adventurer and pirate, and his mistress, the actress Harriet Gray, invested the fortune they made during the gold rushes of California and Australia in a theatre and hotel called the Golden Goose, which has become an internationally acclaimed tourist venue, famous for its Murder Mystery Weekends. Guests gather, and a fake murder is staged, and it is up to them to find the killer. But this hugely successful venture is now at great risk. Timothy Dexter, an American of dubious ancestry, threatens the inheritance of the Golden Goose Hotel, and the Gray family gathers to hold a council of war, interrupted when a real murder intervenes. And a young tourist, Cissy Miller, entrusted with a Harlequin costume and a very strange mission, may be the only one to hold the key to the mystery.

Seymour Hamilton

River of Stones

Only three stones of power remain, and only the eight descendants of Zubin can wield them. A ruthless and power-hungry man is intent on stealing the stones, murdering the three leaders of the fleet, and torturing the secrets of navigation from their children. Grand master Astreya gives his daughter Mairi command of a ship with instructions to keep the younger members of his family far from danger. However, safety is elusive. Mairi must face political turmoil ashore, resolve conflicts with her twin brother Trogen, and lead her young crew through storms, dangerous passages, and battles at sea before she can discover the secret that will lead to the river of stones.

V E Ulett

Blackwell's Homecoming

In a multigenerational saga of love, war and betrayal, Captain Blackwell and Mercedes continue their voyage in Volume III of Blackwell's Adventures. The Blackwell family's eventful journey from England to Hawaii, by way of the new and tempestuous nations of Brazil and Chile, provides an intimate portrait of family conflicts and loyalties in the late Georgian Age. *Blackwell's Homecoming* is an evocation of the dangers and rewards of desire.

Rick Spilman

Evening Gray Morning Red
A young American sailor must escape his past and the clutches of the Royal Navy, in the turbulent years just before the American Revolutionary War. In the spring of 1768, Thom Larkin, a 17-year-old sailor newly arrived in Boston, is caught by Royal Navy press gang and dragged off to HMS *Romney*, where he runs afoul of the cruel and corrupt First Lieutenant. Years later, after escaping the *Romney*, Thom again crosses paths with his old foe, now in command HMS *Gaspee*, cruising in Narragansett Bay. Thom must finally face his nemesis and the guns of the *Gaspee*, armed only with his wits, an unarmed packet boat, and a sand bar.

Antoine Vanner

Britannia's Innocent
The Dawlish Chronicles: February – May 1864.
Political folly has brought war upon Denmark. Lacking allies, the country is invaded by the forces of military superpowers Prussia and Austria. Cut off from the main Danish Army, and refusing to use the word 'retreat', a resolute commander withdraws northwards. Harried by Austrian cavalry, his forces plod through snow, sleet and mud, their determination not to be defeated increasing with each weary step . . .

Alaric Bond

Sea Trials
HMS *Mistral* has emerged from a major refit with one vital element missing – her captain. But Tom King is many miles away aboard a different warship and facing an apparently unbeatable enemy force. Will he survive to claim his rightful place, or is *Mistral* destined to sail under another's command? With graphic naval action, danger from the elements and a major conflict of loyalties, *Mistral*'s sea trials quickly turn into a testing time for her crew as much as their vessel.

Made in the USA
Las Vegas, NV
13 December 2021

37432767R00177